Beloved Exile

ALEXANDER CORDELL

BELOVED EXILE

PIATKUS

Copyright © 1993 by Alexander Cordell

First published in Great Britain in 1993 by
Judy Piatkus (Publishers) Ltd of
5 Windmill Street, London W1

**the moral right of the author
has been asserted**

*A catalogue record for this book is available
from the British Library*

ISBN 0–7499–0179–9

Set in 11/12pt Times by
Derek Doyle & Associates, Mold, Clwyd
Printed and bound in Great Britain by
Biddles Ltd, Guildford and King's Lynn

For Robert Dallen

Acknowledgements

I am grateful to many librarians for assistance in my research during the writing of this novel: not least to Mr J. Iowerth Davies, F.L.A., Assistant Director of Education of Mid Glamorgan County Council. Another librarian who needs special mention is Mr John Edward Thomas of Clwyd County Council Library and Information Service, one ever willing to come to my assistance.

Finally, my thanks are due to the authors listed under 'Further Reading' in the end-papers herein: their detailed historical research into what is virtually an endless supply of material on the subject has provided and crystallized for me the facts necessary for the writing of this book; which, it is hoped, will provide the stimulus for greater public interest in a violent period of British colonial history.

Alexander Cordell
Wales, 1991

SWINDON: *What will history say?*
BURGOYNE: *History, sir, will tell lies*
as usual.

George Bernard Shaw

It appears to me that, from the point of
view of our Imperialism, Afghanistan is nothing
more than a looter's paradise.

William Cobbett
(House of Commons)

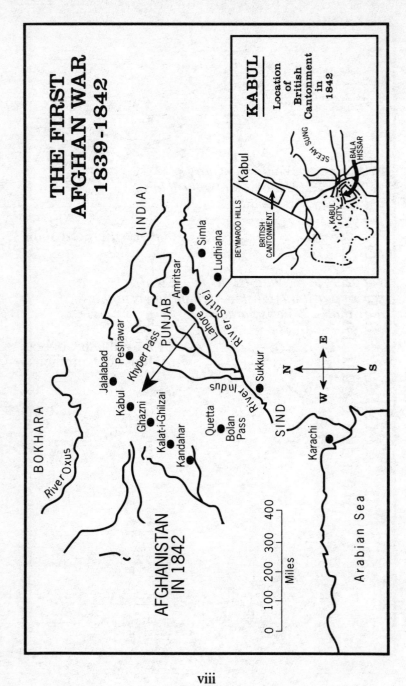

THE FIRST
AFGHAN WAR
1839-1842

KABUL

Location
of
British Cantonment
in
1842

BEYMAROO HILLS

BRITISH CANTONMENT

Kabul

SEEAH SUNG

BALA HISSAR

KABUL CITY

(INDIA)

Simla

Ludhiana

Amritsar

PUNJAB

Lahore

River Sutlej

Peshawar

Khyber Pass

Jalalabad

Kabul

Ghazni

Kalat-i-Ghilzai

Kandahar

Quetta

Bolan Pass

Sukkur

River Indus

SIND

Karachi

BOKHARA

River Oxus

AFGHANISTAN
IN 1842

N
E
W
S

0 100 200 300 400
Miles

Arabian Sea

viii

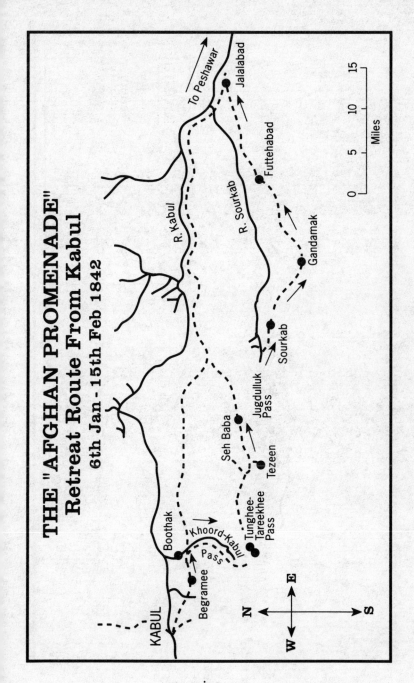

THE "AFGHAN PROMENADE"
Retreat Route From Kabul
6th Jan - 15th Feb 1842

To Peshawar

Jalalabad

R. Kabul

R. Sourkab

Futtehabad

Gandamak

Sourkab

Jugdulluk
Pass

Seh Baba

Tezeen

Tunghee-
Tareekhee
Pass

Boothak

Khoord-Kabul
Pass

Begramee

KABUL

N

E

S

W

0   5   10   15

Miles

ix

Prologue

Cae White House,
Near Llandilo,
Carmarthenshire.

Soon I will have two children.

The first, Jonathan, was born of Mari Dirion, a barefooted girl from Carmarthenshire; the second (and I am praying that it will also be a son) is now in the womb of the Princess Durrani of Afghanistan, she whose people call her the Pearl of the Age.

It is said in the East that a woman can be assessed by her industry: of silken sewing Durrani can make an inch a day, while of plain stitching Mari could turn out half a yard: therefore, through Eastern eyes, the new could scarcely compare with the old: in other respects, believe me, the old cannot compare with the new.

As I sit here writing this, I can see them both in memory: Mari of the laughing eyes; Durrani whose eyes are black, gentle: the first of fiercely Celtic temper, the second of the sensuous glance above her yashmak . . . yet, on form, Mari could achieve more with a Welsh wink than an Afghan princess with fluttering lashes.

But I am not writing this for the benefit of my lovers; it is for my sons, for a man who does not so perpetuate his loins, say the Afghans, is but a meteor flashing across the sky.

It is still autumn. The season being late this year, Wales is dressing herself up in shades of brown and gold. The trees of the valleys are discussing the last beautiful summer. Is it really fourteen years since I left my beloved Gwent, and only months since I escaped from Afghanistan?

From the window where I am writing this I can see Squire's Reach where, they tell me, Jethro, my young brother, courted the squire's daughter before she died.

Morfydd's grave I still have not found, and I don't want to ask too many questions here lest the villagers become suspicious: it's not that the Welsh are nosy, it's just that they like to know what's going on. Certainly my mother married Tomos Traherne, which confirms something I already knew.

Birds are shaking down their nests for dusk; ravens are floating in the wind above the marshes like handfuls of burned paper; curlews are calling from the bogs where Mari's grandfather died – this according to Sixpenny Jane, the Boar's Head barmaid; she's knocking forty now, but still romantic – some things never change, especially in Wales.

Before me are my rain-stained diaries and the ragged manuscript of *Rape of the Fair Country*, which I wrote in Afghanistan; all about me are the wraiths of my past.

For an exile once beloved of the family, I might have hoped for a better welcome than this – sitting in a damp old farmhouse, wondering what has happened to them all.

Strangely, the old black clock (I remember it from my boyhood in Shepherd's Square, Blaenafon) is ticking away above the empty fireplace, so somebody must have been in here recently . . .

A ghost . . .?

Morfydd, perhaps . . .?

Meanwhile, it's no good sitting here dreaming: if I'm going to write this book I'm going to have to get something down on to paper.

A title?

Beloved Exile?

That sounds reasonable . . .

It is getting cold.

The wind is buffeting in the chimney.

Autumn – 1854   *Iestyn Mortymer*

xii

Book I

Afghanistan
1840

1

The Indus River

The chunk-chunking of the paddle steamer beat in my head within a crucifixion by heat; it was mid-summer and the north-west frontier was coming up on the port side.

Through the smudged glass of the chain-locker porthole I saw the bright Indus River, its rippling wastes a quicksilver of astonishing brilliance; refracted light glowed and fired a scintillating brightness; the purple ranges of the surrounding country shimmered in lambent flame.

Big Rhys stretched his body beside me and rattled his chains. 'What the hell we're doing here, Iestyn, I don't know,' said he. 'If this is transportation, give me Botany Bay.'

Earlier, loaded to the gunwales with the paraphernalia of war, the rearguard of the Forty-Fourth Regiment of Foot had left Karachi some four hundred miles away and begun the eight-hundred-mile journey up the Indus River in support of the main army stationed in Kabul; yet another jewel in Victoria's crown acquired by political bribery.

With a minimum of bloodshed, the fierce tribesmen of Afghan – the Alfredis, Ghilzais, Durranis, Pathans and half a dozen more – had been cajoled and threatened into passive acceptance of a puppet king, and watched their true ruler, Dost Mohammed Khan, sent by Britain into exile.

Now the gates of their ancient kingdom had been thrown open to British trade on British terms: soon the primitive

3

Afghan homesteads and bazaars with their embroidered silks and leatherwork would be flourishing with imports, from Welsh coal to Lancashire cotton. All political enemies had been silenced: never again, said the counting houses of London, would the Russian bear roam the steppes of the ancient silk route through the Khyber Pass to Persia.

Where foreign arms had been rendered impotent by the courage of its patriots, Afghanistan had lost the war of diplomatic guile.

'I tell you what,' grumbled Big Rhys, 'we're England's last hope, the broken rubbish of the Chartist cause.'

'Ay, ay,' replied Owen Howells, 'and it's folk like that old John Frost who's landed me in this chain-locker. I'd give me soul to be cuddling up me missus back in Nantyglo, instead of sweating cobs in this bloody place.'

'Count yourself lucky,' I said. 'They could have hanged us.'

'Ach, forget it,' retorted Big Rhys, sitting up. 'Next stop could be the harem.'

'Kabul, here I come, girls,' added Owen.

They talked more, but I did not really hear them above the thumping of the paddle wheels, for I was up on the mountain at the Garndyrus furnaces, watching the iron coming out; and kissing Mari in the heather on Easter Sunday.

Two days later we were clear of Sukkur and the sacrificial glow of funeral pyres, where, they told us, widows cast themselves into the flames of their husbands' bodies: on past loading bays where the main army of the Indus – some forty thousand men – Ghurkas, cavalry, infantry of the line and a dozen other units from Bombay Horse to Indian Sepoys, had months earlier left for the seven-hundred-mile march to Kabul via Kandahar . . . while we, chained as convicts, fumed and sweated in the stifling chain-locker amid stinks of curry, burned maize and dead animals.

The steamer, now motionless, was misted on the vaporous river; an open sewer that drained the onion-gold roofs of fabulous minarets . . . where tortuous alleys wriggled like amputated earthworms through the slums of India's

4

terrifying poverty.

After taking water aboard near Peshawar, the General Officer commanding the rearguard decided that he wanted to interview us.

'Iestyn Mortymer?' cried a voice, and sunlight shafted the locker.

'Here,' I said, and rose on the hay-strewn floor.

'Rhys Jenkins, Owen Howells!'

Both, drenched with sweat, shambled to their feet.

Big, bull-chested, the Sergeant of the Guard barred the entrance and, indicating me, barked, 'Follow me, Mortymer,' and I did so along the heat-scalded deck, aware of the eyes of the civilian passengers.

Elegant women, the wives of military officers joining their husbands in Kabul, shrank away as I passed; children stared at me with unfeigned curiosity, babies were snatched aside. Now we climbed companionway steps to an elegant stateroom of silver and gold decoration: here sat an epauletted general surrounded by aides in their braided panoply of rank.

'Sit,' said someone, and I sat upon a form placed before the general's table. Rustling papers with a professional flourish, he raised a thin, ascetic face, saying:

'Convict Mortymer?'

'Yes,' I replied.

'Yes, sir,' said the sergeant.

'Yes, sir,' I repeated.

The eyes before me, cold in a flushed red face clearly new to the tropics, burned their steely grey into mine. He read from a paper:

'Sentenced to twenty-one years' transportation at Monmouth Assizes for rebellion against Her Imperial Majesty the Queen. Is that correct?'

I nodded.

'In that you, on the night of the fourth of November in the year 1839, did assemble with divers others armed with weapons of a dangerous description in order to take possession of the town of Newport, in the County of Monmouthshire, in an attempt to supercede the lawful

5

authority of the Queen as a preliminary step to a more general insurrection throughout the kingdom . . . ' His voice droned on, dead upon his lips in the stifling atmosphere of the room; the steamer rolled gently, creaking to an incoming swell.

The General asked, 'To this you pleaded guilty?'

I nodded assent, and he fixed his gaze upon me.

'Answer me when I ask you a question!'

'I pleaded guilty.'

'And presumably – for I happen to know you damned Chartists – you have not yet repented your abject disloyalty?' His voice rose shrilly.

'I have not repented.'

'Indeed, given a similar opportunity you would doubtless behave in the same manner!'

'Yes, sir.'

Sighing at the ceiling, the General rose with the apathy of a wounded stag. 'Merely another camp follower, Gentlemen; the rubbish being inflicted upon us in the name of technicians; a typical example, I may say, of the lower orders with which we are going to be burdened.' Raising a weary hand, he added, 'When you reach Kabul, Mortymer, you will report directly to the residence of the Assistant Envoy, whose office will attach you to the civilian department of a Mr Caleb Benedict . . . ' A hint of merriment entered his cold eyes, and he added, 'In passing, I trust you find our Envoy less accommodating than the army, which has had the unfortunate duty of transporting you this far.' Rising, he stalked out, followed by his aides.

One officer remained, a peak-faced lieutenant who took the vacated seat; he said, his eyes expressionless, 'You are aware of your purpose in Afghanistan?'

'No, sir.'

'Then I will tell you so you can pass on the information to your two companions.

'The Army of the Indus, having conquered Afghanistan and sent Dost Mohammed Khan into exile, has appointed Shah Shuja as its new king; he now reigns in Kabul, and it is to him that you owe your freedom.'

I nodded, and he continued, 'Since you are ironworkers

and your trade is needed by the Shah, you are to work for him instead of being in a chain-gang, which is what would have happened if I'd had a hand in it. You follow me?'

'Perfectly.'

His vacant eyes wandered the empty room. Then:

'You will disembark when we reach Peshawar in three days' time, and continue the journey to Kabul on foot: on the march you will be attached to the army for rations and discipline; you will march unchained, since it is not desirable for British personnel to be seen manacled. But, attempt to escape and you will be flogged on a gun wheel, if the Afghans don't get you first, which I would find acceptable. Understand?'

'Yes.'

He rose from the table. 'Now get back to your confederates and acquaint them with these facts, and God help you if you come up before me for the slightest indiscipline.'

The guard called me to order and marched me back to the chain-locker.

It was on my way there, along the steamer's slanting deck, that I first saw Durrani, the child princess. Earlier, we had learned that she was aboard.

She was standing by the starboard rail: tall, dignified in her silken robes of green and black and gold, there was little to distinguish her from the retinue of attendants about her, save that the colour of her skin was considerably lighter than theirs. I judged her age at fifteen, but a female's age is difficult to assess in the East. As I clanked by, preceded by the guard, she lifted her face.

It was her eyes that held me, and always will; there was about them a lustrous sadness; then the vision passed, and the door of the chain-locker clanged behind me.

'What happened?' Big Rhys and Owen were instantly upon their feet, clamouring in their chains, but I did not immediately reply; I was still seeing the sad eyes of the young princess.

Those few days before we reached Peshawar will stay forever in my mind; the sweating pain of being cooped up in the steaming chain-locker; fried all day by the refracted rays of an incinerating sun, shivering all night in an almost arctic cold.

At midnight on the last day on the river we had a visitor.

I was nodding in the vacuum of approaching sleep when a shadow fell across the bars of our prison.

'English, please . . . ?' whispered a voice.

A native lad was crouched outside the bars of the door. His eyes, their whites like bedsheets, rolled in his dusky face. I moved closer.

'What do you want?'

For reply he gave me a note.

Unfolding it, I turned it to the light of the moon, and read:

I, the Princess Durrani, granddaughter of Dost Mohammed Khan, the true king, am being taken from England to Kabul. Soon, says my grandfather, Akbar Khan, my uncle, will come and drive the Franks back to India, killing all but one, and take the throne.

Only a prisoner will help a prisoner, says my grandfather in Ludhiana, and great wealth will be yours if you help Durrani. Tell the Kohistani, yes or no, immediately.

'What the hell's happenin'?' demanded Big Rhys.

'We've got a visitor,' I whispered. 'He has brought a note.'

'At this time of night? Who from?'

'Listen,' and I read the note to him.

Rhys stared at me, his eyes great pools of shadow in the light of the moon. 'What you going to do?'

'What can we do?'

'In or out of here – nothing. Ain't we in trouble enough, as it is? It's politics. Get mixed up with her and you'll wish you'd never been born,' and he leaned over, reached through the bars, shook the lad's sleeve, and said:

'Hop it, you savvy? Hop it!'

'Wait,' I said, restraining the lad. 'You talkee English?'

'I speak English excellently,' came the gentle reply.

8

'Then go back to your mistress and tell her I will help her, if I can,' and if anyone had asked me why I'd sent such a reply, I could not have given a reason.

'You want your head read,' said Rhys, after the boy had gone, at which Owen sat up, scratching.

'What's on?'

'Nothing,' said Rhys. 'Just somebody gone off his nut. Go back to sleep.'

I did not know that my decision to help would cause his death.

2

Kabul (The Army of Occupation)

The residency of Sir Alexander Burnes was worthy of his station. 'One thing's sure,' exclaimed Big Rhys, 'these buggers do 'emselves well.'

It was an understatement.

This, a typical colonial mansion of the period, looked more like the habitat of a Sultan's zenana than the abode of a civil servant: its ostentatious white-walled arches vied for beauty with an oriental harem.

Here bloomed midsummer flowers – gardens of riotous colour and perfume; its patio tiling traversed by a dozen scurrying servants, each apparently bent on reaching somewhere regardless of obstacle.

The walled vegetable garden through which we passed was laden with cabbages of giant proportions; turnips, radishes and potato plants flowered in abundance; cauliflowers from England bloomed their white roses as happily as in Kent.

Entering a door garlanded with sweetpea and geraniums, it was difficult for me to believe that I wasn't in Wales.

A white-gowned man approached, one Mohun Lal, the Hindu assistant to the Envoy.

'Whom do you seek?' he asked in English.

I replied, 'We seek a Caleb Benedict.'

Somebody at my elbow said, 'What do you want with Benedict?' and I turned to a distinguished-looking, plump little man in riding-habit.

10

'We were told to report to him,' I replied.

'Were you, indeed! And who the devil might you be, for God's sake?' He looked my fatigue uniform up and down with undisguised disdain.

I judged his age at thirty; of aristocratic appearance and air, he was slapping his riding-crop impatiently against his leg.

Rhys said, 'Sir, we are attached to the Forty-Fourth regiment . . .'

'Ah yes, the Chartist prisoners!'

His brown eyes, flickering with hostility, looked us over.

'Captain Broadfoot mentioned you. It isn't enough, apparently, to be saddled with internecine war – we're to harbour criminal elements to assist the process of political dissent. What happened? Didn't they want you in Van Diemen's Land?'

I repeated, 'We are to report to Mr Benedict.'

'Really! Well, it so happens that you've bumped into the *Elchi*, and it is I who will decide your future here, not a junior officer.' He turned away.

Owen began, 'Beggin' ye pardon . . .'

'*Silence!*' Burnes snapped his fingers, and a passing servant leaped to his side. 'Take these three over to Havildar at the racecourse and put them on the big roller. Obtain a signature for them, and bring it here to me.' He moved closer to Owen, glaring up into his face. 'Address me again without my permission and I will have you flogged, you damned anarchist. Now *move!*'

'Jesus,' whispered Owen.

Momentarily, I met the man's cold stare: he smiled, but not with his mouth.

'You, your name?' His tongue moved over his lips. Handsome beggar, give him credit.

'Iestyn Mortymer.'

'Repeat it.'

I did so.

The eyes shifted in assessment.

'A Chartist, eh?'

I did not answer; strangely he did not appear to expect one, but I knew that a pact of hostility had already been

11

forged between us.

A word about Sir Alexander Burnes.

In his diary, it was discovered after his death, were expressive descriptions of the life he led in Kabul.

'I am now a highly paid idler,' he wrote to a relative, 'being paid 3500 rupees a month as Resident, and for which I give paper opinions. I lead, in fact, a very pleasant life, and if rotundity be proof of health, I have it.'

It is to be hoped that he enjoyed it while he was able; his life of luxury was not to last long.

A decade earlier Alexander Burnes was a cavalry officer in the Bombay Horse, an unknown lieutenant in the East India Company.

By lucky circumstance he was appointed to deliver political bribes to local chiefs, in return for commercial British expansion. In so doing he appreciated the growing threat to British interests posed by the Russians, and expressed this forcibly in Whitehall circles.

Recently knighted for his services in replacing Dost Mohammed Khan, the King of Afghanistan, by the puppet Shah Shuja (one who more readily agreed to British exploitation of his country), Burnes had his future as an Eastern potentate assured.

Now, at the age of thirty-five, he had been installed as an *Elchi*, Assistant Envoy, in Kabul: only Sir William MacNaghten was his superior in rank and power . . . he who also was soon to die.

On our way out of the Residence we passed through long chains of hanging flower-baskets of every hue and perfume: convolvulus and clematis competed for beauty in a man-made paradise of wealth and privilege, yet its loveliness stank: it brought to me a presentiment of disaster; as if the future had been suddenly hauled back into the present . . . painting a fleeting vision of the deaths of thousands.

'Did ye see those dusky beauties looking out of the upstairs windows?' asked Owen.

'Trust you!'

'Ye know somethin'? I reckon that lad's got a harem goin'

. . . the young sod!'

'If they're Afghan beauties, he'll catch it,' Big Rhys said, voicing my thoughts.

In the event, he did.

Now under the ministrations of the gigantic Keeper of the Racecourse (one Havildar, an overseer who worked the local bad hats), we were to know a month of unremitting labour under the sun of Kabul's blazing June . . . pulling a two-ton grass roller – work usually done by donkeys.

It gave me time to reflect upon an unequal contest – Chartist agitators incurring the displeasure of the British Raj . . . through a political representative who was the lion of the day.

We could not have fallen foul of a more important person.

Meanwhile Havildar, once the King's Master Cannoner, but fallen from grace after an affair with a harem lady at Court, had a magnificent chip upon his shoulder, and was giving us a bad time.

3

'In the name of God,' shouted a voice, 'why are ye heaving that bloody great thing around?'

Rhys, Owen and I straightened on the towing harness: the big roller came to a stop.

The man before us had an alcoholic nose; was as fat as he was tall and as bewhiskered as a stage Irishman; he bowed, his top hat, battered by years, at a cocky angle.

'Are you the Chartist criminals, then?'

We said we were, and he pulled out a snuff-box, took a pinch, sniffed it, coughed himself blue in the face, patted his chest and cried, 'Jesus, I've been lookin' all over Afghanistan for ye, so I have. I'm Caleb Benedict,' and he offered his hand.

I unstrapped the pulling harness, saying, 'We're the three you're lookin' for, Mr Benedict, and we've been here weeks.'

'At the pleasure o' that young upstart, Burnes, they're telling me!'

'He fixed us proper,' said Rhys.

'Do ye always do everything you're told? Sure to God, if you'd mentioned me name to that wee numbskull, he'd 'ave run a bloody mile.'

Havildar, our outsize Sikh gaoler, approached with fawning servility, saying, 'I greet you, Mr Benedict, sir,' and touched his breast and forehead. 'How is your health?'

'When I know meself you'll be the last to hear it, ye big oaf. Have ye nothin' between your ears? There's me waitin' for me Celtic furnacemen, and you've got 'em on a bloody roller!' And the other answered, bowing low:

'It was at the command of Sir Alexander, the Assistant *Elchi*.'

'Is that so? Well, this is at the command of Sir Caleb bloody Benedict, so get the harness off those fellas and hand 'em over, or ye'll never hear the end of it.' He came to us. 'Are you all in one piece, my lovelies?'

'Now you've come,' said I.

'Are ye Irish?'

'Welsh.'

'Ah well, we can't have everything. Do you know why you're here?'

We shook our heads.

'That makes four of us,' said Caleb. 'But I tell ye this free – it won't be long before they'll be bootin' us out o' the beloved country entirely, so make the best of it. Have you heard about the need for iron on the Frontier?'

We said we hadn't.

'Well, I'll tell you,' said Caleb. 'The first idea was to hammer swords into ploughshares, but the locals got other ideas, so you're here to make iron for war – plates for fortifications, a narrow-gauge railway, iron for repairing gun-limbers – and it's all got to come out of Caleb's wee furnace. Have you heard of that even?'

I shook my head.

'Jesus, Mary and Joseph! Didn't they tell you anything?'

'Only that we had to report to you.'

'If you're tradesmen, gents, welcome aboard!'

Preceded by his little fat stomach, he led the way.

The Caleb Furnace, about a quarter of the size of those we'd worked back home in Blaenafon, stood in a tiny furnace compound near the Kabul Gate. As old as Methuselah with its ancient pig moulds, it used a stone in its bung to halt the molten flow.

'But it works,' cried Caleb, tipping up a flask, and he drank deep and gasped, 'Sure to God, there's no finer iron cast in the Orient. Are ye listenin'?'

We said we were.

'Now I'll take you to Captain Broadfoot.'

15

Broadfoot, a Royal Engineer officer in charge of the Shah's sappers and miners, looked us over. Red-haired, silent, dressed in fatigue uniform like us, he was possessed of that commanding dignity that raised him above the herd of regimental officers abounding in Kabul.

'Your names?' he asked, and noted them on a pad. 'All puddlers?'

Big Rhys answered, 'Me and Mortymer, sir.'

'I'm a firer,' said Owen.

'Right, we can do with you, for things are starting to move. You've seen Caleb's furnace?'

I nodded.

'And you've no political bees in your bonnets?'

'Not these days.'

'Keep it that way.' His bright blue eyes drifted over us. 'We've enough local discontent here to suffice us all, otherwise what you do in your private time is nothing to do with me. You'll mess with the Other Ranks and as far as I'm concerned have the run of the place. But step out of line and I'm your boy, so remember it. Stand by me, behave yourselves, and I'll see you right, understand?'

We said we did.

'What about the Envoy?'

'Burnes? Forget him. Just do your job and leave him to me. You got that, Caleb?'

'Aye, sir.'

'Oh, one last thing,' said Broadfoot. 'We'll be working up in the Bala Hissar, the fort. Keep away from the women or you'll be confronted by eunuchs with knives. Emasculation is their stock-in-trade, so keep it in your trousers.

'Meanwhile, Caleb will find you a tent and work out your shifts – you've got only six labourers and they're all Hindus – never mix them up with the Afghans. Racial prejudice. Any questions?'

He spoke more, and I took good note of him. I speak of him now mainly because he is worth it, though we didn't even have him with us on the Retreat from Kabul.

Surviving this, he was killed at Ferozepore, living a little

16

longer than his brother William, who was soon to be assassinated.

The parents of the Broadfoot brothers, gentle vicarage people back in rural England, gave three fine sons to Asia, the first to be sacrificed being James, who had already died under knives in the valley of Purwandurrah.

Some men are worth more than a passing mention: one was Captain Broadfoot.

On the day we officially started work up in the Bala Hissar I began to keep a diary.

4

Now the autumn broke in fiery splendour: mists of morning barged across the gullies of the sky from Beymaroo to Seeah Sung and northwards, beyond the barrier of the Hindu Kush, the Country of Light; here the Russians lay, seething at the stolen prize.

In colder sunlight, the fortress of Bala Hissar, the barbarian of the centuries, glared down upon our military cantonment, the invading British cancer laid out far below it.

The cantonment had not been the same for us since Captain Broadfoot had left us for a military foray with General Sale: he alone, it appeared, understood the workings of the Other Ranks' mind; we missed his fine authority.

But his place had been taken by another of the same ilk – a Captain Sturt, and he took up our work programme where Broadfoot had left off. The continuity was essential; that autumn proved a testing time for the cantonment's defences.

Under Sturt's supervision we made shell-proof the many isolated forts around the perimeter of the military cantonment; labouring bare-backed in the searing heat, propping and reinforcing what was now called Sturt's Bridge over the Kabul River (later to prove a focal point in our defences) and we even fortified the ruins of Sergeant Deane's House and the Orchard Magazine. Around us *chuprassies* (messengers) on horseback came and went; drill squad sergeants barked at raw recruits, and the military band of the 'Little Fighting Fours' (the 44th Queen's) marched past us up and down the square, blasting martial music.

Along the cantonment lines black-faced Indian Sepoys sat bootless in the sun, braces down, contemplating ease; the guard blancoed and polished for yet another Afghan day of leisurely pursuit: all appeared well with our particular world.

The white façades of the administrative buildings glittered in that eerie, translucent light that spells an Asian morning; strange smells arose and perfumed the wind; the stink of camel dung (later we used it as an antiseptic for wounds) clashed with the scent of flowering convolvulus; from the cavalry lines came the hammering of farriers shoeing the sturdy little *yaboos*, hitherto wild Afghan ponies. The morning was filled with the shrieked protests of overburdened camels being prodded down the military lines, from dragging earthwork carts to hauling six-pounder gun-limbers.

Freed from regimental duties now that the political climate had settled into dull routine, the officers of the Army of Occupation lazed in the sun, played polo and drank gin and bitters before tiffin; made assignations with local Afghan maidens for the next night of debauchery, and commended the assiduity of Assistant Political Envoys like Burnes who had presented them with such congenial opportunities.

Meanwhile, these same officers were being aped and ridiculed by the beggars of Kabul, and their wives were threatened and insulted.

Our political people were also being warned by pro-British factions that an uprising was about to take place out of hatred for the puppet King, Shah Shuja.

Violence was growing too. Tit for tat vendettas ensued, as in the case of Private Collins of the 13th Light Infantry – 'a gallant soldier but a great ruffian' as the inquest put it.

Collins, recognizing a 'harmless' beggar as one who privately cut British throats, seized the man by the scruff of his neck and, holding him face down in a rain puddle, 'drowned him like a dog'. The guard was called upon finding the body, but apparently, 'didn't see anything, sir . . .'

Despite warning signs (the Commander-in-Chief made

19

light of them), the Afghan tribes, it was said, had an inherent inability to combine against a common foe, preferring to squabble among themselves . . . This was wishful thinking.

The nature of the opposition was easily recognized, so there was no tactical excuse for not noticing it: clearly the time had arrived when the Afghan patriots had decided upon action.

One, a certain landowner from Pisheen, deciding to be rid of a brother competing for land, had him buried up to the neck in the ground with a rope attached to his neck: he then attached the other end to the saddle of his pony and whipped it around in circles until his relative's head parted company with his shoulders.

Such 'squabbling among themselves' being cited as a particular instance . . .

And while disturbing news was coming in about minor insurrections down south, these soon came to an end with quick British victories.

A score or so of Afghan rank and file having been blown from the cannon's mouth (a fashionable punishment officially recognized in London), the tribal chiefs then received their tribute of 100,000 rupees annually: but the Treasury in Whitehall, impatient at this drain upon its resources, cut the bribery by half soon after we arrived.

It was a mistake which cost 20,000 lives, and very nearly mine.

The three of us were working stripped to the waist, making shell-proof a magazine: this was situated opposite the Mohammed Shereef's fort, a focal point in the coming conflagration; it was still unfinished when we were running for our lives.

We were building iron plates into its roof timbers; Caleb and his native labourers were bringing these up from the furnace by temporary rail, and the day was flourishing in wind and sunlight, with just enough nip to warn of approaching winter.

'Have you heard the latest?' asked Rhys.

He looked immense, his muscles bulging, and a chest on

20

him like a ship's prow: he continued, 'They're sending us into the Bala Hissar at last: just heard – Captain Sturt has drawn up plans for a new wing in the palace to house Shah Shuja's harem.'

'Rather me than him,' added Owen. 'Hundreds of wives, daughters, nieces and aunts!'

I didn't heed him; from all reports Owen was doing all right for himself up by the city's Kohistan Gate; at least one dusky Hindu lady having reason to be grateful for favours. Now he said with fine male gusto, 'As fast as they can pull 'em from under me, boyo. Ye know, since I landed here I anna missed a night on the nest.'

I was tired of Owen, once my companion: when living in Blaenafon I respected him, for he was a first-rate Chartist. After his nightly sojourns up in the Bazaar, his lurid descriptions of his amorous conquests brought me visions of Mari, and I longed with shameful lust for a woman.

It was all very well playing the Simon Pure with naïve manifestations of celibacy, but the rigid intimacy of my loins brought me a thousand doubts. Was Mari, who was as ardent in her demands of love as I, also resisting youth's temptations, I wondered; or would she, having no news of me, fall wife to another? And in my fevered longing I would awake in the mornings like a stag that has soiled its pit . . . empty, listless, cold: a man expired within a Chinese dream of fruitless ecstasy. Banishment and imprisonment restrict liberty, but their real torture lies in the loss of a woman's warm companionship.

We were surprised to discover Lady Sale, the wife of General 'Fighting Bob' Sale, abroad at that time of the morning.

This woman, even then, was a tradition in the encampment; later, during the retreat, she became a legend.

Tall, of severe looks and stern matronly grace, she dominated the officers' wives, and also her husband; he, at the moment, had been sent by our General Elphinstone to clear the Khoord-Kabul Pass fifteen miles east of Kabul.

Here a raiding tribe of Ghilzais were encamped and

blocking our line should retreat prove necessary. This was a serious blunder; the brigade, its return to Kabul also blocked, was forced to march east to Jalalabad. Although we did not know it then, the tribesmen were drawing their net around us.

History relates that the Afghans knew exactly what they were doing.

Clearly we did not.

'Who is in charge of this working party?' asked Lady Sale.

Not by any stretch of imagination could she be called a beauty, and I'd had enough of her within a minute of our meeting.

'He is,' answered Rhys, indicating me, and touched his forelock.

'Ah yes, the time-serving Chartists. English, are you not? You totally surprise me.'

'Welsh,' I said.

My coolness annoyed her, and I was glad: she lifted her chin and her dark eyes shone: I'm over six foot, but gave her only inches.

Dressed in a white woollen skirt that reached to her ankles, she was wearing a native *poshteen*, a sheepskin, over her shoulders as a woman at Ascot might wear a fur: upon her head was a scarlet turban of Afghan style. Her hands were large and veined, her features angular, borrowed from a man; she spoke again, her voice a deep contralto.

'Really? Well, Welsh or English, I'm the wife of the General, so try to remember it. In future refer to me as "Milady", understand?'

Smiling, I bowed to her, and she put up her nose and walked past me as Caleb, two sheets in the wind at that time of the morning, staggered up to us, his arms wide in effusive apology.

'Milady!' cried he, and bowed low, sweeping up the gutter with his top hat.

'Get up, Caleb, you'll do yourself an injury,' and she glared about her. 'The more I see of the shambles called organization around here, the more I realize that the only safe place for officers' families is up in the Bala Hissar fort.'

22

'That is not the wish of the King, beggin' ye pardon, Your Ladyship,' said Caleb.

'Perhaps not, but it is mine. And were Broadfoot in this cantonment now, instead of miles away with my husband on some damn-fool mission when we need them most, he would agree with me.' She stared up at the palace fortifications wreathed in cloud. 'You are working up there now, I hear.'

'About to start, Your Ladyship.'

'Doing what, may I ask?'

'Doin' up the harems, ma'am – 'tis essential, don't ye see, to make the big fella comfortable in all respects, for he's only got a few hundred females to cushion him against the ravages of life.'

'You are a fool, Caleb, for now you are slandering the King.'

'Aye, rightly so, for if I had any sense in me noddle, I'd be keepin' a few o' the wee darlin's meself, instead of drowning me sorrows wi' the hard stuff – sure to God, it'd be a glorious end. Was it Captain Sturt you're after, milady?'

'You know, Caleb, you are the most pitiful object,' she replied. 'With a University education and every prospect of ending up as an Irish gentleman, you are bound for Satan on the back of a pig. For the sake of your Catholic soul, man, is it not time you returned to Ireland?'

'Sure, when that happens, Your Ladyship, I'll be in me box, so I will,' and his sunlit face creased up into a bunch of laughs. 'It being me intention to stay alive to witness the downfall of England for what she's done to the green land of Erin,' and here he crossed himself.

'Now you're a double fool, my friend, for the sun will never set on the British Empire – and do you know why?'

'Because God never trusts an Englishman in the dark, milady.'

She was beaten, and knew it. '*Touché, touché*, you silly old faggot!' she said and, dismissing him with a gesture of futility, turned her attentions, clearly hostile, to me.

'You, your name?' She prodded me in the chest.

'Iestyn Mortymer.'

Her eyes danced. 'Ah yes – the diarist, so this idiot tells me. You'd do better writing home to your family instead of scribbling what are probably political tracts, for I know you revolutionaries, Caleb included. You have a family?'

'Not allowed to write home, Ma'am.'

'Why not?'

'Convicts – secrecy, they say. Captain Broadfoot said he'd see to it, but now he's been posted away.'

She pondered this. 'Who made this rule?'

'The *Elchi*, Ma'am,' replied Caleb.

'Not Sir William McNaghten, surely!'

'Sir Alexander Burnes,' I said.

'Did he now! On the grounds of secrecy? Oh, God, preserve me from the diplomats! Write home, all of you, and leave the politics to me,' and she moved away, shouting, 'you stand indicted, Caleb. Bring in anarchists if you will, but for God's sake draw the line at educated Welshmen. Meanwhile, send Captain Sturt, my son-in-law, to me. I will be in my quarters.'

'The lovely old bitch,' murmured Rhys, as she got into her palanquin, an ornate chair carried by bearers who trotted off with her: lounging soldiers leaped to attention as she passed, while a small boy ran beside it, holding down her skirts in the wind.

'Who the hell does she think she is?' asked Owen.

'She's God Almighty round these parts,' replied Caleb, putting his top hat on sideways.

5

Through Captain Sturt's intervention we were now excused fatigue duties, so pitched our own bell tent in the furnace compound; this had the advantage of privacy, and a drawback. Any passing savage, if taken with the urge, could slip out of the Bazaar one night and cut the throats of the three of us.

Happily, though, we were officially placed 'on detachment', which meant that we were rationed direct from the Quartermaster's Store and not dependent upon 'Family Messing' – the system used by the soldiers – where those doling it out at the top of the table got plenty, while those at the bottom were on a restricted diet.

True, we had to observe military rules; rising with the dawn reveille and retiring with 'Lights Out' at dusk. Worse, as time-serving 'Prisoners of the Crown' (this was stamped upon our identification papers) we had initially to report to the guardroom once a day, but Sturt got this rescinded also, since it interfered with our shift-working.

'Take it from me,' said Rhys, 'there's no Chartists in the Empire having it easier than us. Three square meals a day and a six-hour shift – it's better than I got back home.'

Owen, I noticed, did not reply; his was a silent intimacy of private thought in these early days.

Rhys shouted, 'What's wrong with you – you've a face as long as tomorrow. Are you missing your missus that much?'

Owen shook his head.

'What's wrong then?'

'Wales,' said Owen.

Now, in a blazing August, stripped to the belt, we worked with our native labour, one shift on and two off; casting ten-foot lengths of bull-headed iron rails (25lbs per yard run) on prisoners' rates of twopence a day. And Sturt's levies were laying the rails like mad things on sleepers to a gauge of one foot ten and a half, nailing them in with home-made dog spikes.

Caleb's old furnace (while he lay on the slag with his feet up) rocked and moaned like a sow in labour, shooting up sparks into the clear blue air and settling soot and smuts on the washing of the cantonment; the married pads played hell about it.

Spewing out her molten iron that old furnace didn't know if she was in Kabul or China; but Caleb had built her well, and she spat it out into Owen's sand moulds while Hindu labourers cleaned off the sludge.

Every dusk brought Sturt's Ghurkas with their little Afghan *yaboos* and carts, to haul the rails away for another day of laying, lifting and packing.

'Watch it, watch it! Iron coming out!' Big Rhys used to bawl and, hearing this, out of the Bazaar would rush the Afghans, Turks and Ghilzais, Persians, Hazaras, Durranis and Baluchis. Jabbering and shoving for room, they'd crowd into the furnace area, pointing and shrieking as Big Rhys bent to knock out the bung.

'Watch her, watch her, she's an old cow so treat her gentle!'

And the natives shrieked their delight.

Later I made an entry in my diary:

15th August, 1840. Today we tapped the Caleb Furnace for the fifteenth time. As always, the people came rushing out of the Bazaar to see the miracle of the molten iron. Be it in Blaenafon or Kabul, the sight is as marvellous.

Great is the ingenuity of man that he digs rock from a mountain and boils it into iron. The firebox door swings

26

back and there is a blaze of white heat as the flames curl up in smokeless red and gold. The people shield their eyes from the glare as the plug is knocked out. I see the lip of the moving iron, sheet white at first as it strikes the misted air: steam rolls as it takes its first wet breath of the mountain; a hiss, a sigh, and it is down, down, a writhing globule of red life flashing at the plug. Now black it turns, the white water in pursuit of the impure in the sand moulds; popping, cracking, its fingers diverting into flaring streams. Flame gathers along the moulds and a shining bed expires into a mist of purple, growing rigid in shape and colour to last for a thousand years. The plug is sealed; the firebox belches relief: the watching people gasp in disbelief.

I wrote again. Most nights in the tent I wrote something:

Meanwhile, the whole cantonment, a mile by a mile of tents, marquees and white stone buildings, fires up out of the dusk like a city aglow: light beams and flashes red tongues across the eastern sky – scintillating rainbow colours of orange, purple and gold . . . then comes the dark again and Kabul suspires into another night of dreamful sleep: it needs a priest to build a chapel here where the iron comes out; or a chalice of holy water to sprinkle on the earth . . . it is a miracle.

Big Rhys, picking up this diary entry in the tent later, said, 'I'll say this for ye, Iestyn lad – you got all the words.'
'Like his sister, Morfydd, remember her?' asked Owen.
'Leave it,' said Rhys, frowning up, and his features, in that glowing blackness of the solitary candle, had the primitive stamp of the ape. 'Let his sister be.'

I put my head on the pillow and thought of home; of my first day at work when I watched the iron being made, as I had done today, now thousands of miles from home.
Garndyrus and Blaenafon, Nantyglo, Blaina . . . and beautiful Abergavenny, the gateway to Wales!
Where were they now, these places?
Had they left me on the rush of my father's tears . . .?

27

Morfydd, Mam, Edwina, Jethro . . . and Mari; Jonathan, my son . . . where were they now? I wondered. Were they, like all my hopes, blown to the winds of heaven?

Somewhere up in the crags beyond the palace of Bala Hissar a bird of prey was squawking over its kill. Tonight, I thought, with hopes of September, a matron in a russet-brown cloak would be tiptoeing in the Valley of the Usk, painting up the trees: a nightingale might be shouting above the torrents of the Afon Llyd. Would coloured birds be singing over the Usk, she who wound her ancient path through Gwent?

6

In a fever of excitement in our tent that night, I wrote by the light of a candle.

Military Cantonment,
Kabul, Afghanistan.

Mari *fy ngariad*,

At last I am allowed to write to you. Rhys Jenkins, Owen Howells and I were sentenced to twenty-one years' transportation at Monmouth and we arrived here last June to work as furnacemen. I am not able to impart to you what is in my heart, since this letter is not for your eyes only: unfortunately, they will not allow me to write in Welsh.

This is to tell you that we are alive and well, and hoping we will return to Blaenafon one day, to continue our lives with our loved ones.

I am sending this letter to Cae White, Grandfer Zephaniah's house in Carmarthenshire, to which the family was going when we parted last November. Kiss Mam, Morfydd and her Richard for me, and tell Jonathan that it is my dearest wish to hold him, and you, again in my arms.

Your loving husband,
Iestyn Mortymer.
15th August, 1840

At midday the Grub-up was bugled for dinner and we grabbed our knives, forks and spoons and went down to the

29

army lines; recently they had put us in with some new Welsh lads.

Now here's a palaver, with everybody banging the mess-tent tables, bowls of steaming *cawl* coming in from the field kitchens, and the language going up enough to curl the hair of Satan.

Brown-faced and muscular, these were soldiers on brief detachment from the Welch, the 41st; one of the regiments later to form an Army of Retribution. From the Welsh counties they came, mainly, and it was good to be with our kinsmen.

Fiercely Celtic, on to a quarrel at the drop of a hat, they were boys from north to Anglesey and west to Swansea; come to sing their Welsh songs over the bouldered plains from the Bolan to the Khyber, but few would live to tell of it to their grandchildren: others would die in the battles of Alma and Sebastopol in the Crimea, over a dozen years later.

They got us coming into the mess-tent; not misses, the Welsh.

'O aye, lads, what we got 'ere, then?'

'Strangers, eh?'

'Jesus. I don't like the look o' that big sod.'

They *oohed* and *aahed* about us, spooning up thin lob-scouse; breaking off huge chunks of coarse black bread and tearing at it with their strong white teeth, and there was about their vulgar banter an innocence that I will remember.

'Who called the cook a bastard?' shouted one, and came the reply:

'Who called the bastard a cook?'

For these lads from the Welsh farms with sweethearts back at home were soon to die under the scimitars of the Ghilzais; form British squares along the road that led to Jalalabad, which they would never reach; see their comrades stripped and methodically cut to pieces after the castration that was every soldier's nightmare.

This was the bloodstained fodder that Victoria had sent to push out the boundaries of her already bloated Empire; to die of thirst, fever, mutilation.

'Any complaints?' bawled the Mess Corporal, and we all stood up, not a man replying.

30

This was a personal institution ordained by our new Commander-in-Chief, and was well before its time in Army regulations; the food being poor in the vicinity and the protests many, though I hate to think what would have happened had anyone even hinted that the rations were under par. As it was, we all sat down again and recommenced eating.

I recall this incident because the Duty Officer standing beside the Mess Corporal was tall, distinguished, and new to us; having just been posted in for special diplomatic service – the rescue of a Colonel Stoddart, now a prisoner somewhere beyond the mountains of the Hindu Kush.

'That fella's out of the top drawer,' mentioned Big Rhys, between spoonfuls, and he was; exuding that indefinable dignity which all great men possess . . . one about to write his name, Lieutenant Connolly, in the annals of military heroism.

Next morning I collected Big Rhys from his cabbage patch on the compound; he, though a furnaceman, was close to the earth – never happier than when he had his hands deep in the rich Afghan soil.

Sweet peas and geraniums bordered his vegetable plot: potatoes, artichokes, Kabul lettuces and cauliflowers poured forth in profusion. Even Lady Sale had accepted some of his turnip radishes. Nor would he kneel to the soil, this one, but made it his servant.

'Bala Hissar, here we come,' I said. 'The work programme says we're up there with the King on repairs to the palace.'

Rhys did not reply. Winter was already decorating the mountain peaks, I remember, and I will always see him as I saw him then, his big body, stripped to the waist, shining in the sun.

The Bala Hissar had to be seen to be believed. Capable of housing an army of defenders, its past stretched back through the bloodstained centuries.

Pivot of Afghan's northern defences, it had barked its defiance at the Hindu Kush (the 'Hindu-killer'), so named

31

after the Indian slaves who had died in thousands on forced marches into Asia.

Alexander the Great had fought among its crags. Long before the coming of the Durrani Empire under Ahmad Shah, the warring tribes had sacked and ruled it. He who held Bala Hissar, the legend said, held by the throat the ambitions of Iran, Persia and Russia: Dost Mohammed Khan, its rightful king, had held court here, until London had exiled him and enthroned the puppet Shah Shuja.

With Captain Sturt leading the way on horseback and followed by twenty Ghurka sappers with tool handcarts, Caleb, Rhys, Owen and I plodded along behind; up to a fort perched like a waiting eagle, its talons thrust out in silent threat at the tented British Army below.

This, our military chiefs planned, would prove a haven should hostilities break out: a fortress capable of resisting siege while awaiting British reinforcements coming in from India.

On the edge of a vast hall, with our boots clear of beautiful Persian carpets, we were ushered into the Hall of the King.

This was a pirate's lair of beauty, its walls inset with rosewood embellishments, silver and gold: furniture of Eastern origin was carved with intricate and beautiful designs; its lofty ceilings were panelled and decorated with metopes studded with jewels: at each door, and there were many, vaulted ornamental arches crowned side rooms, their walls shining with gorgeous brocades: at each of these, erotic in statuesque poses, stood half-naked statues, the eunuchs: a sumptuous example of Eastern splendour, all in conflict, said Captain Sturt, with the more confined religious beliefs of Dost Mohammed Khan, its original and more conservative tenant.

At one door, stripped to the waist and bulging with muscle, stood two gigantic guards, each gripping a scimitar against intrusion.

'The women's quarters are behind them,' whispered Caleb.

The floors, of glittering mosaic, their vast borders inlaid with quartz, gleamed with tiger's eye: the ceilings, marvellously decorated with scenes from Afghanistan's past, were lofty, the walls interspersed with segmental arches draped with tapestries.

Here stood more turbaned eunuchs of the Imperial Court: white-gowned servants floated about on Ali Baba slippers; flowering azaleas decorated the glaring whiteness of marble furniture and friezes: through openings to courtyards I saw white fountains blooming in light-sprays amid the chattering of parakeets and love-birds; from suspension hooks hung flower-baskets of jasmine; black persimmon laid out its sombre loveliness like an English funeral train. Nothing moved save the fountains of the courtyards, their wet mosaic flashing in the sun.

Here, I thought, were the court intrigues of Afghanistan: the priceless talismens, the jewels, the garroting cords of hired assassins; all this within sight of the steaming alleys of *Char Chouk*, the chief bazaar, where lived the fawning hucksters and middle-men merchants, the chicken and pork sellers. It was a perfect paradox.

At the far end of the room was a gilded throne: empty, it was approached along a length of yellow carpet; around this stood six courtiers, their rank denoted by their coloured turbans: motionless in their robes of braided silk they stood with their documental scrolls, passively awaiting Shah Shuja's arrival, for he was a beggar for keeping people hanging about, said Caleb. It was nothing, said he, for General Elphinstone, our Commander-in-Chief, to be made to wait three hours for an audience with the King, badly crippled with the gout though he was.

'Don't look now, but we're being watched,' I whispered to Rhys.

Above the Great Hall ran a marble balustrade, and at the far end of this, looking down upon the royal scene below, stood a young woman wearing a golden yashmak; dressed in beautiful robes of yellow, black and green, she stood motionless.

'Who's she?' somebody asked.

'The Princess Durrani,' replied Caleb, 'but don't stare, for God's sake.'

33

'We shouldn't really be here,' added Captain Sturt, 'but if we move now they'll see us.'

'We've been seen already,' I said, for the young princess was looking in our direction, her chin tilted up with arrogant disapproval.

It was a time of great excesses; of unbelievable treasure in money and jewels, when the rich lathered themselves in luxury and the poor begged for scraps. On one hand the British, if Sir Alexander Burnes was an example, denied themselves nothing in the heaped-up profusion that was Kabul: he stated, 'Anyone who cares to drop into my establishment can do so over a rare Scotch breakfast of smoked fish, salmon grills, devils and jellies, and puff away at cigars until midnight . . .'

After which, of course, arrived the dancing girls.

And he went on, 'For the good River Indus is a channel for luxuries as well as commerce, remember; I can place before chosen friends cases of hock, madeira, sherry, port, claret, sauternes and champagne, not forgetting a glass of excellent curaçao, maraschino, and sealed salmon: I tell you, I also serve hot-pot all the way from Aberdeen, and deuced good it is, with the peas as big as if they had been soaked for bristling.'

And from what then happened in the Great Hall below us, it was apparent that the new king, Victoria's puppet Shah, intended to enjoy an equally lavish existence, now the more austere Dost Mohammed Khan had been sent into exile.

The Shah now entered attended by a dozen courtiers, with all the pomp of a ruling Caliph.

Literally dripping with jewels he came, backed by a bevy of tax collectors who plundered the poor and taxed the Kabul merchants almost out of existence: clearly he had surrounded himself with every known refinement, including a harem of eight hundred females; and began by handing out medals and a fountain of honours to his British masters.

With a belt encrusted with flashing gems around his waist, he wore a turquoise-coloured tunic interlaced with pearls: clearly he had not suffered much in the way of privation since his incarceration at Ludhiana; his immense privileges, as one observer put it, vying with those of the British 16th Lancers, who, after a brief and pleasurable sojourn in Kabul, returned to India with their personal pack of foxhounds.

Now the King, enthroned, indulged himself in a casual snap of his fingers, and our poor old General Elphinstone limped forward with his business of the day, but I did not see more because we were then discreetly ushered away.

The impression I gained in the Bala Hissar that morning remains with me still: Whitehall's conquest by diplomatic deceit was matched only by the profligacy of its occupying army and a corrupt and unwanted puppet – 'One of the greatest scoundrels who ever existed', as someone put it. And the last I saw of the Great Hall where a new king had the power of life and death over his unwilling subjects, was the girl wearing her yashmak . . . in her silken robes of yellow, black and green . . . staring fixedly in my direction.

It was the *way* she stared: I began to wonder if, at last, she had recognized me.

7

Winter came, thumping the craggy earth and shrieking her Irish banshees over the dull, forbidding country: haloes of cold mist wreathed the ice-pinnacles of the roaring peaks from Charikar to Ghuznee, whose charred ruins later became the mausoleum of British hopes.

We chattered that first winter, Big Rhys, Owen, Caleb and me; shivering in the bell tent, we huddled together in the howling nights; and in the long, grey days of unending labour, flung ourselves about in freezing temperatures.

The military lines lay deserted; within the tents white-faced British soldiers played black-jack, warming their frozen fingers over stubs of candles. Dark-skinned sepoys, born to warmer climates, cursed the day they had joined this mad-cap army; lost children, wandering off in the darkness, were frosted corpses within an hour; the canal froze solid; rills and streams, once merrily running across the cantonment plain, became gruesome ice palaces, changing colour to each rush of a reluctant sun.

Then came spring and the Afghan sun rose red and hissing in the east; the days now dawned in terrifying splendour.

I wrote in my diary:

10th April, 1841. I cut a spoon for Mari in springtime. It was still cold and there was a stillness over the land as if the sap was breathless with waiting. And it was dark on the night of our meeting. We met most nights, of course, but this was special; necessary, too, for very strict about herself was Mari, wriggling and slapping, and not a decent kiss would she part with unless things were done properly, she said. Which meant a love-spoon, of course; although I could hardly expect her to ask for one. So I cut a spoon for her, being full of ambition to lie with her, and so far getting nowhere. . . .

I put down the pen and blew on my fingers for warmth. Caleb came into the tent, puffing and blowing, for the wind still had a bite.

'You doin' that diary again?' he asked perceptively.

'No, I'm writing a book.'

'God preserve us! What you calling it?'

'*Rape of the Fair Country.*'

'What?' He stared down at me, and I repeated it.

'Jesus alive and reigning!' he exclaimed. 'Are ye after getting us topped and mortified? Sure the Bishop himself will have the tabs off ye for even contemplating such a title. What's it about, for God's sake?'

'It is what happened to my country. Violated, outraged, carried away by force, just like this one.'

Coming closer, he thrust his lined face into mine, and I saw the soiled visage of a face that had died: he said through cracked lips, 'If that bastard Burnes hears of it, he'll put you in chains!'

'I'll write it just the same, Caleb. Colonial conquest. England is doing the same here as at home – and all over the world,' and his bleary eyes drifted over me.

'Is that a fact! Your manhood cries out like mine, at the injustice? Do ye realize what the sods are doin' to me lovely Ireland? Write it, then, but you'll get no thanks for it, son. And if the political bastards round here find out about it, they'll tie you to a gun and flog the skin off your back.'

'That's the chance I take.'

With the coming of spring British imports doubled.

In came caravans from Herat to Persia: camel trains carried gorgeous embroideries from Turkistan; long lines of *yaboos* scrambled down the flinted roads from India: the Khyber Pass, once hostile to all, became a revived trading route for silks, cotton and dried fruits; tea and sugar from India: asafoetida, craved by the peoples of the Sind for food seasoning and hides, was bartered from the backs of protesting camels who screamed their rage at impossible loads.

The factories of Kabul spewed out buttons, leather and tanned hides: but the cotton mills of Jebal-us-Siraj and the wool factories of Kandahar, once prosperous, were now silent. Hunger gripped their workers as up the Indus sailed every kind of craft since the Creation: paddle-steamers, Arab dhows, Malayan junks and sampans, all crammed to the gunwales with cotton from Lancashire, wool from Yorkshire and iron from the Black Country.

Afghan tribesmen thrust their hawk-like faces around the eastern bazaars and honed their knives. Feuds arose in the lust for profit.

Afghanistan was fast learning the doubtful benefits of opening its doors to foreign traders.

Colonial Britain was taking over.

Come May, the yellow briar-rose was in bloom, decorating any wayside places where it could get a hold: asphodels of multi-colours – pink and brown persisting – shone their beauty into a glowing sun; blue sage embellished the stones of wells and waterways, flowering in fine profusion. And as the first wheat harvest began to festoon the arable fields, an aura of tranquillity descended over all that belied the seething hatreds of a captive population. For, while the British were at pains to offer largess to tribal chiefs, nothing was done to allay the growing hostility of a Moslem population languishing under a king they despised. Taxes rose higher, for the Shah had a galaxy of retainers.

'God help him if the balloon goes up,' said Big Rhys. 'They'll have him out of that Bala Hissar like a winkle on a pin.'

8

In the summer of that year an official durbar was celebrated at the Racecourse: an event guaranteed to pull in every Afghan for miles.

With cymbals clashing, trumpets blowing the most ghastly noises and his howdah swaying precariously upon the leading elephant the King arrived, unseen behind the silks and brocades that hid him from the common herd.

His elephant, in turn, was preceded by an ancient, stumbling Wazir: he, fallen from grace, had been relieved of his nose and ears by his ungrateful monarch. And behind these came several palanquins carried by sweating Hindu bearers. Within these was a small army of British; the officers and gentlemen of the social clubs now mushrooming in Kabul; their ladies in white, fanning vigorously against the heat, and their myriad of children.

It was the Indian Raj at its worst and best, now repeated in a newly conquered territory.

Everybody, it appeared, was going to the races, including us.

And the unprivileged Afghans, from a distance, sharpened their knives, and watched.

After the Europeans, administrative and military, trooped Nubian slaves carrying great silver bowls piled high with fruit – musk, melons, almonds, quinces and pomegranates: the slaves draped in coloured scarves and muslins giving the appearance of black ghosts floating in the wind. And Caleb, shouting above the martial music, for now the brass band of the 44th Regiment had arrived, cried, 'The second and third elephants – look!' and he pointed.

Two smaller elephants padded steadily after the first.

'The Princess Durrani,' said Caleb, 'is in the second of these: her intended in marriage – Prince Timur, the King's son – is in the first one.'

Vaguely I wondered if she had now accepted her position in the hierarchy of conquest by marriage.

This was just another day in the social round.

Clearly, the British believed the invasion of Afghanistan to be nothing more than a military saunter. From the moment the main body of our troops arrived in Kabul, military discipline was exchanged for the Raj conception of colonial pleasure.

Although going to war, British officers were determined upon comfort: whereas soldiers carried their all upon their backs, even subalterns rode; their bearers carrying items ranging from perfume to armpit powder; and delicacies such as jams and salted meats; lamp-oil, eating pottery, cutlery and bed-linen; foot and canvas hip-baths were looked upon as necessities.

All officers were given beasts to carry their wardrobes into battle. Our general employed sixty camels to carry his belongings, but another demanded four times this number, and got them. Indeed, it was said that most officers would rather have left behind their weapons than have to manage without their mess-kits and insignias of rank; the epaulettes of silver and gold, the 'bum-freezer' uniform and dressing-cases so necessary for living it up with the locals.

Balls and soirées were given weekly for local Afghan dignitaries, where officers' wives could disport themselves with Afghan gentlemen; candlelit music of quadrilles and minuets echoed down the cantonment lines.

Coffee mornings enticed rich merchants out of their mansions in the Kuzzilbash quarter, to be introduced to the latest fashions in male evening dress.

In secret, women flirted behind their fans while their menfolk, lusty in spurs and out of them, sought capricious, dusky eyes.

*

East met West in giddy coquetry. Even Lady Sale received at her mansion a procession of elegant Afghan gentlemen for morning tête-à-têtes ranging from poetry readings to lessons in Persian and Pashto; the first the language of the upper class; the second the conversation of servants.

There were dog shows; summer durbars when the rite of afternoon tea was taken and foreign guests regaled with nostalgic talk of honey-bread eaten on vicarage lawns; cucumber sandwiches, colonially English, were consumed in quantity.

Bewitched, the Afghan wealthy proved apt disciples of British culture . . . when horizons of profits rose before their eyes.

And while subalterns played polo, the senior officers hunted wild boar imported from the Punjab. This, a bloodsport like fox-hunting, entailed pursuit of the animal on horseback in case anyone other than the boar got hurt; the *coup de grâce* being performed with a cavalry lance up the boar's anus while it was running; individual success ensuring a round of gin and bitters in the Mess.

Come summer, there were tiger shoots, with safari trips into India at the invitation of local maharajas; one of whom, at the age of fourteen, had over a thousand tigers to his credit.

The rite of killing wild boars extended to stag Mess nights, when rumbustious subalterns (their horse-play looked upon with benign understanding by their seniors) chased one another around the Mess with swagger sticks and bowls of after-dinner trifle, leaving the Hindu waiters to clear up after they had carried the drunks to bed.

Military culture, however, was best served at the residence of the Assistant Envoy, Sir Alexander Burnes, where he and his brother, Charles, were living the life of Riley; local ladies taking time off to assist. All-night parties and romantic attachments did nothing to increase understanding between the British and the more conservative tribal chiefs.

41

Rumours abounded, and as more British wives began arriving, Shah Shuja saw no reason why his ladies should not join him, also: so our defenders of the Bala Hissar were turned out to accommodate his enormous harem.

Meanwhile, the fact that one of the Burnes' entourage, a Captain Warburton, was married to the niece of Dost Mohammed Khan, was not to save him. Significantly, this lady was then pursued by Akbar Khan, the fanatically nationalistic eldest son of the Dost; a frightening situation that confronted me later.

Now, the population of the Great Bazaar was flooding on to the racecourse, and six sturdy little *yaboos*, Afghan ponies, were raked into line. A bell rang and they were off in their racing colours, with the equivalent of tick-tack men making books with the zest of an afternoon at Ascot.

Placed discreetly apart from the masses on the grandstand stood the three palanquins of the Royal party; the King in the centre, the Princess on his right, and Prince Timur on his left.

The afternoon sun beat down, slanting in refracted rays off the gilded palanquins standing motionless in the heat; flanked by stalwart bodyguards decked out in armour-plated breastplates, chain-mail and decorative robes.

Between races, black slaves took round silver trays of ice-cold champagne, with orange juice and lemonade for white-frocked English ladies and nothing for the scores of yashmaked ladies of the Court; clothed from head to foot in black, these stirred occasionally to peer in disbelief through the curtains of their stifling palanquins.

Caleb returned from the bookmaker's tent in the saddling enclosure, his face jovial as he counted his winnings.

'How old is she in there?' I asked, and nodded towards the palanquins.

'Young Durrani? About fifteen, they do say.'

'And Prince Timur?'

'Over thirty.'

'So she's half his age?'

42

'That's nothing. Age don't count. In India they splice 'em at the age of seven.'

'According to her she's been abducted,' I said casually.

'O aye! Who told you that?'

I said, 'I know. That's all there is to it.'

'If you do, you're better informed than me, old son.' Caleb made a wry face. 'Perhaps you'd better write and tell the Dost about it – after all, he's her grandfather.'

'Him? He's in exile.'

He looked at me with renewed interest.

'Abducted? Where from?'

'From her school in England.'

'Dear me, we are a mine of information, aren't we! Now tell me where you got such silly guff. She's here to marry Timur, and that's an end to it.'

I didn't reply.

Now the sun was setting and the racecourse was bathed in variant hues of rosy light: slowly, the people dispersed, counting their winnings or bemoaning their losses: on the heated air came sounds of martial music – the band of the 'Fighting Fours' marching back to the cantonment. The retinue of elephants, still outrageously attired, wound their way towards the Lahore Gate and the long ascent back to the cloud-ringed palace, the fort of Bala Hissar.

9

By September even the rank and file of the army were suffering premonitions of disaster, for the population of Kabul was showing us increasing hostility.

Our General was too unhealthy for active command, and his Second-in-Command, Brigadier Shelton, a rough, courageous officer, was disrespectful enough to drop off to sleep during conferences.

Personal animosity, growing at the top, began to filter down to privates; it deeply affected morale.

But the troops still passed their days in the usual frenzy of spit and polish: the usual drill orders were barked by NCOs; the usual squads of bored soldiers stamped on the cantonment square and presented arms to non-existent generals.

Bayonet practice was emphasized on the usual text-book theory that cold steel struck terror into enemy hearts, a British guarantee to save unhappy military occasions. And the Afghan tribesmen, who actually relished close-quarter fighting, honed their scimitars to a razor sharpness.

Yet, despite the growing threat, the social rounds of the officer class continued unabated: delicacies continued to be served to visiting dignitaries, who came from afar laden with expected bribes. Arab, Turkish and Armenian merchants, treacherous, cruel and utterly unscrupulous, vied with each other for military con- tracts: Afghan nobles brought the choicest wines for officers and perfumes for their wives. A condemned British generation danced away the Kabul nights in a heady combination of nepotism and sexual favour.

44

The Afghan chiefs, their religious sensibilities now outraged, waited, and the boil began to fester.

Now a great concourse of camp followers – the traders, bearers, drivers and body servants that always battened on the armies of the East – began to organize against possible British defection; an army pulling out being a source of provisioning and safety.

At this moment lodged in the mansions and hovels around Kabul, this great army of over 12,000 now prepared to move in under our protection at the first sign of Afghan hostility; to be left behind would bring retribution for consorting with the enemy.

In the interim, the same air of indolence and inactivity continued to dominate our High Command. If the worst came to the worst, the generals said, Shah Shuja must be protected.

If necessary, it was argued, we could all move into the Bala Hissar Fort and there hold out until reinforcement marched in from India; the Raj would always survive, they said, despite the threats of barbarians.

As convicts we drew a few rupees a week, which kept us officially out of slavery: Rhys bought vegetable seeds for cultivating his little cabbage patch; Owen bought women and I bought Turkish coffee; there was nothing I liked better than to sit at a café table in the Kuzzilbash quarter, sipping it, and watching the antics of the Bazaar humanity.

On this morning in early November I hadn't been there long before a lad came up and sat beside me; I recognized him; it was the Kohistani boy who had brought me the princess's message on the steamer.

'You remember me, Sahib?' He bowed.

He was darkly handsome; dignified, despite his rags.

'Certainly.'

His arrival evoked in me a nagging distrust, as happens when someone appears unannounced, and I knew what would happen next.

The sun burned down; the jabbering of the people, now

45

pressing about us in smells of sweat, was interjected by the wailing of the hawkers and vendors; every tongue in the world must have been wagging in Kabul's filthy alleys that morning.

'My princess. You promised to help her, remember?'

'Things have changed. Now I am not interested,' I said, and sipped my coffee.

He replied with great sincerity, 'Sahib, while you drink coffee, she prays for her life.' He glanced nervously about him, clearly afraid of listeners. 'You made her a promise. In my country promises last a lifetime. Shall I tell her that you now dishonour yourself?'

It was all very smooth, and I was nervous; he had the smell of death about him. I answered, 'We keep promises in my country, too.'

'Then follow me and I will take you to her. She is with the old Vizier, deep in the city.'

Rhys, I knew, would warn against it: you could get your throat cut in the Kuzzilbash without getting mixed up with a vizier and a royal house.

I asked, 'Is it far?'

'As the raven flies, but half a mile.' His boy's face was now bright with sun.

I followed him through jumbled stalls and past criss-crossed mud hovels where fruits of a dozen hues were roof-drying in the sun: buildings, we discovered later, that defied the fire of our heavy artillery, which, we hoped, would destroy Kabul City at the first incendiary shots; in the event, the roofs collapsed, smothering the flames.

Through steaming alleys and courts we went where beggars called for alms, holding up their mutilated children. Now came food stalls where plucked poultry, a thousand heads swinging on scrawny necks, stared sightlessly as we passed; slaughtered pigs, turned inside out and crucified on doors, were ending their sacrificial days in a haze of blue-bottles.

British soldiers were lounging on the streets, slopping their ale-mugs, their flushed faces turned up to the sun: their more tipsy comrades sat with their boots up on chairs or tables, and they hip-hurrahed at us as we went by, in a country where consuming alcohol was a social crime.

Others with dusky beauties on their arms sought secret doors that opened into unofficial brothels – the 'Wives of Officers Committee' having forbidden official ones.

Here hundreds of Hindu girls – Bazaar Women, as they were called – plied a lucrative trade at a couple of rupees a time: syphilis, the perennial disease of our army of the East, was flourishing.

Slushing through inch-deep mud, we now threaded a path through the carcasses of dead dogs and cats; dancing bright-eyed children barred the way: leaping the body of a dying donkey, we entered the better quarter, the *Char Chouk* or Chief Bazaar; stopped, and went through a low iron-studded door. A drape moved on the curtained wall and an Afghan dwarf entered; he had the body of a starved raven and a beaked face to match.

Bowing low, he snapped his fingers at the Kohistani lad, who retreated: then said, 'Greetings, Sahib. I am Abaya, the Vizier. It was good of you to come. The Princess Durrani awaits you,' and he led the way into an inner chamber.

Here, in an ornately beautiful room, was a gilded chair; upon it was sitting the Princess Durrani.

'You will please kneel to show respect?' asked the Vizier.

This I ignored, remaining standing and saying, 'Tell me what you want of me.'

The eyes of Durrani slanted at me above her yashmak; dressed in a mauve gown that reached to the floor, she made no sign of recognition.

'The Kohistani boy explained nothing?' asked the Vizier.

'Only that the Princess wanted to see me,' and I added, 'can't she speak for herself?' and his hand went up.

'The situation needs careful explanation. When you first saw the Princess on the Indus River, she was being abducted from her school in England. This you know?'

I nodded, and squatting on the floor he raised his ancient face, saying tonelessly in halting English, 'Great misfortune has befallen our royal house, Sahib. As you now know, Durrani's grandfather, the rightful King, has been sent into

47

exile by your government and replaced by Shah Shuja: so, where before there was peace among our tribes, all are squabbling.'

I looked at Durrani. She was so expressionless that I began to wonder if she was drugged. Her Vizier continued, 'Our Princess has been stolen against her family's will, for marriage to Timur, the son of the Shah. By this the Sadozai hope to weld the tribes together.'

'A political marriage?'

'A loveless one born of intrigue, when she should either be safe at school, or in the arms of her grandfather, the Dost Mohammed Khan.'

I interjected, 'Nevertheless, would not such a marriage bring peace?'

'It will not. When her first son sits on the Afghan throne, it will bring war. For the Sadozai are hated and the Barakzai are loved, as is the Dost.' His face twisted up. 'For which your country will be rightly punished. Akbar Khan, this girl's uncle, has sworn that when he has finished with you only one Feringhee will be left alive to carry the news to India.'

And I answered, 'If that be so, Vizier, I will not be around to assist you.'

'Ah, but you will be spared: I will see to it.' He shuffled closer on the carpeted floor. 'Are you not convicts; like our King, rejected people? To whom do you owe allegiance, to your Queen whom you tried to overthrow, or yourselves?'

'We still give loyalty to our country.' And he smiled at this, exposing broken, yellow teeth.

'And to a young woman who has been equally condemned? Think, man, think! What have you to lose, if only your lives?' and he shuffled away, bowed before Durrani, and added, 'Now let my Princess speak for herself and you will learn the evil of Britain's intrigues.' From his robes he drew a scroll and handed it to Durrani, saying, 'Read, child: let him hear it from your own lips.'

She said, unrolling it, 'This letter from my grandfather was sent to me while I was in England.' She read aloud:

'To The Princess Durrani, Granddaughter of Dost

Mohammed Khan, the Barakzai Ruler of Afghanistan, by the Grace of God.

'Ludhiana, India.

'Beloved Child,
   'I languish here in constant thoughts of you, for you also are in exile.
   'Soon Shah Shuja, the usurper, will send viziers to England to bring you back to Kabul for marriage into the hated Sadozai.
   'Being far away I am unable to help you. Resist, my daughter, for you are not of common blood, but that of the Afghan Royals.
   'Seek the help of patriots in the struggle to stay free – noble men who fight injustice in the name of our country: trust nobody, least of all Akbar, your uncle, who has a greedy eye for monarchy.
   'When we return to Afghanistan your bed shall be of inlaid gold: jasmine and eglantine shall perfume your chambers, in the love and felicitation of your beloved grandfather.'

Durrani lowered the letter, adding simply, 'The letter is addressed to me at my school in Sussex. Within a week the officers of the Shah arrived and brought me here to Kabul.'
   I asked Durrani, 'You have no relatives here?'
   'None that she can trust,' answered the Vizier. 'Durrani's mother, a European lady, died at her birth in Simla; her father was killed in Lahore.'
   'A European mother? I didn't know this.'
   'That she is of your blood? See her skin – is it not almost as white as yours?'
   'And if my comrades and I decide to help, where and when do we come for Durrani?'
   '*Ah*!' The Vizier made a long-drawn whistling sound with his teeth. 'This is the smallest problem. *Listen*. Within the month the Shah is turning his great harem out of the Bala Hissar to make room for more defenders. When this happens, Durrani will be brought to my hunting lodge at Seh Baba, which is on the route of your retreat to Jalalabad.'

'Always assuming we intend to retreat!'

'It will happen when the first snows fall. I know it, so does your High Command.'

I got up. 'I will think about this, but I am making no promises – certainly I cannot speak for my two comrades.'

The old man bowed to me, saying, 'Allah wills it, Sahib. The future of my country is in his hands, not yours. One day he will return the Dost to his rightful throne. He commands; all, including you, obey.'

It was doubtful if the others would entertain similar views, I thought, as I took my leave of them: and cursed myself for becoming involved in such a mad-cap escapade.

Clearly, if the army didn't get us, this old man would: there was about him a smell of evil.

10

Sacred to the genius of torture, as the army began to organize for a possible retreat back to India, things came to a head at the beginning of December when the first snows of winter covered the land.

'Top o' the marnin' to ye, me son,' cried Caleb, coming into the furnace compound, his face creased in smiles. 'Are ye healthy this foine day, Iestyn?'

'Aye, for people about to get their throats cut, we're doing passably well.'

'Is your mood poor, then?'

'The mood's fine. It's meeting bog Irishmen first thing in the morning.'

'Is it really true that these bloody fanatics are after killin' us dead?'

'They're going to hit the livin' daylights out of us,' replied Rhys. 'Incidentally, have ye seen that big oaf, Owen, in your travels?'

'I have not.'

Caleb glared around the glowering faces of the Hindu labourers, who were standing about in moods of undisguised hostility.

'Aren't these sinners working, then?'

I replied, 'There's been rioting up in the Bazaar: last night shops in the city were plundered, so they're windy. Didn't you hear the firing?'

'Och, forget it!' Caleb waved me down. 'Sure, it wouldn't be Kabul if they didn't loot it from time to time,' and he raised his stick and threatened them, shouting, 'Back to work, ye lazy spalpeens, or I'll lay ye end to end, so I will!'

With disgruntled stares they obeyed.

Later, he asked, 'Where's your Owen got to, then?'

'We were asking you.'

We were casting shell-proof beams for the roof of the Commissariat Grain Fort, which appeared utter lunacy, since it was a mile south of the cantonment, an outpost: its threatened capture would starve us out.

The Magazine Fort, which we were also repairing, was worse situated, being beyond musket range of the 44th. Indeed, the cantonment's defences were scandalous, being dependent on a shallow ditch which a donkey could leap across.

Caleb said, 'The last time I saw Owen was up in the Kuzzilbash, and the lad was doin' foine, with a pretty wee bitch in one hand and a bottle of gin in the other.'

Big Rhys frowned into the weak sunlight. 'It's time he was back, the fool; things are hotting up in the Bala Hissar.'

'Worse since they started blowing Ghilzais from the guns,' I said.

'You wait till Prince Timur really gets going,' replied Caleb. 'He's running the palace now, they say. Tomorrow he's turning out the rest of his father's harem to make room for more defenders.'

'I'll believe that when I see it, that old boy's fond of his women,' said Rhys, and he opened his shoulders and, grunting, lifted a long cast of pig-iron, put one end under his belt and began breaking it on a stone into convenient lengths.

Caleb observed, 'Ladies of the coin, women of the pave! I've no conscience about 'em – let the buggers freeze.'

'Eight hundred harem beauties loose will put the skids under Kabul, that's for sure.'

And Caleb cried, his arms up to the sky, 'And turn the Promised Land into another Sodom and Gomorrah.

'Sure, I like women well enough in their place, like comin' out o' Church on a Sunday with the sun in their bonnets, and I like best of all Our Lady of Sorrows,' and he crossed himself.

'But street women are the spawn of iniquity, and when God

swipes a hand at that mate of yours he'll die of pneumonia.' He did a jig on the slag. 'Bless and reward ye, I says to me Maker, for with me hat on sideways, I'm havin' a wonderful time in His world. But that Welshman's nothin' but a bloody jack-rabbit – he does everything but eat his dinner with it.'

This raised my eyes. 'And whose fault is that? Is it his, or the shifty buggers who sent him here, thousands of miles from home?'

'Aye, me son, there's a lot in that,' agreed Caleb. ' 'Tis the English Parliament ye look for if you're after a rat in the barrel, and there's naught between any of 'em, Whig or Tory.'

'Are you well informed on the subject, then?' asked Rhys sarcastically.

'More than you, ye numbskull, for I powdered me wig in Parliamentary debate before you two were on tits, and I'd do it ag'in if I thought I'd bring some sense into them.'

'Don't tell me you were one of the layabouts,' I interjected, to madden him, but I was surprised at his reply.

'Listen, you! For a century Parliament has been nothin' but a talking shop where silk-hatted battalions meet to crack jokes, spout nonsense, and make private fortunes in public time. It's a game o' shuttlecock, me darlin's, where the debutantes amuse themselves by tossing about high sounding phrases that have no basis in fact. And an uneducated nation accepts the farce in the belief that it's payin' for intellectualism. *Bah*! 'Tis a sham, said Cobbett, where all are comrades when it comes to profit and all thieves in the plunder; while the Upper House is a home for dozies, foot-proppers and chinless wonders,' and he spat.

'It appears you've had some bad experiences,' said Rhys. 'Have you really been a Member of the House of Commons, then?'

'I'll not answer that, my friend. Come on, get movin', or I'll have ye both on jankers for a fortnight.'

It gave us something to think about; but meanwhile, as usual, Owen was our main topic of conversation – he had been missing for two days now, which meant that soon we would have to go in search of him; a sensitive issue with

Kabul at boiling point.

It was time for another furnace tap that dusk, and I was cleaning off a firing-iron for Rhys when the Kohistani lad appeared again in the shimmering light of the compound; he came like a genie bright in a sudden glow, for Rhys had just knocked out the bung and the sow and her molten piglets were alight with rainbow fire. This brought crowds of people racing out of the city, as usual, so the lad's presence was unnoticed.

'A letter, Sahib,' said he, and disappeared into the crowd as quickly as he had come.

Later, in the privacy of our tent, I lit a stub of candle.

Within an envelope was a little map attached to a note, and I read:

My Friend,

I write secretly, because everybody in the fort here is being watched. Tomorrow, as the Vizier told you, Prince Timur is turning out his father's women to make room for more defence troops. This, as we thought, should enable me to slip out unnoticed with them, and make my way to the Vizier's house in Kabul city. From there I will be taken to the hunting lodge at Seh Baba, where I will meet you during your retreat to India. I enclose a map showing its position in Seh Baba village.

May Allah reward you for your promise to help me to reach my grandfather.

The letter was unsigned.

Next evening when Owen had still not returned from the city, Rhys and I sat together at the furnace, sheltering in its warmth. I said, 'If he isn't back by dark we ought to go in after him.'

'But where to look, for God's sake?'

'Down in the Kuzzilbash first, the brothels.'

'*Duw!* It's one thing after another. What about that note you were sent last night?'

'What about it?'

'Seh Baba? It sounds to me like a trap.'

'No, I told you – I was expecting it.'

'Where is it, anyway?'

'About twelve miles east of here on the road to India.'

'How will she get there?'

'That's up to her. We're due to meet her at the hunting lodge of the Vizier loyal to Dost Mohammed Khan.'

'You know how to get there?'

I showed him the little map.

'You've met this Abaya, you say?'

'I told you in detail. Don't you remember anything?'

'Can you trust him?'

'No farther than I could throw him.'

'Then aren't we taking risks?'

'Probably.'

We sat together. The grasses whispered about us. Overnight the first snow of winter had fallen, a portent of the cold to come, and the wind had shivers in him.

Rhys said, 'Back home in Blaenafon folks used to talk about the mad Mortymers, now I know why. Give me one good reason why I should lift a finger to help this princess.'

'Because she's been abducted and it's the decent thing to do – also, her mother was a European.'

'That makes no difference.'

'Which accounts for her lighter colouring.'

Rhys grunted. 'She's a pretty little bint, and if she gets clear she'll be luckier than some.' He nodded towards Kabul, and I saw beyond the smoking maw of the Caleb furnace the sea of the city's mud-flat hovels, where smoke of the rioting was rising against the redness of the sun; faintly came the staccato rattle of desultory firing.

I said, flatly, 'Murder will be done when the patriots get their hands on those zenana girls.'

'Perhaps,' came the reply, 'but meanwhile, I'm more concerned about Owen,' and he proceeded to fill his clay pipe, an insanitary thing he kept cocked up in the corner of his mouth, and gave me a look to kill. 'We're convicts, mun, not nursemaids to princesses.'

I eyed him. 'If your Dathyl got into a jam, wouldn't you see her through it?'

'Maybe, but this one ain't my Dathyl. Meanwhile let's go and find Owen.'

We didn't have to look far, for Owen had returned to the cantonment during our absence, but not in one piece.

They must have wired him up before they carried him out of the city, and in the dark erected him upon the cross that held him upright, what was left of him. His eyeless sockets were staring up at the moon; he had been castrated, and his hands and feet were missing; upon his naked breast were scrawled the words:

All dirty Feringhees, get out of Kabul.

11

Owen was not the first casualty of Afghan revenge: the corpses of British soldiers, disobedient to Standing Orders, were nightly being picked up on the outskirts of the cantonment and the streets of Kabul, and our people made unavailing protests to the Afghan authorities.

This activity coincided with the beginning of our night defence, ironically called by the troops the 'Gelding Patrols'; castration being automatically guaranteed if one fell into the hands of one of the local tribes: rumours abounded that during such military action the seriously wounded were being left behind by those most active in escaping. And soon there developed a banter which named this practice 'The Nelson Touch': this, based on the death of Nelson, proclaimed the navy's system of throwing overboard the more seriously wounded: some wag suggested that, in addition to the dying words of 'Kiss me, Hardy', was appended the plea, 'And please don't feed me to the sharks like we do the ordinary seamen, poor sods.' Fears of being abandoned thus subscribed to decreasing military activity at a time when good patrolling might have given clearer indications of the Afghans' intentions.

Yet, despite such terrors, the troops' escapades continued; our soldiers slipped out of the cantonment under cover of darkness: Owen's death was a prime example of such indiscipline.

Minor rioting began, which swiftly grew in intensity, the mobs sweeping through the alleys of Kabul, killing and looting. The home of Sir Alexander Burnes, the Assistant

Political Envoy, was burned, together with the Treasury Office, a fact which the taxpayers at home officially deplored; as no doubt Sir Alexander would have done, given the opportunity.

To this day it is astonishing to me that he couldn't see it coming.

'I hear they got Burnes,' said Big Rhys.

'So the rumours go.'

We were waiting for Caleb to arrive, which was dependent on how much he had consumed the night before; anything more than a bottle could bring him as late as midday.

Clearly the time had come for revenge upon Burnes, a man who had flouted their principles and religious beliefs under the Afghans' noses; this man's profligacy had forged its own outcome. Dragging him out of his house with the rest of his companions, the tribesmen stripped them naked and methodically cut them to pieces in the street: the same fate was then meted out to seventy of the guards next door, after the theft of the Treasury coffers.

This was the signal for Afghanistan to rise in rebellion against the British; a precursor of the Indian Mutiny against the Raj five years later. British colonialism in the East was now under fire, the long fuse being lit by Afghan tribesmen.

'More fool Burnes for living so far out,' said Rhys. 'Cool little beggar. Apparently he said to his secretary, as the mob started coming through the windows, "It would appear, Mohun Lal, that it is time I left the country." I could have told him that a year ago.'

Caleb, arriving with bags under his eyes like the flesh-pots of Kabul, said, 'They got the Assistant Envoy, did ye hear? Him, his brother, and young Willie Broadfoot, our captain's brother; plus all the Treasury staff and eighty of the Sepoy guard – blood is running in the gutters, and the lads will be on half pay.'

'Thousands of pounds stolen – Whitehall's going to love it.'

'We'll be on half rations, too,' said Caleb. 'Last night they burned the Secondary Grain Store: if they get the Main Commissariat we'll have nothing to eat – thank God for the High Command.'

'Like the elephant's backside,' said Rhys. 'The higher the formation the bigger the balls,' and we trooped disconsolately up to the furnace compound.

That night I wrote in my diary:

The Afghans have occupied the Zoolficar's Fort, an old tumbledown north of the cantonment, and within the range of their *jezails*; our tents are now being peppered. General Elphinstone ordered an attack upon it, but his 44th Foot broke when Afghan cavalry got among them. Many dead and wounded, mostly raw recruits. Sir Alexander Burnes and scores of his employees have been murdered and hacked to pieces and the Army Treasury, which was next door, looted. Now the Afghans are gradually surrounding our encampment. Rumour says that scores of young harem girls, thrown out of the Bala Hissar by the King, have been butchered on the streets of Kabul. Meanwhile for our protection, the three of us are moving out of the furnace tent, deeper into the cantonment.

16th December 1841
The enemy is now on top of the Beymaroo Heights to the north of us. All this morning they bombarded us: tents and men blown to pieces. Brigadier Shelton, leading the 44th, stormed the hill, but thousands of Afghan infantry and cavalry rushed out of Kabul, and our men came tearing home pell-mell. The Afghans have taken the grain fort and we are now surrounded; food running out; camels and horses already starving. Soon we will begin a retreat to Jalalabad, just as the old Vizier predicted.

20th December, 1841
It is snowing hard. Everything is iced up. We have begun to slaughter the animals; expecting it, they scream horribly. The ponies are eating each others' tails. Just heard that Akbar Khan, the warrior son of Dost Mohammed Khan, has arrived to take command of the tribes in Kabul: Lady Sale says he is a fiend, that

59

he once skinned a captive alive. Certainly I could never hand Durrani over to such a relative. The troops are utterly dispirited; the camp followers are dying of the cold: on half rations for weeks, I'm as thin as a Handel flute now. Caleb seems to thrive on whiskey. Lady Sale inspected us this morning; she looks healthy enough, also her daughter, Mrs Sturt, our new captain's wife, who said that the general is thinking of taking us into the Bala Hissar whether the King wants us in there or not. How they change their minds!

Imperious, autocratic, Lady Sale strode the lines outside our cookhouse – I swear she was six feet tall. She cried, 'What did the General say? Skulk under the beds up in the Bala Hissar? A bunch of cowards? Is this the role of the British Army? Cold steel is what they want, Caleb – the bayonet would teach them better manners – can you hear me?'

'They can hear you on the other side of the Hindu Kush, milady,' replied he, and ignoring this, she shouted:

'Don't stand there grinning, man! Are your convicts ready for the evacuation?'

'All present and correct, milady, ready to retreat.'

'Retreat? *Evacuation*, you fool. Who's talking about retreat? I'll have you know that retreat is not in the English vocabulary.'

'It is in mine, milady,' said Caleb. 'It's all right for the ladies, for they've got nothin' to lose, but it's me intention to meet me Maker with all spare parts attached, beggin' ye pardon for the affront.'

'Caleb, you are beyond redemption!'

'Aye, well make the most of me, for me days are growin' short. Every time I see those Afghan fellas with their knives out, me soul breaks into an English canter.'

'Make the most of it, then, for you'll get no help here. Anyone who slanders England, slanders me.'

'That I will, for I'd rather be scratchin' a tinker's bum in the gaols of Galway than living the life of Riley in enemy country.'

She went off, waving him down with laughter; how he got away with it beats me to this day.

With her grandchild in her arms she went, not bothering to duck the whizzing Afghan bullets.

Now, with the tempo of the attacks increasing, events came to a head.

Our Envoy, Sir William McNaghten, in an attempt to parley with the Afghan chief, Akbar Khan, now suffered the same fate as Burnes: a terrible death, and the first real sign of Afghan treachery; until now the tribal chiefs had been reasonable in their transactions with us.

With iron-making now ceased and in an attempt to turn my mind to peaceful things, I concentrated on my diary.

23rd December, 1841
Soon it will be Christmas; peace on earth and goodwill! God help us. You should see the state of us! This morning Sir William McNaghten and three other officers rode out to parley with Akbar Khan, who promised them a safe passage: our Envoy's idea was to offer a bribe in return for our safe retreat to India, but treachery was in the air. Akbar Khan suddenly cried *'Begeer! Begeer!'* ('Seize! Seize!') and his chiefs attacked our party: two of them, Captains MacKenzie and Lawrence, managed to escape, but Sir William and Captain Trevor were cut to pieces on the spot, the standard Afghan death. There is now a terrible gloom over the cantonment as the enemy continues to plaster us with *jezail* fire, killing men and animals and shredding the tents. Rhys, Caleb and I, huddled behind a little stone wall to escape the bullets, heard that the trunk of Sir William's body, its head and limbs severed, was dragged around the alleys of Kabul, then hung above the gateway of the Great Bazaar.

Christmas Day, 1841
The enemy now control the Seeah Sung heights north of us and keep up artillery fire upon us; the cantonment is mushrooming with detonations. Our dead and wounded are numbered in hundreds, many being

among the camp followers who swarmed in for protection after hostilities began. We bury them without shrouds in nameless graves. Every day now there is talk of a truce being arranged, so that we can pull out of this hell and retreat to Jalalabad: our forts – Rikabashel, Mahmood, Zoolficars, Auguetil and Magazine – are now occupied – hundreds of men have died trying to defend them; now they are turned against us with raking fire. As fast as the Afghans come at us, we kill them: yesterday we killed 150, we ourselves losing twenty-six dead of the 44th – mere boys – and over fifty of the 37th. It is dreadful slaughter; the lines of muddy alleys between the tents are churned red; the tattered tents in which we crouch for shelter from the snow are blotched with blood: beyond our defence ditch from where now the enemy fire at will, our dead lie unburied.

A cannon-ball fell between Big Rhys and I this morning, dislodging an earth embankment which buried him. Under *jezail* fire, I dug him out.

'They can keep this bloody army,' was all he said, 'I'm off back to Wales.'

We lay together in the mud while the rain pelted down and bullets sighed over us.

'You hungry, boy?' he asked.

'Bloody starved.'

'Old Owen was lucky, I reckon.'

'At least he had a few ups, before he went down, poor sod.'

'That's the last thing I've got in mind.'

Cross-fire from the *jezails* increased about us, and after another explosion I was aware that Rhys was lying on top of me; I shoved him off.

'I forgot,' he said, 'I thought you was my missus.'

We lay together in cold, shivering friendship.

He asked, 'You think we'll get back?'

'Bless me soul to hell,' interjected Caleb, diving down into the mud between us. ' 'Tis furthest from me intentions to

62

leave me bones in this pagan place, I'm off to Ireland and into a monastery. Who's comin'?'

We ignored him.

'Only last night I was thinkin' of me past, ye see,' continued Caleb, 'for I spent me youth in a most unusual manner. From the age of ten, since I planned to be a monk, I spent me spare time adding up the full stops in the Bible – do you know how many there are?'

It is wonderful how a man's thoughts turn to God when in the thrall of danger. Caleb started it, and Rhys and I were willing communicants.

We didn't reply, so he continued, 'Right, I'll tell ye. There's two million, six hundred and fifty-four thousand, nine hundred and forty-three – would ye believe that?'

'No!'

The Afghans had turned one of our own nine-pounders on to us now, and it was raking the cantonment, but nothing bothered Caleb, who said, ' 'Tis an arithmetical fact, son, it took me three months to count the commas – four million, two hundred and twenty-two thousand, eight hundred and sixty-four. . . .'

'Wrong,' said Rhys, 'you've not counted Revelations.'

'And do you know the number of semi-colons and colons?'

'I never got round to it,' said I.

Mud and stones rained down upon us.

'And the shortest sentence?'

'Jesus wept,' said Rhys. 'And I bet He's at it now.'

'More than likely, and the word "Lord" occurs only once, as if God only just remembered to slip the thing in. Will ye have any more of it, for I've got some other shockers.'

The bombardment suddenly ceased; side by side we lay there shivering while the rain, turned to snow now, began to cover our faces with great white flakes, like frosted lotus flowers.

Rhys said, sitting up, 'So what will you do with all this biblical information?'

'State it before the hand of St Peter when I get up there, it'll likely help me cause.'

'Have you thought you might have added up wrong?' I

asked, getting to my feet, while Caleb followed me in grunts and wheezes.

'Aw, ye wee bowsie, stop coddin' me along! Would St Peter be likely to add up all the full stops and commas in the Bible?'

'He could ask his boss,' said Rhys. 'He'll know.'

Caleb scratched his ear.

'You'd best start a recount,' said I. 'It'll be hell and damnation if they find you've been making it up.'

'Jesus,' said Caleb, 'I never thought of that.'

Parley after parley went on day and night, with much coming and going of military deputations and the issuing of political documents; every effort was made to obtain Afghan protection of our women and children.

3rd January, 1842
It is bitterly cold. I am writing this in the open with freezing hands. We are appalled at the utter imbecility of our Commanding Officer. Knowing that we are about to retreat, the people of Kabul, ignoring our levelled muskets, gather along the perimeter of the cantonment: from there they hurl abuse at us, and we are forbidden to drive them away. At night thieves roam among us at will, lifting everything movable, from ammunition boxes to tethered animals; sleep is impossible, lest one awakes with a knife in the ribs, and the poor camp followers, huddled together in the snow, are special targets of Afghan hatred, who are now paying off old scores; five of them, two women and three men, were found this morning with their throats cut. One of their leaders, an Armenian merchant, asked our General for a dozen soldiers: with these, he said, he would drive the murdering tribesmen out of the cantonment; the offer was refused; it is essential, said the General, not to anger the enemy more than is necessary! The man cursed and swore (his wife had been murdered), calling Elphinstone and his staff a bunch of English cowards. Now comes the Afghan promise that Akbar Khan's own tribesmen will escort us safely on to the Jalalabad road. Can this be trusted?

Lady Sale said to Caleb, who had taken her a little bottle of gin, 'We march tomorrow, they tell us. We have no money, no firewood and little food. Yet, some of our officers' ladies are quite ready to leave – lying in their night-dresses in the warm blankets of their palanquins! They are straight out from England, of course, but can you believe it – expecting to be carried by native bearers! We are quite unprepared for a retreat of ninety miles through icy mountains to Jalalabad: these people, who are more at home playing croquet, are going to prove a tremendous liability: and the crass stupidity of this General Staff has to be seen to be comprehended.'

'What did you reply to all that?' I asked Caleb.

'With that old girl you don't reply, you just listen.'

5th January, 1842

This might be my last diary entry. What comes after this can only perhaps be jotted down in odd moments. The camp, the whole forbidding country, is covered in a mantle of glacial whiteness; snow continues to fall, covering everything. Ravenously hungry, we shiver in a gale howling over a scene of panic. Animals and men are struggling to prepare for the retreat, which is constantly delayed by poor administration. The Indian sepoys are already ill. As fast as an animal dies the camp followers ravenously fall upon the carcass like famished locusts. All Rhys, Caleb and I have eaten in three days is a handful of flour mixed with buffalo milk. We melt snow, for drinking-water is frozen; also, the Afghans now command the nearby river, which soon we will have to cross. The whole army – some 4,500 men – and its 12,000 camp followers (and God knows how many children) will have to march along one main road through Begramee to Boothak: after which the terrible Khoord-Kabul pass lies before us: there, no doubt, Akbar Khan and his tribesmen will be awaiting us.

Meanwhile, the situation here is unbelievable. Hundreds of ponies and camels are stampeding under the continual bombardment. The agreed truce to get our people and baggage out has been broken; musketry fire from the hills cuts down the drivers; overturned carts and dead animals litter the cantonment roads. And the Afghans, although they promised us a safe passage, are now sending in fanatical groups to kill and loot. The night is filled with the cries of humans and the shrieks of animals; the confusion of rat-a-tat *jezail* fire is punctuated with shrill bugling as the companies try to form up for the march.

Ricochets add to the explosions and clamour: wandering toddlers beseech any passing stranger, for the bearded Ghilzais are among us now, yelling their battle cries. Tents and buildings are ablaze, the flames lighting up the icicled peaks of the mountains. Along our useless defences, the bearded Afredis and Kakrese perform their ritual dances with threatening knives; or jeer at us, for retreat, to them, is dishonourable.

Now separated from Caleb and Rhys, I searched through the milling mob of camp followers. Hauling impossible loads of grain, they fight to control splay-legged, bucking camels: elephants, tethered for gun-hauling, are trumpeting and kicking at their chains. Now the Indian cavalry, more than a thousand, is moving through the cantonment followed by the Sepoy battalions and six hundred of the 44th: these, carving a path through the camp followers, are marching down to the Kabul river; a black serpent of humans and animals trudging across a scene of dazzling whiteness. And in the train of the main exodus of 20,000 men and animals, the already exhausted, ill-clad labourers and their families, like scattered leaves of a ravaged forest, are already lying down in the snow to die, though the march has only just begun.

12

At seven o'clock that morning the funeral cortège moved off; the first obstacle to be crossed being Sturt's Bridge within a mile of the cantonment.

This, a temporary bridge of gun-limbers over the Kabul river, we had built at General Elphinstone's insistence, despite protests that with the water level low, we could safely ford it at a dozen places. Now the bridge had proved a bottleneck; a turmoil of disorder where every unit, frantic to escape, was bunching in a congested mass.

It was being said that Shah Shuja was at the bottom of the insurrection, in order to get rid of us. . . .

A weak sun clothed in whirling snow glared down upon a struggling mass. Bunching up at the bridge approach, shrieking men and animals were now being attacked head on, shredded by point-blank fire from the Afghans.

'Iestyn, give a hand!' shouted Rhys, and I waded up beside him and righted an overturned palanquin where a woman and her infant child had spilled into the river: camp followers, instantly using the palanquin as a stepping-stone, were scrambling over it.

'For God's sake – my baby!'

Seeing a child floating downstream I dived after it, snatching back the soaked bundle out of a mêlée of plunging horses and flying whips: seeing a flash vision of the mother's face, I put the little one into her arms.

'Come on!' bawled Rhys, waist deep. '*Come on!*'

The waterproof packet containing my diary entries came out of my pocket: I snatched them back before they were swept away.

We were in the van of the 44th Regiment, a mass of red coats struggling to cross Sturt's Bridge. The cavalry, behind us, were lashing at the bullocks hauling the gun-limbers: fires were burning all over the cantonment.

With but a quarter of the camp followers out, the Afghans were already looting; making bonfires of the rails and pews out of the Mission Church; carrying off everything movable from altar cloth and chalices to the carpets, beds and wardrobes of the Padre's House next door.

I saw two giants, their bearded faces alight with exultation, pause in headlong haste above a woman beseeching them upon her knees: one held her, the other cut her throat.

Dancing against the fires like outrageous pygmies, yelling their battle cries, the tribesmen methodically murdered and pillaged.

Adding to the panic came more elephants; lumbering into the crowd with their big gun carriages ploughing up the mud behind them.

Temperamental under fire (and a long-range bombardment had now started again from the Beymaroo Hills), these titans trumpeted their terror, trampling underfoot the wounded and dying.

Now the Bala Hissar guns joined in the detonations, mistakenly cutting red swathes into the black serpent fighting to cross the river. We of the vanguard, having gained the eastern bank, were now tramping miserably, soaked and shivering, along the road to Jalalabad.

At our head was Brigadier Anquetil; after him came Captain Sturt's sappers and miners, of which we formed a part: a troop of the King's Cavalry followed us, hauling small mountain guns: Brigadier Shelton, commanding the rearguard, was fighting off the enemy gnawing at our backs.

The country was covered in whiteness; the snow a foot deep on the roads, and hedge-high about us.

'Aha, the convict, is it not?'

It was a woman's voice cutting through the chattering musketry: I glanced up, having heard that voice before.

Lady Sale, of course – always the bad penny; now as much at home sitting side-saddle amid a holocaust as when riding to hounds in a country park.

I replied, with bad grace, 'The name's Mortymer, lady.'

'Ah, so! Help me, please? I am looking for that drunken Caleb.'

'Not with us, ma'am.' I gave her short shrift, expecting my head to be blown off at any moment.

'Do you know where he is?' She asked this of Big Rhys, who, head down, was lumbering along beside me.

'Somewhere up front with Captain Sturt, missus,' he called.

'So I hoped, for I saw them earlier; actually it is my son-in-law I seek.'

The pony shouldered me, and I shoved it away: women, snow-encrusted and shivering, raised imploring hands from the berm as we passed, so I wasn't very interested in English gentry just then. Nor was Rhys, by his glowering upward glances.

Reining in her pony, milady cried shrilly, 'So if you see Captain Sturt, kindly inform him that his wife and little girl are now safely with me.'

The snow swirled; the wind blustered about us, momentarily obliterating the wails and yells, the screaming of horses, the hoarse lamentations of the camels, and I saw in Lady Sale's face a friendly smile; she cried above the din, 'You saved my granddaughter, Mortymer. I am obliged to you, and will repay it. Remember that.'

Now the snow changed from gentle flakes into a blizzard: encrusting our eyes, it painted up our clothes. The wind sang an eerie song, howling down from the frosted peaks, hammering the dull forbidding country with the fists of January. From Boothak to the Khoord Kabul, the land

69

became sheeted ice.

Shining and beautiful were the peaks of the Tarekhee Pass looming up before us: ranges of mountain peaks awaiting us in diadems of brilliance, comrades to a watery sun: she, as bejewelled as a Turkish harlot, sat in the majesty of the sky and beckoned us on towards ravines and chasms we would have to cross to reach Jalalabad.

Rhys frowned up into the driving snow. 'Look at those mountains! Do you think we'll get through?'

'If we do it'll be a miracle.'

Tramp, tramp, tramp on the icy road, the poor bloody infantry: boots, boots and still more boots: ranging cannon shots from Kabul were now whining over our heads; distantly came the rattle of musketry, the dull booming guns and the howls of animals.

Rhys said, 'You're a cheerful sod, aren't you!'

I jerked my thumb. 'Back in Kabul they're chewing up the rearguard.'

We marched on into the sunset, a clanking army of soaked, dispirited men moving amid protests, curses, or in the quiet of those already condemned. The dull thudding of boots on snow was accompanied by the clanking of water-bottles against bayonet scabbards.

Eastward, ever eastward we marched, under a blood-stained sky.

Here, I remembered, the cavalry of Alexander had perished under the knives of pursuing tribes: the crunching of our gun wheels had been heard before in the cruelties of Genghis Khan, he whose gilded pennants had flown in another age of torture.

Lost in this macabre reverie, I did not immediately see the little Indian child lying naked on the roadside, for of corpses we now took no heed, but this child was alive.

'God help me, what do we do about her?' asked Rhys.

'All right,' said a voice, 'I'll take her,' and a young colour sergeant stepped out of the marching ranks: stooping, he lifted the child against him. Pressing his face upon hers, he breathed upon her icy body.

'Just look what Jesus did!' said he, and patted the baby.

'Ay, ay,' called Rhys above the guns. 'He's havin' a right old time back there, ain't he – killing off the bloody rearguard.'

'Oh, aye? Then who started this war – us or God?' and the sergeant opened his buttons and pushed the baby down against his chest. 'We're bound for Hell, man, so best not make a song and dance about it before ye meet St Peter.'

'No offence, mind,' said Rhys, for a full-blown colour sergeant could make your life a misery.

'None taken,' came the reply, 'but I can be a rough young bugger when I meet the Infidels and disbelievers.' Bending, he patted the baby's head. 'What's your names, you two?' he asked. 'I ain't seen you before.'

We told him.

'Ho ho! Bad lads, ain't you! Got caught wi' your hands in the till, eh?'

'Not that bad,' I said, 'we only wanted to hang the Queen,' and told him more.

'Ach, me lad, now you're a-talkin'!' said he. 'If you'd had me along I'd 'ave helped to string her up.'

'Not so loud,' said Rhys, glancing around.

'Ach, to hell – who cares? We'll all be in bloody strips afore nightfall,' and he opened the top of his tunic again, whispering, 'you all right down there, my lovely?'

Night fell: we dropped down into the snow and slept where we had fallen. Many froze to death before the coming of dawn. And with the dawn came the ragged, exhausted rearguard who had been fighting off the enemy on our tail . . . just in time to start again the onward plod. Many fell down in the snow, crying with the cold; others staggered in, supporting wounded comrades.

'God help us, this is a shambles,' said Rhys.

13

Friday, 7th January, 1842

Caleb, on this second day of the retreat, came down from the vanguard, and said, 'D'ye know somethin'? I helped deliver a woman up from there – twins, as dead as doornails. Then on the way back here I came across the band conductor – remember Conductor MacGregor? He was standing against a tree with Cornet Hardyman of the 5th Cavalry beside him, and the pair of them were statues of ice, so I rubbed his ear, shouting, "Are ye alive in there, Conductor?" and the corporal began to fall, so I grabbed his arm, and the thing came off in me hand. Be Jesus, I was away like a hare. Ach, it's terrible – what's happenin' to us?'

'We're all dead, but we think we're alive,' I said.

'But, we've only come to Boothak – five miles; it's another ninety to Jalalabad.'

'Don't remind us.'

Not much time for aimless discussion, Rhys and I, for the column had halted when it should have been marching, and I mentioned it.

'Aye, well we've madmen in charge of us, haven't we!' replied Caleb. 'We're supposed to be east of Khoord-Kabul by now.'

' 'Tis military intelligence, ye see,' said Rhys. 'We've got to give the Ghilzais time to crown the heights of Khoord and shoot us to ribbons tomorrow morning – what say you, Sergeant?' and the reply came:

' 'Tis the elephant's backside again: they collect all the

nitwits they can find in Oxford, and send 'em out here as the General Staff. Is there owt to eat?'

'Nowt,' said a passing soldier, and his face was grey with hunger.

'What about the Commissariat Stores? There's wheat and flour there; didn't it get out of the cantonment?'

'Caught at the bridge, Sarge.' The man squatted in the snow.

'The Afghans filched the lot,' said another, and his face was bloodstained. 'I saw the melted ghee go up in flames with the wheat wagons, and they carted all the barley off into Kabul. The *otta* and *bhoosa* carts were knocked off, too – I tell ye, I never saw an ounce o' grub come out of that cantonment. What the hell are we supposed to eat?'

'Cattle food?'

'Don't make me laugh. I'm cavalry, and our horses have been on twigs and tree-bark for weeks.'

'Is there any other news coming out of Kabul?'

'Only that this new fella, Akbar Khan, has taken over command of the tribes.'

I pricked up my ears.

The man added, 'He knows more about makin' war than any of our lot, according to accounts.'

'Where is he now, then?'

'Still in Kabul, they say.'

'I hope he bloody stays there.'

'If he gets around here, God help us,' said the sergeant.

Earlier, he had purloined a horse blanket which he had cut into strips and wound around the baby, swaddling her up like an Egyptian mummy.

'She'll give us some stick when she wakes up,' observed Rhys. 'When did she eat last?'

'Any time now,' said the Sergeant. 'Has someone given birth, did you say?'

'A Hindustani.' Caleb put up his nose.

'I don't care if she's an Indian squaw,' said the sergeant, 'put this one on her,' and he gave him the baby.

'*Bejaysus*, are ye serious?'

'Do something with your life, Irishman. If you can deliver a child, you can see one fed. And make sure it's good clean

73

milk; I'm takin' this baby home.'

The moment Caleb had gone, the full rearguard under Shelton's command started coming in; this, the standard tactic of leap-frogging during action.

They came like men half dead, having fought for every yard since leaving the cantonment: with tribesmen hanging on to them like leeches, they had fought with musket and bayonet, carrying wounded comrades back in the retreat, for to leave them on the road meant death by cutting. . . . After dark, the Afghan women crept out to chop up what remained.

In hundreds, at first light, they began to stumble in; men and boys, their bloodstained wounds stiff with ice.

These, mainly of the 54th Native Infantry, being barefooted, were enduring the agony of toe frostbite. Interspersing them and leading their exhausted horses, came the 5th Cavalry, or what was left of them, minus their guns. And as they came in, disorganized and weary, they were shouting for the regiments from which they had been separated.

'Any of the Fifth up here?'

'Straight on up – keep going, son!'

'Not me, lad, I've been down Piccadilly.'

'Seen our cavalry?'

'Back in the cantonment, I reckon.'

'Where's the Horse Artillery, then?'

'Up in Nellie's room behind the clock.'

'Anyone heard the three-pounders?'

'Christ, what a bloody shambles!'

Another, no more than a lad, told me, 'They came at us like bloody dervishes, and as the lads fell they pounced on 'em, stripped 'em, and cut 'em up alive – I heard one calling for his ma.'

Another, with a scimitar cut across his cheek, said, 'We passed a fort a mile back there and it were as dead as a dodo, then hundreds of 'em came swarming out and got the baggage and the three-pounders.'

'The *yaboos* and mules went an' all.'

'They was howling like Red Indians!'

'They ain't human, I tell ye!'

Rhys said, 'But they've gone quiet now, thank God.'

'Aye? You wait, man. They're only sleeping so they can come ag'in tonight.'

Now the camp followers also came thronging up from the rear, seeking army protection.

In droves they came, carrying their children on their backs and their wounded in litters; some fell upon their knees imploring our help, and the snow behind them was stained red.

From them came a doleful wailing like that of distressed souls. Snow-covered, starving, they surged through our serried ranks, their food and tents abandoned in their rush of self-preservation.

Among them, amazingly, limped some of the harem girls turned out of the Bala Hissar by the Shah; these, their hair ice-encrusted and their bare feet bloody from the march, clutched about their half-naked bodies the silken scarves that marked their prostitution: wild-eyed, they gaped their chattering mouths at us.

Following these came the orphaned children of dead merchants and compradores, from stalwart young lads to bawling toddlers.

We did not march on the second day. For some reason known only to the General Staff, we halted in the freezing wind while the snow enveloped us; hour after hour went by in frozen inactivity. With no food, no wood to make a fire, we stamped up and down the icy road, getting what shelter we could, while the rearguard poured in with their tales of massacre and destruction. Night followed day with relentless misery; at sunrise on the morning of the third day of the retreat, Lady Sale arrived like one attending a royal durbar.

Wearing a white poshteen that braided her head like an Afghan turban, she sat her horse, surveying us; and Rhys and I, preparing to renew the march, glared up at her with unrelenting hostility. But Caleb, now returned (and an obsequious beggar if ever I saw one), rose from the ground, fought a path through the press of camp followers, and swept up the snow with his hat, saying, 'Good day to you, me sweet cockalorum! Sure, me heart beat with a surfeit of joy the moment I set eyes on ye. Are you safe, milady?'

'Little better for your asking, Caleb.' She brushed snow from her riding-coat. 'I have brought Mrs Sturt and my granddaughter, so please assist them as best you can,' and she waved an airy hand. 'Come, the pair of you, all is well now we have found Caleb.' And the three sat in the snow while the infantry and camp followers trudged by.

Passing Sepoys, bending to their horses with hammers and chisels, were dislodging from their hooves great chunks of ice. The wind increased, howling down the ravines and buffeting in the hollows: even the air we breathed froze in its passage from the lungs, forming dripping icicles on the mouth, decorating beards with spikes of ice.

'And so,' said Lady Sale, 'another day is lost. I find it impossible to contemplate the imbecility of this General Staff. The Sepoys – and I have just left them – have been without food or water since leaving Kabul. And here we sit bereft of tents or even a blanket, while these damnfool generals talk about safe conduct. On my saddle is a bundle of firewood, Caleb. A cup of your excellent tea would be most agreeable.'

'In these circumstances, milady? Sure, tea would scalp ye thorax – don't ye remember . . .? Wouldn't a dram o' the hard stuff suit ye better?'

She smiled, saying, 'Actually, this is why I've come, you old thief – I saw you stealing from my decanter, so I will have some of it now,' and she drank, adding, 'normally, a glass of this can make me quite unladylike, but now I can swallow half a pint with no visible effect. Have you watered this, you old rascal?'

They sat together, Caleb and Lady Sale, and we were on the edge of their conversation; such being the affinity of their friendship that it seemed churlish to intrude.

'Are ye returning to England when once this stunt is over?' asked Caleb and, shivering, sipped his whisky.

'Of course not,' came the sharp reply. 'It will take more than a handful of barbarians to shift me out of the Raj,' and she tossed her head. 'But you, I suspect, will defect at the

76

first opportunity, you old libertine.'

'In fact no, me darlin', I won't. I once worked a furnace for the Amir of Bokhara, ye see, and if I snapped me fingers the day after tomorrow, the old crook would come a-runnin'.'

'You would make iron for that despot?'

'Why not? His rupees are as good as English sovereigns. Besides, I could spend me retirement with me feet up in the sun,' and he slipped her a wink. 'For there's life in the old dog yet, ye know, and I'm sick to death o' being one of Mary's Children with twice to Church on Sunday. Indeed to God, I could pass me days in the arms of lonely maidens and beget meself five hundred children.'

'Really? One lonely maiden would be the death of you, you old soak!'

'Ay, ay, but 'twould be a marvellous way to go.'

She held out her hand; he took it, kissing her blue fingers, and she said, smiling, 'Where ever you be, what ever you do, may God preserve you, Caleb – until we meet again.'

'If only on the other side o' the Great Divide, milady?' He bowed to her, and I saw the affection in their faces; a stranger would have been forgiven for thinking that they had once been lovers. . . .

Certainly, it was the only time I'd heard Caleb mention the Amir of Bokhara.

I made a mental note of it.

14

I awoke after a night of tossing, shivering cold, having sunk into a drowse of exhaustion; and saw on a far horizon a sunrise of astonishing beauty, a contrast to the desolation and death about me. Men and animals were sunk in the torpidity of sleeping death: Lady Sale, with her arms protectively around her granddaughter, had her eyes clenched in a fraud of sleep. Beside her, spilled from her saddle-bag, was a little book fluttering in the snow: trembling I reached out for it, and she opened her eyes, saying, 'Hohenlinden? Would you be interested?'

'Of course. It is a book.'

She smiled, her eyes haggard in her pale face.

'Ah yes, the autobiographer – of course! I had quite forgotten! Would you care to see an interesting page?' She offered the book, and I read:

> Few. Few shall part where many meet,
> The snow shall be their winding sheet;
> And every turf beneath their feet
> Shall be a soldier's sepulchre . . .

Somewhere down the line a bugle was blowing discordantly for the march. She said, 'In a happier place than this I shall remember that we shared a funeral verse; the convict and the general's wife. Bizarre, is it not?'

'To say the least.'

The circulation of my half-frozen feet was returning and I gritted my teeth to the pain.

She said casually, 'We will get through, you and I, Mortymer, because we are survivors. And we will share in the victory; it is unthinkable that it could be otherwise. So, I say to the devil with old poet Campbell and his defeatist rhyming. The Raj always wins the last battle, does it not?'

Caleb said, struggling to his feet in grunts and wheezes, 'All the time we got the likes of you, milady.'

'What say you, young sergeant?' asked Lady Sale.

But he was still only half awake and, raising his face to the peaks of the distant pass, said, forgetting who was listening, 'I say sod the Raj. We gotta shift those bastards off the top o' there afore we start for the Khoord-Kabul or we'll get blown to bloody pieces.'

'Quite,' said Lady Sale, without a blink.

And so we started off again with the frost-bitten infantrymen of the 44th ranging themselves into some semblance of line, and began the snowy trudge up the gradient of the Khoord-Kabul pass. Before us were what was left of Shah Shuja's 6th Infantry, the remnants of those who had deserted and returned to Kabul, and I mentioned this.

'Preferring slavery there to death here,' added Caleb, rolling along on frost-bitten feet beside me.

'Stop that, please,' Lady Sale commanded. 'It is defeatist talk.'

About us surged the frozen camp followers, their ranks still as thick as a mob, though many had last night perished of cold: they went sobbing; many with tongues so swollen with hunger that they were speechless.

'They look a ferocious lot,' said Rhys, and pointed, and the people about us broke into new cries of terror; for now along our flanks troops of Afghan horsemen were riding with drawn sabres; steel flashed in the early sunlight.

'That's him!' cried the sergeant, and jerked a thumb at the trotting cavalry. '*Look!*'

'Who?'

'Akbar Khan, the sod who's supposed to be giving us safe

conduct,' and as he spoke a horseman from the rearguard came galloping through our ranks.

'Take cover! Halt and take cover!' he shouted and, with his sword waving, dashed off up the line, scattering everybody.

So we halted again, not having covered two miles. With arms and ammunition plentiful (deserters in the van had tossed theirs away) Rhys and I, lying in a cluster of men, primed and loaded our muskets. Almost paralyzed with the bitter cold, we lay within a vast cathedral of ice, and trained our foresights on to the trotting tribesmen; these, fed and warm on their little *yaboo* ponies, looked more like entries at a local point-to-point than murderers who planned to cut our British throats.

'Hold your fire! *Hold it*!' came a new command. 'Get up, all of you, and march on – ignore them!'

And so we continued the march; upward, ever upward, and the crags of the towering Khoord-Kabul engulfed us; the peaks rearing above us in the morning sunlight, yet our valley was encased as in night darkness.

And the Afghan cavalry followed us with the design to end our lives.

'They ain't coming at us yet, though.' The sergeant shouldered his musket. 'They know these mountains.'

'They're waiting for us to get up into the Pass, then they'll crown the heights.'

He pointed upward and I saw the crags above us suddenly crawling with men; knives gleamed in the sun; a mirror flashed, a heliograph.

'They know what they're about, that lot,' said the sergeant.

Again we were halted. While awaiting the order to advance again a new sound arose, the tinkling of the icy streams; little white waterfalls were bursting in cascades from crevices in the mountains and as we climbed upward began to pour down the slopes like spouts of white blood in the sun. The air grew warmer.

Blood grew warmer, too, for some artillerymen had

broken into a keg of brandy found in what was left of the 54th stores; this, saved for the officers, was now distributed around to anyone who fancied a gulp. I had some and so did Rhys, and Caleb drained what was left of the keg. Then along came an officer who berated the tipsy gunners, abusing them and calling them drunkards. This was when we were between Begramee and Boothak, and had the enemy attacked at that moment, they could have slaughtered us. Even so, one Afghan detachment succeeded in slipping into our ranks (after the 5th and 37th Regiments had passed) and carried off camels and baggage without opposition. Such are the magical qualities of brandy.

'Advance at the double!'

The order was flung from mouth to mouth, and in a sudden hail of *jezail* bullets we quickened our pace into staggering, disjointed rushes; barging into each other; falling, to rise again and struggle upwards into the hissing rocochets: the ravine was filled with singing lead.

Now the tribesmen were attacking from the rear, expertly swerving their little ponies through the terrified camp followers. Men were throwing up their arms and falling: children were being trampled beneath the pounding hooves. Oaths and cries came from the ranks as soldiers dropped to the shredding bullets of the mounted *jezails*: and I saw above me a stone breastwork shooting fire and smoke, the main ambush.

Thousands were fighting to get through the narrow defile of the pass; hundreds more were wandering out of the line, to sink down into the snow and await death. The tribesmen, their knives out, came out of cover and pounced upon them, methodically cutting them up.

'Come on, lads, up that slope and at 'em!' bawled the sergeant, and I saw the clean outline of his face as he leaped up and ran.

With Rhys and I following him, he went, and half a dozen Sepoys after us: full pelt we raced up the side of the ravine. Slipping, sliding, ducking to bullets from the breastwork as the Ghilzais fought to reload, and reached it in a mêlée of men and bayonets; clubbing down the defenders as they turned for escape, shooting down those who fled.

81

The strongpoint gained, we turned our attention farther upwards where the Afghans were manning new positions; and caught them with such a gush of enfiladed fire – for the old Brown Bess was grand at close range – that they, too, retreated.

With the temporary danger removed, we marched again.

Overtaking us, their camels' bellies deep in the valley brooks, came six British wives and their children in their *kajavas* – the little basket howdahs carried either side of their camels. And the red faces of the children peeping out over the baskets looked like a row of smacked bums. From our higher position we looked down upon them; one woman having nothing covering her but the nightdress in which she had left her bed at Kabul: in this she had lasted two bitter nights at temperatures below zero. Being a tough North Country woman she was still alive: in the event she froze to death on Sunday morning.

As I marched, the first Ghilzai attack over, all was silent save for the wind: and in this temporary respite I saw the face of a man I had killed on the ridge. Bearded and handsome, he was in the bloom of his youth; his eyes, untrammelled by war, were cobalt blue . . . in the second before I cut him down with a bayonet slash . . . and saw him fall, his arms outflung in the moment before death took him. He was gone, yet for me his eyes remained; the bright blue eyes of an Alexander in a tanned Afghan face.

They tell me that you always remember the first man you kill.

'I got two of the buggers,' said the sergeant, wiping blood from his bayonet, and I envied his self-satisfaction, but liked Big Rhys's better.

'One of mine got away, thank God,' said he.

We had lost three Indian Sepoys; I saw their bodies chopped to pieces, lying up there on the ridge. Nobody mentioned them: I saw in my mind's eye a woman weeping.

Now the pace slowed, for the attacks had lessened, and we marched on upwards through the pass . . . from the 4,000 feet of Boothak to the 10,000-foot peaks of the awesome

82

Khoord-Kabul. The muffle of our tramping in the snow was that of an Army marching to its doom. And there came up the line a dozen more officers' ladies and their children, accompanied, as always, by their faithful Hindustani servants.

Gathering about Lady Sale where she was now holding court, they brought with them little scraps of food they had foraged on the journey; the children eating ravenously of raw meat stripped from the less putrid parts of a dead animal.

These infants, now small primitives, tore at the feast with the voracity of young savages: nor offered any to passing strangers who stared with yearning eyes. The greater sympathy was reserved for the families of our loyal Sepoys, who had been either butchered or carried off for sale in the slave bazaars.

I saw trudging towards us a young wife I had often seen in the cantonment. Picking a path through the dead, she came with her newlyborn baby in her arms and four-year-old little Mary Anderson, somebody's child, hanging on to her arm. With her came a Mrs Boyd, and she was calling pitifully for Hugh, her three-year-old son who had been snatched from her arms by an Afghan horseman.

As if working to some obscene timetable, the tribesmen attacked again within minutes of their arrival.

Enclosed on three sides by walls of mountain, there was no other escape from the Afghan bullets but to lie down and pray. And within moments, their cavalry, having broken through the vanguard, came charging four abreast down the icy road at us. At the gallop they came, yelling their shrill battle cries, their scimitars slashing down left and right, and the unprotected people fell before the onslaught; a few to rise, only to be knocked flat again by new cavalry coming the other way.

It was a mass of flashing swords and bayonets, the ferocious close-quarter which the Afghans loved. I saw Big Rhys, his face streaming blood, clutch upwards as a horseman galloped by; dragging him off, Rhys clubbed him senseless.

Children were wandering aimlessly, crying unheeded: and

83

I rose from the snow and flung myself at a bearded ruffian who had Mrs Boyd by the throat. Bowled over, he crouched, snarling, before I pinioned him with his own scimitar. Now came another, cutting at me, but I rolled away as his horse was shot from under him. And saw a flash vision of our sergeant kneeling in the road, now calmly rising to thrust and slash with his fixed bayonet; collecting Afghans one by one with text-book bayonet fighting.

Caleb I saw, too, his youth regained, crawling among the unhorsed enemy, cracking with a cudgel the skulls of the living, battering the dead to make sure.

Now another wave of enemy cavalry tore down the ravine slope upon us, their little *yaboos*' unearthly neighing adding to the din. I pulled a musket from the grasp of a dying Sepoy, levelled it and blew away an Afghan from behind Big Rhys: men and animals were now in bellowing entanglements of arms and legs, for the impetus of those behind bore down upon those in front so that the pass was littered with scrambling hooves and fighting men; a chopping, stabbing confusion where friend fought comrade in muddle and disorder. And still more waves of Afghan cavalry came storming down the sloping road; an indiscriminate chaos of cut and thrust.

Now the Khoord-Kabul, up and down the pass for as far as I could see, was a heaving mass of indiscriminate slaughter, with tribesmen hauling out victims for individual cutting.

Fighting clear, I now found myself on the edge of the conflict, and Rhys was beside me: I glimpsed his face beneath the body of a dead horse: finding his leg, I dragged him clear, instantly coming face to face with a tribesman, but got him with a fist and hit him flat.

Now there suddenly fell upon the convulsed heaps of combatants a strange and terrible quiet. Foe and friend, listlessly moving, seeking to disentangle themselves from the whole, and stagger away, seeking space . . . to wander aimlessly, or tumble head over heels on the ice . . . But one horse scrambled up with its rider still upon its back. Reaching a little knot of cowering British wives, its rider bent low in the saddle. With astonishing horsemanship, in passing, he swept up little Mary Anderson with one arm, and galloped with her up the mountain slope. She was never seen again.

Exhausted, the sergeant, Caleb, Rhys and I sat motionless, panting for breath in the snow, and this was now blotched scarlet: even the torrents cascading into the plain below were red with blood.

All was silent.

There was no sound save the groaning of the wounded, the crying of children, the sounds of falling water: the peaks of Khoord-Kabul, tomb-like in their whiteness, were sole witnesses of the final barbarity: silent sentinels of the blankets of mist spreading slowly over the road to Jalalabad.

Ten thousand people lay dead or dying.

15

On the morning of the third day of the march all hope had died.

Said a later historian: ' . . . the pale wildness of terror was exhibited on every countenance.'

For my part, however, I knew no actual fear; only the numbness of death's inevitability, and an abiding sadness that never again would I see Mari and my son. As for Rhys, he accepted the situation with fatalism.

'What about your princess?' he asked as we started the march, for now we were through the Khoord-Kabul and approaching the narrower defile of Tezeen; at an altitude of 10,000 feet its narrowest point was four yards wide.

'By now she'll be awaiting us at Seh Baba,' I said, and he laughed.

'You'll be lucky! If they have the same trouble getting her there as we've had getting here, she'll never see the skies over the place.'

'There's a difference, she's an Afghan.'

He made a wry face. 'You realize that if we leave the column we could be shot for desertion?'

'It's a chance I'll take – we're as good as dead here, anyway.'

We marched on amid a crush of exhausted people. With the Khoord-Kabul receding into the mists behind us, we went in halting advances while the vanguard laboured to remove piles of mutilated bodies, some still moving faintly, which were blocking the road: a ghastly testimony to Afghan cruelty.

One or two of the corpses I recognized – Lieutenant Jackson of the Horse Artillery, flung haphazardly among the dying, was one; he was a lad from a village in Kent, and I gave a thought to the inevitable stone tablet that they would raise to him in the village church where his father preached – 'Killed in action in Afghanistan' . . .

Now only his fair hair identified him from the other slaughtered.

Others I recognized from the Kabul cantonment: three Hindu women, lying hand in hand in the comradeship of death, their young bodies stripped and grotesquely entangled among the naked limbs of men: women whom I had last seen laughing in the canteen of the 44th . . . serving steaming meals to lads they were pleased to address as sons, yet young enough to have been their lovers. Clearing parties had piled the dead on either side of the pass that led to the gorge of Tunghee Tareekhee; a bottleneck which might prove a winding sheet for what was left of us.

Rhys said, 'After seeing that we'll be lucky to reach the Huft Kotul let alone Jalalabad.'

Always, in the extremity of peril, men talk about women: it is as if, their antecedents before life being womb darkness, they seek to regain an intimacy with their female maker. Also, though still weary beyond description, we seemed to be now living within a vacuum when time and misery held small account: and when, as if by magic, a bag of meal and bread was thrust into our midst (the result of Caleb's foraging) and we had found the comfort of a wayside fire . . . the conversation – as soldiers say – became normal.

'I once had a girl in Huft Kotul,' said the sergeant.

He was indefatigable; until now marching steadily with his Brown Bess and bayonet, ready for yet another dash up the slopes to kill Afghans.

'She were a miller's wife,' he continued, warming his hands at the fire, 'but the miller were grinding his corn down in the mill and me and his missus was up in the loft wi' the bags of flour.'

'That,' said Caleb, affronted, 'was a disgusting situation.'

'That's what I reckoned at the time,' said the sergeant, 'but I still done it,' and he sighed in deep reflection. 'She were a prime little piece with a little yellow bodice, and though we didn't talk each other's lingo, Hindu women speak with their eyes. . . .'

Cried Caleb, 'Ye must have had a ridge tile loose – consorting with a Hindu wife.'

'Ay, ay, I thought of that, too,' came the reply.

Rhys asked, 'Was her hair dark? My wife's hair is; she's got black hair down to her waist . . .'

'Blue-black,' said the sergeant, 'like a raven's tail; it had a plaited braid across her brow, and at her temple she wore a white frangipani flower. And as we tied bags of flour, her hair came down and fell between us, and I held it in me fingers. . . .'

Caleb shouted, 'Away wid ye! If the Lord heard that he'd he reportin' ye to the Pope, ye scurrilous popinjay!'

'Will you hush up, ye boot-faced bloody puritan,' cried Big Rhys.

'Tell us more, Sarge,' I said, and remembered Mari bathing in the Usk down at Llanellen. . . .

The sergeant continued, 'That hair, I tell ye, smelled like musk, and there was little husks of wheat in it, because it was harvest time. And as we began talking with our eyes, I said to her with mine, "How about you and me, my charmer? What about a bit of the old up-in-the-attic with Nellie?" And she giggled and went all soft, and her eyes said yes, but her hands said no when I tried to touch her.

'But a wink is a wink in any language, ain't it? And that wink took her all girlish and opened wide her eyes above her yashmak.

"Ye'll no regret it, never fear," I told her, closing up, and I thought I'd got her going till she became fearful and humped and heaved tremendous and drew her finger across her throat and her eyes grew as big as pies.

"Never you fear, my lovely," I said, "for he'll never find out," and I reached over the flour bag and drew down her yashmak and kissed her lips, which were full and wet, like the mouth of a sucking child.'

'Dear me, God bless all bandy women,' said someone.

'Was she warm?' asked Big Rhys, shivering.

'She were warmer than a muffin on a toastin' fork come Christmas, and as juicy as salted farm butter. I'm telling you lads, I've caught some slicers in me life, but I never met the likes o' that miller's wife. I had a yellow Chinese up in Peking, I frightened a novice nun in Calcutta, and got knifed by a big black fella for goin' over his missus in Ceylon, but they was never a match for that miller's wife when I gave 'er the old up and under. Mates, being in that lady made the world all sunnybuns.'

Caleb, shocked, shouted, 'Now he's a poet! The bloody rapscallion! If He hit the Philistines hip and thigh for Sodom and Gomorrah, can ye think what He'll do about your fornication?'

'And she had a pair o' gold-tipped stunners canoodlin' and courtin' under her chemise like a pair o' cookin' apples. *Jeez*! And it's her I'm going back to, for her old man should have kicked off by now. Six months I knew her, day and night, but ne'er a child of her belly she gave me that I could call mine.'

I asked, 'And this is where the Hindu baby comes in? The one Caleb took up the line?'

'Right first time, me lad. "Don't you worry about making babies, me lovely one," I told her, "for when I'm done me time for Queen and country, I'll bring you back a little fat daughter." No sons for me, I told her – there's only one pair o' balls goin' up my stairs. So in the mornin' I'm away up the line to fetch that baby girl, and when I get her to Huft Kotul I'm handing her over to that miller's wife, give her the stars to play with, and wash her clean with water from the moon.'

I stared at him.

Poets arrive in very unexpected places.

'Now there's a thing!' ejaculated Caleb. 'The blessings of God be on ye for the foine Christian gentleman you are, Sarge! It just shows ye, how wrong you can be about people!'

89

'And if her old man is still activating, I'll put him down in a wooden suit within five minutes of arrivin',' added the sergeant.

In the middle of that night, when we were half-way through the pass of Tunghee Tareekhee the Afghans attacked again, this time in force.

In the sepulchral whiteness of the moon they came, rushing down the ravine slopes after two hours of bombardment, their little two-pounder mule guns going like marrowbones and cleavers.

These cannon shots, whistling through the confining air of the pass, carved bloody paths through our ranks. Soldiers, those still alive, wandered with vacant eyes: women were actually throwing away their babies; or handing them up to their ferocious captors, watching apathetically as they were cut in half, a standard Afghan method of despatching children. So Tunghee Tareekhee became a place of final massacre: one of the greatest five-day slaughters known to mankind, and the greatest military defeat then known to the British army in Asia.

Under a cold moon the killing continued. Hidden behind stonework up on the slopes above us, the enemy poured volley after volley into us, and the Sepoys, those courageous defenders of the British in India, flung away their arms and fled in wild disorder; or sat shivering on the wayside berm, awaiting death.

By dawn, the enemy, aware that their victory was almost complete, now thronged into disciplined, killing groups; bearded fanatics slaughtered at will the few remaining camp followers: even the children of the enemy now entered the fray, savagely stabbing at the wounded. One, caught by our sergeant in the act of trying to cut off the head of a dying Sepoy, found himself stuck by a bayonet, lifted bodily, and dropped over the nearest chasm.

The Afghans, it was discovered, had a particular relish for killing Sepoys: not one was left alive; and of the 4,500

90

fighting men who had left the cantonment five days earlier, less than five hundred entered the Tunghee Pass. More than 12,000 camp followers now lay dead or dying along the road to Kabul, for the tribes simply did not have time to kill them all: later, they returned to finish the job.

Only one man, Dr William Brydon of the Shah's Medical Service, would ultimately be spared to carry the fatal news back to Jalalabad: thus was the prophecy of Mohammed Akbar Khan fulfilled, that one man, and one man only, would survive to tell of the massacre.

16

Monday, 10th January, 1842

That morning Lady Sale arrived with the body of her dead son-in-law, our respected Captain Sturt.

In a lull in the firing we stood in pious groups while he was buried by the roadside; the only body during the actual retreat to receive a Christian burial.

Sturt had left the column to rescue a Lieutenant Mein, and had then himself fallen with a dum-dum bullet in the stomach; Mein, himself seriously wounded, had brought him in over the back of a pony: now we stood respectfully while Lady Sale spoke a few biblical words: her hair down, her clothes now in tatters, she yet retained her usual dignity, making no mention of her granddaughter, aged five, who, like little Mary Anderson, had since been carried off by a Ghilzai horseman. In the event, the child (according to my diary) was later bought in Kabul's bazaar by an escaped British hostage for a trifling sum, and returned to her distraught parent; but Mary Anderson was not so fortunate.

Blood was forming in a little pool at Lady Sale's feet; I was the first to notice this, and she asked Caleb, 'You will please perform a small service for me . . .?'

'Milady,' cried he with his usual gush of words, 'I'll be in service to ye till death puts his chill hand on me brow . . .'

She replied wearily, 'Stop being an idiot, man, I need a surgeon.'

Hearing this, our sergeant said, 'There's a medic up the

line, ma'am, but he's workin' blind.'

'Blind?'

'Snow blind.'

'Then kindly ask him, blind or sighted, if he would be good enough to cut this confounded thing out of my arm, for it is restricting movement.'

The medic, without the aid of laudanam, then cut a half-pound musket ball out of her forearm, and, before the wound froze, bound it with silk torn from her petti- coat. Later, we discovered that she had also been shot in the side, but since treating this meant exposing herself in the presence of men, she made no mention of it.

That morning had broken when we were within sight of Tezeen: thunder clouds shouldered across the chasms of the sky, threatening us with death by water.

Lady Sale said, marching near me, 'Despite this misery, Mortymer, I would like to speak privately to you both,' and Rhys and I, sick to death, did not reply, but trudged on either side of her in the thin ranks. She continued, 'As you might have heard, there's been a meeting between the Political Agent and Sirdar Akbar Khan.'

I nodded, and she said, 'In return for certain hostages he promises us safe conduct to Jalalabad for all our women and children.'

'How many?' asked Big Rhys with bad grace.

'Fourteen in all, but Major Pottinger further negotiated, and he has agreed to twenty.'

I interjected, 'All British, I suspect.'

'Why yes – is there anything wrong with that?'

There was much wrong with it. Thousands of women and children, the relatives of our Ghurkas, Sepoys and camp followers, had already perished; their survivors were still on the march, but there was no talk of clemency for these.

Later, it became clear that male officers also, from General Elphinstone down, were to become beneficiaries of Afghan mercy.

This, and the earlier cowardice exhibited by elements of the fighting regiments, especially the 44th, was to become a password for infamy whenever the retreat from Afghanistan was mentioned.

Not every unit which took part in the 'Afghan Promenade' can today read their names in its battle honours.

Indeed, one military commentator represented the campaign as 'a sombre welter of misrepresentation, unscrupulous intrigue, moral deterioration and dishonour unspeakable'.

Darkness fell with startling suddenness; the stars glimmered and gleamed; a ghostly galleon of a moon wandered across the frozen peaks where victor and vanquished lay sprawled along the road to Kabul.

We lay in black heaps. Clutched in each other's arms for warmth, we spent a shivering night amid dreams of death by knives in the morning.

With the thermometer below zero, we lay tumbled in icy misery without food, fuel or fire.

Somewhere down the line thin wisps of smoke arose: shivering Sepoys were burning their caps to warm their frozen hands.

Now it began to rain, gently at first, then spitefully, in stair-rod vehemence, drumming off the road, foaming in the gulches. Lady Sale said, 'Can you hear me above this din, Mortymer?'

I nodded.

'Akbar Khan's agreement to a truce was to be expected. With the Dost, his father, and two of his brothers held in British hands, he's on a short rein. Then, of course, there is his niece.'

I looked at her through the slanting rain and the wind buffeted us, bringing us together while Rhys dropped behind us.

'The Princess Durrani,' she said.

I did not reply.

'You know of her, of course.' And she sighed. 'Let us stop playing games, for the lives of you and your friend could be forfeit – the Sirdar knows of the Dost's intentions.' She continued, 'Knowing I had knowledge of Caleb's labourers, the General called me into the hostage conference, and I was questioned. "You know these convicts?" Akbar Khan asked me.

' "Two of them," I replied. "The third is dead." '

' "The third, one named Howells, is dead because I had him executed for immorality against our Holy Law," said Akbar Khan, "but before he died he talked of a plot to kidnap my niece, Durrani, and spoke of two others, but we do not know their names." Are you listening, Mortymer?'

I tried to appear calm, but my heart was thudding against my shirt. 'I am listening.'

'You are involved in this, of course?'

There was nothing left to do but explain it all, and I did so.

'I see, but are you aware of the danger you are in?'

'Nothing like that of the last five days – a man can only die once.'

'Perhaps, but the manner of dying is also important. Luckily, however, Akbar believes you are both dead – killed at Sturt's Bridge, I told him. So now what do you propose to do?'

'Keep our promise to the girl,' said Rhys, pushing up behind us, for he had ears to hear a nit in a wig-sack. 'We said we'd meet her at Seh Baba, and we'll keep that promise.'

'You could lose your lives, remember.'

'Likely all of us, missus, hostages or no bloody hostages.'

She ignored this, saying, 'Tell me your intentions.'

'Lady,' said Big Rhys, 'we don't bother nobody, we're just taking her home to her grandad.'

The wind howled between us. The column had temporarily halted and we sought shelter behind a bluff of rock.

Lady Sale said, 'All of which is very heroic, but I doubt if you'll get away with it. According to the Sirdar, Shah Shuja has also been after her from the moment she absconded from the Bala Hissar.'

'Then that makes three of us,' said Rhys. 'What you doin' putting your oar in, anyway?'

'Merely trying to save your lives,' came the cool answer. 'Now tell me how you propose to get to Seh Baba?'

'Make a bolt for it when we get nearer. We should be at the river's mouth tomorrow,' I answered.

'Food? You're going to need food.'

'We'll scrounge it on the way,' said Rhys, and she put a finger in her mouth and looked at the wintry sky.

'Best you stay out of it, missus,' said Rhys, as if reading her thoughts.

'Oh no, I love a bit of action, and I thoroughly approve of what you're up to, after what I've seen happening here. Nor do I approve of abduction from an English school and watching a child being kicked around like a political football. Therefore, it's a pity that your scheme is flawed. *Listen.* Seh Baba, on the road to Jalalabad, has always been a meeting place, mainly because Abdoolah's Fort is in the vicinity – Akbar is taking us there tomorrow to be interned . . .'

'*What!*'

'And on the way he doubtless intends to capture your Durrani.'

I said wearily, 'Jesus, we're walking right into it!'

'And why not?' Her eyes momentarily danced with merriment. 'Why not use the journey for your own ends – become hostages.'

'You could arrange it?'

'Certainly. Henceforth, why not become my bearers? I am injured, am I not?'

'It's a big risk for you. We're nobodies.'

'Taking risks got me this far,' she said. 'Did not someone say, "Gentlemen, your danger is great, but I know you would not have it otherwise, for we are Englishmen"?'

'Welsh, missus.'

'Welsh or English, remember that this particular Sirdar once skinned a man alive for entertainment.'

17

The hostage party, of which Rhys, Caleb and I were now members, set off at midday after a local truce had been negotiated.

Glowering above their beards, the Afghans gathered about us in the pouring rain. And one, a fine figure of a man on an ornately decorated horse, reined it in and drew up beside Lady Sale.

'You are the Feringhee lady?' he asked, in English.

'I am Lady Sale.'

He saluted. 'The wife of the general called "Fighting Bob"?'

She glared up at him, not replying.

'And now he fights no more, eh?' The horse wheeled and he expertly controlled it, grinning down at her.

'Do not worry, Sirdar,' said she, 'he lives to fight again.'

It delighted him, and he dismounted and stood before her, a fine sight in his silver-mounted helmet. 'My respects to him, Lady, when you reach Jalalabad, for I pray to have the privilege of removing his head,' and he bowed.

Returning his bow, she replied, 'You will need a bigger army, Sirdar. Had my husband been in command here you would now be a dead Afghan.'

He indicated us with his whip. 'Who are these?'

'My bearers.'

'Are they on the roll of hostages?'

'No, not until I added their names,' came the reply, and

she opened her girdle and showed her bloodstained dress. 'Do you expect me to walk into this captivity?'

'They are not in the uniform of soldiers . . .'

'Of course not. How can lowly bearers wear the clothes of our noble Queen?'

'I understand,' and he snapped his fingers at Rhys, Caleb and me. 'Follow my horse and keep in line.'

With Lady Sale slung undecorously in a rough hammock between us, we went like Chinese coolies, bouncing her on shoulder-poles, and thirty other hostages followed, drooping in the rain.

At this point, in substantiation of facts, I now refer to the official diary of Lady Sale.

The following is her description of the journey to Seh Baba and internment:

11th February, 1842
We went to Seh Baba, and thence to the enemy fort following the bed of the river.

It would be impossible for me to describe the dreadful scenes through which we passed, the road being covered with dreadfully mangled bodies, all naked. Fifty-eight Europeans we counted in the Tunghee Nullah alone, and innumerable bodies of natives; also scores of camp followers still alive, frost-bitten and starving, some perfectly out of their senses and idiotic. I recognized the bodies of Major Ewart, 54th, and Major Scott, 44th, among others: the sight was dreadful, the smell of blood sickening: indeed, the corpses lay so thickly on the road that it was impossible to remove them from one's sight, lest, in passing, we trod upon them.

Reaching the Abdoolah fort, she continues:

Our whole party, both ladies and gentlemen, were crammed into one room, one side of which was partitioned off with mats and filled with grain. Here an old woman cooked chupatties for us, three for a rupee;

but, finding the demand great (everyone was starving),
she raised the price to a rupee each . . .

Now the stars, large and glittering, paled in the heavens, and
all of us hostages sat in a circle on the earth floor of the fort;
only Caleb had money, and paid for our chupatties; and we
ate greedily, our first real food for nearly a week.

I looked about me at the bowed heads of the hostages;
women, children and men, some wounded, ravenously
chewing like cyphers in a chorus of grunts and moans; the
badly wounded pausing to stretch their filthy bandages, the
children with eyes like jewels in the lamplight; masticating,
swallowing, their hungry eyes searching for more.

Only one, Lady Sale, ate daintily; placing morsels of the
unleavened ottar cakes between her lips like a selective bird:
nothing, it appeared, neither pain, weariness nor starvation
could seduce her from her well-mannered, Victorian
placidity.

Later, she put a portion of her meagre ration aside, and
distributed it among the children.

Akbar Khan now arrived with his entourage, the junior
chiefs.

Of medium height, he possessed the air of one ordained
by God: in the course of time, as the eldest son of Dost
Mohammed Khan, the throne of Afghanistan should rightly
have been his, but he and his father were at odds with each
other, so he was never to gain it.

His features bore the stamp of an Alexander, his eyes
strangely light in an aristocratic, bearded face. Vigorous in
every movement, he exuded a fine sporting air, more as one
of life's tumblers than that of a man slaughtering a British
army.

Dressed in gilded chain-mail armour, a single diamond
flashed at the crown of his leather helmet. In Pashto he said,
and I knew enough of this to understand him, 'Greetings,'
and he bowed; his sirdars following his example.

We, the conquered, rose to our feet in respect.

'My guests have eaten?' He addressed Major Pottinger, a
small, tubby man now our acting Political Agent.

99

'They have eaten,' he replied tersely.

'My hospitality is poor, I regret, but since it is the will of Allah that you have fallen into my hands, you will be granted safe conduct into your captivity.'

'We are grateful, Sirdar,' said Pottinger, and spoke the old language. 'May God grant you a tranquil existence.'

'In return I will show you mercy.'

'Mercy?' asked Lady Sale, coming to the fore. 'We only ask for justice.'

Akbar smiled faintly. 'You Franks! When will you know that you have been destroyed? I will leave but one survivor, and he shall carry the news of your defeat to Jalalabad, who will report it to your Queen.'

'A defeat, Sirdar, that is not complete,' replied she, while others there tried to wave her into silence. 'Already an army of retribution is gathering, for the blood of our soldiers is upon your head.' She came closer, pushing men aside. 'This massacre will be the talk of Asia; we would be dust in the mouth of the Raj, if London did nothing, every death will be avenged.'

And Akbar replied, 'I quote my father, Dost Mohammed Khan, who said to the British, "I have been struck with the magnitude of your resources, your ships, your arsenals; but what I cannot understand is why the rulers of an empire so vast should have crossed the Indus River to deprive me of my poor and barren country," and the question is still in my mind.'

'To improve your lot, Sirdar!'

'Really so?' Akbar smiled. 'If you think that our poor lives are so important in your plundering, I say that it is the will of Allah that will decide it in the end, for we have been fighting in these mountains since the days of the Mongol empire, even among the golden tents of Saladin and the massacre of his ten thousand warriors, which is the way all here will die.'

'Then I make a prophecy, too, Sirdar, and it is this – that Britain, to punish this rebellion, will not rest until your country is conquered and your name humiliated from Peshawar to lands beyond the Hindu Kush.'

Akbar Khan replied with equal authority, 'Even my viziers who know of divination, cannot foretell all the stars,

Great Lady – to confuse prophecy with sorcery can be dangerous . . .'

Lady Sale replied, 'If this be so, then find me guilty, for what I have threatened will come to pass. No man alive can pull the nose of an English queen and live to a ripe old age.'

Akbar spoke again, but his words diminished into silence, for there had come into the room a low whimpering sound, like that of a trapped animal. And people stared at one another, wonderingly, as this sound grew into a low and mournful keening, like the sighing of lost souls.

The deputation began to fidget nervously, for when it comes to Irish banshees, said Caleb later, an Afghan can show the quickest pair of heels in Christendom. As we stood there the moaning grew, and a sirdar, a man of great size, said gustily, 'It is the crying of lost souls! It comes from the places where the tamarisk blooms . . . it is the Beluchis' hymn, they of the long hair and knives. By the beard of the prophet, this is terrible!' and, turning swiftly, he opened a door behind him, and fled.

Streaming outside, we saw an army of naked people come thronging along the road from Seh Baba, all as bare as bones; men, women and children stripped for the final cutting. And as we pushed our way outside, I saw, as far as I could in the moonlight, this wailing mass of naked humanity: the once wealthy compradores of Kabul, expectant mothers, ancient crones and toddlers . . . stumbling along aimlessly, for the enemy, tired of slaughtering them, had stripped them and left them in the frost to die.

Lady Sale's voice in my ear raked me from the horror of it.

'This is your chance, you two – run for it! Caleb, you stay here with me . . . Run, the pair of you – *run*!'

18

Wednesday, 13th February, 1842

With the moon a misted banjo above the mountains, we dived into the ranks of the wailing people and went like Satan after saints through the main fort doors, across a courtyard, vaulted a low parapet wall and ran for open country: among whizzing Afghan bullets we ran for the foothills of the Tezeen mountains, then back down the slopes of the dried watercourse of a river; and an hour later still lay there, panting, listening for sounds of pursuit; but there was nothing except the wind sighing among the boulders.

'Where's the map?' Rhys was first to come to his senses.

'Here.' I spread it out in the moonlight, but he had his finger up.

'What's that?' he whispered, for he had ears to hear a rustling mouse.

I nodded. 'The Tezeen River. If we follow it upstream, we'll come to Seh Baba.'

Our eyes growing accustomed to the cold, blue light, we followed the river, putting up scores of saddled horses, the survivors of another massacre; some British mounts of the fruitless cavalry charges, some the tough little Afghan *yaboos* whose warrior riders had long since gone to Paradise. Stopping me, Rhys pointed.

'Eastward – look!' and the road to Jalalabad rose up sharp and clear in a sudden surge of moonlight, 'the silk route to India. What is left of our army will be on it in the morning, to die at Jugdulluk.'

It was an astonishing prophecy; had he named the killing ground as Gandamak, where our patriots made their final stand, it would have been miraculous.

Within a quarter of a mile we stumbled upon the last stand of an Indian Sepoy regiment. Men lay in twisted attitudes of death; these, seeking escape up the slopes of the pass, had been cut down by pursuing tribesmen: the crags about us rose up like feasting bears, for this was a killing ground. What the Afghans had begun by methodical slaughter, their wives had ended by ritual torture.

'Our turn next, if we don't get moving,' I said, and we struck out along the east bank of the river until mud-walled homes made shape out of the darkness, and this was the hamlet of Seh Baba, an oasis of peace nestling in war's corruptions.

'Which house?' asked Rhys.

'The biggest here, I suppose.'

'Jesus, we could be knocking on doors for a fortnight,' and then, almost at my elbow a small voice asked in perfect English:

'You are the Franks who seek Abaya?'

It was the Kohistani lad who had guided me before in Kabul; this time he was leading two horses with another tethered behind.

'Now you come to lead me again?' I asked.

'I do,' he replied, 'this time with Afghan ponies, for this Abaya is not your friend, but your enemy, and before the night is out you will have need of horses.'

'Why?'

'Because he has imprisoned my princess and now awaits the coming of her uncle, Akbar Khan. Follow me, please?'

We did so.

The Kohistani indicated a little door in a rock face. This opened to our knock into a room of beautiful proportions; an ornate hunting lodge, this, its walls decorated with trophies and talismans. And old Abaya, still as shrivelled and malignant as a leprous crone, opened up silk-clad arms to us in greeting, crying, 'Ah, here you are at last, my friends! Long have we awaited you! Princess, they have come! May Allah preserve you, gentlemen. Enter my humble house!'

An inner door opened now and there entered a man who had the appearance of a gigantic bird of prey: a monster of hairy body and brass-bound biceps: on tree-trunk legs he towered above Big Rhys, eyeing him with hostility.

'This is my slave, Gargoa,' cried Abaya, and the man bowed low, one hand touching his forehead in acknowledgement, the other gripping an ancient double-barrelled hunting *jezail*, which he now placed in a corner with its flintlocks cocked; and his deep-set eyes, fixed upon Big Rhys, smouldered contempt from his flat, Mongolian face. His features betrayed his tribal ancestry, for he was a Hazara, a fact that later played an important part in the business of our survival. Like antagonized boxers before the opening round, he and Big Rhys continued to weigh up one another, looking for weakness.

And the Hazara was first to turn away as Big Rhys asked, 'Where's the princess, then?'

'Patience, my friend!' Abaya gently admonished him, and added, leading us into an inner courtyard, 'there are enemies everywhere, and time is plentiful. Indeed, upon reflection, tonight may not be opportune to take her,' and he made a gesture to the giant Gargoa, who left us.

'The time is now,' I said.

'For you, perhaps, but not for me, for I have recently received a message from Akbar Khan, who is in the vicinity: he may be calling for her in the morning to take her under his protection.'

'That is not what she wants – the Dost himself warned against it,' I said. He replied with suave charm, 'With the Dost exiled in India, what he wants is of small consequence; it is I who must take responsibility for her safety,' and he pushed at a door which silently swung open; within a small red chamber Durrani was sitting; she made no sign of recognition when I greeted her.

She was dressed in the finery of an Afghan court lady: either side of her scarlet bodice her black hair hung in waves to her waist: two rows of braided pearls she wore upon her forehead, and above it a magnificent headdress, an insignia of Royalty; from this fell trinkets of gold encrusted with gems.

Her purple corselet, laced tightly about her waist, was interwoven with silver ornaments; her scarf was yellow, her pantaloons of white Persian silk: over her shoulders was loosely hanging a white fur coat; upon her feet she wore boots that reached to the calf.

Abaya said, 'See, she is dressed for travel, because she now awaits the arrival of her uncle, who has guaranteed her safe conduct to Ludhiana. Here she will receive him, robed appropriately, as befits his rank.'

And in that moment, as Gargoa returned, Big Rhys whispered into my ear, 'You realize she's been drugged? If I could get one good shot at this big bastard's chin. . . .'

'Do so,' I whispered back, 'when I go for the gun,' and said to Abaya as I followed him through the door:

'As you please. It is you who must decide, Sirdar.'

Abaya replied happily, 'Excellent, so surely you do not want to leave at this very moment? Akbar will reward you well for such fealty to his niece. See here . . . ' and he led the way into the other room, saying:

'Unfortunately, Allah has decreed that I am now beyond the charms of women, but should he ever relent, I keep three slave girls, one white, one black and one yellow, for the entertainment of guests . . . ' and he pointed at a window bower. 'See, they have arrived for your inspection,' and he cackled from a crimson mouth. 'All three know more tricks than the Whore of Babylon. Are you interested?'

'We lack time,' I answered, and he raised his hands in disbelief.

'Certainly, one must not pursue the delights of love in haste – but surely, a mere few hours of entertainment until Akbar arrives?' and he smothered us with his attentions. 'Food, then, if not women? For even those who enjoy a voluptuous life count the blessings of Abaya's table, I who am unfairly known as "The Impaler". Besides . . . ' and here he threw up his hands, 'to leave here before Akbar comes? The wrath of the Dost would fall upon my head were

105

I to allow his granddaughter to roam in the dark with strangers – see my position!'

I replied, 'It is a position which has changed much since we last met, for then you agreed with the Dost.'

'But at no time have I rejected the protection of Akbar Khan, remember? As I say, mine is the responsibility, not her grandfather's. Surely, she would be safer with a responsible relative?'

'The gun,' I whispered, and dived for the *jezail* in the corner, reaching it just as Big Rhys caught Gargoa with a right-hander that must have shifted his relatives over in the Hindu Kush: the man toppled like a tall pine, then fell upon his face, but the gun butt, as I snatched it, stamped the floor and the flintlock fired and Big Rhys, taking the bullet in the head, fell also.

One moment peace, next bedlam, with the Vizier jumping up and down calling for help and the three slave girls at the window yelling blue murder. Shrieking, Abaya ran at me with a scimitar, but I dropped him with a backhander, and knelt to Rhys, who lay motionless.

The bullet had taken him across the right temple; blood was pulsing in streams over his chest. Three times I called his name, my hand upon his heart, but it seemed that his life had been snuffed out by the single explosive wound. Then suddenly the Kohistani lad arrived, crying, 'Quick, the Princess!' and I ran into the other room and snatched her up in my arms just as two servants entered it: one grabbed at me and I kicked him flat; a shot cracked out and the second man fell across the unconscious body of Gargoa; a smoking pistol was now in the hand of the Kohistani as he knelt beside Rhys.

'He is dead,' he said calmly, and rose. 'The door, get out!' and I followed him through it into the night, snatching up the *jezail* as I went, only to come face to face, with no free hand, with a guard coming in from the garden. Struck from behind, he also fell, and I found myself running beside the Kohistani.

'Shall I take her?' His arms went out for Durrani.

'No, you hold them off!'

'Come, Sahib!' and I followed him, first through a little orchard and then into the shadows of overhanging trees.

Here the three ponies were waiting and, with Durrani's

senses revived by the cold night air, I put her on one horse, and mounted the other; with the three of us at first trotting uncertainly, we then broke into a gallop.

'God go with us!' cried the lad.

And with Big Rhys, I thought.

We did not stop until reaching Bareekub, which is three miles from Seh Baba, and entered a cave in the face of the mountain; here the road turns off to Jugdulluk.

With Durrani sleeping and the Kohistani watching over her, I looked upon the dawn breaking across the Nullah, the short road back to Kabul: and there, like a snake slithering on the road below, I saw the remnants of our army labouring along to Jalalabad, but this tragedy did not dominate my thoughts: I was thinking, instead, of Big Rhys, the friend of my childhood; of Dathyl, his daughter, and the wife to whom he was lost.

Standing there at the cave entrance, I could not see the dawn for tears.

'Come back, Sirdar, or you will be seen,' said the Kohistani.

No sooner had he said it than a volley of bullets splattered the cave entrance.

Lady Sale later observed in her diary:

Wednesday, 13th February, 1842
Being in captivity I cannot now personally record the fate of our poor army, which is still fighting its way to Jalalabad, but the following information comes from an impeccable source.

Thursday, 14th February, 1842 (with the retreating British Army)
All the bearers have either deserted or been murdered now: all camels either stolen by the Afghans or eaten by the camp followers. Men are so cold that they cannot hold their muskets; scores are found dead every morning. To add to the wretchedness, many are now snow-blind; others, too faint to march, fall to the knives

of the enemy. All sick and wounded left in the rear are immediately cut up.

Major Ewart, commanding the 54th, had both arms broken by *jezail* bullets before he died. Lieutenant Morrieson, carrying the colours, was speared in the back, took a sword-cut that laid his head open, was knifed in the neck and, while crawling, took another spear in the chin: he was then left to die.

In the dip of Tezeen Nullah the scenes are horrible, the ground covered with dead and dying. Here the last gun was left behind, and poor Dr Cardew laid upon its carriage to await inevitable death.

In fine moonlight the army reached Bareekub, a place of caves and water about three miles from Seh Baba, and here Dr Duff, the Surgeon-General who had his left hand cut off with a penknife, lagged behind through loss of blood, and was murdered.

At daybreak on the 15th, the valley of Lughman bore fearful testimony to the night's battle; some 200 bodies were seen, mostly Europeans, naked and covered with gaping wounds: also, scores of poor wretches appeared out of wayside caves, all quite mad and covered with gashes. At first light others were seen through telescopes at a higher cave entrance and, probably being the enemy, were fired upon.

Clearly this was the Kohistani and I, as we had stood watching the army's retreat to its annihilation in the valley.

Meanwhile, Durrani lay like one embalmed, her white face turned up, sleeping off the drug.

'She is beautiful, is she not?' said the Kohistani, looking into her face.

I nodded, my mind with Rhys.

'She is my Princess, and I would die for her,' he added.

The lad intrigued me now.

I replied, 'Do not be too eager. How old are you?'

'I shall be sixteen in the month of White Dews.'

'Yes, well you'll probably be prepared to die for a few more before many years are out,' and kneeling, I wrapped the fur coat closer about Durrani and covered her with a saddle cloth taken from one of the ponies.

19

'What is your name?' I asked the Kohistani.

'My name is Karendeesh,' said he, standing to attention before me.

'It sounds like a sneeze,' said Durrani, disdainfully.

It was our first halt after a gallop to safety; soon, we would have to descend into the valley and take the road to India.

'Treat him gently,' I told her. 'You are safe because of him.'

'I am here despite him,' came the reply, 'since he did not have time to betray me also. He is a *bosh*, and not to be trusted.'

The boy bowed his head at this.

'A *bosh*?' I asked.

'A humbug, a nothing-person.'

They stood silently above me while I tried to light a fire in the snow. The three ponies, tethered nearby, lifted their heads and snorted at the smoke.

I asked, 'Where do you come from, Karendeesh?' and his eyes glowed in his brown, handsome face.

'From the Indus River, Sahib; there I lived on a steamer with my father, but he died.'

'And your mother?'

'I caused her death when arriving out of her womb.'

'As you would cause ours also, given half a chance,' added Durrani.

I frowned up at her. 'You treat him harshly.'

Wrapped in her white fur coat, she glared down at me. 'I treat him as he should be treated, for I never trust a Hindu,' and she stood commandingly while he shivered before her in his rags. Said she, 'Listen, answer me truthfully, or I will have you whipped. You came to me on the steamer outside Peshawar, and said you would take a message to the sahib here, remember? Who sent you?'

'The officer in charge of the *chuprassys*, Lady.'

'You were an official messenger?'

'Like my father, working on the boats, and his father before that.'

'Right. Now tell me, how did you know where to find me when you led this sahib to Abaya's house?'

'It was written in the message, Lady.'

'It was not; no marking was on the envelope.' She added, 'So, by opening envelopes and reading the messages inside – that is how you get about, is it?'

'Of course.'

'You discover everybody's whereabouts by reading their letters?'

'Yes. How otherwise could a *chuprassy* get a living? A good messenger is the servant of the customer, my father told me. He must read and write in English and have good eyes and ears.'

'Also a long nose?'

'Certainly.' Karendeesh was unabashed. 'This is how I heard that the Vizier at Seh Baba was going to betray you to Shah Shuja.'

I glanced up at this.

'Ridiculous!' said Durrani, and turned to me. 'See, he lies! Did not Abaya say that he was going to give me to my uncle, Akbar Khan?'

'Ah yes, lady! Perhaps that is what he told you,' came the gentle reply, and he added, 'But Timur, the King's son, was galloping in from Kabul.' Karendeesh spread his small hands. 'Who would get there first? I wondered. But then Akbar Khan reached Seh Baba a mile or two away, so the Vizier was in trouble.'

'Not the trouble my friend Rhys is in,' I said to Durrani. 'He is dead. Are you as ungrateful to him?'

It stilled her, and I put snow-water in a can on to the little fire and distributed what was left of the wheatcakes into

111

their cupped hands. 'Be friends, for God's sake,' I said. 'You can bully him afterwards.'

This infuriated her. 'I know these people and you do not! He is a *bosh*, and he will sell me in Peshawar to the highest bidder. I say tie him to a tree and leave him. With luck, a passing bandit may cut his throat,' and she spat at my feet like a man.

'Hang around here, and they'll cut ours too,' I said, and we drank hot water and ate the wheatcakes, and did not speak.

Meanwhile I was learning more every moment about the Princess Durrani.

And began to wonder what Big Rhys had died for.

Within a little quarry face alongside the road to Jalalabad we came across about fifty slain people.

Clearly, they were a small band who had advanced in front of the vanguard and had been caught by Ghilzais in their escape.

Young soldiers of the 44th were among them, also a fat compradore, a man I had seen in the Kabul bazaar; and a young girl of about Durrani's age – clearly out of the Shah's harem – was lying beside him; I touched her body; it was still warm; it was eerie, that scene of death, and told that Ghilzais were in the vicinity.

Later the Afghan women would come and finish the job of mutilating the bodies: meanwhile, in my imagination I saw a Hindu girl with a yellow bodice and blue-black hair braided across her brow; at her temple she was wearing a white frangipani flower. She who was the wife of the miller of Huft Kotul, the woman the sergeant loved, and I hoped that they were alive.

'I am not travelling with a *bosh*,' said Durrani, and mounted her pony and sat there, the reins loose in her hands.

Karendeesh and I mounted ours; it was ridiculous; we just sat and stared at one another.

'He is a commoner,' she added, 'and not a true believer. I will now travel alone.'

'Do that and you will die,' I replied. 'Come, Durrani, he is

112

a human being like us.'

'He is not like us, and I will not travel in his company.'

'Then do what you like!'

Spurring the pony, I left her and the lad followed me, saying, 'Sahib, she is a princess and is superior to us. Please take her.'

I shook my head. She was a challenge to my authority. Give this spoiled brat an inch, I thought, and she would swarm all over me.

In some strange way, unknown to me then, perhaps, I needed to avenge the death of Big Rhys, and so at that moment hated her.

Later, with dusk dropping over the earth, the boy and I stopped amid monstrous encompassing rocks, and I shivered, but not with cold; my recklessness in abandoning Durrani began to rake me with terrifying possibilities. Such was the bite in the wind that I wondered if she would survive the night.

Karendeesh said, as I held him under my coat, 'Lady do not come, Sahib . . .?'

'Lady can do what the bloody hell she likes,' I said in Pashto, and his eyes were like diamonds in the moonlight.

When the moon rose I shot a buck rabbit and cooked him on a bakestone, turning the young meat this way and that, and a perfume floated up that must have tempted the beggars out of Karachi: we ate, Karendeesh and I, and lay together under the saddle cloths while Durrani's portion simmered on the stone. And she, following her nose like a starving pariah, came out of the darkness and stood, unspeaking, at my feet.

'You are hungry for our company?' I asked nonchalantly.

'The food called me, not you.'

I took her ice-cold hands and drew her to the fire. After she had eaten her fill, I spread out her saddle cloth on the ground, saying, 'Here now, come and lie between us.'

'Beside him? He is a Hindu.'

'Hindu or Moslem, he is warm and you are cold.'

Dawn was fingering the clouds as I melted more snow and cooked their breakfast, and this I took to Durrani and

113

Karendeesh, but did not awaken them, for they were sleeping close together.

Shivering without my blanket, I watched the sun come up, and the road was a purple ribbon through the mountains to Jalalabad.

We travelled again, meeting nothing on our way, for the last stand of the 44th was raging to the west of us; we heard booming guns and the faint rattle of musketry.

When another night fell, we fould shelter in a little ruined fort, an outpost to the big military headquarters at Jalalabad, said Karendeesh.

Here were two rooms, one up, one down, and in the lower one we built a fire.

Then, with the ponies tethered, we slept again among a horde of Afghan fleas, none of which bothered either Durrani or the boy, but who nearly ate me whole. I was still scratching when dawn came; this probably saved our lives.

Hearing a camel's cry, I got up and peered through a musketry loop-hole.

Three Afghan tribesmen had dismounted from their camels: one, urinating in the open, luckily stood with his back to our tethered ponies: the second was wandering aimlessly: the third, whistling to himself, was coming straight for our entrance door, which was creaking in the wind like a squawking vulture.

I shook the others into wakefulness.

'Quickly, *upstairs!*'

Karendeesh, instantly aware, dragged a protesting Durrani after me up to the room above, while I grabbed the *jezail*. Flattening Durrani against an upstairs wall, I put my hand over her mouth: furious, she snatched it away.

'English?' she asked.

'Ghilzais, *look!*' and she peered, and as she did so the entrance door went down.

Through a break in the floorboards I watched one of the Afghans enter the room below; pausing before our fire, he stirred it with his foot, then knelt, touching the ashes with his fingers.

114

He stared up, I stared down, wondering if he could hear the thudding of my heart.

Durrani had her hands over her face: Ghilzais had perfected infamy when it came to women.

Such as these roamed the battlefields like wingless vultures, robbing the dead, killing the wounded, and marching the rest across the Hindu Kush to the slave markets of Bokhara: I made a mental note to take Durrani with me: the boy must take his chance, I thought, and I saw him draw his little skinning-knife. I held out my hand for it and he tossed it to me.

'The man comes,' whispered Durrani.

I could hear his sandalled feet mounting the stone steps and flattened myself behind the door, while Durrani, unbidden, took a position in the middle of the floor. And as the door creaked open and he momentarily stared at her, I had a hand over his mouth and slid the knife between his ribs: lowering his body to the floor, I stared into his bearded face. He was young, and I pitied him.

'You did him good,' said Karendeesh, and knelt, joyfully searching him; finding some rupees, he bit one and dropped the rest into his own pocket.

'Look, they have seen the horses,' whispered Durrani, 'the other two are coming,' and I went full length on the floor with the *jezail* freshly loaded with the Afghan's powder and shot.

Karendeesh said, 'They will hear that gun as far away as the English forts, Sahib. Let me go down, and I will kill them coming in.'

'You stay,' commanded Durrani, just as the next Ghilzai appeared at the room entrance.

Light flashed as I fired, momentarily blinding us, and in that confusion I saw the man's body, instantly contorted, dance like a puppet before collapsing. The third tribesman leaped across his comrade's body and up the steps, his scimitar upraised.

'Not so easily does a Ghilzai die!' he cried, as I scrambled to my feet.

Ducking his sabre slash, I closed with him: he was a big man and powerful, and his garlic-laden breath pumped into

115

my face as I tripped him: together, we rolled like nailed logs down the stone steps. His thick brown hands closed upon my throat and, as I fought for breath, I saw the thin body of Karendeesh above me as he leaped for the Afghan's sword, kicking it across the floor. The man rose, threw the boy off and came again with clutching hands, and I got him with a right smash that would have felled an ox, but his impetus bore him onward, bearing me down, and his hands gripped my throat again. Suddenly, as we fought, his eyes widened; gasping, he slipped easily into death.

Durrani, dropping the skinning knife, said calmly, 'Now we go before the English come, eh? For they are bastards worse than these, remember?'

'We stay,' I replied, astonished at her language.

'That was good!' said Karendeesh. 'You do him well, Sahib.'

'It is disgusting,' said Durrani. 'All you men are disgusting.'

We pulled the dead Afghans outside and slept for the rest of the night.

At dawn we travelled again, and within a mile Karendeesh's pony broke a fetlock, and I had to shoot it with a muffled gun.

'Now, my brave young friend, you will have to walk,' said Durrani, and this he did for six miles until his bare feet began to bleed.

Earlier, I had mentioned a strain in my thigh, caused by the fight with the Afghan, so Durrani said, 'You expect me to walk while you two ride?'

The sun was weak in the heavens, and there was a threat of rain.

'Of course!'

She glared up at me. 'I, the Princess Durrani, am to lead a damn horse?'

I emptied my hands at her. 'I am injured. The boy has sore feet. What is the alternative?'

'Perhaps it would be better to ride off on my own.'

'You tried that before, remember?'

Karendeesh said tearfully, 'Sahib, it is wrong that I should ride while my princess walks.'

'Look at his poor old feet,' complained Durrani sarcastically. 'Whatever are we going to do?'

'You get down off your pony and he takes your place, it is simple.'

'This,' said she, 'is terrible! My ancestors would turn in their graves.'

She let the boy limp for another mile, then, her face furious, she got off her pony: next time I saw them, Karendeesh was riding while she was leading the pony.

At sunset, within two miles of Jalalabad we camped again and neither would speak to me although I addressed them several times; and when the moon came up both were kneeling.

Either side of the road, yards apart, they knelt praying (with Durrani facing Mecca). And before we bedded down for the night in the open (it did not rain, instead the stars came out like magic lanterns) Durrani came to me with their horse blankets and said, 'For a man supposed to be our friend, you act strangely. The feet of Karendeesh are bleeding badly, yet you do nothing.'

'We all have to share discomfort in this life.'

'His feet are bleeding, I say, and I do not know what to do, for I have no ointment, and no bandages.'

'Then he is out of luck, is he not?'

'Sahib, you are a hard man. Are all Englishmen like you?'

'That is my trouble,' I answered. 'I am not an Englishman.'

'He is a boy with a man's heart, and because he is a Hindu, you despise him, is that not the truth?' She wandered about in the wind. 'He has not fed properly when young; this is why, although he is the same age as me, he is smaller.'

'Oh, certainly! He's as skinny as a flute, while you go in and out in all the right places. Clearly, you haven't gone short of anything since you left your mother's breast.'

She looked like a child standing there. 'I am a woman, and he is only a boy.'

'Then act like one!'

'But you are a man. How can you ride in comfort when

117

one of us is in pain? Will you take your turn at walking, while he rides, in the morning?'

'I will consider it,' I answered, and wrapped myself up in the blanket.

As the sun went down I watched her go to a quiet place of bushes and there lift her robe: tearing off strips from her petticoat she then called Karendeesh and made him sit before her: first she plastered his feet with dung droppings from the ponies, then she bound them up with the silk from her petticoat, meanwhile talking in harsh words to herself and sending looks to kill in my direction.

'He is not as I thought he was, but a brave little boy,' said she as she put her coat over him. 'He is thin and cold. You ought to be ashamed of yourself.'

'I am, positively,' I replied, mimicking her preciseness.

'So move over, please. I prefer not to sleep with you, but with Karendeesh. Is that not so, Small One? We will sleep together,' and she turned her back to me and put her arm about him.

It was an astonishing change of attitude: I decided to keep an eye on her.

20

At the end of February, a cold dawn found us within Peshawar's crumbling walls: this, the grim gateway to the Khyber Pass, now echoed to the shuffling feet of animals carrying gorgeous embroideries smuggled in from Turkistan: the melting-pot of a dozen nationalities.

Camel trains laden with Cashmere silks and the produce of lands beyond the Aghil mountains padded by in brilliant winter light as the sun set fire to the day; and the air was filled with the wails of beggars and cries of fruitsellers, whose carts, despite war's shortages, were laden high with madder, cotton bales and the choicest asafoetida.

Everywhere we walked was a jumble of coloured awnings and the tables of money-changers clattered with gold and silver.

'You have money?' Durrani asked me.

'Ten rupees.'

'If we are taking howdahs on a caravan train to Amritsar, we will need plenty,' said she, and held up a ruby under a money-changer's nose. His eyes grew big in his lined walnut of a face.

'A hundred rupees,' she demanded.

He suspended the jewel in his taloned fingers. 'For you, Daughter, fifty, no more,' and he sighed with the face of a thrashed dog.

'A hundred and ten for two,' said she, and held up another. 'And no bargaining – I know you long-nosed thieves.'

'Oh, beloved of God, where did you obtain such wealth?'

he croaked, and held the rubies up to the sun, his shifty eyes moving under their hooded lids.

'None of your business, man of low caste. Are you buying or not?'

'If you have more, Daughter.'

'These only,' and she pocketed the rubies, walking off.

'Come back, come back!' His voice was a wail of misery.

The people pressed about us in smells of camphor and burned cloth.

'A hundred and fifty now, my friend!' and she rattled the rubies before him: her brown face was sweating, I noticed. Clearly it was a risk, but we needed the money.

'By the bones of the Prophet,' said the money-changer, 'you drive a hard bargain,' and he bit the rubies in his teeth and counted the money into her hands.

'Now mingle with the crowd,' she whispered, and we did so.

'Wait, wait! O my beautiful!' It was a braying jackass of a voice.

Durrani, now hot and as agitated as a fevered rose, said, 'These are not my people; it is dangerous.'

'You have more where these came from?' I asked.

'I plucked them out of my jewels. I have diamonds also, but dare not trade them here.'

Earlier, we had watched the erection of a five-starred gibbet at the border crossing on the frontier: full twenty feet high, its inscription proposed to hang from it the scarlet-coated corpse of a British soldier with his hands and feet cut off – fulfilling the threat that never again, even if crawling, could a foreign invader pollute sacred Afghan soil. Yet, with the threat still warm upon Afghan mouths, we British were already making preparations for a spring offensive.

Whitehall, pledged to win the last battle whatever the cost in lives and treasure, had issued orders to invade again and exact retribution for the slaughter of our army. Nor had Victoria yet abandoned her hopes of stealing the infamous Koh-i-Nor diamond for her Crown Jewels. So a new force under General Pollock was now blocking the narrow courts and alleys of Peshawar, mobilizing against the state that had dared to twist the tail of the British lion.

Therefore, new contingents of army units were already landing off steamers along the Indus River.

Brushing aside the screeched protests of hawkers, pedlars and tallymen, its cavalry and gun-limbers were thundering in, overturning the stalls of the money-changers, collapsing the coloured awnings of the cheap-jacks, and sending the water-tubs of the *bheestees* rolling in the mud.

Threats and curses arose as the big 18-pounders came next, following the mules and ammunition carts of the 3rd Bengal Irregular Cavalry: then arrived a thousand men of the Bengal Native Infantry marching to the skirl of pipes. With their kilts and sporrans swinging to the march came Scots led by one in full ceremonial dress.

'*Look*!' cried Karendeesh, 'The Indian Rope Trick!' and we entered a little knot of people in a place clear of soldiers, for the first performance of the day was about to begin.

Here an ancient fakir, all haunches and bones, was squatting on his heels before a wicker basket; eyes slitted against the sun he sat, his yellow turban a blaze of colour: and as he played on a little tin whistle the tail of rope appeared out of the basket and began to sway in time with his music.

'You have ever seen this?' asked Durrani softly.

I shook my head.

'Then watch carefully,' and I looked around the intent faces of the people.

All eyes were riveted upon the basket.

The end of the rope now rose in the air as the fakir's whistling continued; higher, higher, uncoiling out of the basket between his knees, and a silence fell upon the watching crowd; the whole market-place was silenced, as if by the slam of a lid.

Higher, higher went the rope; now ten feet up, now twelve, now fifteen feet high . . . where it methodically turned and looked down at our staring faces. And in that suspended moment of disbelief, an urchin boy appeared at the fakir's elbow. Leaping on to the rope he began to climb it hand over hand. Reaching the top of the rope, he then passed his hand above it, giving proof that nothing was attached: then, as quickly, he lowered himself to the ground and disappeared into the crowd.

The rope, descending slowly, curled itself back into the basket; the fakir reached out and replaced the lid.

'Can you believe your eyes?' asked Karendeesh, his small face upturned to mine.

'I do not, it is impossible.'

Durrani smiled, narrowing her eyes above her yashmak. 'Nothing is impossible. This is the East.'

Until now I had been holding the folds of my robe against my mouth; but now, safe in the hay of a barn which we had rented for the night, I was at ease, and Durrani removed her yashmak.

'You are far too European to be seen around, and we must do something about it,' she announced.

Having gathered from the wayside the leaves of henna, she now mixed these with the shells of walnuts. Squatting before me now, she boiled these together in Karendeesh's cooking-pot; making a dye, she said, which would turn me into an Afghan.

Karendeesh had watched this performance intently until, with a glance, she ordered him away.

There was a wonderful serenity in lying there while Durrani knelt above me, applying the dye to my face and throat and, as she did so, saying, 'You, my Welsh friend, possess a man's beauty: with your blue eyes and strength of body, you could be mistaken for an Afghan noble; one of my tribe fighting the great Alexander when the world was young. Your breath is sweet to me, while the breath of our princes reek with garlic: nor do you stink when you sweat, and this pleases me.'

'I will remind myself to be delighted,' but the sarcasm was lost upon her.

Now she bent above me and her robe was loose upon her body and I saw the divide of her breasts: like most young Afghan women, she did not go short in this direction, and I found it disturbing. Clearly, she had arranged to give me this particular treat.

*

'You realize, I suppose,' said she, 'that we know little about each other?' This she said in Pashto, in which I was now almost fluent: often when she spoke to Karendeesh, she did so in Persian, knowing that this language I did not fully understand.

'Have you wondered what will happen, for instance, when we reach Ludhiana?' she asked.

'Only that we will have to part.'

'Need that happen?'

'It is the way most journeys end. For a start, I cannot imagine your grandfather tolerating a convict in the house.'

'Then what will you do?'

'Give myself up to the British.'

'But they will imprison you again!'

'Probably.'

'Cannot you go home?'

'Not until I am given a ticket-of-leave – I told you this before, remember?'

With her fingers she applied the dye, and the touch of her, and her nearness, were having upon me an erotic effect. She said, deep in her throat, 'And what if my grandfather asks you to stay in his service?'

'That's unlikely.'

'Why?'

'I am British, and Britain is his enemy.'

'But just suppose?'

'Supposing is the business of children – this is not a game,' and her face puckered up.

'There you go again! Always when we are serious, you speak to me as if I were a child. But I am nearly sixteen years old, and in Afghanistan that is being a woman.'

'Not in my country,' I said, and she was beautiful in anger.

'No? Well, in my country a girl can be married at the age of twelve!'

'There'd be the devil to pay if that happened in mine.'

'Anyway, what have you got to go back to? Once you told me that you had nothing,' and she put her chin up, looking down at me with her slanted eyes, adding, 'you had no

123

woman there, you said.'

'It depends. Perhaps I have, perhaps not.'

'See now, you are playing with me again,' which is not what she said, but what she meant.

'Perhaps I have a woman waiting for me. I am not certain.'

Now she smacked on more henna and walnut, this time upon my chest and emptied her stained hands at me. 'There you go again! But I tell you this. If you are doubtful about her patience, she is not worth having.'

'Ho, ho! Now it is the woman talking!'

A silence came between us, and a small sadness.

'O, Iestyn!'

It was time to go, and I raised myself in the hay, but she gently pushed me back, whispering, 'Will you not stay for a little while when we get to Ludhiana? True, you are a white-faced Frank and I am an Afghan, but they tell me that I am beautiful. Do I not please you a little?'

That's the trouble, I thought.

'Because, when we reach my grandfather's house a new spring will be rising all about us, and the garden of Ludhiana, I am told, is just the place for lovers.

'We will laze together all day and eat wild honey, which we will take from the hives with our fingers; if you are stung once, that is but one love in a lifetime, and if you are stung twice, that is two . . .'

'It's good to know in advance what is about to happen,' I said.

Now the sun had turned over in his sleep and shadows were hording up in the barn's corners: in this twilight I lay, hoping that soon Karendeesh would return, yet fearful of the sounds of his coming. For there was a lovely unity in lying here beneath Durrani's hands; it was a little oasis of beauty beyond the vices of the world; a place of scented hay and the light of the crescent moon.

'Make no mistake,' said Durrani, close to my ear now. 'It will certainly come about.' And she drew up her gown to her thighs and raised her bare legs before me, saying, 'Do you not think, for a start, Iestyn Mortymer – or whatever she calls you at home – that I have pretty brown legs?'

She was having an elemental effect upon me, and knew it.

It was over two years since I had made love to Mari, but I knew a small potent nagging . . . that this was a child within my reach: to take her into my arms would be a transgression of all I believed in.

Until this moment, in our journeyings, I might reach out and touch her; perhaps her hand would brush mine unobtrusively in the intrinsic acts of eating and sleeping, or when one clasped the other for warmth. But now, quite suddenly, all this was forbidden, and I heard her words as an echo.

'What must certainly come about?' I asked.

'You and me, Iestyn. Together always.'

She rarely used my name, but did so prettily.

'Why are you so sure of it?' I asked, and her eyes slanted up so high at the corners that I thought they were never coming down.

'Because it is written in the waters of the moon.'

'Are you so easily forgetting my wife?'

'I told you. I am here, she is not. Better the girl in the bed than one in the moonlight, we Afghans say.'

'Grandfather will have other ideas about that!'

She joined in my laughter, saying, 'Grandfather is a dead old trout, like you. But do not let us talk of relatives. What about the other bits?'

'Other bits?'

'Oh, come! What will happen if you take your shirt off? If you are going to be an Afghan, you must be one all over,' and she laughed again; head back, she laughed, and I saw the tip of her tongue and the straight white lines of her teeth between her vermilion-painted lips.

Then she was no longer a child, but a nubile young fawn; and in the moment I reached out for her, Karendeesh, as if dropping the curtain on the scene of Act I, came through the barn door hooting like a maniac.

'Come quickly! The caravan train is about to start for Amritsar. *Come*!' and he dashed out again.

'Saved by the bell,' I said, putting on my shirt.

125

Durrani's eyes became big in her face. 'A bell? I heard no bell!'

But there was no need to explain it; her eyes danced and I knew she understood.

21

Toko Oolie was his name. His title was Master of Camels, and he owned the caravan which was about to leave for Amritsar.

Here's another old reprobate if ever I saw one: his flaccid jowls hung loosely from pin-bone cheeks; a broad, black beard decorated a massive chest upon which hung medallions pinned upon a coat of turquoise interwoven with scarlet thread: born of a vulture, this one, his eyes drooping in the somnolence of the over-heated tent.

He said abruptly, 'The distance is over four hundred miles, so the cost of journeying to Amritsar will be considerable.'

'Name it,' said Durrani, erect before his table.

This one, like most of his kind, dealt not only in the transport of goods and people.

His camel train, loaded to breaking point and consisting of a hundred protesting animals, was not his sole means of livelihood: he would be engaged, also, in slave-dealing with merchants who lived on the other side of the Hindu Kush. Not for nothing had this range of mountains earned its name – the 'Hindu Killer' – for slavery had been flourishing there since the days of the Mongol Empire.

Whole populations of warring tribes had been transported in chains from the unfertile mountains of the hinterland to the savage fastness of rulers like the Amir of Bokhara; one whose reputation struck terror into Hindu hearts.

But there was another trade in humans, one still prevalent

today, and I was aware of it. His abacus clicked. Smiling up at us with interest, the Master said, 'Five hundred rupees?'

'That is ridiculous,' Durrani snapped. 'We are not buying the camel train.'

'Perhaps not, but see my predicament,' and he raised red-palmed hands upwards as if in prayer.

'If Allah ordains that we safely reach Amritsar, he only does so for those who help themselves, for the cost is heavy. Water has to be carried, since wells are known to be poisoned: animal fodder also, and new camels and donkeys purchased, since many expire under the whip. Armed guards are required to protect us against attack, for bandits now roam India; brain-thudders lie in ambush.

'Taking all this together, Memsahib, it can readily be appreciated that I have difficulty in keeping body and soul together; also the journey, taking a month or more, includes your howdah, food and every comfort.' He sighed unhappily. 'In your case, however, I could make an exception. Four hundred and fifty?'

'It is still too much,' said Durrani.

'You drive a hard bargain. But that is for three, remember. The boy is handsome. Throw him in for the entertainment of my guests on the journey, and I will cut the cost by half.'

Durrani stared at me, not understanding. Toko Oolie added, 'A woman, for all her beauty, is but a duty, remember; but a boy of such good looks is always a delightful pleasure.'

The early sun was turning the room into a light of burnished gold, and small palls of cluster-flies, horrible to contemplate, began their swarming within the smells of sweat and perfume: the same swarms that had pestered India for countless generations; their staccato buzzing akin to the ceaseless singing of night cicadas, in days when child-dealers bought newly weaned children from their starving mothers and tortured them into monstrous shapes for service in maharajas' palaces as objects of derision . . . or for professional begging in market-places from Bombay to Calcutta.

128

Such a trader sat before me now, his thick lips pursed in sensual anticipation.

India was not alone in such trading.

China also had its trade in famine children: their limbs, exhibited on butchers' slabs, could be bought for coppers during famine: while Hong Kong, the Anus of the East, ensured that profits were prolific from Mui Tsai, its infamous child-selling still flourishing under the protection of a regal Britain.

Even Wales, my own land, supplied its crippled innocents for the iron and coal trades, their limbs especially malformed for the lower underground coal seams. One did not have to travel East to observe man's inhumanity; Britain was to the forefront when it came to exploiting cheap labour; her record in the Slave Trade being squalid enough for international contempt.

The animal sitting before me now was no better, or worse, than an English mine-owner dining in his country mansion.

Now I said, taking from my pocket a small diamond Durrani had passed to me, 'It is a privilege, Master of Camels, to do business with one of such ethics,' and I held up the diamond. 'This is all we possess in the world, my sister, I, and our small brother. Take it and carry us to Amritsar, and let there be an end to this.'

'Great fat pigs!' he exclaimed, taking the diamond, 'I am now your slave! May jackals feast upon my bones if I do not serve you all the days of my life. *Kabakan!*' and an Arab entered the tent.

The Master said, 'Treat these guests with all hospitality. Good food and my best howdah shall be theirs until we reach Amritsar. Peace be unto you, travellers; may Allah heap countless blessings upon you,' and as he left he benevolently patted the face of Karendeesh in passing, whispering to him, 'Charming boy. Would that my poor loins could sire such a handsome child, for a man without a son, as I, is but a dead star in the Universe,' and he bowed to us.

Now back at the barn, with Durrani collecting up our few possessions for the journey, Karendeesh listened to me intently.

129

'You know the road to Amritsar?' I asked him.

'Like my hand,' he answered.

'And beyond that – to Ludhiana, the King's home?'

'I do not know that road, Sahib.'

'But you have a tongue in your head, have you not?' asked Durrani over her shoulder.

'Listen,' I told him. 'Take both ponies in case one goes lame, as before. Ride one, lead the other,' and I took from Durrani the envelope she offered, saying, 'Take this letter. It is from the Princess to the King. Give it to the King himself, no other; but first say that you have been sent by his granddaughter, understand?'

'I understand,' he replied, 'but why cannot I travel with you in the caravans?'

'Because for you it is dangerous,' said Durrani. 'Do not ask more, leave it at that. After you deliver the letter, my grandfather will feed you; also, perhaps he will give you clean clothes and a medal to wear on your chest telling that you are now a King's Messenger. What about that!'

His eyes grew big in his boy's face.

'Also something painful on your rear if you fail us,' she added. 'More. Give my name to anyone on the road and I will personally skin you. This letter asks my grandfather to send guards to meet us at Amritsar. It is rice paper, so eat it rather than yield it to anyone but my grandfather. Understand?'

'I will not speak of you, Lady,' said Karendeesh and, going full length on the floor before her, he placed his right hand under her foot.

Durrani raised him, saying, 'Ride well for us, boy, and you will live for ever in the gardens of Allah,' and, to my astonishment, put his face in her hands and kissed him.

Things were changing every moment in the social order of Afghanistan.

The camel being the ship of the desert, Durrani and I had now spent the first week of our journey within a howdah strapped to one of their backs. I could think of worse ways to travel, for the somnolence induced by the rolling gait of this beast is guaranteed to induce sleep in the worst insomniac, and I am not good at sleeping with Durrani around.

130

The howdah we travelled in was formed in two parts; while travelling, I was on one side of our camel and she was on the other, with the camel in between.

However, when the caravans halted for the evening meal in a circle around a blazing fire (tigers were about) the Master's servants then took the howdahs off the camels and laid them on the ground, where they formed a primitive double bed. This was at a place of water, with all the freshness and brilliance of an Indian summer: nearby was an orchard containing date trees, also apple and quince and pomegranate trees, all displaying a profusion of blossoms and skirted with willow and mulberry trees where fireflies danced and the night was pin-pointed with a thousand lights from clustering glow-worms. Here, also, legions of silk-worms laboured.

'Are you awake, Iestyn?' asked Durrani.

As weary as a dying sloth, I tried to sleep, but Durrani had other ideas. On my side of the couch, within the intimate warmth of the howdah's waterproof walls, I stared up at the stars through its unrolled roof, for they were bright enough that night outside Islamabad to faint right out of the sky.

'Go to sleep,' I replied.

'Sleep?' she repeated. 'I can do that any old time,' and she elbowed me under the rugs as the camel rolled onward.

In an effort to canalize my thoughts to less earthly things, I watched the constellations stepping over the wayside trees.

Sirius, I saw flashing her scarlet and gold, and the Great Bear, who was really the beautiful nymph Callisto, said my father once: she who, having aroused the jealousy of Hera, the wife of the god Zeus, was changed into an animal in revenge.

Each had their own story, and my father seemed to know them all; from the Swan and the winged horse, Pegasus, flying in an eternal race, to Perseus carrying the slain head of Medusa and Andromeda struggling in her chains. How small and insignificant we are, I thought, half dreaming; as I am here – lying with an Afghan princess, journeying on the back of a stupid, protesting camel in a mad world of war and foreign tongues . . . while watching the lights of other

131

worlds step by within constellations long vanished before my world was born.

What Great Hand, I wondered, had fashioned these galaxies within the eternity of a Grand Design?

'You,' exclaimed Durrani, 'are a dozy old Welshman, sleeping when I want to talk.'

There was nothing else for it. Sighing drowsily, I sat up on my couch.

'Tell me of Mari. Was she beautiful?' asked Durrani.

I said, 'Rooms light up when she enters.'

'More beautiful than me?'

'Mari wouldn't have asked that.'

The admonishment silenced her. The camel, shrieking his disgust at his double burden, swayed on; the stars swung over the sky.

'Was she fair?'

I feigned sleep again, and was elbowed. She repeated, 'Fair, like most of your women?'

'No, dark; her hair is black, like yours. But her eyes are blue; yours are brown.'

'Which colour do you prefer?'

'I have never given a thought to it.'

'Did you love her?'

'Of course.'

'But you may never see her again.'

'Perhaps not, but I will always love her.'

'Like the perfume that lives in dead flowers?'

I nodded. 'Something like that.'

'You had no children?'

'Oh yes – surely I told you.'

'You did not, you tell me so little. Sometimes I think I know nothing at all about you.'

'We had a boy.'

'Tell his name.'

'Jonathan.'

She turned her face to the moon and a pattern of clouds crossed her features, as water darkens when the wind makes ripples. She said, 'What a ridiculous name! Why not Afzalorapa or Poonkataara – something easy to say.'

132

'Because he is not an Afghan.'

'He lives still?'

'I hope so, for I have made him a promise in my heart –
that every winter after I return, I am going to dress him in a
sailor-suit and take him to see the swallows fly away, as my
father did with me.'

'But you are not even sure that he is alive?'

'How can I be? I left him soon after he was born.'

'Then it is ridiculous to make such a promise, even to
yourself. A sailor-suit, indeed! He would look ridiculous.'

The camel, shrieking out of habit, broke wind merrily
beneath us. Usually when this happened we turned the
obscenity into humour, because Durrani was refined. But
now the bloody thing became a strident wind-bag that could
not be ignored.

'He has a bad stomach,' said Durrani, but I did not reply,
for I suddenly saw my small son in the arms of my sister,
Morfydd . . . when I first laid eyes upon him in the disused
ironworks of the Nantyglo, where he had been born. And
Mari's eyes, I remembered, were large and glittering in the
dim light as I kissed her, and the taste was salt upon my
mouth, being the sweat of her labour.

Durrani asked, 'Your wife, she will wait for you, you
think?'

'Who knows? It has already been two years. She may
think I'm dead. Look, I already told you all this!'

'I would wait for you until the end of the world.'

'You are only a girl. How can you say such things?'

'Because I have pain for you in here,' she said quietly.

I did not reply to this, and she added, 'I know you think I
am a stupid child, but I tell you, I am in pain for you,' and
she held herself.

'Oh God, don't start that again!'

'Is it so terrible that I should want you?'

'It is only terrible that nothing can come of it. Go to sleep,
for God's sake.'

This sat her up. 'And do not keep saying that! All the time
you call upon God with anger in your voice – taking Allah's
name in vain. He hears, and will punish you.'

'All right, all right, I am sorry.'

133

'And always you are so sorry. Perhaps I will get down off this old camel and walk, then you will be sitting up here by yourself – how would you like that?'

It was the argument of a child. I said, 'Sleep, Durrani, please . . .?'

'There you go again!'

I turned over, seeking release from her. In the darkness I thought I heard her sobbing.

The old camel plodded on, night and day; ever onward south-east: with Peshawar and Rawalpindi far behind us now and the River Indus to the west, we journeyed down the road to Gujranwala where the stars were the brightest I have ever seen: we went with our guards galloping up and down the lines of the caravan, and the moon changed from a Turkish slipper to big-bellied and full, as the golden roofs of Lahore made shape on a far horizon.

Other camel trains passed us coming up from Delhi and Bombay: laden to the girths with rice from Ahmadabad, cotton from the factories of Jodhpur, jute from the fields of Gwalior and indigo from Patiala: a trade reviving, said the camel-masters, now the Afghan war was over and the enemy had been kicked over the Khyber Pass . . . but they know better now, because the British were coming again; new slaughters were about to begin.

On the twenty-first day of travel, the road widened and the town of Amritsar made shape, green and gold in sunfire, and the caravan train of Toko Oolie (other travellers having joined it on the way) now stretched for as far as I could see across an endless plain.

Then, to my astonishment, I saw approaching along the road from Ludhiana, a small convoy of armed horsemen. At their head, in the green uniform of an official Barakzai messenger and as elegant as a young prince, rode Karendeesh. Reining in his big horse he dismounted, calling our names: and we seized his hands and danced him in a circle of joy, to the embarrassment of Toko Oolie and his staring merchants.

'Now,' cried Durrani, 'I am going to show you the pleasures of Ludhiana!' and, throwing her arms about my neck, kissed me. The objective of getting her safely back

134

into the arms of her relatives having been achieved . . . (and *virgo intacta* also, upon which I quietly congratulated myself) . . . the greater difficulty now, it appeared, was to maintain a semblance of decorum before the eyes of strangers. But the outlook, as Durrani kissed me again, this time on the mouth, was still unsettled, to say the least of it.

Meanwhile, Karendeesh, with all the dignity of a visiting potentate, put his hands together as if in prayer and bowed low to me on the road.

'The King awaits us, Sahib,' said he.

22

The India period of my life, given the complication of Durrani's presence, became an interlude best expressed in diary form in order to give it shape: for in the listless, soporific laze spent in Ludhiana, time and events dropped into the unrecognizable; merged into the bumbledore hum of summer in the Punjab; a wing- blue, dragonfly somnolence that diminished all effort. No wonder the white-duck civil servants with their sweating faces and baggy trousers took to the bottle, and thirst wasn't the only thing rising in Ludhiana with people like Durrani around.

My attitude towards her alternated between anger and joy: one moment a palpitation of pleasure; next a slough of despondency when I was wishing her to the devil.

Talk had it that the Dost, in whose service I was now bound, had plans to marry her off to a tribal chief in Persia, thus annealing the bonds of two rich families. For such a future was Durrani born, said the gossiping servants; granddaughters of the royal House of Barakzai being expected to do what they were told. The only trouble here appeared to be that nobody, to date, had informed Durrani.

I knew her, they didn't. Hell and high water would come loose at the first unacceptable suggestion.

The Dost, for all his kingly wisdom, appeared unaware that, far from nurturing a pliant granddaughter in his bosom, he had collected an asp. But I must not be unfair. In those early days in Ludhiana, while sweating out my diary entries in what was a sylvan paradise, Durrani treated me with the

136

care and consideration of a lover instead of what I was – a bum-faced, stinking Feringhee . . . a description applied to Britishers who had desecrated their country.

In the interim, while I was safely at Ludhiana, poor Lady Sale and the other hostages (who I believed, wrongly, to include Caleb) were being moved around the country from one destination to another to avoid their rescue.

In her diary published later, her ladyship wrote:

> We marched, leaving behind all servants who could not walk. It would be impossible for me to describe the feelings with which we pursued our way through the dreadful scenes awaiting us, the road being covered with dreadfully mangled bodies, all naked. Fifty-eight Europeans we counted in the Tunghee Nullah alone, and innumerable bodies of natives; also scores of camp followers still alive, frost-bitten and starving, some perfectly out of their senses and idiotic.

She ended her record of events with an entry which epitomized the total disaster of the 'Promenade' in Afghanistan:

13th February, 1842
From Sourkab the remnant of the column moved towards Gandamak. The force now consisted only of some twenty officers, fifty men of the 44th and about 300 camp followers. Major Griffiths, the senior officer and a Mr Blewett, who spoke Persian, called for a truce, but the Afghans snatched away their weapons and our small force was surrounded on a little hill, where the enemy reduced it further with musket fire. Then the Afghans bore down upon our soldiers, and knife in hand, slaughtered everybody except Captain Souter and seven or eight men.

Thus, out of an original army of nearly 17,000 which had left Kabul not a fortnight before, there was officially left alive (apart from the few hostages) only one man to carry the news of the slaughter to General Sale at Jalalabad.

It was inevitable that an Army of Retribution, as it was now called, would be unleashed to avenge this defeat, or India, sensing British weakness, would surely rise against us. (Hence the Indian Mutiny.)

Meanwhile, the Afghan people were about to suffer unimaginable consequences.

'It is impossible,' announced Wellington (the Iron Duke, writing to the Governor General of India), 'to impress upon you too strongly the notion of the importance of restoring our reputation in the East.' He then described the loss of Afghanistan as the result of the 'grossest treachery and imbecility . . .'

In this he was probably right. But the people in the immediate firing-line were now the brave Afghans, who had done nothing but defend their country against colonial aggression.

The new army under General Pollock attacked them again through the bloodstained Khyber, while General Notts with eight thousand camels carrying his war stores, marched on Kabul from the south.

The blood-letting was about to begin again, leaving me, after the loss of Rhys, with but one consolation: we had helped to save at least one small princess from what was again to become a holocaust.

During the next six months while I lazed in the beautiful Punjab (Ludhiana was the cool, upland country used by India's privileged classes), the war rumbled on. But I found no peace in my Elysian serenity, for my nights were filled with bearded ruffians and descending scimitars: my days wandering haphazardly in the King's gardens were fraught with my loss of Big Rhys; grief swept over me in waves of increasing intensity.

'You have a consolation,' Durrani had said. 'His death was instant.'

'He didn't even have a decent burial!'

But hers was a woman's practicality. 'Had you delayed for another moment, it would have been death for the three of us.'

Meanwhile, no soldier in any army could have enjoyed a better posting than this one: I was living in an Arcadia beyond belief: an enchantment of balmy days and torrid nights in which a human, if not bound by conventional worries, could luxuriate in mind and body.

My quarters, removed from the enormous Rest House which was the King's up-country mansion, was a little log hut, previously the habitation of the head gardener, sparsely but comfortably furnished.

Set by an ornamental lake, it possessed its own small garden where an industrious man could grow everything required of a family; even owning a tiny jetty where a communal fishing-boat was moored for his use.

About a hundred yards offshore flourished a verdant islet of luxuriant trees and ferns, the home of a plethora of water-birds. Often, if the day had been hot, I would swim out to it in the cool of darkness, not deigning to use the row-boat, and there laze in total isolation, dreaming of home.

It was an oasis of peace into which I could step at my own choosing; communing with Nature's tranquillity.

Sometimes, too, I would catch great home-bred trout there and toast them on a fire spiced with delicious onions left over in the gardener's plot: it was also a haven where I was usually free of a tempting Durrani.

This, at least, is what I had fondly hoped . . .

Here beneath the willows strutted pheasants: coloured birds winged the placid waters. My days were filled with birdsong from tree warblers, with nightingale music to soothe my longings for Mari.

After dark, came the drowsy singing of the cicadas, where great bouquets of marigolds and convolvulus showered their petals at the moon; and surely, no moon is larger than the one that hangs above Ludhiana.

But more, apart from occasional visits from Durrani (whose home was a wing of the King's residence not a quarter of a mile distant) I had the company of a huge cock pheasant, a friend of an earlier inmate: an aggressive bird feathered in white and black who strutted on crimson legs and chuckled his appreciation of the wheat germ I fed him: and who, when his rations ran out, adopted a pugilistic pose of a screeching yellow beak and ruffled feathers.

Such birds are kept by the Afghans for fighting; as indeed, are certain breeds of camels; dozens of which, hobbled to prevent escape, grazed in every area of the royal gardens: ill-tempered, diseased creatures whose main interest in life appeared to be sex and squabbling, and in that order.

The whole of their working day appeared hinged to one ambition – to cover the nearest neighbour.

Even a passing, doleful donkey, bent on his own privacy (camels, as is generally known, spend their waking hours in composing obscene rhymes) would fall victim to romantic attentions. Their presence was a reminder of a bawdy ditty which poor old Owen Howells used to sing when in his cups:

> The sexual urge of the camel
> Is greater than anyone thinks.
> And in a passionate moment
> One tried to roger the Sphinx.
> But the Sphinx's sexual favour
> Is blocked by the sands of
>   the Nile
> Which accounts for the hump of
>   the camel
> And the Sphinx's inscrutable smile.

I was feeding Albert, my cock pheasant, when Durrani came wandering along the edge of the lake: I saw her coming against moonlit water and flowering frangipani, and beyond her the dome of a mosque that called the faithful of Ludhiana to prayer: a muezzin tower nearby was glowing like a burning roof of Tamburlaine.

I saw her clearly, for she was dressed in white; a gown she used when wearing nothing underneath: sorely she tried me, and knew it . . . my only protection these days being her lady-in-waiting; a new rule born of her grandfather's insistence, thank God: clearly he was wise in the ways of Welshmen and granddaughters.

Sitting in the boat when she arrived, I was writing home: the white gown, I thought, suited her rich darkness; her hair, usually a plaited braid, was blowing free in the wind.

She bent above me with her usual flirtatious smile.

'You are writing to your wife?'

I nodded.

She contemplated me as one does a wayward child. 'And how many letters have you sent her since you arrived here?'

'Probably half a dozen.'

'And still you receive no replies.'

'Nor do I expect any – I have told you this before. A letter to Britain from Karachi takes an eternity.'

'There's something wrong in your beloved Wales. If I were Mari, you'd hear all right!'

She spoke the precise English of the upper class, and her words annoyed me; I longed for Mari's sing-song, ungrammatical Welsh. Therefore, at any opportunity, I indulged myself in a small sharpness: yet always Durrani maintained her smile, forgiving my vexatious moods. My coolness to her was necessary; she was now sexually available and her ambitions were frightening.

Having managed to keep my head during the slaughters of Kabul, I didn't intend to lose it through the antics of a moony adolescent.

Durrani was now speaking earnestly to me, but I obliterated my replies with memories of Mari.

It was late July and the royal gardens were in full bloom, with hanging clusters of white and pink blossoms shining brilliantly in the afternoon heat.

At lonely places, with their chins sunk on their chests, the worked-out gardeners of another era, now pensioned off by royal decree, dozed in odd corners and wrinkled their noses to pestilential flies. Bees hummed harmonic interjections into the fruitful music of summer in the Punjab: and behind the white-shuttered windows of the Rest House white-coated British administrators worked clinically in sweating subservience.

This, beautiful Ludhiana, the upland escape from heat where, a century ago, a white man came and built a summer cottage and a thousand grateful exploiters followed; to pore over Hindi text books, listen to lectures from impious God-botherers, and bow before portraits of an already gross Victoria.

And so Ludhiana was a hybrid of clumsy Anglo-Indian manners where East met West in hypocritical union; a place of bloated political dilettantes, and a bubbling pot of Indian mutiny.

Now the day became one of sweltering heat as the molten ball of the sun rose to its midday zenith, and we walked, Durrani and I, amid flowering fruit trees where long-plumaged birds stalked by with stately precision, and dignified hollyhocks, long planted by early British settlers, caressed little pools of roach and golden carp: the air moved with sultry diffidence, perfumed with the scent of musk.

Sometimes, in the shade of a mango grove down by the river, we would spread out rugs on the lush grass: Durrani would clap her hands, and, like a genie out of a bottle, a white-gowned servant would appear, spread out a tablecloth and bring salads of tomato, garlic and spiced pepper, with delicious shredded lamb and a ratatouille of aubergines. Sufficed, we would wash this down – she with iced goat's milk, I with the King's wine, which was brittle to the palate: now, as we wandered in the cool of dusk, a servant with a silver platter of wild apricots would follow at a respectful distance.

For a convict on a stretch for treason against the State, I was doing passably well.

'As I say,' said Durrani, returning to her favourite subject, 'you British amaze me. If your wife really wanted to know where you were, could she not make enquiries – even assuming that she doesn't get your letters?'

'I am a convict, remember,' I replied. 'The authorities aren't remotely interested in my whereabouts. Also the new Penny Post is terrible.'

'It is not the post, and you know it. Please do not be perverse. This is the King's address; the authorities would

142

not dare to treat it insignificantly. I myself have written to my old school in England, and have received replies.'

'The Penny Post is not reliable, I tell you.'

'It is excellent, and you know it!' She got up and stamped about, her expression furious. 'It is clear that they do not want you. I hate to see you wasting yourself on people who do not care. Are they ashamed of having a convict in the family, perhaps? This sister of yours – might it be so with her?'

I rubbed my chin and grinned at the thought. 'Morfydd? She would be delighted!'

She flounced away now. 'I do not know why I even bother to discuss it with you, you must have a very strange family.'

'You can say that again!'

'If you became a convict in an Afghan family, you would be garrotted.'

'Very probably.'

'You fought against your own country – for this you could be put to death?'

'I fought *for* my country, not against it, Durrani,' I answered quietly, and it brought her tearfully to her knees on the grass beside me.

'Oh please, Iestyn! Forgive me, do not let us quarrel.'

She was getting close again; I got up, wandering away.

One moment I was wishing her to the devil and back; next I was waiting for her by the lake, worried because she had not arrived.

Schoolboys, not grown men, get themselves into such a predicament.

23

Dost Mohammed Khan, 'The Great Amir' as his people called him, was the first of his dynasty to rule Afghanistan from Kabul. But, when Zeman Shah (deposed and blinded in 1801) ruled there, he was given by fawning courtiers the title of 'The Pearl of the Age' (it was said that so loaded was he with jewels that he could not rise from a chair without assistance).

This title the Dost had now given to his beloved granddaughter, the Princess Durrani.

Within a few years the Dost had been replaced by the Shah Shuja, Britain's puppet. Therefore it was unreasonable of me to expect mercy from such a man, even though I might have saved Durrani from a fate worse than death.

It was significant and worrying that although he had passed me several times in his gardens, the exiled king had never given me a glance.

Of distinguished appearance, he had made war in his youth, and his eldest son, Akbar Khan, was living proof of a warrior dynasty.

The Dost's hatred of Hindus was apparent in his opinion of the Sikhs, to whom he referred as a 'diabolical tribe'. Now given to the conservatism of advancing years, he once risked an horrific death by appropriating a jewelled waistband from the wife of a royal prince, and in other diverse ways, 'treated her much rudely'.

Clearly, therefore, he'd been quite a boy in his time. Luckily for me he considered his granddaughter to be a

144

treasure above rubies, a view I shared in terms of self-preservation.

Now, called before the official Court, I awaited instructions.

'Sit,' commanded the King's Vizier.

I sat cross-legged on the cold mosaic floor of the Ludhiana Rest House and faced a dozen red-carpeted steps that led to a gilded chair.

It wasn't Dost Mohammed Khan sitting before me, however, but the highest paid official of the Royal Court.

'You understand Persian?' he asked me.

'A little, Sirdar,' I answered, 'but Pashto better,' and made to rise, but his guards either side of his chair – giants in chainmail, gripping ferocious halberds – moved threateningly, so I subsided, sweating freely.

The Vizier said, 'I greet you in the name of Dost Mohammed Khan; may you live in amity, he says, for delivering his granddaughter from the hands of barbarians and sorcerers.'

So far so good, and I relaxed. We sat unspeaking, but his eyes were fixed upon me with unsettling intensity.

He wore a gown of green silk cloaked with red brocade, and his curved visage (denoting his Aryan ancestry) gave him the appearance of a turbaned hawk.

He asked, 'How then, says my King, can I reward this conjurer? With diamonds at a time when our lives are a nightmare of adversity? With honours, when even princelings cannot enjoy the gifts of victory . . . or the company of women with eyes of black amber and breasts of gold? – with whom, young man, you could drink and love hilariously.' Pausing, he lifted a silken tassle stuffed with aromatic herbs, sniffed deeply, and added, 'Indeed, I begin to wonder at the health of a young man who disdains dreams of such fair women. Or is it only Unbelievers who cherish thoughts of home when beautiful women abound? Do you not long for the soft, round arms of the maidens?'

'No, my only wish is to return to my own people.'

His old eyes momentarily shone. 'But is that possible? As a convict you would be immediately re-arrested.'

'It is the chance I take, Sirdar.'

'And if the King were to offer you further service here, would you not accept?'

I replied, since it could have been a trap, 'If the King wills it, all is possible.'

'Then that is settled. You have heard talk of the young Captain Benson, no doubt?'

I shook my head.

'That being so, he is of small consequence, though if you wish to know his story, the Princess Durrani will doubtless appraise you. *Listen*,' and he rose and wandered about me, saying, 'but to change the subject . . . beyond the mountains of the Hindu Kush are the lands of the Amir of Bokhara . . . you have heard of him?'

I nodded.

'His prisons are many, his slave markets filled, but that is of no concern to us. However, he has recently obtained the service of a man who makes the best iron in the eastern hemisphere – a European for whom you once worked . . .?'

I interjected, 'A man named Caleb Benedict?'

'The same. Listen again. Soon the war will be over and the accursed British will return whence they came. Let India consume them, since they are now reviled. But let us, too, take heed of what small benefits they have brought; one is the making of iron of excellent quality. You were engaged on this work in Kabul, were you not?'

'Yes, Sirdar.'

He weighed his words with care. 'As I say, Benedict, once in the employ of Bokhara, has now returned there, and our King wants his skills. Such is the quality of his iron that even our heaviest artillery makes little impression upon it.

'But there is more, much more, and of even greater importance. Our spies tell us that he is working on the design of a gun that can fire a shot of even greater weight than the big *Zabber Jang* which you British captured at Ghazni: were such a design to stay in the hands of our enemy, the Amir of Bokhara, it could succeed in forcing even the Bala Hissar to capitulate, and spell the end of our dynasty in Kabul. Soon the Dost will return to his throne as the rightful King of Afghanistan, and it will be necessary so to fortify the walls of his fort that no new barbarian will ever

146

again set foot within it.'

I interjected, 'Sirdar, you astonish me that Caleb Benedict is living in Bokhara . . .'

'But he is. Go there and bring him back to the service of our King, in friendship.'

'No one man can achieve this,' I answered. 'It would need an army.'

To this he smiled wryly, and said, 'Go, for the King has faith in your powers of persuasion, but not until we march on Kabul; meanwhile, prepare yourself for the task. If you succeed, you will know great reward.'

It was a ruse, of course; an excuse to remove me from Ludhiana, but for what reason I could not think. I said, 'Not only Caleb Benedict can make good iron, Sirdar. I also know the colour of the flame for perfect iron.'

'The King demands the services of Benedict.'

'And if I refuse, for it is almost certain death?' and he smiled, his eyes dilating in his aged face.

'I suggest you agree, Feringhee. Better a live cat than a dead tiger.'

With which he waved me away.

When one is so dismissed in Afghan circles, it is safer not to hang about.

It was cooler in the garden.

'You have been received by the King?' Durrani asked me.

I shook my head. 'By the Vizier. Your grandfather was not there.'

'But he is in the Rest House – I have just left him. He tells me that you are to be sent away.'

'Yes, to Bokhara, to find a man and take him to Kabul.'

'If you go to Bokhara you will never return. Oh, Iestyn!'

'You know about this?'

'Yes, but why, after such loyal service?'

The moon flooded light: the lady-in-waiting hovered close, intent upon our words. I took Durrani's arm and moved her away, saying softly, 'The Vizier spoke of a Captain Benson. What do you know of him?'

'Who?' Her face was beautiful in that dim light.

'A Captain Benson . . .'

147

'Ah, you are talking of *The Great Love*!'

'I do not know of this – what of it?'

Durrani looked at the moon; shadows were fashioning blackness beneath her eyes and the night seemed suddenly brought to silence; not even the corncrakes of the river spoke . . . the lady-in-waiting moved nearer.

Durrani said, 'It is the talk of all lovers discussing Afghan lore. There was a British officer named Benson who fell in love with an Afghan princess in Kandahar; but her father, the King elect who loved them both, feared a mixing of the blood . . . ' She suddenly hesitated, staring up at me. 'The Vizier talked of this, you say?'

'And said that you would explain it . . .'

'The two lovers eloped, the Englishman and the Afghan princess, and the King searched to find them, but could not. But another tribe, the Hazaras, a fierce people of Turkish stock who were descended from the Golden Horde, found the lovers asleep.

'The young officer they tied to a stake and tortured, forcing the princess to witness his pain until he died. Then the elder of the tribe arrived and heard the tribe leaders quarrelling about who should possess the princess, for she was of great beauty. To settle the affair, he cut off her head, saying that none should own her.'

'And that was the end of them?'

'Not quite. The lovers were buried yards from one another. But when the King came to claim the body of his daughter, she was found in the arms of her lover; not even death could keep them apart. And today, from their grave, have grown two trees of beautiful perfume, one perfume blending most beautifully with the other, so that the air is scented for passing lovers.'

'A likely tale,' I said. 'Probably invented for our benefit?' for I was trying to distract her from this romantic mood.

'It is true, I tell you; it is written in the stars.'

'It is also written that your grandfather won't rest until you and I are separated, that's clear.'

'He has already told me this,' said Durrani. 'This is why you are to stay here while I am being sent to Persia. There I will die without you.'

'Unless I'm much mistaken, you'll manage.'

'Why are you so cruel?'

'I am not, only practical.'

Durrani raised her face and her eyes were large and shining with tears above her yashmak. 'You saved me from Prince Timur only so I could be sent to Persia, for another marriage of convenience. Out of the frying-pan into the fire, as your English schoolgirls say.'

'A liaison with Persia?'

She nodded. 'Beyond the Hindu Kush the Russians watch and wait, says Grandfather, and once the British are gone, they will move upon India, which is the prize. Turkey, he says, will first fall to The Bear, then Persia, and then Afghanistan, and that will be the end of the civilized Eastern world.'

'You have learned considerably of politics.'

'When one is a pawn in the game.' She turned away.

'So now you are to marry a Persian prince?'

'He is forty-eight years old, heir to the Persian throne; his name is Ayab.'

'You are to be his first wife?'

'His third, and he has many concubines in Baghdad.' She took my hand and raised it to her lips. 'Please take me with you to Bokhara?'

'It is not possible.'

'When do you leave?'

'I do not know. Probably after the King returns to his throne in Kabul.'

'Kiss me, Iestyn . . .'

'Do not be ridiculous, we are being watched.'

'I do not care. Take me to your room and make love to me.' She began to untie her girdle.

'Durrani, it is not possible!'

'Iestyn. I beg you! Do not let them take me. If I have your child, Persia will not want me.'

'If you had my child, they would kill the pair of us.'

She wept, her hands over her face; I held her, and the attendant watched.

Durrani said, sobbing, 'Had I been a bazaar girl, we could have known each other in loving. Why must it be so different

149

because I am a princess?'

'Because you belong to Afghanistan, I to the other side of the world. Now come, pull yourself together.'

'That,' she said, 'is what the English teachers said every time I wept.'

'Your Highness,' called the lady-in-waiting. 'It is getting late. Come?'

Durrani bowed her head.

I stood watching as she disappeared into the darkness where the lake was rippling silver under a crescent moon.

24

I could not sleep, but lay awake within a doleful, shuddering drowse on the edge of oblivion. It was as if, by some eerie phantasm, Mari had returned and was within my room. Indeed, she appeared to be performing a macabre dance of death: in black she was, without identity; the drapes of her skeletal form swaying in and out of my consciousness. And every time I endeavoured to snatch at her and bring her to reality, she swayed out of my reach; a juxtaposition of dismembered limbs that filtered from darkness into light with terrifying clarity.

It was a delirium from which I awoke in a sweating fever. I sat up in bed and stared at the moon-stained window.

After a little while, cooled in mind, but still sweating like a Spanish bull, I opened the hut door. Moonlight blazed; the world was like daylight under the star-fire and a grinning, whorish moon; grinning at me, perhaps, a solitary soul in a foreign place . . . when I should have been at home in the arms of Mari.

Naked, I wandered down to the edge of the lake, listening to the chattering of night-birds and the croaking of a corncrake from the marshes.

The cool, wet arms of water enveloped me, cleansing my nightmare dream.

Automatically, I struck out, swimming with lazy strokes towards the greenness of the distant islet; and did not notice on the silvered water behind me, that the little lake-boat had gone from its moorings.

151

*

Now my feet touched bottom: I waded up the shingled slope to lakeside ferns, and there flung myself down, watching waterlights playing on my naked body; it was an unusual phosphorescence, for this was tainted water; an inland pool of unfathomed depth (the local fishermen said) which reached down into salt caverns formed before the world was ice: but it was cleansing, and I slept, but not to dream; in utter purity I floated in suspended quietude. Mari, the chains of captivity, the threat of Bokhara were banished; even my fears for Durrani did not invade this perfect tranquillity . . . until reality came storming back, transfigured by the fading moon.

A solitary figure was standing before me; in shape so unclearly defined, that at first I thought it a gibbertykok, an Afghan troll, until it came so close that I could have touched it: then the figure spoke.

'You are awake, Sahib?'

Karendeesh.

'I called to you,' said he, 'but you did not answer.'

'What are you doing here?' I struggled up, trying to cover my nakedness.

'I do not come alone, Sahib; it is the Princess; she desires to talk with you.'

'For God's sake, man! Why didn't you bring her to the hut?'

'I did, and she saw you swimming here. "Do not bother yourself, Small One," she said, for by this name she sometimes calls me. "Take me to the island in the boat."

' "But – the Sahib is without his trousers, Your Highness",' I replied.

' "What are trousers between friends?" she replied, "take me," and she got into the boat.' He emptied white-palmed hands at me. 'What could I do? I am her servant.'

'Where is she now?' I got to my feet.

'Behind you,' said Durrani.

'I will go,' interjected Karendeesh, 'until I am called for service,' and bowed low, enjoying every moment, the sod.

'Come back!' I cried.

'Goodbye,' said Durrani.

There are times in literature when floors swallow people; this time they stayed solid. I sat down again with attempts at decorum, but she was having none of it, and sat cross-legged on the ground before me, saying; 'Small One considers that you are not only attractive with your clothes on, but that you are quite beautiful with your clothes off, and I agree with him.'

'Really? Tell him I'll give him something to get on with when I lay hands on him. What the hell are you doing here?'

'I am visiting my lover before they make me an old man's darling.'

'I am not your lover.'

'Not yet, but it is an imperfect world, Iestyn. "What would you do?" I asked Karendeesh, when we saw you swimming here.

' "I would go back to bed, Your Highness," he replied.

' "But if they were sending you to Persia in the morning, what then?"

' "I would go over to the island to say goodbye," said he. "For does not the old Afghan proverb say, 'He who departs a friend without a last farewell is no more than a comrade?' " '

'It sounds fine,' I replied. 'But if your grandfather knows of this, you'll lose your prince and I my head.'

'Would you not be prepared to die for love?'

'I do not love you, Durrani. How many times must I tell you?'

'But I love you. So will you not get up and walk with me?'

At which I hesitated, which is the way of men who are without their trousers; for while the body of a woman is a poetry of loveliness in youth, that of a man, at any age, is but a temptation to short-sighted ducks; nor did my modesty approve, being part of my strict Methodist upbringing. John Wesley, who frowns every time a Welshman sinks a pint, would have been outraged. Though Mari, I remembered, thought clothes of very small importance . . . from the time I first saw her bathing in the Usk down at Llanellen. So many

153

years . . . a lifetime ago. . . .

'You are lost to me,' said Durrani sulkily.

I smiled at her. The tipsy moon, always on the grin when lovers are activating, pulled up her petticoats in harlot anticipation.

'You are back with me again?' asked Durrani.

I said, pressing her hand to my lips, 'No good will come of this, Durrani. You are a princess. I am a commoner.'

'So I will do my best to change that, shall I?' and, drawing her gown over her head, she dropped it at my feet. 'Now,' she added, 'you are a man and I am a woman: I am only Durrani, and you are pompous old Iestyn who cannot be seen with his trousers off – but a man, nevertheless, by the look of it from here. *Whee-oh!* And a Frank as well, are you not? Even a hated Feringhee, but a girl can't have everything,' and she took my hand and led me down to the water's edge. There, on tiptoe, she folded her arms about me and reached up for my lips, and there was not an ounce of shame between the three of us.

'Really,' said she, 'this is the most delightful situation and we should do it more often.'

Meanwhile, being the only one with a gram of sense, I was trying my best not to do it now.

Durrani had other ideas.

There was a secret place of rushes and moonbeams where shadows hid prospective lovers, and to this place some unknown sense guided us. There we sat, Durrani and I, contemplating one another, as lovers do before the tumult of intimacy.

Yet, though there was no real reluctance in me, there remained the old nagging conscience because of her tender years, though in knowledge of the subject she clearly could have passed for my grandma: meanwhile, I was also concerned about her grandfather, and his fury should I bring her to child. Nor did the harlot moon assist me, for now it was painting Durrani's face from a girl's into a mature and beautiful woman's.

So I clenched my eyes and lay within her breathing, and held her, and did not move.

154

'Iestyn, please?'

Anthony had the same palaver with Cleopatra, as history relates.

'Durrani, I cannot!'

'Unless I'm mistaken, you certainly can. What's wrong?'

'We must not!'

'Then shall I assist you, my pious Welshman?'

'You'll regret this!'

'Dear me, are there any more at home like you?'

'Think of the consequences!'

'I have, and I'm not going to that rotten old prince in Persia without you have me first. Don't I please you?'

It was the last straw.

Her love-making was much like Mari's, being filled with abandon, wild whispers and senseless exclamations: indeed, it could have been Mari lying beneath me, stuttering words in a foreign tongue that I had not heard before . . . she of the long-spread lashes lying upon her cheeks, she of the glistening mouth . . . but Mari's body was white, her small breasts pink-tipped, until Jonathan suckled them, while Durrani's were mounds of brown alabaster under the moon.

Now lost in time, I entered her again and again, and within her richness knew a physic of pleasure I had never known before; it was not an assault upon her, but a sharing, a celebration of unity. And she, suddenly tuned to unexpected quiet, lay within a sloe-eyed placidity which could have been indifference while I enjoyed her . . . as if, her plan having been laid and successful, she could now know resignation. But for me it was a resurrection of all I had known with Mari; as if some elphin genie of invention had returned her to me.

Yet her beauty was not that of my wife's. And the eyes that opened to me were not cornflower blue, as were Mari's, but black amber moving in dusky cheeks: and the lips, though full and red like my girl's, were but twin crescent shadows born of darkness. And Durrani's smile as she lifted her face to mine, as radiant as the sun, was foreign to me; though her body, like Mari's, was alive with a rhythmic beauty within the disorder of the loving . . . painted by the

155

unreal light into black ivory. It was a time when men forget their sisters and dismantle the edicts of ancestry. . . .

Now the conflict over in a sweet subsiding. . . .

'That is what I wanted – just you and me, Iestyn. . . . ' Durrani sighed and closed her eyes, and slipped easily into a silence that could have been death . . . to awake almost instantly.

'Again, please?'

Just like Mari.

I did not reply, being now filled with a searing contrition that, having at last floundered into possessing her, I had transgressed the rule of manhood. The passion over, I was, by cold reasoning, an adult who had exploited the yearning of youth; taken her virtue. More, I had done this practically within sight of an adoring grandparent who had the power of life and death over us both: even the moon seemed to hide herself dolefully.

Now a little wind moved over the lake, bringing it to silver ripples, and the ancient scent of frangipani touched my nostrils; scenting this too, Durrani opened large, lustrous eyes.

'Now we've done it,' I said.

She giggled like a child. 'I know! Wasn't it absolutely marvellous!'

'In more ways than one,' and I added, 'you realize, I suppose, that you've lost your virginity?'

'Virginity?' She thumbed her chest. 'You must be joking. I lost that ages ago in my first year down in Sussex.'

'*Whisht*!' said someone, and I looked up to find Karandeesh staring down at us over a boulder.

'What is it?' demanded Durrani. It didn't seem to occur to her that he had probably witnessed the entire performance.

He shouted, 'The lights have gone on in the Rest House! Dogs are barking. Soldiers are coming!'

'Run for it!' cried Durrani and, pulling on her gown, went past me like the wind.

As for me, I must have beaten the hundred yards record and, with Karendeesh rowing like a mad thing, we leaped out at the hut mooring and scattered in three directions.

156

Without even drying myself, I was under the blankets as the door of my room went back on its hinges.

'The Princess Durrani?' asked the Vizier, panting, in his night-shirt.

'Not here, Sirdar,' said I, rubbing my eyes and, bowing, he retreated.

Albert, my fighting cock pheasant, saw him off the premises with claws and ferocious screeching, and I never saw the going of him.

25

Now events followed with astonishing rapidity.

Durrani, in a welter of tears and protestations, was hauled aboard the leading howdah elephant and, with an armed guard sent by her suitor for her protection, began the journey to Persia for marriage: nor was I given the opportunity to say goodbye to her; I doubt if she even saw me wave.

Also, Shah Shuja, the puppet king of the British, had been assassinated while inspecting troops in Kabul; it being hinted in Court circles in Ludhiana that the Dost had had a hand in it, which, knowing Afghans, did not surprise anyone.

Then the King gave orders that he wished to see me, and I was ushered by flunkeys into his presence; this, a king who clearly had not forgotten his youth, for he said, 'It appears that you have gained the respect, even the affection of my granddaughter.'

No reply was called for. I stood humbly before him.

His English was perfect, his presence commanding, though he wore but a simple purple gown.

This, the king who was about to return to Kabul by the authority of Britain, which had now no further use for Afghanistan; his people proving unconquerable, as others have since discovered.

His Sadozai Dynasty had stretched back a century to the reign of Painda Khan, who had been put to death by heretical priests in 1801: now the River Indus was again his wash-pot; over Karachi in the south, to the Caspian in the west, he had cast his slipper. Afghanistan, rid of British

158

infidels, could now enjoy comparative tranquillity.

'But,' said the Dost, 'in the eyes of your compatriots, Mortymer, you are still a convict, and I have no authority to ask for clemency on your behalf. You understand me?'

'Perfectly, Sire.'

'So the question remains unanswered – what to do with you now?'

He was possessed of the classical features of an Alexander; the hook nose, the high forehead; a grey beard decorated his narrow chest; a small man, but big in personality, he emptied blue-veined hands towards me. 'What do you wish for yourself?'

'That I continue in your employ, Sire.'

'And not return to your own country?'

'That is not possible, until I receive my ticket-of-leave.'

'Which means completing your sentence?'

I nodded. 'Could I not travel with your Court to Kabul, and there make iron?'

The reply was instant. 'That, I fear, is not possible. Within a few months my granddaughter will be back in Kabul, with her betrothed.'

The inference was obvious, and I sensed his anger for the first time. It was said in Ludhiana that not much missed the Dost.

He said now, 'In one way only can you serve us – my vizier talked to you of this – by finding Caleb Benedict, the great ironmaker, and persuading him to return to my service. It is said that he is in Bokhara.'

'Bokhara?' I asked. 'That could be dangerous for Mr Benedict, for is it not rumoured that the people there are on the edge of revolt against their Amir?' He did not reply to this.

Rejecting his formal stance, he now wandered down the red-carpeted steps towards me. 'The damage your soldiers have caused is considerable. Ghazni and Kalat, my beautiful towns, lie in ruins; Kabul itself has been looted and burned, but luckily the Bala Hissar was spared. Therefore the need for Benedict is not immediate, so I suggest that you remain here with the palace rear party, and seek him out when you get further orders from my headquarters in Kabul.'

'Remain here? For how long?'

'Ah now, Mortymer, that is in the lap of the gods, as you English say! Allah being wise in the ways of men, I will not captivate you with artful words . . . except to say that you can live here in peace and amity as a reward for returning to me my Durrani – a courageous action which cost your friend his life.' He smiled, his white teeth appearing in his bearded face. 'Think of the benefits, Mortymer, for I will leave behind for your pleasure half a dozen slave girls; from what I hear, you are not averse to female company.' He smiled thinly, adding, 'I envy you your youth, Mortymer; such could prove a feast of love for such a beloved exile.

'Kabul is still a city of war, one ravaged by tribal feuds which I will have to put down; but here in Ludhiana lies tranquillity. Many days of fishing could be yours, which is your hobby, I understand; also there would be time for your writing, for are you not a perverse diarist? Without the perfidious temper of my Durrani to set your life by its heels, such munificence could be yours for years to come: indeed, come to think of it, you could spend the next dozen years in such a paradise, until your sentence is fulfilled.'

We stared at one another; it was the oldest trick in the world; he was flattering to deceive . . . before sending me into exile with Durrani miles away from my influence.

'You agree to this, Mortymer?'

I could not do otherwise.

'It would be most suitable, Sire,' I said, and thought, If you think I'm settling for half a lifetime here, old man, you've another think coming; but I would never have then believed that it would be five years before I escaped from Ludhiana.

'Meanwhile, Mortymer, to show our appreciation of your service, a small gift to take with you when you eventually return to Britain? Let it never be said that we Afghans cannot show gratitude, even to Feringhees who hate us and in their spare time pursue our relatives,' and he gave me a little leather string-bag.

Within were fifty small diamonds.

160

*

Calamity, the old Welsh say, often brings with him a companion, and this preventative detention in Ludhiana was no exception.

Karendeesh arrived next with his own particular adversity.

'I am going from here, Sahib,' said he.

Karendeesh had grown both in size and stature: the beggar-boy in rags, now beautifully attired, was as handsome as Lothario.

'You are leaving with the Court for Kabul tomorrow?' I asked him.

'That is so, Sahib. Therefore we must part in friendship.'

'Could it be otherwise, Karendeesh? We owe you much.'

'You are to stay here, I understand?'

'I am, but God knows why.'

'Because of your love for the Princess?'

I raised my eyes to his. He added, 'And her love for you.'

I shrugged, and he said, 'You make a face, eh? Does not Karendeesh tell only that which is true?'

'I have a wife in Wales,' I answered. 'How can I be in love with both?'

We were down by the lake, near my hut; the wind was cool, although the autumn had been one of raging heat, and I pitied Durrani in the enclosing tapestries of her elephant howdah, swaying along dusty roads to Persia.

'That,' said Karendeesh, coming closer to me, 'is what I could not understand. How is it possible to love two women at the same time, one near, and one far away?'

'It is in the nature of men.'

His face went up at this. 'It is not the way of Karendeesh. For years, since first I set eyes on her, I have loved but one – Durrani. Always I have been prepared to give my life for her, yet I have not even touched the hem of her gown. How strange is this grown-up-love – all wet kisses and many vulgar noises?'

This was a new Karendeesh. I said, 'You gave no hint of loving your princess in this way.'

161

'Of course not, for nothing could come of it. Durrani had eyes only for the Feringhee. Yet you are a white body, and she is brown, like me. True, I am a Hindu, but not once has she raised her eyes to me, except in anger.'

'That is not true!'

'Her heart was all for you; nothing was left for me to enjoy. Do you not realize the hurt in this?'

I said, 'She did not know of your love, Karendeesh, and neither did I.'

He said bitterly, and I was astonished to see tears upon his face, 'Now she has gone to a foreign marriage and she is not here for either of us. Soon she will bear an old man's children, and will not know of me.'

'Perhaps that is for the best. Then neither of us can have her.'

He said vehemently, 'Yours is the fault of this, Sahib! All was well between us before you entered her life.'

'I am sorry you feel that is so . . .'

'Sorry is not enough. You did things to her that are against the laws of God; she was pure until you brought to her your nakedness, and you will be punished for making her a woman when she was a girl.'

'It is the rule of Nature, Karendeesh, as well as the law of God. These are things that will always be between men and women.'

'Not the women of whom my father spoke. They are weak, he said, and are to be protected. What would a child of her sweet loins say if it were conceived before marriage to her prince?'

I had no words for him; he appeared to possess them all.

Vaguely, in the deeper recesses of my memory, there came to me words of another, a youth out of the Middle Ages . . . 'She was a lady great and splendid, I was a minstrel in her halls . . .'

'I will go now,' said Karendeesh. 'Later, I will come to you again, for I have further news of importance.'

This was at sun-go-down, as Durrani used to call it: later the boy came when the moon was high, and in his hands he carried a postal packet. Said he, 'This came for your friend

162

Rhys Jenkins many weeks ago – two letters, Sahib, each of which I read, which is the practice of a good *chuprassey*.' That was debatable, but I did not challenge it.

'Read this one first,' said he, and gave me one of the letters.

It was addressed to Big Rhys, and was from his daughter, Dathyl. I opened the envelope, and read:

2 Staffordshire Row,
North Street, Blaenafon,
Monmouthshire.

Dearest Dada,

Today Mam and me got your letter, the first from Afghanistan, and we hope you get this reply from us. It come on Gwynfor's fourth birthday, and we hoped Will Blaenavon would remember it, but not likely. Some do say he is alive and puddling somewhere, but even Uncle Silas don't have proof of it, and he do get around the valleys a lot, being a coach-driver. We three are doing good; I'm down the Coity Pit and Mam's on the washeries, so don't worry about us and money. Tomos Traherne have gone from the valley some say to marry some old girl, but maybe it's just pew talk like, for our new pulpit chap be an English raver, telling only of damnation. Fair set the Ebenezer alight do he. When you asked about Iestyn Mortymer's folk, I say they anna round by here now, since they all went down Carmarthen way, three years back. Remember his Mari's relatives lived down there? Uncle Silas says he'll ask around about them when he drives westward, but one thing's certain sure, tell Iestyn, they anna round these parts now. But I'll get the letter-writer to put it down to you if we gets any more news. All the folks in North Street send good luck and come home soon.

Your loving Wife and your daughter,
Dathyl Jenkins.

The letter was undated.

'Now read this one,' said Karendeesh, and gave me the other letter.

Such was the expression upon his face that I tore at this envelope with shaking hands, and read:

2 Staffordshire Row,
North Street, Blaenafon,
Monmouthshire.

Dearest Dada,

I hope you got my last letter.

Uncle Silas has just come back from Carmarthen, and talked to neighbours of Cae White, outside Llandilo, at the address you gave me. It's an old farmhouse, he says, all dead and deserted with the front door broke down and on the mat he found Iestyn's letters to his Mari, which we packed up inside here so you can give them back to him, but no hide nor hair of the Mortymer family, so he made enquiries at a Black Boar tavern, an old boozer, and a barmaid called Sixpenny Jane do tell him as how Morfydd, the sister, got herself killed down a pit called the Gower after Mam Mortymer spliced old Tomos Traherne and went up north after marrying . . . remember I told of his wedding? Then this Jane tells how Jethro comes sweet on Mari, his sister-in-law, for gossip had it that Iestyn had been killed at the Westgate battle. Some old girl called Effie Downpillow tells how her chap saw Iestyn dying of the redcoats when trying to escape, and yesterday Uncle Silas comes back from Carmarthen with the mail again and says how a farmer called Osian Hughes, gone soft on Morfydd, spoke about Jethro taking Mari and the two lads off to a new life in America, thinking Iestyn dead and gone; tell him from me, I dunna think she'd have done this if he'd been alive, though.

I lowered the letter Big Rhys's daughter had written to him, then tore up the letters I had written to the family at Cae White; letters which Mari had never received. The bitterness was like alum in my mouth: it had taken the family only three years to forget that I had ever existed.

And Dathyl had clearly not received the letter I had written to her telling of her father's death. . . .

After Karendeesh had said his last goodbye, I went down to the lake's edge and looked over the expanse of moonlit water. Albert, my cock pheasant, came clucking up and rubbed his body against my leg, but I did not turn to him.

Everything was lost; my world was barren.

Morfydd had died; Jethro had taken my son Jonathan and Richard, Morfydd's boy, off to God knows where: Mam had married Tomos Traherne, sullying the sweet memory I held for my father.

But worst of all, I had lost Mari.

In this bitterness I did not pause to repent my own adultery.

26

Now years of idleness followed in wearisome procession.

At the age of twenty-three I had progressed from a convict in chains to a privileged guest in the lap of enforced luxury, for now, apart from a few house servants who trod the corridors of the Rest House (presumably awaiting the next banished Royal) I was the sole occupant of Dost Mohammed Khan's abode in exile – Ludhiana palace.

No letter arrived from home: clearly everybody there except Big Rhys's family believed I was six feet down, and I grieved for the loss of Mari and Morfydd.

But it was something beyond the loss of those beloved; I now longed for Wales with an emotion approaching lust; it was as if a part of me had become dismembered; an irretrievable loss that could never be replaced.

And there came to me a longing to put down on paper the honey-sweet memories of a life that had departed; never, it seemed, to return. And so I continued with the task begun years ago in the tent I shared with Big Rhys and Owen Howells.

Sylvan visions of my country returned to haunt my nights; my days now were filled with elegiac hymns: praiseful choirs of exultant melodies which echoed down the streets of my fevered dreams.

Blaenafon in all its sooted glory rose monumentally amid Welsh choirs: Rhyd-y-nos (Dark-as-Curtains Street) blanketed the chapel-haunting dusks, and Broad Street opened its arms to greet my wandering soul. Here, the lych-gate where I had first kissed Mari; there the marble

washstand and its little white mouse engraved at play. Now
the tiny window where Morfydd waited for her lovers, and
the door that led out the back to neighbours in Shepherd's
Square. Lost, irrevocably lost to me, and the metallic ringing
of my iron-tipped boots beat again within my head as I went
with my father along North Street to my first day at work at
Garndyrus, aged eight.

In earnest now, I began to write my autobiography, and
that walk with my father stood clearly in my mind. . . .

But now the moon was bright above the jacaranda trees of
beautiful Ludhiana and, although my body was there, wandering along the jasmine-scented bank of Shalimar Lake, my
mind was shivering in the starlight of a winter's night on the
Blorenge Mountain, when I had my fight with Mo Jenkins.

An icy wind was tearing at my clothes when I awoke to the
cold, wet breast of the mountain.

> Most pleasant it is to be floating in a dream, and
> awake in your father's arms.
> 'Very handy you are with fists, my son,' said he.
> 'But since you will rarely fight with gentlemen, next
> time I'll teach you how to miss their boots.'
> 'Christ,' I said, 'there's a tooth missing,' and felt my
> mouth.
> 'Two,' said my father. 'I have another in my pocket.
> Up on your feet now, do not make a meal of it.'
> I looked at him as he brushed water from his eyes.
> 'Up a dando,' said he, with business, and lifted me in
> his arms. 'All right for you, mind, for you have kept
> warm fighting, but I am freezing solid – look, I am
> streaming from the eyes. And your fight, remember,
> not mine, for Mam plays hell with pugilists.'
> My father did a strange thing then; bending, he
> kissed me.
> A first day at work to remember, aged eight. A
> bleeding nose, a tooth in one hand, another in Dada's
> pocket, and a boot in the belly.
> There's a mess to take home to Mam, and all for
> twopence.

I put down my pencil and walked to the hut window. Memories, I thought, all memories. Yet the same moon shining here in Ludhiana would also smile on Mari's face, and my brother Jethro's . . . as they lay together in the belly of a bed on the other side of the world.

Summers came and went, and still I received no letters, even from Durrani, who, according to reports, was now married to her Persian prince and living in splendour with her grandfather in Kabul: yet the lake, shining in noonday heat, brought aching memories of a love that was fast replacing my love of Mari, who had so completely rejected me.

I dozed and dreamed in renewed thoughts of Durrani; her true loss began when those lonely seasons turned into years. I was in love with two women; the longing for Mari still persisted.

Mari returned to me in the quiet hours before the dawn, when the song of a cicada or the screech of a night owl would revive memories.

I heard again in imagination's ear, the noisy chatter of the customers of the Drum and Monkey on pay nights: the sound of Morfydd shouting from the back, laying the blame on one or another: my father's bass voice in the pews of the Bethany Baptist, the song of the cauldrons of the North Street furnaces when the iron was stirred.

The years passed; new springs were born. More and more, as memories faded in my mind, I turned again to Wales for half-forgotten dreams . . . and wrote:

Very pretty was Poll Morgan, aged thirteen; her lips curved and red as if in hope of a kiss.

'Oh aye!' said Morfydd. 'So who was walking someone round the mountain a week last Sunday?'

'She is not my girl,' I replied, hot.

'Pleased I am to hear it,' she replied, 'for the moment she is I'm cooling her down with a bucket of water – leave her to the likes of that Mo Jenkins. Now get down to the Drum and Monkey for Mam's whisky,' and I went like lightning, for Polly was the barmaid there.

'Good evening,' said she, her elbows on the bar.

'Good evening,' I said back. 'Two penn'orth of whisky for medicine purposes, please,' and I pushed the bottle towards her.

'Dear me,' said she, 'what a pretty boy you are, Iestyn Mortymer, so if you fancy some time in a haystack, just turn up, mun, never mind the hour.'

'I am too young for women,' said I, sweating, but she reached out and caught my fingers and the touch of her was like a burn.

'Good God,' said she, 'you don't know what you're missing. Up on the mountain at eight o'clock next Sunday and grow up two years earlier?'

'I shall not be there, Polly Morgan. According to the deacons you are a harlot.'

'Ay, ay,' said she, 'and I'm making the most of it before I blister,' and she leaned over the bar and kissed my lips, the shadows deep in her breast.

There's forward for a bare thirteen; but now she was on my pillow and it took me six weeks to get her off.

Also, I was there to meet her up on the mountain.

'For somebody not coming, you're pretty well on time,' said she, and laid back on the grass and pulled up her skirt to show her red garters.

It must be marvellous to be a loose woman.

Mind you, I wasn't the only one in a bother with the deacons: old Morfydd got her share as well. I wrote:

Bang bang on our door in Shepherd's Square.

'Good gracious, who's that at this time of night?' asked my mother, and my father opened it.

Very smart was Iolo Milk, the chap keen on Morfydd, with the carnation he wears in his buttonhole especially for lady-killing: all six-foot-two of him he stands there, cap in hand, his white teeth shining.

'Good evening, Mr Mortymer,' says Iolo.

'Good evening,' says Dada. 'Very fancy you look in

that Sunday suit, Iolo. Up with the chest to show it off, mun – in with the stomach by here,' and he tapped it. 'Courting, is it?'

'No violence, remember,' whispers Mam, looking under Dada's arm.

'God forbid, woman, is it Morfydd you are come for, Iolo?'

'Please God. But with your permission, mind.'

'For a little stroll up the mountain, is it?'

'Just a stroll, Mr Mortymer. No harm in a bit of a stroll with a maiden as respectable as your Morfydd, not like some I could mention.'

'Back before dark, is it?' asks Dada.

'Back in half an hour, if you like – the quicker the better when a decent girl is involved, if that do suit you?'

'It do not,' said Dada. 'Head on one side, if you please, for I can scarcely see you in this light. And bend a bit, for you have grown inches since I saw you last. And smile, mun, do not look unhappy.'

And Iolo, the fool, held his chin up, beaming.

One hit and he was out, flat out in the yard, with his hands crossed on his chest, ready for burial.

'*Diawch*!' exclaimed my father, 'and me a deacon,' while the women screamed. 'This house is open to Christians, Chapels and Church of England, but pagans and fornicators stay without.'

And still I wrote:

Winter came and hoar frost painted up the trees of the canal back home; the hills became April-misted, the old sun red and rosy after his winter's sleep.

Out of bed at first light, me, and down the canal to Llanellen, and I tell you this, of all the villages in Wales, God loves that place best!

Across the fields I went like something demented, to crawl on hands and knees to the river's edge. Quiet you! Listen for bailiffs now. Steady. Peep . . .! Nearer, nearer, as quiet as a cobra, and there he is a foot below you, all two pounds of him glittering among the reeds, dreaming of fat bugs and flies; now he spits and rolls an eye at a water-beetle, dozing and swaying with lazy delight . . .

I reckon you never saw a trout like this one. For years now I've been tickling 'em out of the Shalimar Lake, where I made love to Durrani, but this chap took the biscuit.

Narrow the eyes now and reach down into the river. Two Pounds flaps his tail six inches from your fingers: for two million years he's been frozen, no wonder he waddles to meet you . . . Now tickle him, the silly bugger, and watch him grin. There's a daft old fish, old enough to know better: smooth his belly, rub him under the gills; cup your hand and get ready to throw him; the river swirls, the wind sighs, and Two Pounds rolls in the eddies, paralyzed with pleasure . . . Crook your fingers and throw him wide. . . .

Too late he remembers what his old mam told him; down he comes – *Flop*! – a silver crescent of terror flapping on the grass. . . .

Tears fill my eyes as I remember . . . it was the first time I met my Mari. . . .

Suddenly a salmon started to jump downriver, making enough palaver for a man diving: leaving Two Pounds on the bank, I parted branches and peered. Here's a salmon for you – five feet long if it's an inch, and well over a hundred pounds – a hen salmon, by the look of it, standing on its tail in three feet of water, throwing its long white arms about and combing out its long, black hair.

Lovely is a woman naked, bathing in a river. . . .

Nearer, nearer she came, wading towards my hiding place. Now opposite my position on the bank, she stood upright and swept the water from her face.

'Good morning,' I said to her. 'There's strange where you came from . . .'

171

So long ago now that I can scarcely remember my Mari's face. Now I sat at the edge of the Shalimar lake, bowed my head, and the tears were a scald to my eyes.

Mari and Durrani; Durrani and Mari: it was possible, I was discovering, to be in love with two women at the same time: one calling to me out of my adolescence, and the other reaching up dusky arms for me out of the cool waters of the Shalimar. And it seemed, sometimes, as if neither they nor my beloved Blaenafon, not even my childhood, had ever existed.

Meanwhile, during my long exile in Ludhiana the wind was fragrant with the scent of jasmine and the yellow roses of the south.

Then, suddenly and unexpectedly, like a genie out of Dost Mohammed Khan's bottle, Karendeesh arrived, and with him came instructions.

I took the letter he offered.

'You have read this, of course,' I said, cool.

'Naturally. It is necessary, as I have said before, that a good messenger reads all the correspondence,' replied he.

The letter from the King read:

Now fulfil the order which once I gave you. Bring to me the great ironmaker, Caleb Benedict, he who is in Bokhara.

'You have news of the Princess Durrani for me?' I asked Karendeesh.

'I am instructed not to speak of the Princess,' came the curt reply.

The years dividing us had turned him into a man.

Book Two

Bokhara
1848

Thou wilt go to Bokhara?
O fool for thy pains.
Thither thou goest, to be
put into chains.

Mesnevi, quoted by Vambery

27

Having left Ludhiana six weeks ago on Dost Mohammed Khan's orders, I was now deep in the mountains of the Hindu Kush, the old Slave-Killer, following the route taken years earlier by a certain Lieutenant Wyburd: this unfortunate, an early emissary, appears to have been out of luck from the moment he left Whitehall; ending his days by crying to his tormentors as they led him to the scaffold in Bokhara, 'See how a Christian Englishman can die!'

Now I was consoling myself that not only was I Welsh, but my hold on Christianity was tenuous; and vaguely wondered if this might assist me when I reached the Court of the most ferocious ruler in Central Asia.

The fact that Caleb Benedict had been in the Amir's employ for the past five years I found a consolation.

It is said in the East that one can tell the nationality of a man by the way he sits a donkey and I prided myself that the way I was sitting this one called Meg (whom I had bought at the entrance of the Khyber) I could not have been mistaken for anything other than what I purported to be – a travelling packman on his way to Bokhara. For my skin these days had no need of Durrani's artificial dyes, being burned to the dark consistency of an Afghan warrior's; also I was now an expert in Persian and Pashto.

Armed with my identity, I did not fear this intrusion into Turkistan, but was troubled that the Amir might consider my journey unnecessary.

And why did the Dost send *me*?

175

Kabul, from which he ruled, was considerably closer to Bokhara than was Ludhiana . . . could he not have sent a local emissary to invite Caleb Benedict back into his employ?

One overriding consolation sustained me; the promise that, should I succeed in returning to Kabul with the old ironmaker, I would again be near to Durrani. Her unhappiness there, according to rumour, was great, for there had been no child of her marriage; this constituted wifely failure in the eyes of her Persian prince.

Such was my eagerness to get away from exile in Ludhiana, that I gave no thought to the possibility of treachery.

It was evening, with shafts of golden light wounding the endless plains five thousand feet below me, and I saw a purple ribbon winding away into the horizon, and some call this the Golden Road to Samarkand, the way of the ancient caravans.

From this great height, with the donkey slipping and sliding on the mountain track, an almost treeless steppe unfolded before me; a forbidden land with its threat of death to Infidels and Unbelievers, according to the dictates of its successive rulers. These, for generations, had lived from the export of jute, cotton and slave-dealing; the slave-platforms of Bokhara being the human auction houses of the world.

Here pert and beautiful Uzbek girls with their ornamental headdresses of tinker-silver danced in the market-places on jingling feet, waving their long-nailed, expressive hands while *besmachi*, the bandit brain-thudders of the steppes, plied their trade of kidnapping, ransom and arms-selling: jabbering in their high-pitched nasal twangs in the shading charpoys under which was sold everything from a pin to a shroud amid the clucking of hens tied upside down and the squawking of geese having their throats cut. Here teeth were extracted amid wails and protests, and bald elders pored over ancient books of literature while teaching urchin children the art of picking the pockets of unwary travellers.

Here the lowest form of Eastern life, the women, sweated patiently under their donkey-hair *paranjas*, veils that hid them from fornicating eyes. Receptacles of lust to their commanding menfolk, there, but he is guilty of a woeful crime who flickers an eye at a neighbour's wife in villages where a gourd of wine is of greater value than a life.

Under the lurid furnace of an early summer sun the panorama before me stretched out west to the Caspian Sea and east to the steppes of Russia: flashing tributaries of the ancient Oxus River possessed a quicksilver breast of astonishing beauty. In reluctant shading, from blinding golden light into sombre hues of darkness, little clusters of horses stood statuesque in the occasional farmsteads, near the one-man ferry where I crossed the river.

As my donkey descended towards the plain below, the dome of the Amir's palace rose up in the fading light like a great Spanish onion, with a single minaret reaching skyward.

Since it is safer to enter a strange town in the light of day, I decided to rest in the mountains for the night, and led my donkey to the entrance of a solitary cave. There I became aware that I was being watched. The donkey sensed danger, too, and raised her black muzzle above my shoulder, staring fixedly into the cave.

Down in the valley, as if in accompaniment to the action to come, a pack of jackals were howling at the Turkestan moon.

Hearing a faint cry I searched on hands and knees until I touched a body. Kneeling, I struck a match, and before my eyes, instantly contoured by brilliance, was the wasted face of a bearded man: one drawn from the tomb by his looks, my wavering light enhancing his sunken cheeks and shadowed eyes.

'*Aman!*' he said huskily.

'No need for mercy, for I will not harm you,' I said in Pashto, and this he understood, for he relaxed, nearly fainting, in my arms.

'*Bheestee* . . .?' he whispered now.

I held my water-bottle to his mouth and he drank greedily.

Dragging him to the cave entrance I examined him better in the light of the moon. His wrists were manacled across his

177

chest and beneath his tattered clothing I saw the marks of recent punishment; an escaped prisoner.

'From Bokhara, Sahib . . . ' His voice was scarcely audible, and there came to his throat the tell-tale rattling of approaching death.

It seemed wrong to pester him; he whispered, as if anticipating my question, 'From Bemaru . . . '

The name meant 'the husbandless', which was a village near Kabul, so named after its violation by a wandering tribe of Akukzye. His gaunt features told of the Afredis, but his accent placed him farther east.

'I now go to Bokhara,' I said to him, and he opened frightened eyes at this, whispering, 'Do not go . . . to Bokhara,' and, sighing, faded into death.

I did not heed him, for he was a mere passing acquaintance in the business of living; dying easy along the tracks of the Hindu Kush where thousands of slave corpses lay unburied.

All that night I was within touch of him in a shivering companionship: and in the morning, while old Meg watched, buried him beneath a cairn of rocks at the cave entrance; first taking from his pockets his few possessions, as was then the custom; a few annas in money, what was clearly a strangling cord, and something which surprised me – an English prayer-book. This I opened, and read an inscription within:

> To Lieutenant Arthur Connolly, on this
> his twenty-first Birthday: 4th August 1828.
> Love, Mother.

The print of the prayer book was almost indecipherable, as if subject to long and heavy usage, its black cover of ragged leather badly stained; several pages were clearly blackened with blood. On the back end-sheet, written in a firm English hand, was:

> Captain A. Connolly, Bengal Cavalry:
> England, Karachi; Moscow; Persia;
> Afghanistan; Kiva; Kokhand;
> Bokhara . . . (10th Nov. '41)

It was then that I recalled him – the young officer I had seen in our mess tent on his way to Bokhara to rescue a Colonel Stoddart, before our fatal retreat from Kabul.

By an ironic turn of fate, Connolly's prayer book had come into my possession. But I did not read the little book beyond its personal inscription, and, with the intention of returning it to its owner, I dropped it into my rucksack.

Kneeling now, I said a brief prayer over the grave of the dead Afghan then, mounting Old Meg, began the journey down the mountain track to the plain.

The West, then and now, has no conception of the British losses we incurred, not only in slave-dealing, but by operating on the fringe of internecine wars between squabbling Afghan monarchs.

Only a decade ago, when Shah Shuja defeated Kohandil's vast army and was himself attacked by Dost Mohammed Khan, Afghanistan's roads and ditches, after fifty-one days of butchery, were covered with 65,000 bodies of the slain.

Central Asia, through her warring tribes and invasions from Persia, Britain and Russia, had become a charnel house; so the presence of one manacled, whip-lashed prisoner of the Amir of Bokhara occasioned in me neither pity nor regret, for horror mounting on horror dilutes compassion.

Therefore, I steered Meg Donkey onward without a backward glance at the cairn I had built beside the cave; nor gave another thought to Captain Arthur Connolly.

But had I stopped to read his little book of prayer, which proved to be a diary of events, I wouldn't have taken another step towards the tortures of Bokhara.

179

28

Having first buried my bag of diamonds in a safe place, I entered Bokhara by its eastern gate in blinding light, the sun being already high.

It appeared that a festival of some kind was in progress, since the narrow courts and alleys of the town were crowded with hawkers and packmen – I passed scores of them on the approach roads coming in from fields of standing gold, the early harvest.

Camel, mule trains, and staggering donkeys were descending on to the market-place from every point of the compass; wobbling loads of vegetable produce and baskets of mulberry leaves for the silkworm factories: as ancient as Samarkand itself, this industry, having been introduced by the Mongol emperors after Alexander had destroyed the city five hundred years before.

Every tongue in Asia was gabbling around me: slant-eyed Turks and Russians vying with each other in raucous shrieks: Uzbeks, Kirghiz and Turkomans rubbing shoulders with Chinese horse-traders coming in from the Tien Shan mountain.

Here vendors were bawling the quality of Bokhara rugs, their sheepskins flung over their shoulders in preparation for the bitter nights of the steppe: the wind was flavoured with smells of roasting mutton and bitter with distant sandstorms.

Now the sunlit morning was punctuated by screams, each followed by cheering from crowds thronging the central market-place; this led me to the main, iron-studded door of the fort which guarded the royal palace. A man with a proboscis, not a nose, jostled me as he craned his neck for a better look.

'What is happening?' I asked him.

He pointed excitedly. 'Execution Day!'

I looked up into the sun, seeing above me on a towering platform two pygmy figures – executioners pinioning victims eighty feet above: Nasrullah, the Amir of Bokhara, being engaged upon his favourite pastime – the execution of his prisoners.

The method he used was cheap and effective: after being tied hand and foot they were then cast off from the platform, to fall on to the flagstones of the market-place.

I watched in sickened fascination: one by one they came; the watching crowd, silent during the victim's howling descent: thunderous applause as he hit the ground.

Later, I learned that the flagstones bore testimony to these barbaric executions . . . the indentation of the victims' bones, cast to their deaths in thousands, can be seen to this day.

It was in the nature of an initiation ceremony.

Turbaned and helmeted soldiers were everywhere, as were saffron-robed priests who, their bald heads gleaming under the incandescent rays of a midday sun, glided past me intoning incantations of the Kulmah, the holy affirmation of their faith.

These, the root of Bokhara's learning, were the holy men divorced from the ferocious antics of the petty tyrant who ruled them. From their heads sprang scholarship; from their hands the exquisite artifacts that were the essence of Moslem Bokhara – intricate and beautiful jade emblematic of an artistry passed down through generations. They it was who had introduced the four-man plough that tilled the soil of Turkistan before the advent of the bullock: their gentility lingers down the centuries.

The next thing I looked for was a smoke-plume, for smoke probably meant a furnace working and a furnace meant Caleb Benedict, whom I had come to find: Fate decreed that I found him under ceremonial conditions.

181

A little processional group approached me, with turbanned policemen swinging their truncheons to clear a path for a dignitary. And the dignitary was rotten old Caleb, seated like a visiting potentate in an open palanquin. Wearing a white gown and a poshteen threaded with gold, he came, dispensing annas to scrambling urchins; pausing only to take swigs from a whisky flask, his baggy eyes clenched against the sun.

It was indisputably Caleb, years older, but to his credit he instantly recognized me.

Now, amid the plush furnishings of his quarters in Fort Bokhara, he regarded me with affectionate warmth.

'You've been expecting me, you say?' I asked.

'These past weeks, for I got a letter from the Dost in Kabul.'

'And you're coming back with me as he suggests?'

'Me boy, what Dost suggests and what His Majesty here agrees with are two different things, for the beggars are sworn enemies.'

'Not according to the Dost. Didn't the Amir once give him sanctuary in Bokhara?'

'Perhaps, but these lads are comrades one moment, next they're at each other's throats. Meanwhile he's away on business, catching slaves. His family have been at it for a century. Make yourself at home, for I've struck it lucky here and the King thinks the sun shines out of me rear. By the way, where did Big Rhys get to while you were livin' it up in Ludhiana?'

I told him.

'So you're the last o' the Welsh line, is it?' and he popped grapes into his mouth and chewed lustily. 'Meanwhile, may I suggest ye take a bath, son, for you stink to high heaven,' and he clapped his hands and two young women appeared in curved harem slippers, silk veils and not much else.

'Oh no they don't!'

'Oh yes they will; it's a national custom.'

I retorted, 'I was in Ludhiana for years and it never happened there.'

'That was India, this is Turkistan.'

182

What began as a laughing tug-of-war in an attempt to retain my modesty, ended with my resignation to total nakedness, for half a dozen more dusky beauties came in to help the others. Caleb looked on, smiling his satisfaction while I was bathed, perfumed and stood up for towelling while the females elbowed each other amid shrieks while I tried to cover myself.

'Think nothing of it, me lad,' cried Caleb, enjoying it, while more harem women came rushing in. 'Take it as a compliment, for if a fella has anything special round here they turn it into a national sport.'

After the bathing I lazed in luxury with Caleb, eating roast goat and dainty pastries while voluptuous females fed us grapes and wild berries, and Caleb said, 'Time was I was against the ways of wickedness, with fornication a long way down me list, but now the wine is upon me, I wonder why I lasted so long.'

I did not answer.

'When I did the rounds of the pubs in Derry, I'd wear me little white surplice and sing holy songs; then, when I opened me own pub in Galway, me best customer was meself: the essence of me life being a ten pint brew and a plate of tripe and onions, but now I've fallen on me feet.'

'Me, too,' I said, eating grapes.

He tipped up his goblet and drank deep, gasping. 'But I had less brains than a Church of England bishop, for while I was soakin' it, the gloss of Irish manhood was droppin' on the dunghills of England. So I set meself a target for wickedness; goodness, I find, pays small dividends.'

'You can say that again.'

'And what do ye mean by that, ye naffin' scallywag?'

'That you've moved a bit to the left of the Cross.'

'Is that a fact? And who are you to pass judgement on me?'

'The execution jumping, for a start. Doesn't your conscience jib at the things that are happening here? God, it makes me sick, and it seems you approve of it.'

'Perhaps, for when you're in Rome, lad, you do as Rome does. You're not back in Welsh Wales now, ye know, when it comes to crime and punishment. So away wid your hypocrisy. It wasn't so far back that the likes of you were fitting blazing caps to the heads of Irish patriots, and the Good Book says an eye for an eye.'

It was a subject I didn't want to pursue. 'They tell me Lady Sale was rescued, am I right?' I asked.

'Ach, the marvellous woman, yes! Her old man came out from Jalalabad and carried all hostages back to India, and they tell me Akbar Khan wasn't best pleased; especially when you got your princess back to her granddad.'

'And he married her off to a Persian prince.'

'Which left you cooling your heels in Ludhiana!' He grinned hugely.

'For five years. It wasn't easy.'

He rose and wandered the room as dusk began to paint shadows on the windows. 'It was a mite better than leaving your bones on the rocks of the Khoord-Kabul. Do you know what happened to the Sergeant?'

'Never saw the going of him, nor his baby.'

'The plans of mice and men, me darling!' Caleb's eyes grew distant. 'Sometimes I think I'm the only man still alive.'

I was watching him.

Caleb had changed both in looks and character. His morals were diluted: a Hindu serving-maid was hovering near him and I sensed their affinity. I said, 'Everything has changed, and I'd give my soul to be back in the beloved country, for I'm still as Welsh as a leek.'

'But unless you change, too, you'll end up on the wrong side of the street, me lad; this is Bokhara.'

'God, I can't stay here.'

'You can, son; you can work with me making iron until the king comes home. And if ye take me tip, you'll stay on the right side of him; he's a pernickety old boy when he's roused.

'It's iron he's after, and I know how to make it. He rates it as high as gold – weapons of war. D'ye know we're casting twelve-pounder cannon?'

'So what about you coming back with me to Kabul?' I

184

asked. 'The Dost is making ploughshares for peace,' and Caleb threw up his hands in disgust.

'Don't even mention it, or we'll both finish up in the Hole; this chap's dead against peace with anyone.'

'The Hole?'

He waved me down. 'Forget it, I said. But you can put away any ideas of getting me back to Kabul to work wi' that old bowser, for I'm doing all right here. I'm an independent spirit sitting on a fortune in the middle of paradise. Do you know what he's paying me?'

'You're sitting in the middle of Hell,' I said.

'And whose fault's that? All my life I've prayed to a Catholic god who put me into a charnel house. Now I'm eating young lamb stuffed wi' nuts and almonds; I drink the best wine of Bokhara's vineyards. By the balls of me granddad, I'm not giving this up now I've found it.'

I replied, and it sounded trite, 'But you've prospered in iniquity. What does it profit a man to gain the world and lose his soul?'

'Ach, away wid ye! You sound like the drunken priests I knew back home in Dublin city. Dear God, up to now I never knew what I was missing.'

'You'll roast, Caleb, the Bible says so.'

'Then I'll make the best of it before I fry, lad, so away next door to your bed and I'll see you in the marnin'.' He clapped his hands again and a girl of marvellous beauty appeared in the doorway, with enough bewitchery in her smile to shock Satan.

'I don't need her,' I said, and rose.

'Dear God!' Caleb shouted laughter. 'Don't tell me a Welshman's so far gone that he's forgotten the essentials between his knees! Have ye died since I last saw ye?'

'No, you have.'

'Is that a fact! Then may Allah wither your bones for the hypocrite you are,' said he, 'since I know for certain sure that you gave it Durrani.'

'Who told you that?'

'A boy called Karendeesh.'

'What else did he say?'

'Wouldn't you like to know!' said Caleb.

185

29

Bokhara Fort was a village within a town: surrounded on all sides by a high wall with towering ramparts, its embrasures and loopholes being built to deter the most audacious attackers.

Inside the wider city environs stood the market-place, the bazaars, slave-platforms, and a dense, highly populated, mud-walled native quarter.

Within this complex stood the Fort and its adjoining prison, in which were incarcerated the prisoners of the Amir; who, said Caleb, entertained hundreds at any given time.

Within the security of the fort, whose ramparts were guarded day and night, was the Amir's royal palace; a sumptuous affair that vied with Kabul for princely splendour.

I repeat that it was to Bokhara that Dost Mohammed Khan had once fled for protection, only to find that his host had instantly planned his death; the Dost escaping by disguising himself as a woman.

Death to all friends and enemies was apparently Nasser Ullah Khan's maxim; he who had come to power by murdering his father and three of his brothers.

I asked Caleb how he was held in favour by such a man.

'By making good iron, son,' came the reply. 'And he don't need you to help me. Take my tip and make yourself scarce.'

I was about to follow this advice when two armed guards appeared.

'Come now,' one commanded.

Too late I realized the trap that Dost Mohammed Khan had set for me; an effective way of ending my ambitions towards Durrani.

'*Begeer! Begeer!*' bawled a guard, and assisted me along with his boot, down spiral steps, across a courtyard and into the austere presence of Nasrullah, the Amir of Bokhara, the most feared king in Central Asia.

Here was a squint-eyed monster if ever I saw one.

In lavish splendour he sat cross-legged upon a scarlet cushion: a sadist with crossed eyes and a malevolence to match his bearded ugliness. Dressed in a gold gown encrusted with diadems, he sat in motionless ferocity, his ball eyes glaring from beneath his turbaned head, where a single diamond flashed upon his forehead: scoundrels such as he competed with each other for Eastern ostentation.

Spawned from a fat-lined womb, this one; his grossness was an abomination; layers of it being superimposed upon layers of wobbling obesity. Swag-bellied, his manhood long expired into elephantine corpulence, his was the voice of the castrati: a high-pitched soprano piping from bloated cheeks.

'Your name?' he asked in Persian.

'Iestyn Mortymer, Your Majesty.'

'*Prostrate yourself!*'

I did not move, so it was done for me; the guards projecting me forwards on to my knees.

Held thus, face down, my right hand was placed under the Amir's foot, an act of total obeisance, and with the heel of his curved shoe he ground my fingers into the carpet. Then a guard grabbed my hair and pulled my face upward, and I looked into the flaccid features of the King. A Vizier beside him asked tonelessly, 'The purpose of your visit to Bokhara, Feringhee?'

'To work with Caleb Benedict, the ironmaster.'

'You lie,' said the Vizier.

'You lie!' repeated the King, his face inflamed.

The Vizier, an old man of aristocratic coldness, asked, 'Was it not also to persuade Mr Benedict to return to Dost Mohammed Khan in Kabul?'

187

'Was it not?' bawled the King.

I said, with my neck cracking in the grip of the guard, 'Only with your permission, Your Majesty.'

'He addresses me?' asked the King.

'It is so, Sire. He addresses you directly,' replied the Vizier, who was already wandering away, saying, 'Return him to the royal presence when he has learned better manners.'

'Wait!' commanded the King, a plump hand held up. 'You come from Britain, do you not?'

I hesitated.

'Answer!' commanded the Vizier.

'I am a prisoner of the English,' I replied.

'A convict?'

'A convict, Sire.'

'Then you bring no gifts from Victoria?'

'I bring no gifts, Sire.'

'Take him away and beat him,' said His Majesty, and the guards hauled me off.

'May Allah grant the Dost Mohammed Khan a hideous death; you also,' I heard the Vizier say as I went, my feet dragging along the carpets.

They hauled me into the fortress courtyard, struck me down and beat me with sticks: it is strange how I recall, as I slipped into unconsciousness, that the day was extravagant with sunlight and that skylarks were singing in a sky of blue . . . in the moment before the sun faded.

I opened my eyes in almost total darkness, aware that, with a rope tightening under my arms, I was being lowered down what appeared to be a hole in the ground; all about me, chattering into my growing conscious- ness, were the voices of men, and I saw a small circle of blue above me, the sky.

Around me were the faces of the haggard inmates of what was known as the Black Well, a pit which the Amir reserved for special prisoners; apparently, to give them a taste of hardships to come.

They pressed about me, these men, as I found my feet. In a babble of foreign tongues, mainly Pashto, they questioned.

'Who is he?'

'What's your name?'

'How long you in for?'

'You been beaten?'

I had – effectively. Every bone in my body ached, for they had been at me with bludgeons, and I saw the faces of the prisoners about me within a misted conscious- ness; their features strangely contorted in the dimness of the hole.

I had heard of this place before, and I now quote, in service to absolute veracity, from the testimony of one, Saleh Mohammed, a servant of Captain Arthur Connolly: this servant, commonly called Akhundzada, stated: 'I was imprisoned in the *Siah Chah*, which, translated, means, The Black Well. It is a prison for criminals, a circular well 17 feet deep and 21 feet in diameter which has a brick roof with a hole in it: the prisoners are lowered into it upon a rope.'

Immediately I was released from the rope, I found myself standing in six inches of water swarming with snakes and lizards; about me the circular walls were dripping with mud and padded with years of filthy effluent: all was verminous, crawling with cockroaches and sheep-fleas whose bites induced painful red swellings on the skin, and instantly they discovered in me a new and wholesome host.

The other prisoners, all in various stages of filth and nakedness, now clustered about me, pulling at me with wild exclamations, demanding news from the world above.

Some eighty men were incarcerated here, so crammed in together that some were lying on top of others; all having fallen foul of the Amir for one crime or another. Some crouched in postures of listlessness and acceptance of their lot; seemingly unaware of the myriad of snakes that writhed about their feet: oblivious also, it appeared, to the biting sheep-fleas and the incessant chatter of the market-place coming from a world removed, for the well acted as a sounding board.

No light entered the melancholy darkness of the pit save a single ray of sunlight from the sky above; and from the mouths of the prisoners came a lamenting chord of misery like the wail of lost souls. Others, on the threshold of madness, sat pulling at their clothes in whimpering sadness; verminous old lags and fresh-faced young men squatted side by side in the reeking sewage; no form of drainage served the pit.

My eyes growing accustomed to the dark, I stared around me in disbelief.

This was a Gehenna, an abyss created by a modern Satan haunted by his own spectral and demoniacal ghosts: no sane man could have conceived such a monstrous cruelty.

As instantly as they had clambered over one another to question me, so my new companions subsided back into the rut of their despair; either sinking to their knees or lying back against the flowing walls; many were there whose reason had completely gone; staring vacantly upward, their worn faces turned to the single ray of sunlight.

'What is your crime?' asked a voice in English and I turned to it, seeing dimly the outline of a face which was young, though its white beard was down to the chest.

'You are British?' I asked of the speaker.

'Polish,' came the reply. 'Though a man's nationality is not important in this hell.'

'How long have you been here?'

'So long that I cannot remember,' said he, 'for days are nights here and nights become days,' and he raised shrunken arms to me, as if in prayer. 'With the Russian deputation I came, and they are now living in the harem rooms while I am forgotten, being not of their blood.

'You offended by coming to Bokhara, Comrade.' He peered at me in the dimness of the hole. 'And here they give no pardons.'

'It is enough that I am here, leave it at that,' I replied.

'One thing is certain. Now the King is returned we will not be here much longer. May God destroy the house of his mother.'

'You speak of pardons?' I spoke the old language, like his own – the stilted English of the educated foreigner.

'Not of pardons, but of a release from despair,' he answered. 'You have not heard of the Execution Jumping?'

'I saw it when coming into Bokhara.'

'We are the jumpers. One by one they take us, and for this we draw lots.'

The others, sensing the intimacy of our conversation, now began to crowd about us, their haggard faces, malevolent with suffering, looming up like disembodied ghosts; elbowing, nudging like participants in a madness of gossip. Some were naked, others half clothed, pulling their rags closer about them for decency: most were heavily bearded, their matted hair hanging about their shoulders; some bore the stamp of idiocy, evident in their imbecilic smiles. In a corner a man was dying with friends intoning about him, for here the living shared communion with the dead: the rotting corpses of those already favoured being stacked in a burial cairn in a corner.

'Draw lots?' I asked.

'For the privilege of death, my friend; only through death does one escape from the *Siah Chah*, Nasrullah's Black Well. We draw for the privilege of dying. For what is life but a tormented dream in such a circumstance as this? One small jump into the sunlight of the market-place with closed eyes; moments later – Heaven's glory.'

'You are a Christian?'

'I have never been baptized.'

'Baptism does not make you a Christian.'

'In the name of Jesus,' said he, 'do not treat me to philosophy! What is your name?'

I told him. 'And yours?' I asked.

'I have no name. Here I am known as the Pole.'

The conversation over, I sank down into the mud and shut off my senses from the heat and stinks of unwashed humanity; around me odours of filth rose on the fetid air.

They fed us once a day like dogs.

A guard appeared at the top of the well next morning and emptied down slops upon us. The prisoners, stirred from the torpidity of their exhaustion, gathered around with upraised hands in a gabble of excitement as the garbage fell upon them. Some tore instantly at the swill for pigs; others crept away to gnaw at some unexpected prize: for my part I sat in growing languour, my mental alertness already dulled into a resignation to my fate.

The sun beat down through the spy-glass hole down which the winch rope dangled, acting upon those jammed together in sweating misery like the blistering sun-shot of a magnifying glass; it was necessary for all to cower away from the scalding rays of the circling sun.

In company with a legion of rats we moved, our faces ever turned upwards to the single ray of light; and as the inmates died, so they were stowed away in the burial cairn in the corner, there to pollute the air with their decomposition.

On the morning of the fifth day down the hole, I was aware of sounds of jollity and laughter coming from the prisoners, and wondered at this change of mood: finding myself pressed hard against the naked body of a neighbour, I inquired of this.

'It is Jump Day soon,' said he, and his face, though gaunt with hunger, was alight with an inner expecta- tion.

'It is good,' said he in Pashto. 'I will certainly draw a straw. I have no hope of staying alive.'

'An equal chance with the rest of us, surely?'

'No, Sahib English, not equal, for I am not circumcised, and the food, when it is dropped, is smuggled away from me by highwaymen and other criminals.'

The Pole, overhearing, said to me, 'It is true what you hear.'

'So we all draw for the privilege of dying?'

'Those who wish to. Is it not better than rotting here? Besides, there is a chance of life also; straws will be sent down this morning by the guards. But of four only three will die; the lucky one goes free.'

'Truly free?'

'If the Amir keeps his promise.'

'You trust him to do so?'

The Pole shrugged. 'Of course not; it is the chance we take. He promises freedom to the longest straw.'

'I shall not take part in this,' I said.

'Then you are a bigger fool than I believed you to be. Draw, if you get the opportunity; it is a chance to live.'

A man, listening nearby, said, 'There is talk that the man who is given freedom lives but half an hour, before they feed him to crocodiles.'

I stared at him, and the Pole said, 'It is as I explained, my friend. It may be rumour, but it could be possible to have one's freedom.'

'I shall not draw,' I said.

'Don't be a bloody idiot,' said a new voice from the dark. 'You turn down the chance, you might never get another,' and his accent was North Country. On all fours I crawled through the slush of mud and excrement and found him sitting with his back to the wall; cockroaches were crawling over his naked chest.

'You British?' I asked him, and he nodded.

'They calls me Wigan,' he explained. 'In Peshawar, I were a Corporal in the Bengal Cavalry, and got bagged out on patrol: our officer were always puttin' his nose where it weren't bloody wanted, and the women got at him and did him proper. Then they took me for sale in Bokhara, but I was dear at fifty rupees, so I landed up here. And the only way out they tell me is by execution jumping.'

'Have you drawn straws for it?'

'Every time the lads come round I draw, but no luck,' and he raised his eyes upward. 'Reckon someone up there don't want me, neither.'

The day dragged on in plopping water and rustling rats.

Each day of sweating heat turned to night and an arctic coldness, and the prisoners, save for their strange intoning sadness, made no sound: night's blueness came with moonlight, and the dawn broke on another Bokhara day of stifling heat and market noises; then night came again; each succeeding day became one of cramped agony.

And then, on the morning of my tenth day in the Black Well, up to my hips in fouled water, with my legs and feet grotesquely stuck upward, the top of the well opened wider to the sun, and the bearded face of a guard grinned down.

'It is Jump Day,' said the Pole, 'now the straws will come.'

Earlier, I had been reading by the dawn light some pages

from the Connolly diary; the writings of a brave man who had suffered here some five years before: between its blank lines of the print I read:

6th December, 1841
Towards the end of last month reports came that Sir Alexander Burnes and most of the English had been killed in Afghanistan, and that our influence there had now been destroyed . . . The Amir questioned us again about the true object of our mission to Khiva and Khokand, and suggested that it had been our intention to excite the enmity of these states against him. He also demanded to know why our Queen had made no reply to his letter of friendship, and this had clearly infuriated him; also, it made our value of no consequence in his eyes, since all he wished for, he said, was an alliance with England.

I read on.

On December 24th we petitioned the Amir of Bokhara thus: 'If we had unwittingly offended His Majesty, the Amir of Bokhara, we were sorry, and begged him to pardon our error, but that we were only servants of our English government and not the proper objects of His Majesty's displeasure . . .

Nasrullah's response was to send his Topshibashi (Master General of Ordnance) to strip Captain Connolly naked and clothe him in the stinking skin of a sheep recently slaughtered; at the same time informing him that Colonel Stoddart had already been compelled to proselytize. Connolly replied:

My religion is a matter between me and my God, and I would rather suffer death than change it. All the world knew that a forced confession of faith was null, and that Colonel Stoddart had consented to repeat the Kulmah, the holy affirmation of the Moslem faith, solely to avert bloodshed and disorder. We have now been 53 days

194

and nights without means of washing or changing our clothes, and this book will serve as an opportunity in which to write a last blessing to all my friends. May God, our Saviour and Comforter in whom I trust, and for whom I will die, grant them happiness in this world and the next.

Let it not be thought that the Russian mission, which is also in Bokhara, could in any way help us: we feel sure that Colonel Buteyov would help us if he could, but the Amir knows nothing of justice or generosity . . .

On 15th February Connolly wrote: 'Thank God this prayer book was left to me. Stoddart and I have found it a great comfort: how beautiful are the prayers of the Church . . . We doubt if we will live much longer, and have committed our souls to God . . .'

On 16th February several of Connolly's servants were also committed to the rat-infested Black Well, and the two officers remained in captivity (the Amir was away) until June. Upon his return, Colonel Stoddart was violently beaten with heavy sticks, when a pencil stub was found in his pocket: for two to three days he was badly beaten, but did not reveal its source. On Friday, 7th July both men were taken into the town square, and, with their hands tied, watched their graves being dug before a market crowd. Stoddart's head was cut off with a knife, and the Chief Executioner then said to Captain Connolly, 'The Amir will spare your life if you become a Moslem.'

But Connolly answered, 'Colonel Stoddart has been a Moslem for three years while here in Bokhara, and you have just killed him. I refuse, and am ready to die.'

His head was then cut off and the bodies of the two officers were interred.

30

'Ya-hoy! Ya-hoy!'

A ring of bearded, ruffian faces lined the top brickwork of the Black Well, shouting down. We, the prisoners, stared up.

'The bastards,' said someone.

The guards bawled and laughed, making obscene gestures, and a small pannier came dangling down on a rope, lowered by a guard who was shouting obscenities in broken English.

'It is the straws. It is Jump Day,' said the Pole, beside me.

A silence fell upon the vaulting walls, broken only by the croaking of frogs and the hollow plopping of water. A man moved in the crush of men: his bones jutted obscenely through his rags and his emaciated face brushed mine.

'You going to draw?' he asked me.

'He's a fool if he don't,' said Wigan. 'What about it, Taff?'

I did not reply; I was watching the descending pannier; the Pole, reaching up, lowered it into his arms.

Many pieces of bright straw of unequal length lay gleaming in sunlight.

'Jump Day,' shouted the Pole in Pashto. 'Who's drawing?' and the prisoners pushed closer, their haggard faces glaring at the straws, their only hope of deliverance, for the man with the longest straw went free.

I said, 'Let's get this right. The volunteers draw straws, and the man with the longest straw goes free. The three drawing shorter straws jump off the tower in the market-place?'

196

'You're an intelligent fella for a Taff,' said Wigan. 'Set 'em up,' and the Pole, with waving arms, cleared people away.

'Hurry!' bawled a guard, and men pushed forward, then backed away into the obliterating darkness.

'Come on, make up your minds!'

'Count me in,' said Wigan.

Another came, and another: one, I knew, was the highwayman; his Asiatic face bore the stamp of debauchery; another, clearly a Hindu, was no older than Karendeesh.

'How about you?' the Pole asked me.

I shook my head.

'You'll come to it, they all do.'

I didn't trust the Amir. His mind, debauched by sadism, was beyond the reach of human pity: he could be reserving a more horrible fate for the man escaping the execution jump: it was true that crocodiles, kept as pets, abounded in the river below the King's gardens. . . .

The Pole picked up the straws. When he showed his fists for all to see, four straws projected from his fingers; and he held them up to the light.

A single golden shaft of sunlight shafted the gloom of the pit, and fell upon the straws.

'Draw,' said the Pole.

One by one, with shaking hands, four men drew, and held up the straws, and the highwayman drew the longest.

The Pole said, 'You live again, to bludgeon and kill, my footpad friend,' and pushed him to one side.

The three drawing short straws sank down on their haunches in the mud and waited; one had tears coursing down his cheeks, and this was the boy who was as young as Karendeesh.

Now a silence had fallen upon the assembled men; in their rags and ferocious aspects of glowering faces, they stared at nothing. The shaft of sunlight had now fallen on me, and I discovered that the little prayer book of Captain Connolly was unexpectedly in my hands, and I opened it at a page, from which I read aloud:

Unto thee, O Lord, will I lift up my soul; my God, I have put my trust in thee; O let me not be confounded, neither let mine enemies triumph over me . . . Turn thee unto me, and have mercy upon me: for I am desolate and in misery. The sorrows of my heart are enlarged: O, bring me out of my troubles. Look upon my adversity and misery; and forgive me all my sins. Consider mine enemies, how many they are; and they bear a tyrannous hate against me. . . .

As I read aloud I became aware of another voice interpreting my words, and saw that the ring of men had tightened about me, their movements silent in the mud. The Pole spoke first in a low utterance, but all there heard: and even more . . . from the depth of the pit where light did not penetrate, other voices sounded – the whispered intonations of men who understood English and were translating my words to their comrades in different tongues. And as my voice rose higher in this recognition, so their voices rose also; therefore there came from the darkness of *Shih Chah* a swelling volume of prayer that funnelled up to the market-place above, and many guards and the common people came and looked down at those who were praying: the money-lenders and hucksters came; the mule-drivers, hagmen and many others; all lined the top of the pit and looked down at us as our words rose up: prayers that had no meaning to the sects of other beliefs; nor to those of a score of other tongues and blessings. Nevertheless, I read on, and it was translated:

O keep my soul, and deliver me; let me not be confounded, for I have put my trust in thee: let perfectness and righteous dealing wait upon me; for my hope hath been in thee. Deliver Israel, O God; out of all his troubles . . .

The people above stared down; we stared up. And the single shaft of light that lay upon us from the sun became a beam of striking brilliance so that those above covered their heads with their poshteens, and we in the pit below covered our eyes.

198

And so it was that for years this incident was talked about in the market-place; also around the auction slave platforms and in the bazaars of Bokhara; even, it is said, into the ear of the Amir.

'Take the English also,' he commanded.

'*Begeer! Begeer!*' cried the guards above, and came scrambling down a rope ladder flung from above; seized me, and bound me with ropes, as they did the three others.

Therefore, four of us were hoisted up the Black Well and out into the crowds of the market-place.

The guards prodded us onward with their scimitars. And coming to the highest tower in Bokhara (this was not the holy muezzin which calls the faithful to prayer) forced us up its spiral stone steps, which ran externally, in the manner of a lighthouse. In single file we went, all prisoners, to the top of the tower. Reaching it, we were then forced through a narrow doorway and on to a circling perimeter of flagstones guarded by a handrail.

From this great height I looked down upon the market-place below. The distant mountain peaks were haloed with sunlight.

I have never been a great one for religion, save to chapel back home in Blaenafon come Sundays, and while the moaning intonations of God's ministers trouble me, I do believe in the Man who died for us. Never, however, have I held Him in such esteem as at that moment; the prospect of death wonderfully concentrates the mind: it is the death of Jesus, not the gross activities of some of his ministers that a man remembers.

The Hindu boy was crying beside me, miserably calling for his mother. His neighbour, a starved ghost of manhood who would find solace in death, was an Arab, and he was upon his knees in wailing protestations: the third, a Ghilzai tribesman by his looks, showed no discernible emotion – not unusual in the face of death when it comes to Ghilzais. Indeed, to my amazement, he appeared considerably interested in the macabre proceedings.

The sun was blinding, the air still: the guards about us were pushing and shoving us about, their nerves strained to breaking point as the two prisoners wailed; and as they seized the Ghilzai and projected him forward to the open rail, I heard him say, to my utter astonishment:

'Holy Mary, Mother of God, pray for this sinner now and for evermore . . . Holy Mary, Mother of God, pray for this sinner . . . ' and his words floated into a whisper as the guards launched him into space.

He fell as the crow goes; first in a strange gliding flight, legs and arms akimbo, before his body assumed the position of a protective ball at the moment it splashed the ground.

A compatriot? Possibly a Britisher, and English by his accent? I never knew, but judged him by his courage in the face of such adversity . . . in a strange land, without companionship. A spy? Perhaps one of the brave young officers – *agents provacateurs* – sent to the North-West frontier by an uncaring monarch in pursuit of Empire?

Silenced now by the bloodstained flagstones of the market-place, the people turned their faces upwards again in hungering anticipation.

In screeching protests, the old Arab went next, and lastly the little Hindu lad; in what judgement and for what crime none appeared to know, and certainly nobody cared save me . . . I managed to kiss him before he was thrown into the air.

Again, I saw the market-place shimmering in waves of refracted light, and the tiny upturned faces of the people eighty feet below.

They say a man's life flashes before his eyes at the moment of death; for myself, I saw only the face of Durrani.

I saw her every feature in clear perspective; the ever-changing expressions of her moods ranging from joy to sadness. Of Mari I saw no sign: it was as if my whole being had been transfigured by a single outrage, so that all that had preceded my knowledge of Durrani had been erased by the horror of events.

It was the puzzle of my life never explained or eradicated: it betokened, in some strange manner, a new existence; the end and yet the beginning of another era. And as the guards seized me I saw Durrani against fleeting clouds with a clarity so astonishing that it silenced my fears into death's acceptance.

'You enjoy that, Feringhee?' A bearded face was thrust into mine, replacing the gentle face of Durrani: it was the English-speaking guard. 'Now you go down and wait to jump next time, eh? And die many times for me, before you dig your grave in Bokhara?' and he shouted bass laughter.

His time was then, but my time was to come: his name, they told me later, was Basra Topshibashi: I made a mental note to be up with him before I left Turkistan.

Meanwhile, thumping me with the butt of his whip, he bundled me down the spiral steps of the tower and booted me along an alley to the door of a prison. This opened, and into it he flung me full length.

'Good to see you again,' said a face bending over me.

It was the sergeant with whom I had fought in the retreat from Kabul; this time without his adopted baby.

31

Bokhara being the centre of the slave-trade in Turkistan, the Amir's business was to catch slaves in neighbouring villages ranging along the Oxus River, west to Ashkhabad and east to Samarkand. Hundreds he drove in chains across the Hindu Kush, also from as far south as Koh-i-Baba. Many enemies he made along the way, but such was their disunity that none contrived to form the alliance that would drive him out of business.

During these expeditions the Amir sent home thousands to be auctioned on the platforms of Bokhara: slave merchants, their agents operating from as far away as China, came flocking in to buy from every corner of Central Asia: a repeat, if on a smaller scale, of the commerce in humans upon which Britain had built her Empire.

But there was more to the Amir's ambitions than slave-selling. His fittest and most healthy specimens of humanity he kept at home to enlarge his town: always, as Caleb had told me, he employed a labouring population of two hundred prisoners: of these I was one, the sergeant another.

'So where did they pick you up?' I asked him.

'Back in Seh Baba,' said he. 'Six months ago.'

'But you got back safely to the wife of the miller?'

'I got away at Gandamak. There may have been a couple more got off that hill, but I doubt it. I was there till Captain Souter wrapped the flag around his waist, then I was off. Sixteen thousand plus caught it dead; they could do without me.'

'And the baby?'

'That's why I skedaddled; she was entitled, that baby, so I did the Army down, for once. And got back to the woman to find her chap had snuffed it. We was living happy ever after until Nasrullah's hooligans arrived, the bastards.'

'And landed you here for auction?' and he nodded.

'His slave foremen picked me out of a bundle, mainly Chinese they'd landed on an opium run. I were lucky, most got sent to Arabia. But you'll never guess who they put me working for . . .'

'Who?'

'Old Caleb Benedict – remember him, the tipsy Irishman?'

'Remember him? That's why I'm here. What you doing now, then?'

'Breaking limestone for him. Furnace work. Dawn till dusk. You'll 'ave your bellyfull before you're finished, I tell ye. There's eighty of us in my shift alone – look around you.'

I did so. In the semi-darkness of the bare prison room the dozing, half-naked bodies of exhausted men made shape.

'It's one better than the Black Well,' and I told him about it.

They were clearing out a few from there, too, apparently, for within a week two more were thrown through the door: the Pole for one: Wigan, the Lancashire chap, came two days later . . .

They brought the furnace limestone in by horse and cart and we tipped it, labouring under a cooler autumn sun; there were four of us in our gang – Sergeant, the Pole, Wigan and me.

The carts were coming in from a quarry east of the river where a seam of limestone had been found. They came in single line, a convoy of limping mules and flying whips, the fierce cries of the drivers echoing for miles.

The furnace area itself, where Caleb held court, was inside the town walls; we broke the limestone down into manageable lumps, then reloaded it on to the carts: a small army of us were engaged on this, each prisoner with a sledge-hammer that could fell any guard within swinging

distance . . . if it hadn't been for the scimitars they carried
. . . and their loaded *jezails* were every- where; bearded
marksmen, these, who would boot a man to death at the
smallest provocation.

The sun burned down, if with only a hint of autumn; the
work went on day and night without a break. In the distance,
like a pall over the town, hung the smoke of Caleb
Benedict's furnaces.

'Don't you ever see him?' I asked, and Sergeant lowered
his hammer and his big body glistened with sweat in the
midday sunlight.

'Caleb? Neither hide nor hair of him, for he lies low, the
old crook – giving himself to a monster like the Amir. One
day we're having the skin off him for it.'

And the Pole, with black hair sprouting over his naked
back and shoulders, said, 'And after we've fixed him we will
all get out of here.'

'I've heard that every day for the past six months,' said
Sergeant, moodily.

The guards came round; one levelled his *jezail* while the
other beat the Pole; the whipping went on and on, and he
made no sound; just lay upon the ground, shuddering to the
lash.

'You no talk, you understand?' said Basra, the
Topshibashi who spoke English; and he stood by with folded
arms while the Pole collected another ten lashes. He was our
neolithic ape, this Basra, with about a thousand more years
of evolution to go before he made sense as a human.

I looked at the labouring slaves: as far as I could see in the
sunlight the breaking hammers were rising and falling,
making limestone for Caleb's bloomeries; the shrill
commands and threats of the guards filled the autumn air.

That night, back within the prison walls, we stole oil from
the wake-lights and poured it upon the Pole's back, and the
weals of his beating stood out like red fingers on the living
flesh.

'Never mind about Caleb Benedict,' said Wigan, 'one day
I'll 'ave that Basra Topshibashi.'

'You're second in the queue,' I said.

They were inexhaustible; never have I known such men;

neither threats of death nor torture could break their proud spirits.

'Is it bad?' someone asked.

'Do not worry, it is nothing,' said the Pole.

A month later we were still at it with no sign of relief, and another batch of slaves came in from the mountains, the result of the Amir's battles around Tashkent.

In single file the new slaves arrived with their hands tied behind their backs, even the children; all two hundred roped together by their necks.

The slave merchants waiting to receive them were already bickering over prices in huddled, argumentative groups. The whole scene was bathed in a beautiful, roseate hue, for the sun was going down: whips cracked as the wilting slaves were herded into line; six files of them before the waiting auction platforms.

'Soon,' said the Pole, and eased his shoulders to the wrack of his pain.

'Soon what?' asked Wigan.

From somewhere he had filched a stub of tobacco and was smoking this in an evil-looking contraption he called a pipe.

The Pole drew his finger across his throat and scowled.

'I know, I know,' said Sergeant, and waved him down. 'I've been hearin' that for the past six months, too, but it don't come to nothin'.'

I said, 'You'll never stop slavery here. It has been happening for centuries – even before the British had a go at it.'

'I tell you, the time is coming,' said the Pole. 'The Romans never numbered their slaves lest they discovered their strength. So I tell you – one day the slaves in Bokhara will rise . . .'

'And cut every enemy throat in sight,' finished Sergeant. 'We talk about it, but nothin' bloody happens.'

'Soon,' said the Pole again.

We lay together in the stifling air of the prison, amid the grunts and groans of exhausted men. The autumn passed, winter came in with bitter winds and still we laboured out on

205

the steppe, and the peaks of the mountains were covered with ice.

Then spring came again, dancing over the land in bright green clothes.

Once again my dreams turned to Durrani.

And with the coming of that spring came our first hopes of release from the bondage of Bokhara.

The prison door clanged open and the Topshibashi stood there with his whip. 'Four men I want,' bawled he in broken English, 'you, you, you and you,' and he prodded the Pole, Wigan, Sergeant and me. '*Come!*'

We followed him out into morning sunlight.

There, to my astonishment, stood Caleb Benedict.

'I wonder you've got the bloody gall,' I said.

'Aha!' cried he, unabashed, 'here's four foine specimens of manhood I've got a'comin' – Jesus, they're all skin and bone,' and he felt my bicep with one hand and waved the guard away with the other.

'It is as you desired, Sahib,' said Basra, and bowed low. 'You will please sign for them?' and Caleb did so.

After the guard had gone, I said, 'By God, Caleb, I've a mind to strangle you now, and swing for it.'

'Is that a fact?' came the reply, and he was as full of life and cheek as ever. 'And for my part I've a wish to wallop your jaw for talkin' to a priest in that manner,' and he bowed low to the others. 'Being once in holy orders, I'm a pure-tongued chap, see? But once I start I can strip the varnish off communion pews,' and he added, 'do ye think I can work bloody miracles?'

'You're nothing but a two-timing skunk!'

'This is the ironmaker man?' asked the Pole, and Sergeant explained.

'Then what do you want with us?' he asked.

'Just follow me and cut the gabble,' said Caleb.

Through the market-place we went and into the furnace area, and here three bloomeries were simmering; little squat furnaces, top-filled and raked at the hearths, and the Hindu labour, seeing Caleb coming, began to scurry.

Now, in a quiet place away from eyes, he sat on a boulder;

we, in our rags, squatted about him.

'Listen,' said he. 'Jesus protect me, for I loosed meself down into the pit of the Amir's iniquity, but now I'm after making a break for it. Five years I've made iron here, and when the bastard gets back from slave-catching this time, your lives, and mine, won't be worth a fig – ye hear me?'

'I hear you, but I don't trust you,' I replied, and his face screwed up into the old happy merriment.

'Can you trust anybody in this accursed place, Iestyn? Listen, I'm ye best bet, and you know it. It's time we all made a break for it, and if you turn me offer down you've got a ridge tile loose.'

Wigan, already tiring of him, said, 'Look, will you cut the cackle. If you're going to help us outta here, can you just tell us how in words of two syllables?'

'Just this, me lads,' said Caleb, and lowered his voice. 'The Amir's about to begin a different policy. The Russians are threatening invasion from the north and Vicky Victoria's startin' to bang the war drums again . . .'

'And so?'

'And so, when he gets back from his slave-catching this time, he's knocking off every white face he can find east of the Oxus River.'

There was a silence, and the Pole said, 'This could be true. My informers tell me that my Russian friends under Colonel Buteyov are beginning to pull out of the harem rooms.'

'That's it,' added Caleb. 'The Russians return to Moscow, the Jews to Israel and the British agents are off back to London. The writing's on the wall, my lovelies. It's time to go.'

I said, 'You mean we break out, and take you with us!'

'That's it, me darlin' – you've got the muscle. I do the planning.'

'And save your own skin!'

The Pole pushed me aside. 'It do not matter. It is good. More, it is excellent! We all save each other, eh?' and he put his arm around Caleb's shoulders.

Wigan said quietly, 'It sounds all right, but I reckon they'll shoot the lot of us.'

'Isn't it better than jumping off an eighty-foot tower?'

207

'The Huzrut cannot kill all of us.'

'The Huzrut?'

'The Amir – the King,' said Caleb, and we gathered closer about him like plotters crouching over a bomb.

'When do we go?'

Said Caleb, 'When ye guarantee me safe conduct and delivery into the arms of me friend and comrade, the Dost Mohammed Khan of Kabul—'

I interjected, 'I offered you that once, remember?'

'Then I'll see ye all safely back into the bosoms of your lovin' families,' finished Caleb. 'Are ye on?'

'Reluctantly.'

'Arrah, me lovely fella, don't be like that,' said he, and he tipped up his whisky flask and drank deep, watching me.

'A mass break-out?' said the Pole. 'When, you say?'

'The day after tomorrow,' replied Caleb, 'before the Amir gets back from the wars. Listen, this is the plan . . . ' and he winked at the sun.

'First there will be a very large explosion,' whispered Caleb.

'An explosion?'

'We will arrange to blow up the furnaces.'

The Pole said, 'To blow up things, mister, you need gunpowder.'

'I've got ten pounds of it under me bed.'

'Jesus, he means it,' muttered Wigan, his eyes growing large.

'Ten pounds under me bed,' repeated Caleb, 'and I'll bury it where it's convenient for you to find it. Blowing the furnaces is your job, you're a shot-firer.' He prodded me.

'Are you on the level?'

Caleb purpled and became terse, saying, 'Don't put your airs and graces on me, darlin', I'm too old in the tooth. Straight and forthright – I swear it by the Holy Grail.'

I replied, eyeing him, 'Time was I trusted you, you twisted little sod.'

The Pole said urgently, 'Please do not quarrel. When does this happen?'

'The day after tomorrow. That's the twenty-seventh. The Amir's due back on Sunday.'

'There'll be a row when those furnaces explode,' said Wigan.

'That's the idea! A diversion, to allow us to get away.'

'Folks are going to get killed.'

'Scores,' said Caleb. 'It makes me soul hobble to think of it, poor sods.'

'There'll be even more dead if we do nothing,' said the Pole evenly.

Caleb tossed two keys on a ring to Sergeant. 'Your job is to release the fort prisoners – Iestyn will take care of the ones down the Black Well – just kill the guards, open the door and lead them to the armoury – the smaller key opens it, and there's always a dozen or so spare *jezails* in there; let them loose to fire in all directions. We need panic.'

Exclaimed Wigan, 'The guards'll shoot holes in us!'

'It's the chance we take – the more prisoners we can arm, the better; the greater the stampede, the better our chances.' He turned to the Pole.

'You are good with horses, I heard say. This time you collect camels. There's a dozen racing camels in the transport compound. I want them waiting by the East Gate ten minutes after sundown. You got that?'

It was a different Irishman. Even the accent had diminished; he was strong, purposeful; for this is the time when the leader rises, and it was Caleb.

'How many of us are breaking out?'

'Hundreds, if we work it right.'

A silence came to us. We looked from one to the other.

I asked, 'What about you, Caleb – have you got a job?' and he tapped his forehead.

'I've got the brains, you've got the brawn. I've only one ambition, to get me carcass back to Kabul before this murderin' king knocks me off. Are ye with me, or ag'in me – make up your mind.'

People were beginning to notice us sitting there, so under Caleb's bawled instructions we got up and joined the Hindu labour in raking out and loading ash trams now lumbering into the area.

'What happens if we do get clear?' I asked Caleb, before Basra came to collect us for the march back to prison.

'We make for the river.'

I said, with veiled sarcasm, 'Don't tell me you've got a boat waiting.'

'It's been waiting this past month, since the day the Amir went mad. What happens to you and your foreign lot I don't give a damn, me boy, but Caleb's taking these old bones back to the beloved country.'

I still didn't trust him.

32

Luckily for me, Caleb's wish for self-preservation was made
stronger by my arrival in Bokhara. Also, while his intellect
was pickled in alcohol, it yet possessed a sense of morality
that demanded release from the dictates of his Amir. Later,
Caleb acknowledged that his change of attitude had come
with the realization that his King was mad; that the creeping
paralysis of the man's brain was now total.

Further, explained Caleb, my suffering, more than
anything, had done much to convince him that the sooner I
was out of Bokhara and back in Kabul, the better; this I
certainly didn't believe.

'Can you trust him?' asked the Pole, as if voicing my doubts.

Dawn was breaking, and we were being whipped out of
our prison straw for another day of labour.

'In the past I could,' I whispered back.

'We're dead ducks if he goes off the boil,' said Wigan.

Sergeant, already up and waiting, added, 'If I finish up on
a charge sheet before Basra, that fornicatin' old sod'll be the
first to collect it,' and he held up a hairy fist.

We were rousted by a shrieking Basra and his guards, who,
as usual, hit out at anything handy until they got us into line,
a drooping, exhausted batch of men: we were then led out
into a morning of pelting rain and lowering clouds.

The market-place was already alive with an abundance of
new slaves; the merchant population again expectant with
hopes of profit on a typical Bokhara morning.

211

But there existed also an unusual air of jocularity, almost as if the peasant population was inexplicably expecting a change to come when the slaves, chained in groups, were taken to the platforms for the daily auctions.

Entertainers had arrived; flocking in from outlying villages: tumblers and acrobats, sword-swallowers and fire-eaters displayed their antics with more than usual gusto; dancing bears and chained tigers went through their pathetic programmes to the cracking of whips: parakeets screeched and song-birds sang from gilded cages in the burnishing glow of an awakening day.

I took my place in the line of prisoners under the eagle eyes of squat Pathan guards, whose passions could be instantly aroused even by a well-meaning glance. And Basra Topshibashi, happily unaware that he had but a few hours left in which to make peace with his Maker, squatted crosslegged on a boulder and dozed in peaceful somnolence; through drooping lids he contemplated the long line of hammers rising and falling in the sun, one of which was mine.

'Close up the ranks,' whispered the Pole, which was my signal, and men about me obeyed: sinking low on my haunches I raced some ten yards to an overhanging bluff of rock in this, the first test of Caleb's fidelity; and went down on all fours, scrambling like a dog after a bone into the loose earth. Instantly, I found what I sought – a small parcel wrapped with rice-paper; within it were three packets of shot-firer, gunpowder sausages, buried exactly where Caleb had promised.

Momentarily, I crouched, raising a hand to the labouring prisoners: and saw Sergeant's fist shoot out, sending Wigan headlong: shrieking abuse, Wigan rose and flung himself on the Pole, bearing him to the ground. And in a moment Basra, the dozing fool, was off his haunches and among them, lashing out with his whip. Cries filled the morning as the prisoners attacked one another; in the diversion I ran out of my cover and, crouching, sped from boulder to boulder, and did not stop until, unseen, I had reached the confines of Caleb's furnace compound. Here the Hindu labour was working at double time, getting out a record production to celebrate the Amir's impending return. And Caleb, as promised, had stoked the three furnaces almost to melting-point: lambent flame was licking up from the fireboxes even to the maws, where the wheelbarrow top-fillers were working furiously.

A black pall was already billowing over the town.

Casually, I took my place among the compound workers; with my turban well down to avoid detection, I joined a gang in pushing ash trams all day, until shadows began to grow with approaching dusk.

At dusk, I knew, the overseers would tap the furnaces; and at the moment I expected, Caleb appeared looking pompous and full of authority.

'Come on, come on! More coal, more coal!'

His appearance was the signal for increased activity, yet the furnace bases were already glowing red. Soon, the Bokhara sky would be stricken with rainbow colours; a configuration and dazzlement that would turn night into day.

'Rodders out!' roared Caleb. 'Come on rodders!'

Three came running with their firing-irons; the moulders stood by to rake off the sludge. And Caleb deliberately looked over his shoulder in my direction. It was a signal. With the gunpowder pellets hidden in my rags, I moved closer to the first furnace.

Seconds passed; the sun sank lower. In my mind's eye I saw Sergeant, the Pole, Wigan and the other prisoners waiting to attack; all casting anxious eyes at the sinking sun.

The area about me now was a buzz of industry; slag wagons coming and going, top-fillers steadying their wheel-barrows above the gaping maws, and the compound was filled with the hoarse commands of the overseers.

Within a group of half-naked bodies I moved with an unconcern I did not feel, and the spit was dry in my mouth: many here were about to die; if things went badly, I might not survive.

Nearer now, and the heat of the fireboxes was scalding to my face; each overseer, upon Caleb's orders, was pressurizing his furnace to the limit of its acceptance, and the brick walls

213

and base plates were shuddering to the bubbling iron.
Loaded to the brim, all three were sighing like cows in
labour, and I acted when I heard Caleb shout in Pashto:

'Right! Knock out the bungs!'

The labourers relaxed, their bodies shining with sweat as
the rodders went forward: the moulders backed away.

Nobody appeared to notice my first gunpower cartridge
sail up through the swirling steam and smoke. To my horror
there came a moment of delay, as if the furnace I had
attacked was astonished at its impending destruction. Then
it blew up with a detonation of smoke and coruscation that
sent me head over heels: a glittering explosion of sparkling
heat shooting skyward in a brilliance equal to the sun's
corona, lighting up the world.

A moment of silence, then wails and curses filled the acrid
air; and, as the smoke cleared, I saw bodies writhing all over
the compound.

Climbing to my feet I approached the second furnace and
tossed the second pellet up into its smoke: instantly this one
exploded, sending a column of flame skyward. I ran;
swerving through the flailing bodies to the third and last
furnace. The last pellet ascribed an arc against the dying sun,
before detonating in another ball of fire.

Men were rising about me now; one with a firing-iron,
quicker witted than the rest, tried to trip me with it in my
headlong flight towards the Black Well; this, my next task,
to free its prisoners.

Caleb was already here. I saw behind him the guards: they,
slowly recovering from the shock waves, were climbing to
their feet. I kicked one flat, picked up his musket and
clubbed another as he sought to rise.

'Keep 'em off,' said Caleb, as calm as ice, and began to
lower the bucket, while I, reloading, kept up sniping fire at
any guard presenting a target.

Prisoners were running in all directions; the auction
platform slaves, their cut ropes dangling, were coming in
droves out of the market-place, knocking down and
trampling guards who tried to halt them: in a headlong,
shrieking flight they came; men, women and children crying

hysterically at their unexpected release.

The Black Well guards, impelled from behind by the moving mass of slaves and merchants, were also on the move, their impetus hastened by collapsing charpoys, whose awnings were on fire. And onto this crammed panic dropped the molten ash of the exploded furnaces: screams filled the dusk; the world was now alight with an incinerating brilliance as the native quarter sent up tongues of fire.

Prisoners were escaping from the Black Well, staggering blindly after their pitch-dark captivity: and the guards fell before their fury.

I was hauling yet another tattered inmate out of the Black Well when I heard exultant shouts and turned to see the notorious Basra, his arms and legs gyrating in space, plummeting from the crown of the Execution Tower – flung from it by jubilant prisoners. Old debts were being paid off, old scores avenged in those five minutes when Bokhara struck off the Amir's chains.

Yaboos, mules, donkeys and camels were leaping at their tethering ropes in terror, straining to escape from their pounds: harem girls, running in scantily attired groups, were seeking shelter from the molten ash; and Black Well guards, once cock-a-hoop and arrogant, were now going down it head first, thrown by jeering prisoners. It was a reversal of all that had gone before; a Nemesis where vanquished became victors and tyrants paid with their lives; all over the town, said Caleb, heads were being lopped off at thirteen to the dozen: slave merchants, still arrayed in finery, were upon their knees praying for mercy to slaves wielding bright scimitars, while the ancient market-place, the centre of Bokhara's misery, was being burned to the ground.

At the East gate of the town the Pole and Sergeant were waiting; with the assistance of half a dozen excited urchins they were harnessing five of the Amir's finest camels.

'Where's Wigan?' I demanded, breathless.

'Wigan caught it,' said Sergeant.

'Basra shot him before he got ten yards,' added the Pole. 'You go now quick and find the river,' and he pointed south.

'And you?'

'I go in a different direction, my friends. I take the road that leads to Moscow. There I will look for my friend, Colonel Buteyov of the Russian deputation. But a request of you before we part, please? You will grant me the little prayer book that belonged to Captain Connolly? For this is how I learned my Christian prayers.'

'If you see that it is returned to his sister in England; her address is within it,' and I gave it to him.

'I, in turn, will give it to Colonel Buteyov, who knew Connolly well: he will arrange it, all this I promise.'

The red glow of the Bokhara fires could still be seen behind us, as Caleb, Sergeant and I reined our camels towards the Oxus River.

Here, hidden in reeds, was the boat Caleb had promised; a small wickerwork and skin affair used by generations of Sunni Moslems for the export of Persian lambskins along the basins of the great rivers.

'What about you?' I asked Sergeant.

'I go overland, for I need these camels for the plough. And I will plough the land pretty, for I'm sick of war and have always wanted for a farmer. Also, I have the bellies of two women to feed in Seh Baba, and I will see to it proper.'

'God speed ye,' said Caleb, and gave him fifty rupees.

'I can do him better than that,' said I, and told of the grave of the man I had buried up in the mountains, and where he could find a bag of diamonds.

'Beware that old Nasrullah don't catch you ag'in,' warned Caleb.

'He'll 'ave to get up in the mornin' next time, the bugger,' said Sergeant and, riding one camel and pulling the others, he padded them eastward along the river.

Now we were alone in darkness, Caleb Benedict and I, on the breast of the glittering Oxus, and the moon was a silver crescent floating on cloudy seas.

33

Kabul, 1852

With Dost Mohammed Khan steadfastly occupying the throne of Afghanistan, the ambitions of Akbar Khan, his eldest son, had simmered into delusions of distant grandeur, until ended by his death in 1847.

And with that puppet of the British, Shah Shuja, also mouldering in his grave, it appeared that the Dost was safe from ambitious interlopers. But two other sons had love of kingship.

Therefore there still existed the threat of internecine wars; such pretenders being prepared to poison grandfathers to gain royal recognition, and anyone standing in their way would receive short shrift: one of these, of course, being the Dost's granddaughter, the Pearl of the Age, Princess Durrani.

This was the situation she inherited – and therefore to some extent which I shared – as, with Caleb lounging ostentatiously in a silk-lined palanquin (the Dost, now again on his throne, had sent an armed escort under Karendeesh to meet us on our journey from Bokhara) we approached the environs of Kabul.

But there was more to this than family squabbling.

Over a decade ago, when the Dost was ousted by the British, he had sought sanctuary in Bokhara; a move so dangerous (our old enemy, Nasrullah, was King there) that the Shah of Persia warned Nasrullah that he would hold him responsible should anything happen to his friend, the Dost. Nasrullah, planning the Dost's death, therefore released him, meanwhile bribing a ferryman on the Oxus River to 'drown him like a dog'.

Happily, the Dost swam safely ashore, and escaped to Samarkand, disguised as a woman.

Nasrullah, true to form, never forgave the Dost for surviving, and little happened in neighbouring Afghan- istan of which the tyrant was not informed. Certainly, Caleb's escape from Bokhara did little to endear him to his old employer; and I was soon to find that my own name was included on a list of those with whom Nasrullah hoped to renew acquaintance.

Nor was I completely unworried about the Dost's acceptance of me, despite the fact that he had sent an armed escort under Karendeesh to guide us home.

'I wonder,' I asked Caleb, 'how the Dost will receive us . . .?'

'With all the palaver of a long lost friend, me darlin',' came the reply, and he puffed portentously on a cigar the Dost had sent him and, bouncing along, laid back in the cushions.

'Ye see, Iestyn, 'tis a measure of the standard a fella sets himself. Call yourself a puddler like you do, and the nearest foreman will kick your arse from bum-hole to breakfast time. But call ye'self an inventor, like me, and they'll lay the fruits o' the kingdom at ye feet. Ach, dear me, it's a wonderful world! Don't ye realize that we're about to make Afghan history? When that gun blasts off from the Bala Hissar, it'll send the pair of us on a rocket to the stars.'

'The *Zabber Jang*?' I waved him down. 'That monstrosity will be the death of you, me included.'

'Is that a fact?' and he eyed me from the palanquin, pointing his cigar at my face. 'I'm tellin' ye, Iestyn, it's a weapon that will change the face o' the eastern world; the king who owns it will raise a plaque to the man who invented it – me, Caleb Benedict!'

I sent him a look of disgust. 'So you're enjoying yourself, just because you've invented a bloody gun?'

218

'Ay, ay, and for puttin' one over that filthy rapscallion Nasrullah, for if ever I saw a soul wi' both elbows out of its sleeves, it's his – may he rot in Hell.'

'Which is where you'll land, if ever he lays hands on you.'

'Aye, perhaps,' and he sank back in the cushions and puffed smoke at the sun, then tipped up his gin flask, gurgling. 'Meanwhile, me lad, it's a marvellous life, so it is.'

For him perhaps: for me it had been a nightmare, hauling him, protesting every yard, from Bokhara to Kabul.

With Karendeesh riding on one side of the palanquin, and me on the other, we had jogged through a beautiful day. Larks were fluttering above us as omens of peace, I recall, but corncrakes were croaking their harsh messages (this according to Afghan lore) from the marshes of the Kabul River . . . And Karendeesh sat his big mare as contained and silent as an Eastern potentate; a man clearly deliberating my obnoxious presence: the weapons of the escort clashed and jangled on the clear summer air.

All that day Caleb drank like a fish, and when we climbed the slope of the Bala Hissar at Kabul, he was three sheets in the wind; so tipsy that I had to steady him as he stood before the Court.

Caleb Benedict was the only man I had known who could stand drunkenly before a Moslem king, and live.

'Take him away and make him sober,' commanded the Dost.

But that was three years ago, and now I left Caleb's death-bed with a sense of loss that little could compensate: a tippler and a rogue was he, yet there had existed between us that bond of male friendship that few men enjoy: an inner sanctity of affection that the loves of women can neither invade nor understand: no physical contact being needed to bolster its sincerity.

'Mr Benedict is dead,' I said to Karendeesh.

'I know,' he replied distantly, 'and the King grieves.'

Had this been true, I had seen no sign of it: Caleb, born to the bottle, had died of it: the alcohol proving as effective as

219

any potion devised by Court murderers. His illness was long and sad, during which time I had succeeded him as the official furnace master, and now enjoyed the title of 'Furnace Engineer Extraordinary to the Dost'.

Having done Caleb's job to the King's satisfaction, there was now, it appeared, little reason to grieve over the loss of a drunken Irishman whom we buried with full military honours in the furnace compound; with a gravestone at his head of cast iron strong enough to hold up the next Tory government, said he. 'And make sure of that in me name,' said Caleb, 'for I'll be waitin' and watchin', me lovely fella.'

Karendeesh said now, 'The Dost wishes to see you officially, to express his regret upon Mr Benedict's death.'

I did not reply.

Everything had changed since last I was in Kabul: the remnants of British occupation having now been swept away, only the racecourse remained as a training plateau for the Afghan military. But the greatest change of all I found in Karendeesh.

No longer the beggar boy of the paddle-steamer, this one; the tear-stained urchin whose humility was as apparent as his devotion to Durrani. I wondered if his love for her persisted, because in these last three years he had scarcely mentioned her: as if her absence from Court (she had again removed to the Royal House in Persia) had taken her from his mind.

In my presence he evinced an arrogance that did not become his station, for as Furnace Master I was superior to him in title.

About a week after Caleb's funeral, I met Karendeesh in a courtyard of the palace: earlier I had been supervising the casting of Caleb's *Zabber Jang*, named after the great artillery piece, *The Widow Maker*, which had been captured at Ghazni during the Battle of Retribution ten years earlier: having gained Caleb's respect by redesigning it from its early prototype, I had thereby gained favour in the eyes of the King.

Now, in the courtyard I looked Karendeesh over; and he

220

was worth a glance, for the women of the court made big eyes and giggled among themselves at his appear- ance; these he ignored with studied disregard.

Now he enjoyed mature manhood, the years having filled him with muscular intent: he wore his uniform of King's Messenger with a grace so splendid that it raised even my male, disrespectful eyes: he was as handsome as a god.

Yet there existed upon his face a sadness that neither rank nor luxury could erase. Although the lower harem was open to any Court official of rank or distinction, never was Karendeesh found within its silk-lined walls, though I had often fallen from such grace within the urgency of manhood.

Brave in battle, he yet retained a personal isolation; a man of frugal habits and adornment, for he wore no badges of insignia: surviving many captures (always the fatal risk to messengers) he had contrived legendary escapes.

Now he said, 'Yesterday, Sahib, I reported that the King wished you to appear before him, yet you did not come.'

I replied carelessly, 'In my good time. He grants me dispensation.'

'No, Sahib. The Dost orders, we obey.'

'You have heard of the *Zabber Jang*?' I asked, and he nodded.

'I was casting its muzzle; do I leave ten tons of molten iron to cool while I take coffee?'

Karendeesh stood silently; then said, inexplicably, 'It is necessary, says the Princess Durrani, that you stay in good favour with her grandfather.'

I raised my eyes to his. 'She said that? When?'

'A week ago, when I was privileged to speak with her.'

'You were in Persia?'

'In Persia, Sahib.'

My agitation at this news must have betrayed me. 'She . . . she is well, Karendeesh?'

He lowered his face. 'Durrani is well, and sends her respects to you,' and he hesitated. 'Soon . . . she will return to Kabul.'

'That is not possible. She belongs totally to Persia.'

'Not now, Sahib, for Persia has rejected her. In the time of a decade, she has produced no son.'

'But a daughter, I heard. Did she not birth a daughter?'

'A daughter, yes, but it died deformed. But no son, and her husband rejects her. Now it is necessary that he takes another wife, it is understandable.'

'When does she return to Kabul?'

'Within months, at the time of hoar frost, after White Dews Falling.' He spoke the old language.

'In springtime?'

For reply, he bowed, saying, 'Sahib, the return of the Princess will bring danger. For you I do not worry. I put my head on my pillow and do not dream of your pain, but for Durrani's pain to come I suffer night- mares.'

'She'll be all right. Don't lose sleep about it.'

'You will not pursue her?'

He was exasperating; one moment the man, next the boy, and he said, 'She loves music! I have learned the lute, and will play to her, also on the lyre. It is years since she went away.'

I said, 'If they do not want her in Baghdad, it is right that she should return to her people. Meanwhile, I shall keep away for the sake of her grandfather, and you should do the same. She'll have had enough of men to last her a lifetime.'

'Of course. She must not endure further sadness.'

'Nor people like you playing bloody lutes and serenading under her window. She is not for either of us.'

He touched his forehead and retreated backwards.

To this day I do not know why it was, but I always left Karendeesh with an enduring sense of my own deficiency; it could have had something to do with his damnable purity.

Now he paused, saying, 'Oh, Sahib, forgive me – I have just remembered. My Princess sends this letter to you, and for your eyes alone, said she,' and he gave me a little blue envelope heavily scented with jasmine.

'Naturally, you've read it,' I said, taking it.

'Sahib,' came the reply, 'only with my eyes. It is a private letter, though in case I am captured, it is better for a good *chuprassy* to commit all correspondence to memory, whether or not it is written on rice-paper, which can be eaten.'

'Christ,' I said.

222

'My beloved Iestyn', the letter began, which was a pretty good start, I thought, for the wife of a Persian prince to her ex-lover: no wonder it had put the shakes up Karendeesh.

He said now, 'You will forgive me, Sahib, but I beg you not to do to her the thing she asks you to do in this letter . . .'

'Not unless she insists on it.'

34

When the King arrived in the furnace area, I halted the work and stood to attention before him.

In his youth a wild one, age and conservatism had mellowed his capricious nature; proof of his early aggression lay in Akbar Khan, his dead son, who today stands as a paladin of Afghan legend.

Born of the noble house of the Quizilbash, and calling himself Khan, and not Shah, his intriguing allowed him to survive in a state where treachery was abundant: his love of country besetting him, he had returned from his exile by the British in Ludhiana and Calcutta, claiming that it was his ambition to abandon war.

I bowed low as the King approached with his bodyguards.

'You are well, Mortymer?' he asked in Persian.

For reply I touched my head and heart.

He added, 'I gave instruction that you should visit me immediately upon the death of Mr Benedict. You did not receive this order?'

I replied, 'It was impossible to leave the casting of so big an article, Sire. I was about to come.'

He accepted this.

'The gun is here?'

'In the casting house, your Majesty,' and I led him into it.

'You will explain to me what is happening now?' and I did so.

The process of cannon-making has been handed down from ancient times.

First a pit adjacent to the furnace is excavated, and within this the clay mould of the gun is built and vertically lowered.

On tapping the furnace, the liquid iron is then channelled into the clay mould, in which a circular sand-shaft descends to form the cannon's bore, and the impurities of the iron – the slag and sludge – floating to the top, are then creamed off by the puddlers; after which the iron mass is left to cool.

When cold, the rough gun can be then lifted by a hoist, and is placed horizontally on a lathe, after the clay mould has been broken away. Then comes the art of grinding the gun to shape and size, and the boring of the muzzle: this is achieved by turning the cannon, not the lathe, clockwise; the essence of the science being the lathe's cutting edge – the hard tool invented by Wilkinson which possesses in its steel about one in twenty parts of carbon. I knew the process well, having seen hundreds of cannons so bored at Crawshay's works at Cyfarthfa; he who supplied cannon to Nelson's ships-of-the-line.

The King commented, 'They tell me that you are superior even to Mr Benedict in this knowledge.'

'The manufacture of the boring tool is the secret, Sire.'

'And the rifling of which I hear tell, what is this?'

I replied, 'It has been discovered that by grooving the inside of a musket's barrel, the bullet, when fired, can be made to rotate; thus increasing range and accuracy.'

'And it is your intention to so groove the barrel of my beautiful *Zabber Jang*?'

'That is not possible: I intend to groove the shot.'

'How? The shot is round.'

'The shot, as invented by Benedict, is melon-shaped: he has named it a projectile.'

'It will work?'

'It works excellently on smaller prototypes.'

'And the range of such a weapon?'

'Over two thousand yards.'

'Twice the range of a modern cannon-ball?'

'More than twice.'

He drew himself up. 'Such a gun would revolutionize war!'

'And bring peace.'

'Now tell me its disadvantages.'

'There are none that I can foresee.'

He asked, 'Our modern cannons continue to burst, do they not? Occasioning greater casualties to those who fire it than their enemies.'

'I have eliminated that danger with the *Zabber Two*. Premature bursting is caused by air-bubbles in the iron during casting: the casing is weakened by such porous metal; there will be no premature explosions with this gun.'

'You can give proof of this?'

'The proof will be seen during its testing.'

'When will that be?'

'The gun will be erected on the old Racecourse by the end of the year.'

'And up on the palace heights, when will it be stationed?'

'A few months after that, Your Majesty.'

'You stake your reputation upon this?'

'I stake my life.'

He smiled at me and his eyes were good in the brightness of the sun.

'Let us pray to Allah that that will not prove necessary. You have done well, Mortymer. Now allow the men to carry on, for there is not a moment to be wasted; the Amir of Bokhara is a watchful enemy. It could have changed the politics of Central Asia had this weapon been available to him, instead of to peaceful Afghanistan. You did well in bringing me the genius of Caleb Benedict, and your own.'

I bowed and he strolled away, his escort following; then suddenly he turned, beckoning.

'Ah, yes, but I would also speak with you upon another subject; you will please make yourself available?'

'When?'

'Now,' said the King.

To my surprise he dismissed his escort, and led me away from the bustle of the furnaces; here on a mossy bank he sat, indicating that I should sit beside him.

'It is said that to make good honey a young bee needs beautiful flowers: certainly that was true in my own youth, when I spread my net far and wide to enjoy the arms of the maidens . . .'

226

I made no reply, but he raised a silencing finger.

'In that misspent youth I learned that one man's conquest is another man's heresy, for my parents taught me little of the arts of courtship, though they were excellent when it came to their own desires – shoemakers' children are always the worst shod . . .

'But at middle age – which is around your age now, I began to learn discretion . . . .'

His Sepoys, turbaned in scarlet and smartly puttied (a remnant of the British flag who had deserted to his service), marched past with fine dignity, and he gave them a weary glance of disapproval, saying, 'I once had a *bobigree* in Ludhiana, a Hindu servant of some quality whom, I discovered, was lying with his neighbour's wife; I had him executed. "Speak clearly and willingly," I told him. "Even a *bobigree* has the right to know why he is dying", and he replied:

' "Latsahip, my lord and master, have I not sinned only in the manner of many men? The world would soon die for lack of people if every *bobigree* who divided another's wife should lose his head for it."

' "You are not dying for the fornication, *bobigree*," I told him, "but because the sin was performed beneath my roof."

'Happily, he acknowledged the ethic, and, baring his neck to the axe, expired without further protest. You see the connection?'

'With what, Sire?' I asked and he sighed deeply in his beard.

'You British are uncultured when it comes to ana- logies, which accounts for your custom of leaving calling-cards as proof that you are still alive. But be alive to what I am saying now, Mortymer, for your presence here is only tolerated.'

I met his icy stare; he continued.

'When in Ludhiana, I did my best to convince you of the dangers of consorting with one of my relatives, but this advice you chose to ignore—'

I interjected. 'The advice was taken, Your Majesty.'

'Only because you had no option; I exiled you to India, did I not? But now Fate decrees that you return to my service, and still as the favourite of my grand- daughter.

227

Listen! It is not the will of Allah that the Princess Durrani should be so minded; nor is it written on the wind that her desires should be violated by a white-faced Feringhee who is neither of her nationality nor nobility.'

His temper was rising; it would have proved unwise to interrupt him.

'Yours is an imperious arrogance, for you are more likely to gather water from the moon than gain a position in my royal house – other than that of a menial cannon-maker.'

His voice subsided into heavy breathing, and he eyed me, his spade beard trembling.

I said quietly, 'Have no fear, Your Majesty. I will not impose further upon your trust. Meanwhile, the Princess remains safely in Persia . . .'

'Unfortunately, she will not! She will be back in Kabul within the month, being as headstrong as she is obstinate; her marriage has failed and she is again my responsibility. See to it, Mortymer, that she is not yours.'

He rose, and I with him, and he said, 'Women of the coin can be yours in plenty; I have told you this before. When your work is finished here, you can return to your own people with my consent. Meanwhile, be warned. I owe you the genius of Benedict: your own ability also serves me, and for this I am grateful. But do not break your word, or my granddaughter will die by stoning in the market-place – a just death for all princesses who betray their blood. And you will end in the hands of the impalers.'

Without another glance, he left me.

The Dost was wrong about the date of Durrani's return; within days she was back in Kabul.

35

I was not surprised when the Dost moved me out of my private rooms in his harem quarter in the Bala Hissar (living there was the prerogative of very special guests) and settled me comfortably miles away from Durrani on the other side of Kabul; understandably, while needing my technical ability, he didn't want me in close proximity with his granddaughter . . . but I was a little surprised to discover that my new accommodation was none other than Abaya's ornate and beautiful little hunting lodge at Seh Baba.

Wizened old Abaya had fallen from grace since his attempt, when Big Rhys was killed there, to hand Durrani over to the ambitious Akbar Khan: and with Akbar's early death, his adherents had also reaped the dislike Abaya left behind him: more than one, apparently, had gone to an early grave.

Abaya, who had long taken to the hills, possessed a good memory, and I was reminded of this on entering his lodge from which he had been forced to flee the King's vengeance. A note was delivered to me at dead of night, reading:

Most esteemed friend and comrade,
one who stands so highly in Royal esteem:
be aware that one day we will meet again.

Not if I could help it, I reflected, and tore the note into pieces and dropped it on the floor.

Had I known what the future had in store for me, I would have treated it with more respect.

*

It was a traumatic experience to stand in the place where Big Rhys had died nearly ten years ago, with nostalgia quickened by unchanged surroundings: still the same hunting relics on the walls, still the Persian carpets and talismen of amber and jade. And I paused in my walk around the rooms, now emptied, thank God, of the obscene Abaya and gigantic Gargoa, to kneel and examine a dull black mark on a fringe of Chinese silk; this was the stain of Big Rhys's blood.

Touching it with the tips of my fingers I knew again the warmth of his personality; and was filled with an overpowering belief that, should I call his name, he would appear like a genie from the grave, and stand smiling before me.

To compliment me on my life to date? I wondered; or to disclaim knowledge of me?

Had I proved worthy of his sacrifice?

Would he, for instance, have sought relief in the brown arms of harem girls who arrived half-naked at a snap of my fingers? Would he have dispensed his manhood, as I had done, in the face of a lost Durrani . . . to hard-breathing females and the acrobatic antics of chinking Hindu tarts? Or sought a single favour of the womanhood of Asia, where a female is the cheapest commodity on earth?

It was doubtful.

Men like Rhys, I thought then, though of limited intelligence, are schooled in native charm when it comes to mates: taking them in marriage with gentleness, enjoying and honouring them by natural demands; no ghosts looked over Rhys's shoulder when he was making love to his fat little missus: no poetic stanzas, vaporous whispers and half-baked poetic notions would fly to his simple, respectable mind.

As for me, I had pandered to my professed sensitivity; leaving it to others to regret my frivolity and ignore my pranks. It was a dilemma of my nature from which my adolescence had been forged – the absolute necessity to be one and everything to any woman if the chance obtained:

230

caprice had always been my mortal enemy, when the flutter of a black-lashed eye could send me pitter-patter into love affairs I never really wanted.

Harem women had been tossed in my way by an uncaring society: Big Rhys, for all his primitive appearance, would have handled his life less profanely.

Complete with this continued indiscipline, in the knowledge that a woman, or six, was available on a signal, I decided, on entry into Abaya's house, to abandon what principles were left to me and devoutly and thoroughly enjoy in full the remainder of my wanton years . . . in the absence of a beloved who might have anchored me to decency . . .

Mari had left me for another; Durrani was lost to me on pain of death: I would have to be a congenital idiot, I told myself, to deny myself the comfort of a harem lady – one a night if the call required – each and every one of them young and beautiful (even if their charm was a little diluted) in the face of what otherwise appeared a future of monkish irascibility at the randy old age of thirty-three.

Now, at the door of the main chamber, I clapped my hands and a Hindu servant appeared: dressed in white, and yellow of turban, he bowed to me; a man schooled in diplomacy, since he went with the furniture.

'Yes, Sahib?'

'Send me a woman,' I said.

'Which woman?'

Amazingly, he was tipsy, having been at a drink he called 'toddy', the unfermented juice of the Palmyra tree: his name was Khansaman, meaning 'House Steward', and he once was the slave of a Maharaja, a real pukka-wallah who had treated him abominably: he drank to forget his past, this one, so my manner was always lenient.

'Any woman,' I said.

He stood to attention, swaying before me. 'It is wrong for the Sahib to call for any woman; would he have me go to the Bazaar and bring back two with only one leg?'

'Don't be a fool, Khansaman, you know what I mean.'

'Subara, may I suggest? The girl of the bright hair and breasts like melons? Always she do send me very trembly myself, the little bitch.'

'She'll do – send a pankee for her.'

He bowed subserviently, nearly falling over. I said, 'If a vizier sees you in this state, Khan, you will lose your balls.'

'I know, Sahib. You are a very kind master, so you will not tell him. What about Lakita, the harem attendant of the large eyes and long black hair? She is as beautiful as a Hindu girl should be; indeed, if my caste was lower, I would fancy her myself.'

'Any girl,' I said and, bowing, he left me.

For a man seeking love when love is not available, any girl will do.

Khansaman's home was in Calcutta, on the bank of the Hoogly river, a tributary of the holy Ganges: possessing three wives, his plan of life was simple: in service first to Abaya, and now to me, he would earn enough in a year to go back to Calcutta, put his wives in the family way again, and then return to Seh Baba.

Lucky old beggar, I thought, to enjoy such marvellous substantiality.

Unlike me, who hadn't got one wife, he had something to go home to.

Cocooned in Abaya's home-bred comforts in Seh Baba, I now impatiently awaited the arrival of Subara, she of the bright hair, beautiful breasts, and the carriage of a queen: many times in the two years since I had returned to Kabul, she had brought me comfort.

She was a harem lady of Second Order who lived in the Bala Hissar, she and her family enjoying many privileges because of her beauty, though some said she was past her best at twenty-five; harem ladies being in their prime at a very early age.

Once she had lived near the Great Bazaar in Kabul City, and at the age of thirteen had been taken into Shah Shuja's harem. Most of her family had been killed in the explosion when the bazaar was blown up – surely one of the finest examples of monumental architecture in the East – the charge detonated by our Army of Retribution as revenge for the murder of Sir William MacNaghton; his mangled remains having been publicly exhibited over its arch.

Poor Subara, who now lived alone with a sister, had been walking home at the time, she said; fragmentation wounds, though slight, across her young back, gave the appearance of whip-lashing. Her beauty despoiled, she was demoted by the Shah to 'Second Order of Harem'.

Such was the fate of harem girls who, like Chinese concubines, could begin with Royalty and end up with rickshaw boys.

Within a few hours of occupying old Abaya's lodge, and with Khansaman, my servant, dutifully expecting Subara, he first turned on the water fountain within my inner chamber (making love in falling water is a delectable experience) and then hastened excitedly to answer a knock.

Clad in a single white robe, I heard the girl say at the door, 'Servant of the Master, I am not Subara for whom you have sent to serve kindness to the Great Engineer, I am her sister. She has asked me to give him the pleasures denied to her through illness.'

'*What*?'

Coming to the edge of the hall I saw Khansaman draw himself up with honest rage, and heard him cry, 'You are not Subara? Indeed, daughter of a noseless beggar, I can see from here you are not, even though you hide behind your yashmak! Away, alley cat!' and he reached for a rawhide whip on the wall.

'Wait,' I said, coming closer. 'Wait, Khansaman.'

It was her eyes.

It was her eyes above the silk covering her mouth that fixed me with a strange magnetism.

Khan cried, furious, 'But who is this whore? If she is not the sister of the beautiful Subara, for whom you would pay good money, she could be anybody – look, Master – perceive her feet – she is even pigeon-toed.'

'I am *not* pigeon-toed,' replied the girl. 'Son of a pig! Can you not see that it is only the way I am standing?'

'Also, she has not Subara's deportment, Master,' shouted Khan. 'And since she is only half the size of her sister, you will get less enjoyment for your money. What is more, she is

233

dressed like a slut!'

I said, 'You have news of Subara, your sister?'

'Only that she is ill,' came the gentle reply, 'and sends me to replace her.'

I nodded. 'It is reasonable, Khan. Take her to the servants' toilets, wash her, feed her, and then bring her to me. For a little hour she may amuse me until I can find something better.'

'But illness is in the family, Sirdar!' cried Khan, appalled. 'From her own lips she tells you! Who knows what foul disease she may bring to your noble loins. Leave, little whore, or I will have you whipped from here to Kabul!'

The girl raised her face to mine again, and I stood aside in the hall.

'Pray enter, woman.'

'Be it on your own head, Master!' yelled Khan, raising the whip.

'So shall it be.' I bowed to her. 'Enter, little whore,' and, taking her hand, led her through the hall and into the inner chamber where merrily the fountain was playing, and the rugs had been laid on the cold mosaic for my enjoyment of Subara.

Within this privacy I drew down the yashmak of the woman who called herself the sister of Subara and, pressing my mouth upon hers, sought her breasts beneath her peasant gown.

'*Durrani*!'

And took her up into my arms and laid her down upon the rugs of the floor, and entered her with all the hunger of our wasted years, while she clung to me with gasped words which beat heedlessly upon my ears.

After this I carried her again and laid her within the cooling waters of the fountain where once the young Nubian slaves of Abaya had played, disporting themselves with frequent lovers: and there cleaved to her again despite the threat of an impaling death, until the glow of Kabul City faded and the light of the moon came shining over the mountains.

36

It was dusk, and a fortnight later: the night was curled up on a couch of premature darkness. Earlier it had been a day of bone-dry heat, with the sun standing on its ear in swathes of golden corn; under its burning topaz Afghanistan shimmered and sweated.

Down in the furnace area, where Caleb was buried (he had insisted upon this five minutes before his expiry), the grinding machines were silent for lack of water; the paddle-wheels of the little brooks – usually in full spate at this time of year – were stilled.

Durrani, appearing like magic out of the raiment of the sun, stood beyond the grave where I had knelt to place fresh flowers, the little rosebuds of the hedgerows which Caleb loved.

Tethering her pony, she said, 'I thought I'd find you here – the first day of every month.'

'Caleb was a man of routine and practicality,' I answered. 'If I didn't carry out this monthly ritual, he would arise and haunt me. Which is what your grandfather will do if he finds you here.'

Because the June afternoon was one of blinding heat, I had dismissed the furnace workers; nothing could happen, anyway, until the rains came and the ravines filled for the water-wheels.

Durrani, clad in white, took off her yashmak and tossed her hair about.

'Put that thing back on – you'll be recognized.'

'You know what you are, don't you?' she asked, pertly.

I got up from Caleb's grave.

'I once heard Big Rhys call you a belt and braces man, and he's right.'

I nodded. 'I don't take unnecessary risks.'

She made a face. 'But with Grandfather away in Jahore and not due back till Tuesday, cannot the little mice play a little?' and she made sweeting noises at me with her lips.

'Not this mouse. He intends to stay alive.'

'Cannot love be all that sweeter when forbidden?'

'And all that harsher if they find us out. You wouldn't be the first Afghan princess to die by stoning.'

She wandered away, smiling at me over her shoulder.

There was a little sheltering hut on the edge of the furnace area; a place where I kept the site drawings. To this we went. I was surprised to see the pani-wallah still at his post pulling on the wind-blind; the air moved in an unusual fragrance for little summer flowers grew here on neat borders, struggling for life amid a tang of furnace sulphur. Here we sat and the blind creaked kindly above us.

'This is scarcely a place for a lovers' tryst,' said Durrani.

'It will do. Suspicions only arise when we try to meet in secret.'

Her eyes took on a hapless look. 'I have come all the way from Persia to be with you and I am beginning to think I have wasted my time. Perhaps your painted whore, Subara, would have equally served you?'

'That is a stupid thing to say!'

It was fearful here and her presence was bringing me to a testy disregard. Any passing individual could carry the news of this meeting up to the Bala Hissar, and what the viziers lacked in fact they would soon make up through espionage.

Durrani said, 'Let us go from this silly place – I was an idiot to come – and meet after dark on the road to the Bazaar? I know of a place of coolness where a cave drips water so cold that it freezes teeth in their sockets. There we can sit and dabble our feet.'

'When it is really dark, we will go,' I said. 'I'll get another horse from the stables.'

236

*

We rode silently through the darkening country and sat side by side within the silent cave; distantly could we hear the drumming music of Kabul which was beginning its night's revels.

Like a wraith of whiteness, Durrani sat; her eyes dark smudges in her high-boned cheeks, so that her face swayed before me like an undertaker's puppet.

'Tell me of your marriage to the Persian prince,' I said, and she made big eyes and hunched her shoulders like a querrulous child.

'It was a nothing marriage, you understand; nothing for him, less for me.'

'But you had a child?'

'Only a half baby girl, one scarcely formed.'

'But this was surely a proof of your love together?'

'It was not. My prince was more concerned with sleep and sweet foods. Only upon one occasion did he enter my womb, at all other occasions he was as nothing to a woman. This happens often, the doctors told me, when the blood is highly inter-bred.'

'And when you did not birth a son they cast you out?'

Durrani nodded. 'The fault is always with the woman. This wife has a dry womb and breasts of stone, they say, yet often she could spawn a family at the wink of a virile husband's eye.'

'This does not confine itself to Persia; it is the same back home in Wales,' I said. 'So you might even produce a son for me?'

'Six! I'm as normal as any other woman.'

'So I have noticed, but try not to start producing until I give the word.'

'I will do my best, but cannot guarantee it. Meanwhile, is it possible that you love me as much as you say you do? Oh, Iestyn!' and she put her arms about me and kissed my face. 'For the years we were apart you did not write to me. Week after week in Baghdad I sat watching for the couriers, but not a single letter came.'

I said, 'And while in Ludhiana I received only one from you!'

237

'I wrote many times.'

I nodded. 'It was the couriers.'

'It is that Karendeesh, you mean! My letters were written on rice-paper, so that, if captured, he could eat them before execution.'

'But not before reading them. Our Karendeesh is a marvellous original; for one so deeply in love with you, he acts like a barbarian.'

'He is not in love with me: his order came from my grandfather, and he obeys the King.'

'Where is he these days? I haven't seen him for weeks.'

'Tonight he is up in the Bala Hissar, please Allah.'

'I am not, Princess,' said a voice from the darkness. 'I am here,' and Karendeesh moved across the entrance to the cave, obliterating the moonlight.

'What the hell are you doing here?' I got up.

'Spying upon us, that is what he is doing!' said Durrani.

The reply was gentle, as he joined us in the dark. 'That is not so, Princess Durrani. It is as you said. The King orders; I obey.'

'How can he give orders when he is in Jahore?'

'The King is no longer in Jahore, Lady; earlier this evening he returned.'

'*God, no!*'

'He returned before starlight, and already he is asking for you,' said Karendeesh. ' "Where is the Princess Durrani?" he asked me. "She is walking among the fountains," I told him, "and she is worried about your safe return." '

'You told him that?'

'In your name I told him. It is necessary for you to come at once, Lady; he is in an impatient mood.'

'He suspects that we are meeting?'

'He does not, but it will be a great sadness for your people if you continue to make love with a Feringhee, as you have been doing under Abaya's roof.'

'How did you know we were there?'

'Because I followed the woman who called herself Subara. It is shameful, Sirdar,' and here he bowed to me, 'that you should seek the company of painted whores while knowing the love of our royal princess.'

Durrani went to her pony, mounted it and glared down at us, saying, 'Make your opinions known to as many as you wish, Karendeesh, but not to me, or I will drive you out of the palace!

'I gave you many letters when living in Persia to carry to the Sahib in Ludhiana, but you delivered only one: many times he wrote to me, but nothing I received. Keep out of our business, or you will end as you began – a cheap little *chuprassy* working the steamers on the Indus, where no man will give you a second glance.'

Karendeesh drew himself up. 'I am responsible to the King to protect my princess from the evil of the Feringhee; of this he has instructed. Even in death I will continue to be of service to your royal house; Afghanistan is my country, and I am of her blood.

'I know all things: I know your spoken and written words – all whispers, good and bad, are heard by Karendeesh – all intelligence comes my way concerning you. And if you do not like this, Princess, then report me to the King so he may take my head.'

He went to Durrani's pony and caught its bridle, shouting up at her, 'Meanwhile, neither of you will make another outrage upon the house of the Sadozai: continue the evil and I will betray you to the viziers and they will seek an audience with your grandfather.'

At which he turned to me, adding, 'It is finished, you understand? No more meetings. It is better for her to die than stain herself with another touch of a Frank, call yourself what you will.'

I stood watching as, with Karendeesh leading the way, they took the sloping road that led up to the palace of the Bala Hissar.

Another addition to my newly found life of luxury was Abaya's little house in Kabul City, the one to which Karendeesh had first led me when I met Durrani there – now so long ago.

Khan, my new servant, with his usual dedication, had had the rooms decorated and refurbished, and it was here I stayed when I couldn't get away for longer periods to the mansion at Seh Baba.

Instantly we knew, Durrani and I, that as a trysting place the house was ideal; lodged as it was in the depth of the Kuzzilbash quarter; one's misdemeanours could be enjoyed in secret here, or so we thought. And, although I warned constantly of the punishments facing us should we be discovered, all our fears were banished at a touch, which is the way of lovers.

Summer was dying and the air was cooler: song-birds sang in the garden of Abaya's little house in Kabul. The moon, round and yellow, lay her orb of brilliance in the window of my chamber.

'*Iestyn!*' It was a whisper.

I opened my eyes in the drowse between sleep and wakefulness: beyond the lattice window of my bedroom I saw the stars, large and brilliant, and the night was clutched in the arms of sleep: nothing stirred save the rushing wings of a bird.

'*Iestyn!*' Louder now.

I opened the casement and Durrani came in head first, and, drawing down her yashmak, sought my mouth in an anguish of breathing.

'Durrani!' I held her away. 'For God's sake!'

'Yes, yes! I need you. It is only a woman who knows this pain.' Her voice rose to a cry. Putting my hand over her mouth, I held her, but she took it away.

'I do not care. Don't go here! Don't meet there! I love you, I want you, and I am sick of it!'

'*Heisht!* For God's sake, you'll have Khan in here – he sleeps outside my door.'

'Let him watch if he likes. I want you, for you are my husband . . . ' and she kissed my face and hair, putting me into a rare old state, and had Old Nick himself been rummaging around us with bugles and brass cymbals we wouldn't have heard him. For sound and senses fade when in the arms of a lover; a time when precaution is tossed aside and threats are smothered in stuttering breath, a time when unborn children are forgotten . . . and unwanted babies made . . .

240

For me all threat vanished: when with this woman I knew a unity and pleasure I had never known before; even the memory of my love for Mari was banished when in her arms. And, although this new haven was within musket range of the Bala Hissar where lay the Dost in harem finery, there was provided, by the very noises of the city about us, that sense of security that the mansion at Seh Baba never brought.

That our love was wrong never occurred to us: the penalty, if discovered, was our sole inhibition: it was a delicious madness that snatched us up, forbidding coherent appreciation of our danger: that lust was here, too, I have never disagreed; but it was love also, and hope for the future that bound us.

When in Durrani's absence, any harem woman would do, but now that she was within reach, nothing could appease me but her presence.

So we loved that night in the fashion of lovers, giving and taking of each other, as if snatching at a final copulation: lying together in the belly of the bed in the somnolence of love's insensibility; awake but sleeping, aware, yet unknowing . . . while the raucous cries of night-time hawkers peddled in the room, and distant hoof-beats pounded the city into dreamy nothingness.

'What was that?' whispered Durrani.

I stirred and sighed.

Up on an elbow now, she made a little hissing sound with her lips.

'*Listen!*' She had a finger up in the darkness.

I kissed her and drew her down on to the pillow. 'It is nothing, only imaginings.'

Nevertheless, I sensed the tension in her, and as she slowly raised her eyes I followed her look; her finger was pointing upward . . . and I saw, smudged on the window-glass of a little rooflight above the bed, the dark image of a watching face; a face that instantly vanished as I threw aside the sheets and leaped out on to the floor.

Snatching at a gown in my flight, I tripped over Khan's

sleeping body as I ran down the hall. Scrambling up and running out into the night, I was in time to see a figure clad in black slip slowly down from the apex of the roof; landing in bushes, it then rushed headlong into the maze of city streets.

Pursuit being impossible, I returned to the hall. Khan, shivering with fear, was standing there awaiting me.

'The roof, Sahib? He was on the roof?'

I nodded. 'Up on the roof, looking in. Get that skylight covered.'

'It will be done, Master.'

Durrani was already dressed when I returned to the bedroom. She said:

'*Karendeesh!*'

'I doubt it.'

Her reply was instant, 'You are too kind to him! Always it is this damned Karendeesh!' She paced the room, clutching herself in pent anger.

A silence came to us.

I said, 'Let's hope to God it was Karendeesh, and that it was not a spy of the viziers.'

Putting her hands over her face she subsided on to the bed. 'This is impossible, we cannot go on like this!'

'The Princess is right, Sahib,' said Khan, bowing.

'You keep out of this!'

'I am fearful, Master . . . only fearful. The Dost in anger is terrible . . .'

Durrani dismissed him with a gesture. 'Take it from me, it was Karendeesh, and he will not tell the Dost.'

Strange, that at this time a poem should come out of my childhood; one that I had earlier remembered, and then forgotten: the words returned to me now with astonishing clarity:

She was a lady great and splendid. I was a
minstrel in her halls.
A warrior, like a prince attended, stayed
his steed at the castle walls.
Far had he fared to gaze upon her. 'O rest

242

thee now, Sir Knight,' she said.
The warrior wooed her; the warrior won her.
In times of snowdrops they were wed.
I made sweet music in his honour,
And longed to strike him dead!

37

It was over three months before I saw Durrani again . . . when she came with the Dost to see the testing of the *Zabber Two*.

A week earlier, with the assistance of six chained elephants, we had hauled the great cannon up the slope to the outskirt forts of the Bala Hissar, which was to be its permanent home. This was a feat of engineering in itself, being the method used by the British when hauling the siege guns of Gibraltar up to their defensive heights.

In that case using mules, they had adopted a method of hauling them in short distances by driving in anchorage stakes and gaining height advantage by closing upon each in turn. Needless to say, the idea came from Caleb, who had spent his early years in Gibraltar, but I gained the credit for what was then considered an engineering feat.

Therefore, with the dying year, my star with the Dost was in the ascendant.

The day was bright; all the previous night the spit-gob spiders that infest Afghanistan had been at it spinning their gum-speckled webs, and the fields and hedgerows were sparkling white with billows of catch-me-eat-me swathes of the stuff. It reminded me of home; of the darling places where once I had left my heart: the undulating valleys of the Blorenge mountain, the luscious green of the Little Skirrid and the white-blossoming canal which swam amid its drooping alders.

Where was it now, I wondered? Had it been lost in the

careless drifting of my now foreign heart?

And yet, despite the years of absence, the sight of those autumn webs brought to this exile, with invigorating clarity, the sights and sounds of a most beloved Wales.

Havildar, the giant overseer at the racecourse (he who once chained Big Rhys, Owen and me to his two-ton roller), had been relegated to that menial task for touching up a harem lady in passing jest: earlier one of Caleb's best technicians, I reappointed him: now Havildar was my faithful friend.

'Is all prepared for the ranging shots?' I asked him.

To attention stood he, all six-foot-five of him. 'All is ready for the pull of the lanyard, Sahib,' said he, double bass. And added in a stentorian voice, 'Director of Armaments, we now await the King.'

'Master of Gunnery,' I responded, 'it looks like rain, so keep your powder dry. If this thing fails, he'll have the heads off the pair of us.'

'May Allah protect me,' came the reply, and he turned his eyes to Mecca.

I followed him to the firing-platform, which, on rollers, gave the great gun a fifty-five degree traverse, allowing it to be trained on any target between the northern outskirts of Kabul and the most southerly point of the Old Cantonment, where I was once quartered.

Now the deserted cantonment, the scene of such acrimony and blood, stood abandoned by fickle posterity; all that was visible now the British had gone were the scores of square and circular patterns of discoloured grass.

So much, I reflected, for dreams of colonial empires; here, too, had died the dreams of our colonial youth.

The Dost, laden with all the jewelled paraphernalia of a state occasion, arrived on an ornately decorated elephant: upon the howdah of a second elephant came Durrani; viziers and lesser state dignitaries followed upon humble camels.

Reaching the gun trolley, the King descended and, accompanied by Durrani, came to inspect the Mark Two *Zabber Jang*.

Its gunnery team, commanded by Havildar, all dressed in

245

scarlet and gold braid, lined up beneath its massive muzzle. I, dressed in a simple white gown and a poshteen, bowed before him.

The King said, 'I greet you, Mortymer, and compliment you upon completing its readiness for trial on the promised date. All is ready?'

I could feel, but did not see, Durrani's eyes upon me: the wind moved over distant Wazirabad Lake and must have stirred her gown; the air was perfumed.

It is disconcerting to be in the presence of a beloved, and yet have no communion with the lover: it is as if one stands within the cocoon of a self-imposed dungeon, alive yet deceased.

Also I was aware of the King's unremitting gaze; selecting the secrets of my soul for hanging them out in public. And the eyes of his viziers, who were bowing and scraping obsequiously, were equally unrelenting: presumably debating which spike upon which to hang my head.

As for Durrani, she looked straight through me, as if by some trick of Merlin I had vanished, and now saw only the place where I had been standing. It brought me sadness, for although she was now so close that I could have touched her, we were apart.

I could have wept for the chasm of class and blood that divided us . . . yet knew that should I ever shed a single tear for my lost Mari, I would weep for ever. . . .

Remembering this, I suffered conscience, because it is the loves he loses that a man remembers, not the loves available: yet, at the raising of a finger, Durrani would run gasping into my arms . . . while Mari Dirion of the Welsh kisses was gone to the mouth of another.

'I asked you, Mortymer, if all is ready,' said the King testily.

I bowed. 'As you desired it, Your Majesty.'

'Then lead me to a safe place where I can see your monster perform.'

I led him down the brick staircase of an outpost fort.

Durrani, taking a seat beside him, brushed my hand with hers in passing; the effect upon me was like a burn.

246

*

The morning shone in dazzling splendour, with white billowing clouds rolling in from the west from St Peter's weekly wash; the land was bathed in diadems of dew light.

With Havildar holding the lanyard and awaiting my command, I looked down the shining muzzle of the enormous *Zabber Jang* and held my breath in secret prayer: great internal forces would be built up with the first detonation; the first shot from any cannon always inspiring the greatest danger.

I remembered Merthyr in the old years. Nelson, staying with his Emma Hamilton at the Swan Hotel (he had refused to accept Crawshay's invitation to stay at the Castle), narrowly escaped with his life when a tested cannon exploded, killing a little boy.

Now I looked towards the slit embrasure of the nearby bunker: a white flag was fluttering as a signal. I nodded to Havildar and he snapped shut the fire-lock; smoke wisped up and I opened my mouth and covered my ears. The world seemed to disintegrate as the propellant exploded: the *Zabber Jang* leaped up, its muzzle shooting flame and smoke, and the gunners jumped aside to the recoil as the chocks flew up: the heavy projectile whined away into the distance: with Wazirbad Lake focused in its sights, it vanished into the shimmering country. We watched and waited, our telescopes to our eyes. Two thousand yards away the earth mushroomed up in a detonating blaze; the missile had landed; the blinding discharge of the *Zabber Jang* was followed by a distant thunder that clattered and reverberated around the peaks.

Silence. No birds sang. It was like the end of the world.

Then the Dost emerged with Durrani upon his arm, all smiles; reaching me, he raised his hands in greeting, crying, 'May Allah, who knows all things, grant you a tranquil life. You have saved my country!'

Durrani, I recall, was staring hard at me as if trying to tell me something.

'May you henceforth live in perpetual amity,' said the King, and I bowed before him; for this mood, I knew, could change instantly into implacable rage.

247

The notables took their places around his chair, which was a mobile throne of silk, satin and floral decoration.

'Now,' said he airily, 'we can sit and watch in safety, for the danger is over. Another round, if you please, Director of Armaments – instruct your gunners.'

I protested, 'But only one safety shot, Your Majesty? The danger is far from over.'

'My trust lies in your excellence, my new Director,' and he snapped his fingers at a nearby servant, shouting, 'Let us celebrate – in wild regions will I spend my old age if today does not prove that Kabul now rules Central Asia. Death to my enemies from the Oxus to Bokhara!'

Even Havildar and his gang of gunners were invited to the Dost's celebration party; Havildar looking enormous in his scarlet jacket buttoned up to the throat, with the cuffs of his regimental colours, green with traceries of mother-of-pearl. Across his great chest he wore a blancoed sword strap; white duck trousers, with creases to cut his throat, clad his tree-trunk legs; upon his head he wore a tall shako, on the front of which was the badge of the Bombay Horse: all to the approval of the Iron Duke Wellington back at home, who didn't have to wear such trappings in the ferocious heat of Asia.

By contrast I looked significant in my white poshteen and purple gown, which I wore on special occasions, for to be invited to the King's private chambers, as now, was privilege indeed; to which, of course, Durrani was excluded. The evening entertainment was for the entertainment of males; naked dancing girls being in attendance.

The little tables of the banqueting hall being set, everybody sat upon the floor; a mosaic freezing of the bums by interlaced *cloisonné* of gold: opulence was the keynote, nothing spared in terms of lavish beauty. Food was then brought in on the shoulders of black slave girls and long-haired eunuchs.

I sat at the King's right as the honoured guest; on his left sat his viziers and, judging by the gourds of wine being assembled, all palace rules were about to be transgressed.

The opening toast was to 'The genius of Caleb Benedict and his pupil, my new Director of Armaments, recently promoted Colonel-General Mortymer'. This was stated by His Majesty assisted by a goblet of Sikh 'toddy', guaranteed to kill within the hour.

We all rose for this, and then sat down again; the feasting began.

As king of a country recently pillaged by the British Army of Retribution, the Dost was doing pretty well, I thought: this, my first encounter with a regal state occasion, was an eye-opener.

The Dost was wearing an armour of jewels upon a purple tunic emblazoned with gold. From his waist, I noticed, dangling on a golden chain, a splendid diamond which he claimed was the infamous Koh-i-Nor (although this was disputable, as it had by this time already become the property of another).

Course after course was presented by Nubians, partaken first by the Dost, who, swallowing a sheep's eyeball, then helped me to one and with satisfaction watched it go down. Fresh salmon followed this and goat pâté washed down with French burgundy, slices of the choicest mutton, duck liver and pheasants' wings, also the tongues of nightingales and peacocks, extracted to cleanse them of their nocturnal screechings, said the King. And while the consumption of alcoholic beverages might be frowned upon without the environs of the palace, no such regulation applied here, apparently: for within ten minutes all were elated with wine, including me: well flushed for the occasion, the Dost clapped his hands, and on came the dancing girls.

They came from left and right as in entry on to a stage; big and small, all as bare as eggs; some slender, some busty, all wearing the single ruby that covered their navels.

With their naked bodies sprinkled with gold and silver dust, brown, white, black and yellow they spilled out before us, mingling with the squatting guests and pirouetting in time with the music of lutes and drums: bowing, stretching, turning on naked feet, their bangled arms akimbo; now

249

gracefully inclining their long-maned heads in a perfect combination of rhythm and symmetry. And the long-nosed merchants greeted them with suggestive gestures; bleary-eyed with wine were the viziers, their clawing hands contriving to grasp their bodies as they flitted among us; it was a beauteous yet bawdy exultation of art and lust, and as the music quickened so the dancers rose to Eastern passions: their belly-dancing driving the guests into a frenzy of excitement that ended on the floor, each in the arms of a girl; some to woo and cajole; some to join in the whirling of others in giddy adulation, weaving their sparkling bodies into perambulating shakes and spasms.

As the dance quickened the room was packed with bodies, and with the cymbals clashing about me and a dancer gyrating on her knees before me, I felt a hand touch mine, and recognized Subara . . . A piece of paper was lying in my hand and I tucked it away into my robe, while Subara, writhing and swaying before me, now offered herself in abject supplication.

Leaning towards me, the Dost winked perceptively, saying:

'Make the most of her, Director. The opportunity may not express itself so readily in the future,' and he smiled, but not with his eyes.

Later, when he rose to speak, the guests, including me, were drunkenly attentive.

'Today,' he began in Persian, 'has been a milestone in the history of our country. The original *Zabber Jang*, constructed by the genius of our late engineer supreme, Mr Caleb Benedict, had fallen into enemy hands during the defence of Ghazni; rarely in its short life did it fire a shot in anger. But now, Allah be praised, there has arisen in our country the pupil of Mr Benedict – not to be compared with the master in terms of genius, perhaps, but of sufficient technical ability to cast an even larger cannon of incomparable iron under a process known to him in early years.

'So today, after the successful testing of the Mark II

250

Zabber, I give you my new Director of Armaments, Iestyn Mortymer.'

Much clapping now, and toasts being raised to me.

'It is to him, not to the illustrious Benedict, that Afghanistan owes this new success in war: and it is he whom we will remember if ever again the Bala Hissar is under siege, for with this new gun we will blow away our enemies from here to the Oxus; none shall threaten us while this new monster weapon – by the grace of Allah – keeps us safe.

'But there is more to merely manufacturing a great artillery piece than knowing the colour of the flame before the molten iron is poured – take these two examples of Mortymer's engineering ability:

'It is known, is it not, that in an assault two cannons always must be positioned. This is because, under rapid firing, it is necessary for the gunner to "serve the vent" – that, I understand, is the expression. After a shot is discharged small particles of burning material collect within the cannon's bore, and these, fanned by the hot draught of escaping fumes, can still be alight in the area of the touch-hole when the next propellent is rammed in for reloading. Many of our best gunners have lost their lives by premature explosions caused by this enigma.

'But this danger, Sirdars, is now passed, thanks to an invention by our new Director, and the patent belongs solely to Afghanistan. Listen, through an ingenious device known as a snap-hammer, the vent no longer has to be served by the thumb – the cannon being often so hot that the firing-rate is slowed. Automatically, through the application of a little water at this vital point, the burning particles are first drenched and then instantly dried by the cannon's heat, before the new touch-powder is poured. Therefore, our gunners no longer suffer blistered thumbs! Further, the firing-rate is maintained by a clever flint-lock mechanism. With such a contraption – and I may say that only an engineer of quality fully understands its function – is the new *Zabber* fitted. So fire away this great gun to your delight, my gunners: only your enemies will excel in death what this man Mortymer holds as his genius. But more, much more – listen!

251

'The shot the *Zabber* fires now is not a cannon-ball but is melon-shaped, and called the "Wilkinson" Design: when projected, this shot rotates in flight, like the turning of an arrow, thus achieving greater range and accuracy. This will soon be obtained by grooving the inside of the cannon's muzzle by what is called "rifling"; a process of cutting carried out during the boring of the cannon, and apparently invented by the workers of an iron foundry in a place called Bersham, so Mortymer informs me. Note that this man of destiny possesses all the attributes of humility: the inventor taught him such wiles, and we, Sirdars, gain the advantages.'

Tremendous applause now, with every man in the room upon his feet; the wine goblets went up and the wine went down: the *zenana* ladies, their dances over, filed out of the hall.

'Sirdars,' the King continued, The Taj Mahal, that Gem of Buildings in Agra, India, was erected by the Mongol emperor Shah Jahan some two hundred years ago in memory of Mumtaz Mahal, his favourite wife. But, although he conceived its beautiful design in a dream, he could find no architect capable of envisaging its perfection. But, to his court one day came a sorcerer, and to an architect present he offered a drink, saying, "Drink this, and the emperor's perfect vision will be revealed to you," and the architect drank of the potion, and found it so. In all its glory the most perfect building in the world made shape before his eyes: feverishly then the architect worked, and beside the lovely River Jumna, surrounded by Persian gardens, the Taj Mahal became that vision which enthralls us today.'

His guests were entranced; not an eyelid flickered.

The King continued, 'So it is with this great gun, my beautiful Widow Maker: it is the product of a technical vision – first seen by Caleb Benedict, now forged by fire and moulds into the monstrous cannon of death to protect the Bala Hissar.

'From its mass will its children of iron be born, the scythe and the ploughshare, the hook and the knife which will gather in our harvests. Under the protection of the *Zabber Jang* will rise great fields of wheat and grain which will enrich our people. The enemy – Britain – has been thrown

252

out of our land and will no longer pester us: never again will the hated Feringhee march in our ravines and over our plains, sent by the white-faced Queen beyond the seas to rape, pillage and burn. How very strange is Fate that two of Victoria's sons designed the weapon which guarantees our future. I offer you, Sirdars, the genius of Iestyn Mortymer, one of Britain's despised convicts, who brings his gifts to Afghanistan.'

Now, drunk with amiability and a wine-kindness akin to love, the viziers gathered about me, slapping me upon the back in heartiest congratulations, until the Dost silenced them with a raised hand, saying, 'But legend also inspires the greatest of stories, and history has it, though it may not be accurate, that the successful architect of the Taj Mahal was cast off its dome by the Mongol emperor to ensure that never again would he build a rival to such an edifice of beauty . . .'

The viziers were silent. In a low voice, the King continued, 'And while I have no intention of serving the same fate to our esteemed Director of Armaments, it would be unhappy indeed should he leave here for the courts of our enemies . . . and there put his brain to equally effective instruments of war . . . which could lead to our destruction . . .

'Therefore, I have decided to request him to leave my country and return to Britain in peace and felicitation; never again to show his face in Afghanistan. To assist his happy departure I here grant him as an honorarium a lakh of rupees – ten thousand pounds sterling – for his old age – sharing it, we pray, with a woman of his own colour and class . . . in comfort and amity.

'For, although all here wish him a long and happy life, this could be forfeited were he to remain in Kabul. You see, despite our love of him, he is still a hated Feringhee in the eyes of our people; and who could send some fervent patriot to an ignoble end were he to despatch our friend to his death at the time of his greatest conquest? How badly would we feel were this to happen to one who has proved himself such a valorous lover, not only of our land, but of many Afghan women . . .'

The room exploded with bawdy guffaws.

'Indeed, I would go so far as to say that when it comes to a harem – not least, I may add, to one of my own relatives – his inventive genius is matched only by his amorous techniques!'

The chamber was now a crescendo of bawled obscenities, and in the bedlam I rose and made a brief and dignified reply, with the promise that I would take my leave of beautiful Afghanistan at the earliest opportunity.

The important issue governing one's life here was knowing when to make an exit.

The moment I was alone in my own apartment, I took out the note that Subara had given me. Upon it, in English, was written:

Iestyn,
    This girl is risking her life by bringing this message to you. And I am risking mine in writing it.
    Help me, please. I am with child.

38

Khan, my servant, said, 'Master, if you leave Afghanistan, I come with you. The Maharaja and then old Abaya treated me like a dog, but you treat me like a man.'

I finished packing my rucksack for the journey. 'As you wish. But recall that he who deserts the King signs his own death warrant. Is that not so?'

'It is, Sahib.'

'And the punishment?'

'Death by beheading, Sahib.'

'And the punishment for lying with a daughter of the Royal House?'

'Death by impaling.'

I slung the rucksack across my shoulders. 'Then remember that you are in bad company. You still want to come?'

The little man straightened. 'If necessary I would die for my princess.'

Somewhere, I remembered, I had heard this before . . .

'Attach yourself to me, Khan, and you'll be given every opportunity: understand the dangers!'

We left the house in Kabul by the back entrance, and sought the shadows of crowded alleys.

Few people were abroad; the only sounds came from street vendors plying their wares as they did in Kabul from dawn to darkness.

Time was, when British troops garrisoned the city, the courts and alleys were alive with beery songs, and the unofficial bordellos, which so outraged Afghan sensibilities, were crammed to the doors. Now all was quiet as Khan led me through a maze of squalid garrets, moving northward towards the site of the old military cantonment.

'The Princess will be waiting at midnight?' Khan asked.

'At the derelict grandstand of the old racecourse,' I answered. 'From there it is only a quick run to the old military footbridge.'

'We are in the hands of Allah, he who can simultaneously see both ends of a ten-foot stick,' said Khan.

'No, we're in the hands of your boatman,' and I looked up at the enemy moon where a thousand woollen clouds were being shepherded across the sky, sheep most beautiful to see.

It was on such nights as this that the raiding tribesmen had descended on to the cantonment, whirling their scimitars out of the dark. And as the old tented area came nearer the wind blew cold on my face, returning to me the bawdy sounds of its once lively garrison; whose men, rank on rank, had died in the retreat to Jalalabad: and I heard again the soldiers' ditties and epithets that had fashioned the British army since the start of Time: men's tuneless bawling came to me on the night wind, whispering faintly in waving vetch grass, the hair of the abandoned cantonment . . .

I don't want to fight the Afghans.
I'm too scared to go to war.
I'd rather hang around and earn an easy pound
Living on the earnings of a high-born lady.
Don't want a bayonet up me jacksie,
Don't want me bollocks shot away.
I'd rather be in England, in merry, merry
    England,
And booze and booze and booze me life away, Gor
    Blimey!
Booze and booze and booze me life away.

I remembered then the poem that Lady Sale had quoted from 'Hohenlinden':

Few, few shall part where many meet,
The snow shall be their winding sheet;
And every turf beneath their feet
Shall be a soldier's sepulchre . . .

'Can you hear people singing?' I asked Khan, and he inclined his ear to the wind.

'No, Sahib.'

Still I heard it, until reaching the debris of the old racecourse grandstand: this, the rendezvous where we were to meet Durrani and Subara, the harem girl who was to accompany her.

Greeting me, Durrani caught my arm.

Her eyes were black tulips in her face, pale as a corpse.

'Iestyn,' she said, 'We heard men singing. . . .'

I hesitated, and she added, 'Just now – British soldiers singing. . . .'

I shook my head. 'It is not possible. All the soldiers are asleep in death; there are no soldiers of any kind between here and the Bala Hissar, so you are just hearing things. You are ready, and have your things?'

'On my back, like you. Subara carries also.'

'She comes as well?'

The harem girl replied, 'I come to serve my princess.'

'You know the dangers?'

She nodded.

The weedy, undersized Khan and the tragic Subara: we didn't deserve them.

'Quickly, then. The boat is waiting, Khan says. He will lead us down to the river.'

No skin and hide skiff this one, but a fourteen-foot, shiplap-constructed British provision boat, with a pole-boatman aboard it waiting in the reeds; one of many, Khan explained, abandoned by the British Sappers during the Retreat and taken over by speculative ferrymen.

Given a fast current and good luck, in this we hoped to reach the confluence with the River Sourkab; and from there float downstream, not only to Jalalabad, but even to Peshawar and British India. Thereafter, God willing, it was

257

a caravan to Karachi and from there a passage by steamer to Britain.

'How long?' I asked the boatman, and he raised a crippled face to the moon.

'To Jalalabad? – about a hundred miles? – three days if Allah smiles upon us.'

'And to Peshawar?'

'Another twenty-four hours if we are not stopped by bandits, which can happen if Allah frowns. You have money to pay, Feringhee?'

'Son of a decaying bitch!' cried Khan, appalled. '*Animal!* Your words are like wind from a donkey's anus. The Frank, like us, is a child of the sun!' and the boatman replied harshly as he poled us over to the southern bank:

'*Listen!* Once I was in service to the East India Company, and my wife attended to such as these. As a *koi-hais* wet nurse she was not allowed to feed their Feringhee baby-people, lest her milk infect their delicate stomachs. Yet many were contaminated already by the "Colonel Forbes", which is their stupid name for the cholera.

'I have lived among the Feringhees and know their arrogance; always they command, and we obey, but not now, for we are free of them.' And he pointed at me sitting in the stern. 'Let him show his money before we start this journey, and if he has none, out and walk!'

'Are you aware,' asked Khan, with heavy threat, 'that we could tip you over the side?'

'Try it, Frank-lover, and you will not reach Sourkab, never mind Jalalabad. Show his money!'

We sat looking at each other under a bone-white moon.

'Show him, Master,' said Khan, and I opened the belt at my waist and spread out some of the money the Dost had given to me.

The boatman's eyes threatened to drop out of his face; he wheedled, 'Sirdar, the beauty of your two wives would ravish the heart of a eunuch. My soul leaps with joy at the sight of such munificence. I accept your forgiveness with the greatest felicitation.'

'How much for the journey to Peshawar? Already I have asked you twice, you old sod.'

'Two hundred rupees a person.'

'Too much!'

'Then one hundred each; bargain me lower, my beloved prince, and I will starve, my wives and children also.'

'I will give you three hundred total at the end of the journey – think yourself lucky.'

'May guile and malice serve only your enemies, my friend,' came the reply. 'I would prove guilty of a woeful crime were I to ask a rupee more,' and he bowed over his pole. 'Everything you demand shall be accomplished.'

And much more as well, as we were about to discover.

It had been a mistake to show him the money.

We went amid towering mountains, leaving behind us in the dark the mounding monster of the Beymaroo Hills where Shelton's troops had died; heights that had echoed to the tramping legions of Alexander the Great some three hundred years before the coming of Christ.

The boatman kept to the shallows, always within sight of land but never near enough to be assaulted.

Almost instantly Durrani slept, curling herself up like a cat on cushions, while Subara watched over her.

I kept first watch. The gliding bulrushes of the river spiked the autumn moon; rats and water snakes, their nests disturbed, joined affronted wading birds in the panic of escape; but nothing moved in the hinterland beyond the bank. In shimmering moonlight the river sulked and bubbled to the thrusting pole; the Arabian face of the boatman was as one carved from black alabaster.

It was then, I think, that the wind moved from the west and I heard a horse neigh; one of many grazing the fields within hearing distance of the river? With Durrani's hand in mine, I slept.

On the second night of travel, when parallel to Gandamak where the remnants of the 44th had died, the current quickened and we were bowling along at a rare old pace in the moonlight. And when we heard the singing of the river near the confluence with the River Sourkab, Subara, the slave girl, in reply to a question from Khan, said in an

259

educated voice, 'My past? My past, Sahib, is of small consequence.'

'You have always been a harem girl?' I asked her.

'Since I could remember,' and I saw the piquant beauty of her face when she removed her yashmak. 'When I was seven years old my father sold me to a Chinese trader who was buying unbroken *yaboos* for the British near Jalalabad. For many years I was in his caravan, and ate well. Little was asked of me since he already possessed many concubines of beauty and maturity; then one day – on my tenth birthday, I remember – his son, who was an albino, took me to his table. . . .'

The boat drifted on; the swim quickened.

'Tell us,' urged Durrani.

'By this son I came to child, which was then forbidden to a harem girl, and so I was beaten and cast out; returning to Kabul, I gained a position as a sewing-maid in the Bala Hissar.'

She looked at the moon and her eyes were diamonds.

'My boy was comely, his skin being the colour of milk, not that of an Afghan child. And for this reason the harem merchants sold him to a passing caravan at the age of five, giving me one tenth of the rupees they had gained in the sale. This money I took into the palace of Bala Hissar and flung it into the Vizier's face.

'For this I was flogged in the manner in which men are flogged . . . ' and saying this she undid her gown and exposed her back, and the moon traced the white weals with ghostly fingers. Subara said, replacing her gown, 'I lied to you all. It was not the explosion of the Great Bazaar that caused me ill, but the whips of Shah Shuja's eunuchs; it is their delight to beat harem girls. Now I ask your forgiveness, my Princess.'

'And your son?' asked Durrani.

'Still pleasuring the guests of the Chinese horse-traders. But one day, when I have money enough, I will buy him back – that he may enjoy his youth, having lost his childhood.'

Subara spoke more, but we did not hear her: Khan had his finger up for silence; the boatman ceased his poling; all listened to the music of the river.

Khan said, 'I thought I heard the chinking of cavalry . . .'

The boatman laughed bassly. 'Old Kabul River, she sings many songs from deep down where the bones of our ancestors lie. Also, she tells tales like an artful woman who pleads sympathy – like this bitch here, the black-bummed whore.'

'Silence!' cried Khan. 'May Allah appropriate your penis, vile scum! Men will piss in your mother's milk for such an insult – this woman is a friend of a princess.'

'She is still a black-bummed whore,' said the boatman.

We would have done better to have heeded warnings than listen to the woes of Subara, for clearly we were being followed.

During this second night of travel the boatman went ashore; to meet his son, he said, who would buy provisions for us and meet us at a rendezvous on the northern slope of the mountain, a mile or so north of Futtenbad.

'I do not trust this man,' announced Subara. 'So let the one who employed him answer for any betrayal.'

Khan replied, 'He is a boatman of the river. All such as he are great scoundrels, but one has to trust somebody, if one wants to travel.'

'Is that the wise man speaking, or the clown?' asked Durrani.

'Cut my throat if my choice is proved unwise, my Princess.'

'With the greatest pleasure.'

I took no part in such conversation, feeling apart from their squabbling, flowery threats and denunciations.

On the third night of travel an urchin appeared on the river bank in mad dances and gesticulations, bringing the food; this was acceptable; we were down to our last loaf. The boatman poled us into a little inlet and the urchin, his arms full of provisions, splashed through the shallows and tumbled them into the boat.

There, under the autumn star-fire, we drank good wine and feasted on *chiparoos* and chupatties, the little wheatcakes drowned in honey; the wine was strong, the night warm, and it was pleasurable.

Later, we travelled again until Subara heard the chinking

of cavalry. And we saw riding on the southern bank a little posse of horsemen: on the side of the glittering river they went, silhouetted against the moon. As the speed of the boat quickened so they trotted faster: when, in the shallows, the craft slowed, they slowed also. Before the night was ended we took refuge in a little backwater, and there all lay silently, full length in the bottom of the boat.

'They have gone past?' asked Durrani.

'All have departed!' cried the boatman, befuddled with wine. 'As I promised, it is so!' and he opened his arms to us. 'The horsemen have departed! I, the son of Kokran, having saved my Princess, will now place the Koh-i-Nor diamond in her navel and parade her beauty before all Asia.'

'If, on the other hand, you have betrayed us,' said Durrani, 'I will see to it that your pole enters your backside, the thick end first, you damned old reprobate!'

'Allah confirms your gentleness, my beloved Princess.' Bowing, he took her hand and helped her out of the boat.

Instantly, in a mêlée of enveloping foam and flying water, men came splashing into the shallows. Surrounded, we were hauled unceremoniously through the mud to the river bank.

'Do I have to keep telling you?' cried the boatman in the darkness, 'in his possession he has a fortune in rupees!'

'It is not the money I am after,' said a voice, and I recognized it instantly: seconds later I was dragged up the bank and flung down. In the brightening dawn I saw a face.

It was Abaya.

And behind him, his half-naked body obliterating the moon, was his Neolithic servant, the gigantic Gargoa.

39

'Aha!' cried Abaya in his light soprano. 'What have we here? A travelling member of the Royal House of Barakzai and her funeral cortège, too, unless I am mistaken!' and with the four of us held in the grip of his accomplices, he inspected us like a butcher at a meat auction.

Gargoa, towering above Durrani, said, 'Master, you give me this one? and he begged with big hands. 'Let me have a royal princess and never again will I pester you for torture!'

'Have her, and welcome,' replied Abaya, 'for she has caused me more travail than a cat on heat,' and he stooped above me when his men pulled me down upon my knees before him. 'I am much concerned with this spawn of the Devil, and need him as a plaything. You remember me, Feringhee?'

I did not reply.

'Be assured that you will. We, the undertakers, present our credentials, my beloved,' and he swung to his men. 'Tie them! Bind them with ropes. This noble may be thin on top, but not in the head, and he has good recollections,' and he stooped and whispered into my face.

'Abaya, it was, my friend, who swore to deliver Durrani into the hands of Akbar, he who was soon to be King; and you prevented it. It was Abaya's mansion in which you made sport with concubines; and my cherished home in Kabul that you turned into a house of bawds, remember?'

Turning, he kicked the smouldering bonfire behind him into a blaze so that the forest clearing about us burst into redness, and I saw the people about me more clearly:

263

Gargoa holding Durrani, other bearded ruffians holding Subara, Khan and the boatman down upon their knees, the latter wailing to wake the dead.

'But Master, have I not served you well? Was it not my son who brought you word of the Feringhee's money?'

'Silence him!' commanded Abaya. 'And kill all three,' and amid the boatman's shrieking protests he was dragged nearer to the bonfire; two held him; a third beheaded him with a scimitar so that his head, lopped off cleanly, rolled about like a live thing in the ashes of the fire, clucking its tongue like a chicken caught in flames. Khan they killed next; he of the gentle incantation, raising his eyes to me before he fell: Subara, for her part, showed no sign of distress but bared her neck to the knife with Oriental fatality; Durrani screamed; three times she screamed as Subara died.

I could not move; all happened with such obscene rapidity that my brain could not comprehend it; one moment Subara's beauty was alive, next her dismembered body – the standard Afghan mutilation – had been flung into the undergrowth. Others tore off the clothes and hacked at the remains of Khan and the boatman.

Abaya, the while, as withered as an ancient crone, watched my reactions; a hand plucking his beard with undivided speculation.

'Thus your friends have died,' he said. 'And as you have seen, their end was merciful. But no such easy death I have in mind for you, or the bitch dog who calls herself an Afghan Royal, for she has infected her blood with that of an Unbeliever.'

An amputated hand, Subara's by its smallness, was lying nearby, its fingers slowly unfolding in a final paroxysm of death; it held me with riveting force. But Abaya's shrieked command within the sudden monastic quiet returned me to reality.

'Bring the stones! Cut the stake!'

Instant activity again; Durrani was bundled out of Gargoa's arms and tied to a tree; I was manhandled into a sitting position and roped to a stump: strangely I recall, within the confusion of it, the amber drowse of bee-hum;

wild honey must have been nearby; honey that Durrani had pledged we would one day eat with our fingers: and in my nostrils was not the stench of death, but that of the narcissus whose petals were flowering above the rushes; the river sparkled.

In that moment – in a faint redness of the dawn, I saw Durrani's eyes fixed upon me from the other side of the fire. Gargoa had torn away her poshteen; her hair, once alive and beautiful, was now lying in sweated strands about her naked shoulders; brown-gold was once the colour of her skin, now it was smeared with mud and bruised by the grip of ruffians. And as her eyes met mine she had one eyebrow slightly raised, as if in patent acceptance of her revulsion, as Gargoa, squatting beside her, whispered into her ear.

All about us now was the excited activity of guards, relishing the appointed tortures: like small boys driven into an urgency of expectation, they gathered from the clearing loose stones and piled them into heaps beside a squatting Abaya. Others were hacking at a tree beyond the clearing for the impaling stake; this they triumphantly carried to the fire, shaving off its obstructing gnarls and branches: Gargoa, now on hands and knees, was digging a hole for it.

The full dawn came suddenly, bringing autumn brightness. And I reflected, as I saw the sunrise, upon the events which had brought us to this pass: Caleb, doubtless, would have had a word for it; in terms, perhaps, of a bitter retribution . . . but to die in such a manner . . . so far from home. But first, it appeared, I was going to have to witness the stoning of Durrani.

Unaccountably, I then remembered a British woman of the cantonment whom the pursuing Ghilzais spared because she was with child . . . The thought straightened me, a movement Abaya discerned.

'Does the Princess have to die?' I asked him.

'She has transgressed our holy laws.'

'And what of the law of the Dost?'

'The law of the Dost is similar. The woman found in adultery dies by stoning – is that not the same, even in your Bible?'

265

'How can it be adultery? She is not married.'

'It is sufficient that she is guilty of fornication – death by stoning.'

'Who, then, will cast the first stone? This question has been asked before.'

It momentarily stilled him; then, 'It is the law of the Royals; it is that which would be meted out to her in Kabul.'

'But if she were with child?'

This raised his face. 'But she is not with child.'

'But were she to be so, then you could not kill her.'

'It makes no difference to me.'

'It makes all the difference to the tribe of the Ghilzais.'

'But they are not Ghilzais; they are Hazaras.'

I shouted in Pashto, 'Let every man here know that this woman is with child, do you hear me?' and Abaya, crawling over, struck me in the mouth.

I shouted again, 'Kill her, and her blood will be upon your sons, their sons also, down to the third generation. This is your law! You are Ghilzais who have no priests to advise you. This woman is four months with baby – take off her gown and see for yourselves,' and the men clustered together, muttering and pulling at one another, while Abaya, now recovered, held his stomach and chuckled.

Hearing this, the others joined him, guffawing and stamping their feet like excited children, and one cried, 'Alas, Feringhee, you have the wrong tribe! We are Hazaras and have no such superstitions.'

'But I have,' said a voice, and Gargoa, leaving Durrani's side, walked among them.

I glanced at Abaya; he had not accounted for this.

'Is it true that she is with the baby people?' asked Gargoa.

'It is true,' I replied.

'It is a lie,' cried Abaya, ruffled. 'And if you doubt me, look for yourself, she is no more with child than me!' and Gargoa, going to Durrani, pulled up her gown, and pulled down her pantaloons, and the swell of her stomach was plain to see.

'How long?' Gargoa asked her, still holding up her gown.

'Four months,' said Durrani.

'She is with the baby people, she cannot die,' announced Gargoa, as if the argument was finished.

266

'She dies,' said Abaya. 'This white-faced one here has covered her! Would you have her breed a bastard, Feringhee?'

'Nevertheless, she is carrying, and we cannot kill her,' said Gargoa, then nodded in my direction. 'Have sport with him instead,' and, taking the stake prepared by the others, he drove it into the ground in the middle of the clearing, and the new light showed the stake ready for the impaling and the men clustered about it.

Nothing moved, save the river; there was no other sound in the forest; it was as if the birds themselves were perched as silent witnesses.

'He goes to his ancestors when the first red light touches the stake,' said Abaya, 'which was the manner in which the last Feringhee, Captain Benson, died, he who also sullied the virtue of an Afghan princess.'

'You are barbarians!' shrieked Durrani. '*Iestyn!*'

There entered me then, amid the terror of my inner self, a strange and wonderful benediction; a salve conferred upon me by an unseen hand.

It was as if, within the sickening fear, there existed a small light of unrelenting intensity: one that comes to those who are gripped within a final paroxysm of horror? It was a light of hope that grew into a ravishing brightness, bringing me to a cold, soporific calm: its tranquillity so intense that it banished my febrile inflammations of blood and heat.

As the sun rose higher and crept towards the foot of the stake, cold air came to the clearing, brought on a little wind from the river, and my terror had gone.

Pulling me to my feet, the men stripped me, and I saw above me, in a space of branches, the growing brightness of the sun, scudded now by threatening clouds.

Nothing moved before my eyes, neither pictures of my past life nor visions conjured by the future: and only vaguely, within an inner consciousness, did I hear Durrani's unintelligible shrieking as they lifted me for the impaling. After which, I knew, they would leave me to die alone, this being the custom: for a strong man, this could take a day and night.

Gargoa, I remember, was beside me, directing operations; Abaya, like a wingless vulture, was squatting on the ground, his legs akimbo, enjoying the spectacle. Raindrops began to spatter the ground. And I sensed, rather than saw, the small round hole appear in Gargoa's forehead in the second before his jaw dropped and his knees buckled. Then shots echoed in the clearing and horsemen appeared, bursting through the surrounding undergrowth: I struggled instantly, falling from the arms of the men, to lie amid a confusion of cries and trampling hooves. Seconds later I was hauled to my feet.

'I could have arrived long ago, my friend,' said a voice, 'but left you to enjoy it. Of one thing I'm sure – you would have deserved it.'

'See to Durrani,' I replied. 'Next time you may be too late.'

'There will be no next time,' said Karendeesh.

40

Karendeesh, to me, had always been an enigma: certainly, as a King's Messenger, he was reliable in that, reading all correspondence, he had his ear to the ground in terms of current affairs; always knowing which way the political wind was blowing. Certainly, everything that happened to Durrani was his business, which more than once had guaranteed her survival. His private ambitions towards her were equally obvious, so he wanted me out of the way as soon as possible.

Upon Karendeesh's instructions my clothes were now returned to me. The remains of the unfortunates – Subara, Khan and the boatman – were decently buried, and Abaya, chained by the neck, was prepared for the journey back to Kabul and justice.

Reaction from the imminence of my impaling began to sweep over me in jolts of sickening fear, and I fought the · indignity of being physically sick.

Now, removed from the site of the burials, I stood before Karendeesh. Fine and handsome looked he, regally clad as he was in his uniform of green, scarlet and gold: every inch the King's representative, as he announced with regal arrogance:

'I now implicitly follow my instructions, and they are these: you, the Princess Durrani, will return with me to Kabul, there to be received by the Dost. His intention, I understand, is to keep you under lock and key lest news of your flight gets abroad, which would be scandalous politically. You . . . ' and here he tapped my chest with his riding-crop, 'will be escorted out of the country, since it appears that you are having difficulty in finding your way without assistance.'

His men, mounting, pressed about me; two came nearer on foot.

'This time,' continued Karendeesh, 'to ensure your banishment – and the King asks me to state that he will not order it twice – two of my men will escort you, first by boat along the Kabul River and down the Indus; then overland south to Karachi where the *Karmarla*, a steamship, will deliver you back to your own country – in one piece, Mortymer, unless you prefer it otherwise. . . . ' He smiled thinly. 'Even by your standards it will be seen that you have outlived your welcome in Afghanistan.'

I interjected, 'It is not so easy. I have important papers in the palace safe in Ludhiana. . . .'

'I know, and to ensure your swift departure, I have already had them collected.' He turned, took a little leather case from a man behind him and pushed it against me. 'Although of what importance they are to your country's posterity is beyond my comprehension.'

His attitude was that of a Sirdar; his English unblemished, his manner aloof.

I replied, 'No doubt you have read them, which is the privilege of a *chuprassy* who lacks ethics—'

'Thank God for me, you should be saying. Had I not learned of this escapade, you would by now be impaled.' Autocratically, he added, 'I obeyed my instructions in saving your life, but I cannot tell you how much I enjoyed those last few minutes.'

'You are a pig, Karendeesh,' said Durrani.

Until now, appalled by the manner of Subara's death, she had maintained a stricken silence. She stood in the drumming rain, with her hair stranding either side of her face: over his shoulder the other replied, 'Your grandfather doesn't share your opinion, otherwise would he have entrusted to me your safe return to Kabul?'

Turning back to me, he added, 'In the case you will find the money promised to you by the King as reward for your services; also passport documents which will gain you entry into Britain.'

270

I smiled. 'A passport . . .?'

'Yes, a passport. How little you know of your own country! Even before the Black Plague this has been necessary. In it you will find that your identity has been changed to Ahmad Saud, a gentleman travelling in carpet manufacture; otherwise, as a wanted convict, you would be picked up before you got a mile. As the Dost says, you have the appearance of an Afghan gentleman; do your best to act like one.'

'My God, Karendeesh, I give you credit!'

'Finally, if despite our efforts you are captured and land back in a British prison, Afghanistan will deny all knowledge of you.'

I looked him up and down. 'And supposing, after all your efforts, I decide not to go?'

'You'll go all right – I'll personally see to it – dead or alive.'

Durrani said, 'How easily people like you forget! Do you not remember the ragged urchin we picked up off the road?'

'That is the good fortune of urchins.'

'By the same token, my friend, you may never get me back to Kabul, either.'

'God makes the back to bear the burden, my Princess.'

Slowly she approached him, her hands clenched by her side.

The rain was running in streams down her face and throat; shivering in her wet dress, she whispered into his face, 'You work in the manner of the rat. Using everybody to your advantage; you sneak-thief of business in the dark! By subterfuge you gain advantage, and in this manner hoped to gain me. But this will never be, because I am a princess, and for all your pomposity, you are still an urchin.

'You knew of this escape and informed the Dost, did you not? You knew that Abaya was waiting to trap us – indeed, I suggest that you did more than come to save us – you arranged it to be so!' This she shouted into his face, and he raised a hand and dismissed the guards about him, so that he stood alone with us.

Durrani, her temper rising, added, 'You who read all private correspondence, know the whims of the Dost before

271

he lifts a finger, eh? But there are others who also deal in intrigue and espionage.

'Does my grandfather know, for instance, of Persians whose bald heads are tattooed in Futtehabad before being marched to the Bokhara slave markets? – a trade with our enemy for which you receive reward? Ah yes! I learned of intrigue, too, when I was sent to Persia. Nor does one have to be a King's Messenger to practise Court corruption!' She paused for breath while the rain beat down upon us with roaring intensity, then raised a fist crying, 'He who decorates his rooms with gold taken from travelling caravans must first ensure that he has no enemies. And he who works with conjurers must also learn of witchcraft and divination; as he who deals with the desires of strange men must first ensure that those about him hold their tongues. I am not the only one, Karendeesh, who deals in sinful copulations!'

Her words appeared to have no visible effect: he just stood before her, his face expressionless while her accusations beat about him. Durrani lowered her voice, joining me, and said:

'You think you can part us by dividing us, Karendeesh, but this can never be. It was you, little urchin, who brought us together, but you will never break the love between us, nor will the Dost.'

She did not touch me, but stood aside while the rain poured down between us and the wind lashed the encompassing trees.

I put out a hand to her, but she moved away.

Always will I remember her standing there, her elegance and beauty gone, while the storm beat about us.

No gesture of affection could have been dearer; no proof of her love for me surer than that she offered in that silent communion.

'Goodbye, Iestyn.' She closed her eyes to the rain.

'Not goodbye,' I replied. 'One day I will come back for you.'

'Come!' commanded Karendeesh, and led her out of the clearing.

We stood together, the escort and I; nothing existed save the gusty rain. And in that quiet the figure of Karendeesh again appeared out of shadow.

He called, 'I forgot to mention something, Feringhee. Aboard the *Karmarla*, if God wills it, is an old friend; one who will be delighted to renew your acquaintance.'

Such was my emptiness at losing Durrani that I could not contemplate his meaning.

My escort guards, now one either side, peered at me, and I knew a small consolation.

Nobody can discern tears in falling rain.

41

After continuing my journey, this time as a prisoner, to Peshawar, I boarded a paddle steamer going down the Indus for the last leg of the journey to the steamship *Karmarla*; this was berthed at Karachi for the voyage to Liverpool.

Documentation was a formality; as organized by Karendeesh, everything had been cut and dried efficiently. Even my two ruffian escorts caused me no embarrassment, bowing themselves away at the ship's gangplank under the watching eyes of the crew; indeed, Laird, the ship's captain, greeted me at the passenger rail with all the decorum reserved for a travelling Afghan gentleman. No doubt I looked the part, being now heavily bearded and attired in white, flowing robes and a purple poshteen encircled with silver; proof of wealth and class.

'Mr Ahmad Saud?' The captain's accent was Scottish; wizened, undersized, his constitution had long been manhandled out of him by gin, women and the tropics: destined for early retirement by the young board of P & O directors. 'And you, what about you, Mr Saud?'

The quay below us was a bedlam of activity as the near-naked coaling coolies, men and women, toiled in endless files from coal stacks to ships' bunkers, under the reviling commands of overseers.

Above me, high on the white deck of the ship, I saw a lady in white reclining in a chaise-longue; a cruel comparison, I thought, with her sweating sisters twenty feet below.

The captain said, his words sharper, 'I asked about you, Mr Saud.'

I gave him a grin. 'What about me?'

I knew at that moment that it wasn't going to be so easy. 'Explain myself?'

I moved away, but he detained me, adding testily, 'Look, if ye don't mind, young fella, we'll sort out the gold from the dross right now, which will save them beating it out of you when we get to Liverpool, or you'll be goin' into ship's irons five minutes from now.'

I stared at him. 'What the devil are you talking about?'

'Just this, me son. This is me last trip; there's a pension on the end of it, and I'm not blotting me copybook with the likes of you!'

I was suitably outraged. 'For a start, I don't know what you're getting at, but I certainly intend to report your behaviour to the port authorities!'

For reply he called to a passing sailor, 'Ship's carpenter, get this bugger below and tie him to the rig while I sort this out, for I'm not sailing this bucket with an escaped convict aboard – move, man, *move!*'

Two other sailors arrived and I was unceremoniously bundled down companionway steps and into a state- room, and as I went I heard the captain shout, 'I've got a special way to kill this particular bloody goose, so watch me next move!'

With the crewmen standing guard over me, I sat awaiting it, and was astonished to see Captain Laird reappear with an old lady upon his arm; the one dressed in white, whom I had noticed before.

It was Lady Sale.

The years had ravaged her. Never laying claim to beauty, she was now but a pale shell of the woman I had served with during the Retreat: yet I still sensed her inner fire as she feebly approached.

I got to my feet; her eyes, lined with weariness, drifted over me in assessment . . . but without a flicker of recognition.

Distantly, I heard the captain say, 'Your ladyship, as I mentioned, this man came aboard for passage to Liverpool, but his papers are in doubt. His name, he says, is Ahmad

275

Saud, and he claims to be an Afghan manufacturer travelling in trade to Wales. However, a letter accompanying his sealed papers – written by a King's Messenger in Kabul – alleges that he is, in fact, an escaped British convict, and that possibly, since it is known that you are travelling aboard, you would be able to prove this.'

Her old eyes lightened with a hint of inner amuse- ment, and she put her head on one side, regarding me quizzically, then took a lorgnette from her purse and peered at me through it.

'Kindly ask him to remove his poshteen,' she said.

Laird took it off my head.

Lady Sale said, 'One basic error you have already made, Captain Laird. During the retreat from Kabul I did not consort with convicts, but with valorous British soldiers, all but a handful of whom died for their country.' She peered at me again. 'What is your name?'

'Mr Ahmad Saud, milady,' I replied.

Smiling, she nodded, saying to the captain, 'The eyes grow old, Captain Laird, but my ears do not fail me! It is the voice . . . of course, of *course!*' and she held out a white-gloved hand to me. 'Mr Saud, I am delighted to renew our acquaintance. With the Captain's permission we shall take tea together; this time under happier circumstances.'

'Thank you.' After an inner sigh of relief, I shot Laird a hostile stare.

'You heard that my husband died?' she asked, ignoring all there.

'I heard that Sir Robert was killed at Ferozepore. I am sorry.'

She replied, 'No, at Sutlej. He was always Queen and Country, and all that, you know. "Fighting Bob" they called him, as no doubt you remember – always in the thick of it, the darling idiot – rolling on the ground with ruffians twice his age.' Her voice became inaudible; then, 'Eight years . . . it seems like yesterday . . .!'

'And now?'

'Now I am leaving the Raj for Capetown to stay with friends. One . . . one tends to wander when loved ones go . . . but you are too young to understand that, I suppose . . .'

276

She appeared suddenly empty of words, but not of her old quick-witted intelligence.

Captain Laird said, brusquely, 'I apologize for a bad mistake, Mr Saud. I will try to make your voyage as comfortable as possible; meanwhile, Lady Sale, I will send down some tea.'

And the moment we were alone in the state-room, she leaned forward and whispered, 'That nearly caught me out! What the devil are you up to? I want a full and concise explanation.'

'Yes, ma'am.'

'And do not call me ma'am – I am not the Queen. I told you that before, if I recall.'

'Not me, milady – Caleb, remember?'

Later, with the ship at sea, she said, 'Dear Caleb! He died too, did he not?'

'Buried in Kabul, with full military honours,' I replied.

Her eyes grew wistful. 'Full military honours? He wouldn't have liked that, not Caleb. I hope you did your best to prevent it.'

'Dost Mohammed Khan insisted,' I said. 'He didn't understand the Irish situation . . .'

She said nostalgically, 'For a brief period in his early life Caleb was a Member of Parliament, did you know that?'

'He told us, but we didn't believe him.'

'This was the trouble. In his alcoholic state few believed anything of him. It was the death of his young wife that put him on the bottle: he never survived the grief . . . ' Her voice lowered. 'Does anyone survive such bereavement?'

'You have friends, you say. At times like this we all need them most.'

She brightened, touching her mouth with a small lace handkerchief. 'Not I, for I am going home to die. But you have your life before you, so what are your plans?'

'I am going home to find my wife.'

'To whom you wrote poems, I recall.'

'You knew that!' There was a sudden joy between us.

'My son-in-law, Captain Sturt, mentioned it – letter censorship, you know. He also said that they were beautiful.

But more, that you were writing an autobiography.'

'I have written it. The manuscript is with me.'

'But that is magnificent!'

I smiled. 'I've yet to find a publisher.'

'How very interesting.' Her old eyes shone. 'What is it called?'

'*Rape of the Fair Country.*'

'I beg your pardon . . .'

I repeated it.

She was appalled. 'My dear fellow, you cannot employ a title like that!'

'Why not, it is what happened.'

'But you cannot rape a country!'

'Yes, you can. You can violate it, plunder it, carry it away by force.'

'And what country, may I ask?' She was cool.

'Wales, my country. Afghanistan, also – indeed, any country against which the rape is committed, especially in terms of colonialism.' I was hot, and showed it.

'Dear me, Mortymer, the Foreign Office wouldn't like to hear you say things like that, let alone write them. You're aware, I hope, of your position as a convict?'

I nodded.

'And the dangers of re-arrest.'

'First they'll have to catch me.'

She considered this. 'Meanwhile, please tell me where, in literature or art, there is a precedent for such unadulterated language.'

'In literature, *The Rape of Lucrece* by Shakespeare: in art, *The Rape of the Sabines* by Rubens.'

She put her tongue between her teeth like a child, and smiled. 'God help you when you publish it, my friend. Meanwhile what does your wife think about all this?'

'She doesn't know of it.'

'Have you not told her?'

'I don't know where she is. When I was transported, she took my baby son to her grandfather's farm in Carmarthenshire, but despite many letters to that address, I have never received a reply.'

'How could that be?'

A gentler person, this one; the autocratic gesturing had been stilled by hardship; her dominant personality diluted by grief. Life had clubbed Lady Sale into submission. She said softly, 'She loved you?'

'I thought she did.'

'And Durrani? What of your beautiful princess?'

I met her eyes. 'Durrani is another story.'

'A triangle?'

'It could never be. Only one true love can exist in a single lifetime.'

'Do not be ridiculous! Men and women have the potential for a hundred loves.'

I did not reply.

'Where is the Princess now?'

'The King's Messenger who betrayed me, took her back to Kabul to her grandfather.'

'And the future?'

'There is no future.'

'At your age!' She chided me with a glance.

'Because soon there will be thousands of miles between us. . . .'

The ship rolled to a swell coming in from Africa, and I smelled the air, which was sweet with the scent of fruitful groves and the glades of a world as yet largely undiscovered: somewhere out on the wasteful sea the lights of passing ships were flickering; the African stars beamed.

'Listen,' whispered Lady Sale, and took my hand. 'I am an old witch, so hear my words. Once a love is born, Mortymer, it cannot be destroyed; no power on earth can sully it; and only those who prove unworthy of it can suffer it to die. You alone are the enigma, the joker in the pack. But, if you love hard enough in this world, of one, or two, even of three – she whom you love best will one day return to you – the Mari of whom you tell me, perhaps? Or the Durrani of whom you dream? There is no need to search, for she will come . . . as my darling, when the world sleeps, comes to me . . .'

She emptied her hands at me.

'Look at me! Unattractive, angular – mannish, some even say: not in any sense could I be called a beauty. But my Robert comes to me from the other side of the world.'

279

I had no words for her.

A fortnight later we were clipping along out of Karachi at a merry old rate, and the Indian Ocean – scene of a thousand such voyages to come, when the passenger routes, I heard, could be followed by empty beer bottles on the bed of the ocean – the coming and going of nations.

With the Seychelles over the horizon to port and Zanzibar of the British slave trade route coming up starboard, the old rust bucket called the *Karmarla* ploughed the waves, a white heron with her mains'l billowing, running on steam and ballast; her cargo of cotton long since winding its way up the Indus for the profit of British shareholders.

On, on, ever southerly, through the Mozambique Channel, to take on water and coal at Durban; on again around the Cape of Good Hope until Capetown came sliding up out of the morning mist.

'This is where we part,' said Lady Sale. 'And I am wondering, since the ship is in port here for twenty-four hours, if you would be kind enough to escort me to my friends who live on Table Mountain? They will see to it that you return in time for sailing . . .'

Until now I had not really known her: a woman courageous if ever I was privileged to meet one; but more, much more; her intellect was a portal of rich design, her heart a vestibule of unspoken dreams.

I did not enjoy her company for long.

With the porters collecting her ship's luggage and the sun a molten ball in a sky of brass, Lady Sale suddenly put her hand to her face and, closing her eyes, smiled at me.

And, on the pavement of Capetown, with all the bustle of Africa about us, turned her face into the shelter of my coat, and died in my arms.

To this day – and nothing will dissuade me – I believe that someone had sent me to her; to bring to her a last crumb of friendship in a world which had otherwise forgotten her.

Caleb!

Book Three

Wales
1854

42

Liverpool, with its overcast sky and choppy harbour, was doing its worst for me in blustering wind and rain when the *Karmarla* docked there six weeks later.

I spent the night in a seedy tavern, left with more company than I'd come with, and next morning caught the packet steamer down south to Carmarthen City.

Here, two days later, the sea wind of the ancient Tywi estuary was as brittle as October wine; and Wales, garlanded by Nature to greet an exile, was dressed up in gay autumn colours.

There entered into me an excitement that snatched me up and carried me joyfully along the roads of the beloved country; this, the land of my fathers, in whose arms all exiles are carried. The very music of the name seemed to envelop me in its splendour. Wales, the wanderer's dream!

Never, never again would I leave her: this I pledged, as the old Carmarthen to Llanstephan stage coach wobbled and clanged along the road to Morfa Bach.

'Where you say?' bawled the driver in Welsh. 'Cae White?'

I nodded, keeping my identity as a foreigner.

As Ahmad Saud I had arrived in the robes of an Arab; a bearded disguise necessary to continue, lest local tongues started wagging.

The driver's face appeared upside down on the glass of the door: the face of a ferret plus whiskers, this one, with a body to match.

'Cae White, you say, mister?' This in English now. 'Near Morfa Bach, is it?'

I gave him the Arab soprano. 'I do not know. Only the name of the house of my friends I know, sir. Near to Black Boar tavern?'

'By 'ere?'

The coach rumbled to a stop. 'Nobody livin' in it now, mind,' he added. 'Been empty these past five years to my knowledge, for I been a'comin' and a'goin' to Ferryside all me life. You got black relatives?'

I did not reply.

The horses stamped and snorted on the darkening road.

'You know it's haunted, don't ye?' The driver peered down from above. 'You'll likely know what you're about, but I don't, mister,' and he whipped up the horses and was away at speed.

Kneeling, I gathered up from the roadside verge a handful of soil and held it before me in my cupped hands: lifting it to my nostrils I smelled deeply of it, and sighed, as a man sighs when his soul is riven with an exile's pain; a pain which none but returning exiles know.

Now I stared up in the gathering dusk at the old pile that for so long had been Mari's home: the air here would have heard the cries of Jonathan, my son: Morfydd, my sister, and Jethro, my brother, might have walked in the very place where I was kneeling now: Mam, Tomos Traherne, and Richard, Morfydd's boy, in all their comings and goings seemed suddenly to be about me . . . yet even now slipping away in a wraithlike emptiness . . .

The ancient house of gothic turrets and twisted ornamental chimneys now faced me . . .

Heaving up my travelling-bags, I went down the overgrown garden path.

The iron-studded entrance door faced me; I pushed it, and it rasped open as if in a dying welcome; now swinging wide to expose a debris-strewn hall.

In a wire cage behind the door were old envelopes: holding them up to the dusk, I recognized my own handwriting: these; my last letters to Mari from Afghanistan, which she had not received.

As I entered the kitchen there came to me an unusual sense

of foreboding, for the old black clock, which I remembered from my childhood, was ticking merrily away on the mantel above the empty fireplace: proof, if any was needed, that somebody had been in here recently; the sound held me with riveting force.

Now I wandered around the empty kitchen. Passing tramps, perhaps, seeking a night's free lodging, had scattered rusting pots and pans over the floor; relics of what had once been furniture, bits of which I recognized from Blaenafon, were flung haphazardly about, and what the vagrants had begun the field mice and shippon rats had continued; all contributed to a dismal scene of vandalism and lack of respect for another's property. It was apparent, too, that the family must have left in a hurry.

Now darkness had fallen on the house and mist from the distant Tywi began slowly to billow through its broken windows.

It was then that I heard a board creak above me.

Tense, I listened.

The floorboards creaked again.

Under the kitchen door that led to the stairs a dim light appeared, growing into brightness: moving silently I took up a position behind the door.

Seconds passed. Nothing happened. Then a foot slithered on boards on the other side of the door; slowly it came open, pushed from behind.

I raised a fist to club the intruder.

A little woman, cranked with age, entered the kitchen preceded by a lighted candle; its wavering light banished the shadows.

'That you, Sam?' she asked faintly and, turning, raised her candle higher as she saw me behind her.

Not a hint of shock assailed her; indeed, her old lined face (and she was as bald as an egg) showed only a kindly interest, as she added, 'Ach no, it ain't Sam at all, is it! You heard about my chap? Sam Miller they called him, his Pa being in flour . . .'

I found my voice. 'I . . . I do not know him.'

Her face grew wistful. 'Strange that, see – nobody knows

him, but he were some fella in his time, ye know . . . ' and she gazed around the room. 'Best puddlin' man Gwent ever had. Marched wi' the men o' the Eastern Valley an' all – frit of nothin' were my Sam. You listening, young fella?'

I nodded, pitying her; life had taken this one, belted her into skin and bone and stolen everything, including her reason; the madness being clear upon her small, wizened face.

She continued, wandering past me. 'Topped six foot did my lad – you just never seen such a mountain!' and she tossed back her head and cackled from a toothless mouth. 'Big and broad and smellin' o' caulking tar, being of ships down Swansea way, till he heard the call of the iron, and hied 'imself over to Blaina. You know Blaina, son?'

'Like my hand,' I answered.

'Wi' shoulders on 'im like a bull heifer, and an arm that strong he could break a woman's back . . . ach, dear me!'

I interjected, 'What is your name?'

'Me?' She thumbed herself. 'Everybody knows ole Effie Downpillow . . . What's yours?'

'Ahmad Saud.'

'Who?'

'Ahmad Saud,' I repeated, and her eyes moved slowly over my white gown and poshteen.

'*Well!*' she whispered. 'I thought you was Jesus! That's why I weren't afraid, see . . . ' and she clutched the top of her dress as if I was halfway down it. 'What you up to bein' dressed like that, then?'

'I am an African, Miss Downpillow.'

'*Ach-i-fy!* They do come strange sorts round by 'ere these days, an' no mistake,' and she smiled at me with a naked mouth. 'What you doin' here, then?'

'I'm a travelling packman, selling African things from door to door.'

'Well, I never did! It would'a put the frits up the Mortymers had you been a'comin' round dressed like this before!'

'The Mortymers?' I asked.

'The folks who used to live 'ere. Do ye fancy a brew o' tea?'

'Not now, missus,' and I spoke her own language to put her at her ease. 'Come later I'm spending the night at the tavern over the way.'

'That place? You'll 'ave old Sixpenny Jane for a landlady, mind; she'll be between your sheets before ye can say Jack Robinson, and she'll slide your dinners under the door, mean bitch. Ye'd do better 'ere with this old Effie.'

Going outside, she fetched water while I made a fire in the grate, fanning into a flame the letters I had written to Mari.

I said, when she returned, 'You live here permanent, Miss Downpillow?'

'Every winter I arrive; come summer I'm goin' . . .'

'For long?'

She shrugged, putting the kettle on the fire. 'Since Moses were a baby, I reckon – even a'fore that.'

'Did you know the folks who used to live here well?'

'The Mortymers? Like the back o' me hand, sir. And Grandfer Zephaniah a'fore that – I knew 'em all.' She cackled like one of Macbeth's witches. 'He soused himsel' in hops did Grandfer, mind, and one night trapped himself in the bogs wi' a bottle in each hand, poor sod.'

'Dead?'

'Dead and gone. The old place weren't the same after Grandfer snuffed it. I told ye about my Sam, didn't I?'

'You did, Effie. Now tell me what you know about the Mortymers.'

It stilled her hands and she glared at me. 'You wants to know a lot, don't ye?'

Not as daft as she looked, this one.

Later, however, we sat on the floor in front of the fire, and there came to us an unusual sense of affinity, one to the other. The shadows deepened: dusk and bats fell about us, and there was no sound but wind-sigh in the chimney.

I took her slowly; this was a woman who might tell all, but in her own time: the man wasn't born who could rush Effie Downpillow.

'How do you live?' I asked her.

'By selling me hair to the gentry,' said she. 'I rub in oil till I gets a good crop, then shaves meself bald and takes it down to Carmarthen market.

"'Tis good clean hair, mind, for making wigs and pieces – I thatch the old 'uns, young 'uns, county clergy and magistrates – no fleas nor lice. I can turn a dame into a sprite and a hag into a fairy. I'm as bald as a coot one minute, and more hair'n Delilah the next. I'm a friend to all the gentry – tonsured, bearded, you name it – there ain't nothin' this Effie can't achieve in turning sows' ears into silk purses.

'I can earn a bit on the side on wickedness an' all, 'cause I knows their secrets, see? Many a fat old duchess 'as dropped a sovereign to keep this Effie quiet, for I'm likely to loose off me scandals when it comes to suchlike, and they wants a quiet life. For instance! If an old girl's sportin' a cod piece on the quiet, Effie could put it over the country!' She crowed like a rooster.

'Reckon you've got the wig trade sewed up, eh?' I slapped my thigh, shouting laughter.

'I got you sewed up an' all, young fellamelad . . . ' and she eyed me. 'What you really doin' here?'

'Promise not to tell a living soul?'

Probably, nobody would believe her if she did, I reflected.

'Cross me heart and hope to die,' said Effie.

'Then listen, for it's a long story,' I said, and related it.

'Now then,' I finished. 'You tell me all I want to know.'

'How much?' she asked, rubbing two fingers.

'A sovereign?' I spun one up in the firelight, and she caught it, testing it with broken teeth.

'Wait you,' she said, 'and I'll tell ye a tale that'll make your hair stand on end,' and she did.

'You knows I told ye about my Sam? Well, I was up here at the time, selling at the door and a nipsy young maid I were, let me tell ye, tho' no pig-tailed sailor-man had ever shared me breakfast.

'But one night, passing that old Black Boar tavern over the way, I found Sam Miller as drunk as a coot. Pitying him, I stripped him, washed him, and got him home between sheets. Then, it being winter and him freezing, I slipped in beside 'im to keep 'im warm. Was that improper?'

'No. Effie.'

'But me get drunk at night and sober in the mornin', and nine months later I feared wee hands and feet a'wavin' about inside me. So I tracked Sam down to Saundersfoot and the big four-masters going west. "Sam Miller," I said to him, "you shared sheets wi' this Effie and brought me to child" – though he hadn't, mind you. "Make me decent, lest you be judged for it," and he married me, thinking me doubled.'

'That was wrong, Effie.'

'Ay, ay, but it took a woman to think of it, eh? Good clean Welsh, he were – it's a pity such men die . . . '

'He died?'

'Killed in the fighting at the old Westgate Inn, like you was supposed to 'ave done.'

I rose, looking down at her. 'You heard that I was killed?'

'Stone dead, so the tale went – you and others, trying to escape, including my Sam.' She stared at me. 'A man called Shanco Mathews told me, when I went to find my sailorman. Stone dead, you were – according to him – you and a score of others. "Effie Downpillow," said Shanco, "your Sam is dead, so back home you go to Carmarthen City and look up the Mortymer family – they're up there, near Black Boar tavern, too. Find them, Effie, and tell Jethro, the family's son – not the daughter, Morfydd, nor the mother – tell the son his brother's dead, for the women will go mad; as mad as you, Effie Downpillow." ' Her eyes were shining in the firelight.

'You listening, Iestyn Mortymer?'

'Yes.'

'So I came to Cae White and told 'em you'd snuffed it.'

'I know that,' I said softly. 'I had a letter . . .'

'It were the beginning and the end for 'em all. First, Tomos Traherne cut and carried your mam, and took her back to the valleys: than young Jethro, hearing you'd turned up your toes, took a shine to Mari, your wife . . .'

'And took her and my son to America . . ?'

'Oh no! Where did you get that?'

'I had a letter telling it.'

'Then the letter's wrong,' she said. 'Jethro flaked out a soldier and run off on a ship from Saundersfoot, being chased by the military. But your Mari don't go with him – oh dear me, no!'

Her words were beating upon my ears in stupid repetition, louder, louder, in understanding – but I could not believe what I was hearing, such was my joy.

'Are you telling me that Mari is still in Wales?'

'Not 'ere, Mister. Gone off to a place called Resolven in the Neath valley, I heard last; but one thing I know – she didn't do the bunk to America with Jethro; she were back here at home for months after, cryin' for you.'

Reaching down, I lifted Effie to her feet, and put my arms around her, and she clung to me as, a lifetime ago, she had clung to old Sam Miller, her lover, I held her and would not let her go, until she struggled free, patting heself for breath.

'Well, I do say, Mr Mortymer. You certainly know how to handle a maiden . . .!'

'I must go!'

'But you've only just come!'

'Mari's waiting for me! I must go tonight.'

'Ye can't, ye daft beggar! Gawd, you fellas are all the same! Look, I'll make a bed up for you and you can get away first thing in the morning . . ?'

Snatching up my bags, I dropped Effie some sovereigns and went like a madman acxross the fields to the Black Boar Tavern.

43

Side-stepping Sixpenny Jane, the landlady (who had much to tell me about the activities of the Mortymers), I managed to keep my business there on an official footing.

A fortnight later, with the threat of winter winds coming in from Carmarthen Bay, I left the inn with my travelling hampers, every inch an Asian packman: safe employment, this, for Wales, in the 'fifties, was jam-packed full of them.

'Mind, you don't look like a real Asian to me,' said Jane, undone at the bosom and high at the ankle, and she fluffed up her hair and made no eyes to speak of. 'I always thought they shot bows and arrows and went around wiv feathers.'

Jethro, in his teens, must have had a right old time with this one, I reflected.

'Mind, I didn't know the Mortymers much, really speakin',' Jane continued. 'I was bad under the doctor about the time Morfydd, the daughter, were killed down the Gower, and I didn't really see the goin' of 'em.' She saw me to the waiting coach. 'Is it right and true that you're 'aving Cae White done up, like, and coming to live here permanent?'

'Got to live somewhere; Cae White's as good as any.'

'Folks say as how you bought it off the agent up at Squire's Reach. He went off his head, ye know, after his daughter died.'

'Who, the agent?'

'No, Squire Lloyd Parry, ye dafto! Dear me, you foreign gents ain't half dull. Why d'ye want to know so much about the Mortymers, anyway?'

The wind had a sharper bite in him as I mounted the stage

coach for Carmarthen, and from my high perch I gave Sixpenny a grin, for she'd been a girl in her time. However, there was about her these days a maidenly purity, said the coachman – ever since Osian Hughes, a local farmer, carried her to the altar and then walked around on eggs, not knowing what had hit him: though some o' these quiet gents can be beggars when they gets their rags out, he added.

'I'll be back,' I called, as the coach rumbled off, and there was Jane's old man watching points from the pub doorway as she winked and shouted at me:

'Married or single, mister, white, yellow or black – they all come back to Sixpenny, but don't tell me old fella.'

As we went past Cae White I waved to Effie Downpillow, who was seeing the builders in; she may not have been the best housekeeper in the county, but she loved the old place and promised to hold the key during its refurbishing.

Being a woman on the move, she had a further advantage . . . if I managed to find Mari and bring her back with me. . . .

It was only a fifty-mile-or-so coach journey to Neath; we changed horses at Pen-y-groes; then at the Old Ship Inn at Pontardulais, and Neath and dusk were coming up on the early winter day, with the promise of sleet. There I hired a buggy which took me through Morriston and Skewen; here, I was told, I would find the Cuddlecome Inn, a hostelry on the tow-path of the Tennant Canal. Here too, I was advised, I could get a bed for the night from the most generous landlady in the Vale, despite the ageing process.

They could say that again, I thought, for up on the bar counter was Cushy Cuddlecome, the best pillow in the area, and she was beating time to a squeeze box played by a little wizened navvy, and the language going up around her was enough to strip the tune off Irish fiddles.

'Is it a bed you're after, lovely boy?' she asked, getting down. She bawled at the room, 'Will you stop ye slobberin' this minute, for it's an Eastern gentleman from Arabia, and ye'll show respect.'

'Ach, it's a foreign packman travellin' the Vale wi' his wares, Cushy!' bellowed a voice, but the landlady ignored him.

'For the night, is it, sire?' She curtsied splendidly.

'If you please, madam.' I bowed to her and touched my poshteen, taking a backward step, and the tears of ale grew in her eyes, which were black-lashed and heavily mascarad to hide their weariness, for her youth had been well spent.

'Are ye takin' in Cushy an' all, Your Highness?' yelled a navvy.

She threatened him with a fist, saying to me, 'Forgive the lower orders. You're welcome, kindly welcome, sir, like all respected travellers who apply for a night with Cushy,' and she dropped me another curtsey. 'This way, if ye please.' And she led the way to a snug little room upstairs.

I was taking my leave of the inn next morning when down comes Cushy all bulges and frills like a ship in full sail, and her minder (she used to have two, the customer told me, another called Ham Bone, recently expired through a chemical deficiency) raised bleary eyes from a table in the corner, as she bellowed:

'Swillickin', do you know a female round these parts called Mortymer?'

'A fella, is it?' He focused us through his maze of hops.

'A female I said, ye numbskull!'

'The lady's name is Mari,' I added. 'She promised to buy a silk from me, but I have lost her address.'

'Resolven way, did ye say?'

'That is what I remember.'

And Swillickin', with an effort, replied, 'You know young Bryn Evan who comes in 'ere? His auntie's called Mari, ye know.'

'Bryn the Tall?' asked Cushy.

An old man, bowed in a corner, said, 'Bryn Evan. *Mae ef yn dalach na'i dad . . .*'

'Jesus!' cried Cushy. 'Will you lot speak English! The fella's foreign,' and to me she said, 'the old man says he's even taller than his father. Do that make sense?'

'His aunty's name is Mari, they say?'

Others entered, and there was a gabble in English, Welsh and Irish, and a bargee with his knees yorked up, said bassly, lifting a quart:

'There was a woman called Mari who worked a cottage lock on the canal near Tonna, but she went off – workhouse, I heard tell, with her daughter.'

'Not this one, sir,' I answered. 'She didn't have a daughter.'

'Adopted daughter, they do say. Rhiannon? Then a fella called Mostyn Evan took her in,' said another. 'A skivvy, like, round the house, to help the grandma.'

'Big Mostyn?' asked another.

'The widower with three sons. *Bejasus*, them lads were a caution.'

'Ifor, Bryn, and Dewi the Revolutionary! But Mostyn was the boyo of 'em all!'

'The fella who put the skids under the Black Welshman, remember!'

They joyed and barged each other, spilling their quarts.

I asked, 'Who is the Black Welshman?'

'Somebody who tried for the father and got his eyes filled up!' And the big man saying this added, facing me, 'That your pony and trap outside?'

'Yes.'

'Then you get into it, savvy?' and he pointed. 'Go down the road till you gets to Resolven – t'other way from Neath, understand? Go straight till you get to the Resolven turning by the canal bridge, and ask for the Old Navigation.'

I nodded. His friend, a little gnome of a man, added:

'Last time I knew it, Mostyn Evan's lot lived there, see?'

'No they don't – I just told ye,' argued another. 'Last time I heard they was knockin' off the rioting Irish up in Green Fach, Aberdare.'

'Don't mind him,' said a third. 'He's off 'is rocker. Try the Old Navigation first, is it?'

'Meanwhile don't hang around by 'ere much lest Cushy pulls ye boots off!'

Heaven had a place for them, I thought – golden men for golden places, the refuse carriers – all Job's children. One thing was certain, for all their drinking and bawdy banter, they'd make it with St Peter.

Reaching a ruin beside the canal, which a passing urchin told

294

me was the Old Navigation, I entered it and looked around its derelict rooms: could it really have been here that Mari had once lived? I wondered. A paid servant, as one of the navvies had said: and if so, what of the daughter one had mentioned . . .? Wandering, I noticed on the floor among the dust of years, a crumpled piece of paper: picking it up, I unfolded its brittle page and, holding it up to the light, read:

> In certain parts of the island there is a people called Welsh, so bold and ferocious that, even when unarmed, they do not fear to encounter an armed force; being ready to shed their blood in defence of their country, and sacrifice their lives for renown . . .
>
> King Henry V of England

A strange and noble message, I thought, to find amid rubbish.

Out into the sunshine now, I watched the trains coming and going and the floor trembled to the pounding of the ten-ton high loaders going to Aberdare for coal.

Back at the trap now I saw a man standing on the edge of the forest; he was as old as a dead crow; upon his head was a poacher's moleskin cap, and his white beard reached to his chest; four rabbits dangled from his belt.

Crippled with age, he raised his riven face to mine, and I saw in it the tragedy of my generation, for his wrists held the white scars of manacles, and his naked ankles the weals of leg irons.

'You buy a coney, mister?' He shot an anxious glance over his shoulder.

'Depends on how much,' for I wanted to get him talking.

'Penny a piece, sir. And for God's sake don't tell you got 'em off old Shon Shonko, I've done time overseas.'

You're not alone in that, I thought.

'Two for a penny,' I said.

'Jeez, mister, you drive a hard bargain! You a foreign gent?' He eased his wracked shoulders and his face died in the fierce sunlight.

'So foreign that I don't know the money yet,' I said, and gave him a sovereign.

He stared at it in the blinding light, then gave it back, shouting in a croaking soprano, '*Duwedd*! Round these parts they'll 'ave ye done brown before you're up in the mornin' – but old Shonko don't twist nobody, sir – a penny a coney is all I wants – for I only takes what's mine.'

I gave him twopence, and he strung two rabbits on to the buckle of my belt. 'You new round these parts, then?'

I explained to him.

'Young Mari, the bargee's wife, ye mean?'

I stared down at him. He continued, 'Mostyn Evan's missus? Christ, they gone long since – nigh a year, I suppose. . . .'

'Gone where?'

'Up to Green Fach, Aberdare.' He sighed at the sun. '*Dammo di*, she were some lady, that one, and Mostyn were some gent. . . . She were the prettiest thing I ever saw on two legs, and respectful kind to poor old Shonko.'

His eyes filled with tears. 'Don't know anythin' more, sir.'

A sickness of fear was clutching at me. I seized his frail shoulders and shook him to rattle. 'Tell me, old man!' But he tore himself free of me and limped off back into the forest.

'Don't you lay hands on Shonko!' he shouted. 'Go up to Green Fach and find out for yourself.'

Aberdare had just finished weeks of bitter persecution they told me up there. First a vicious strike against starvation pay and working conditions down the Gadlys, the local slaughterhouse they called a coal mine, then forced back to work on Master's terms.

But the October wind had been caressed by God and made it an Indian Summer for its people, and the sun blazed like June down over the Top towns. So now there was dancing in the streets and the hope of better times to come, and the Irish, once battling with the Welsh in rivalry, were now arming it around in the publics to the music of Welsh fiddles, though a word out of place and the fists and shillelaghs would come out of moth balls.

After a struggle among a maze of courts and alleys I found what was nothing less than an open sewer they called the

River Dare; with people still recovering from stomach cramps after drinking water from the polluted spouts of Maes y dre and the Darran, Vicarage Well, a local fever stream, had officially been placed out of bounds.

Local pits like the Wherfa, the Dyffryns, and the Aber Nanty-Groes had closed like the Gadlys, also the big Aberdare after a fifteen per cent reduction in colliers' wages. And, as usual, the children, always the first in Welsh coal, had begun to die of cholera, while owners like Lady Charlotte Guest of Dirty Dowlais had done the bunk to England.

I got out of the buggy and asked bystanders for Green Fach and the family called Evan, and a grandma directed me to Number Five.

I tapped the door and the face of a starved ghost appeared out of the next door window.

'You after the Evan family, my duck?'

'Yes.'

The old girl pointed. 'Their Rhiannon's just gone up to the church, not five minutes back. Her and young Bryn are leaving Green Fach, ye know – making a bolt for it, they do say . . .'

'The church?'

'That's right, straight up the hill, but she'll be back directly. You got business with 'em?'

'Does Mari Evan live here, too?'

At this the window slammed shut, ending the conversation.

In retrospect I have often wondered why the truth of the situation didn't immediately strike me. The reluctance of the Cuddlecome navvies to give more information had become apparent, as had the foreboding of Shon Shonko, the poacher I'd met at the Old Navigation.

All questions concerning Mari were being abruptly terminated by people usually eager to know one's business.

Taking the buggy up the hill, I tethered its pony at the lych gate and entered the churchyard.

Nobody was about. If the girl called Rhiannon had been

here, her stay must have been brief. And then I saw a grave with fresh flowers and a simple wooden tablet with an inscription which read:

MOSTYN EVAN
SON OF BEN THE DROVER
also
MARI, HIS WIFE
Died down Gadlys Pit
9th September, 1854
Interred by their comrades
in the Colliers' Benefit.

It was my Mari. I knew it as certainly as if she had arisen from the grave and come to me with welcoming arms.

Kneeling there, I was with her again at the start of time with my kisses. I was binding her feet after the Hiring Fair. Under the summer moons I was with her in Shant-y-Brain's barn, and now up on the mountain, carving her love-spoon from cedar.

Through the empty years I heard her voice again . . .

'Who do you love?' I asked her.
'A boy from Garndyrus.'
'Do you swear to that love?'
'On the Bible black . . .'
'Who do you love, Iestyn Mortymer?'
'A girl from Carmarthen.'
'Do you swear to that love?'
'On the Bible black I swear.'
'Tell her name, then . . .'
Mari Dirion . . .'

I bowed my head in my emptiness; the tears were a scald to my eyes.

Nowhere to go now, nothing to do . . .
I wandered, lost.
Drawn as if by an invisible magnet, I took the buggy down

from the Top and on to the road to Merthyr, but I did not find Mari there.

Next day, after awaking stiff and cold in the driving seat in October morning frost, I took the pony aimlessly through the dew-laden glades of Rhymney, and behind me the night shift of Crawshay's furnaces were belching their rainbow colours at the sky.

At Nantyglo I stood in the yard of Long Row within the turmoil of Bailey's iron empire, and in the ear-splitting drop-hammers of his iron-making, re- membered the first night of our wedding . . . now rubbing the smoke off the little window of what was once our bedroom, I looked within (where a little girl was getting up) and heard again the firer's song from the compound . . . which echoed through our dreaming as we made love. On again to Blaenafon and the little house in Shepherd's Square where I took her after finding her bathing in the river down at Llanellen.

Now it was dusk, and the old Drum and Monkey was going at it like marrow-bones and cleavers, with the drunks being tossed down into North Street, as in the days of old.

With the moon hanging like a silver orb in the sky I stopped at the Royal Oak and there took a bed for the night – overcharged as usual, the locals said, for the landlord, Selwyn ap Pringle, was a bloody old Shylock if ever there was one, and I don't think he liked having an Arab in the establishment in case I stained the sheets.

Next morning I was off again, this time down the Fiddler's Elbow to lovely Abergavenny: and on, on to the bridge at Llanellen.

There I thought, of all the places in the world, I would find my girl again, but I did not: it was a corrupt and vicious loneliness, and I think I knew, sitting there listening to the song of the Usk, that my search for Mari Dirion was over, for I had found her moulded in the arms of another . . . within the rich tabernacle of the earth.

One day, perhaps, in another place, and at another time. . . .

The wind was ruffling the silver sheen of the river into cold and inhospitable ripples.

'Goodbye,' I said.

*

I had no immediate wish to return to Cae White, for only family ghosts and Effie Downpillow were there. True, I had bought the place and left instructions for its rehabilitation, for I had to have a home somewhere and living with ghosts is better than nothing. Money was no consideration thanks to the Dost's generosity, and I had just deposited a small fortune in the Old Bank at Abergavenny, it being senseless to carry gold abroad.

For there had come to me an urge to lose myself in a world that seemed to have no place for me; nothing of love, little of companionship. My thoughts turned to Durrani, for she was a staunch friend and lover if ever there was one, but she, too, was lost: indeed, I doubted if she was alive.

So I took myself down to Cardiff and the docks, which later they called Tiger Bay, and there signed myself on as a deck-hand on a big full-rigger. She was long and slim and straining at her hawsers, dying to be gone.

The sea, perhaps, would cleanse me of the past and leave to me, in the writing of my books, the one true path along which I might again find myself.

44

1855

A year before the mast as a deck hand on a big sailing ship not only hardened my body but banished all my nightmare dreams; leaving me, at the age of thirty-six, with new and vital ambitions.

Returning to Britain I was now eager to collate my haphazard diary entries and complete the writing of *Rape of the Fair Country*, my first literary attempt at telling of the violation of my country. After this I planned to begin my second book, *Beloved Exile*, which would expose the worst single massacre of our soldiers in the history of the British Empire: an ignominious defeat which would otherwise be ignored by lackey historians employed to twist truth for schoolroom consumption. Britain, of all the colonialists, being expert in the falsification of history, confined its truth to the dates of the battles and glorious antecedents of a parasitical Royalty.

The late summer of 1855, therefore, found me back in Carmarthenshire and in occupation of a beautiful and refurbished Cae White.

Here, almost immediately, I began to write.

Grandfather Zephaniah would have had fits had he seen the old pile now, for the builders had taken full licence of my casual statement – 'I'll be away for a year, meanwhile do what you think is necessary' – and as I took my new pony and trap along the drive, the old house, turreted and spired,

301

rose up before me, its twenty acres of golden corn shining like a jewel in the evening sun.

This was going to cost a pretty penny, I reflected, and it did, for Cae White now competed with my neighbour's mansion up at Squire's Reach.

It was a pity, I reflected, as I reined in the pony, that with money to spend on such luxury, I now possessed nobody with whom to share it: Mari was gone, the rest of the family either dead or scattered to the ends of the earth. And Durrani . . .? God knows what Durrani's fate had been; returned by Karendeesh to an outraged grandfather who was quite capable of executing her according to the law. There was nothing to allay my fears concerning her, though I looked anxiously for a letter. There was, however, a verbal message from Effie, saying that she hoped I had safely arrived home, and that she would be back at the end of her tour of gentile establishments.

Also, there was a letter from my solicitors, whom I had instructed before sailing from Cardiff. It read:

Messrs Arne and Lang,
Solicitors,
2 Bank Buildings,
Cathedral Road,
Cardiff, Glamorgan

Dear Mr Saud,

Acting upon your instructions, we have, during your absence abroad, made inquiries concerning the whereabouts of your son, Jonathan Mortymer, and regretfully have to pass on to you the following information.

Jonathan was killed at the age of eleven whilst working with sub-contractors on plate-laying for the Cambrian Railway Company; his death occurring on June 15th 1850 on the Pontsticill viaduct near Merthyr. Despite exhaustive research, the whereabouts of his grave is still unknown: it is suggested that he probably lies where he fell, somewhere within the earth embankment; this was a usual working custom.

His mother, Mari Mortymer, soon after her son's

302

death, began work as a lockkeeper on the Tennant Canal in the Vale of Neath. The next information we have concerning her is that she became the wife of one Mostyn Evan, a Resolven bargee: both were killed in September 1854 in an accident down the Gadlys Pit, Aberdare: in company with others, they were interred in a churchyard in that town.

Of Jethro Mortymer we have no news other than, wanted by the Carmarthen police for a serious crime (it is thought to be murder), he sailed from Saundersfoot on the *Cestria*, an emigration ship of the time (1843) after which all trace of him is lost to us; his destination, according to the port authorities, was Philadelphia.

We earnestly regret having to give you such unhappy information, which has come about after exhaustive pursuit of our inquiries upon your behalf, and have pleasure in enclosing our account, which we trust you will find to your satisfaction.

Yours faithfully,
J.S. Arne.

4th January 1855

I lowered the letter and stared through the open window at the beauty of Cae White.

This was the first official news of Jonathan, my son, and while all along I had feared the absence of news of him, the impact of his death now struck me with terrifying force: he, of all people, I had hoped, would live on to perpetuate my name, for a man without a son, say the bald elders of the East, is as a star burned out in the middle of the sky; a man without earthly or heavenly representation.

With his death the tenuous link that still held me to Mari now snapped like a silver thread; my world was encompassed by a pall of gloom, and I knew a devastating sense of isolation.

This was the son, who, like so many years ago, I had promised myself to take on my shoulders to see the swallows fly away: nothing, I had sworn, would ever divide me from this simple, personal pleasure.

For days now I wandered the house, magnetized by the

303

whisky decanter – anything that might bring me solace; the distant lights of Black Boar tavern and the soprano laughter that filtered down to Cae White called me during nights of sleepless tossing: but neither women nor wine could heal as they had done before; this sickness was of the soul.

As I buried myself in work, my thoughts turned again to Durrani, and the love I had borne through the years

The onset of the first harvest at Cae White found me rounding up the locals: working stripped to the waist with them, I forgot my grief in calloused hands and the labour of the reaping; sweating in the slanting heat of the sun from morn till darkness; after which I lost myself in the plot and theme of the new book. And then, towards the end of summer, with the harvest in, I sat at the long refectory table in the drawing room, and with my Afghanistan notes and decanter set out before me, wrote:

BELOVED EXILE
BOOK ONE
Afghanistan
1840
Chapter 1
The Indus River

The chunk-chunking of the paddle steamer beat in my head within a crucifixion by heat; it was mid-summer and the north-west frontier was coming up on the port side.

Through the smudged glass of the chain-locker porthole I saw the bright Indus River, its rippling wastes a quicksilver of astonishing brilliance; refracted light glowed and fired a scintillating brightness; the purple ranges of the surrounding country shimmered in lambent flame . . .

For weeks I worked incessantly, caught up in teh magic of nostalgia, and the memory of Durrani. The writing brought her back with astonishing evocation; the girl-woman in the green and black and gold . . . standing in profile against the

304

sheen of the Indus River, which is how I first saw her.

As I worked, sometimes into the early hours of cock-shut time, my being appeared transported from a misty present into a definable past; no longer were people and events unsubstantial, but adopted, within my turmoiled mind, a strange and material phantasmagoria.

It was as if I had become diembodied within time; a vague and ethereal phantom which was not of mine but of another's making: a phenomenon that awakened the past with striking reality . . . in a spectrum of variegated light and blinding colours.

Within this spectrum arose visions of panoramic horizons; of mountainous wastelands that I had never seen before; peopled in my visionary mind by an hypnotic power.

It was, of course, a manifestation enhanced by the fumes of whisky. And the more of this I drank, so more colourful became the visions, racing their pictures down to the cul-de-sac of my mind: reaching it, the visions stopped dead; the phantasm was over as suddenly as it had begun. And the evocation ended, not as one might expect, in sleep and quiet dreams, but in the clattering of hooves outside in the shippon.

Earlier, I had heard hoof-beats and discounted them as coming from the Carmarthen road. But now, imminently embraced in the confusion of an arrival, I rose from my desk.

Draining my glass, swaying a little within the mental hubbub of the whisky, I entered the darkened hall and faced the front door.

Silence now: a pin-drop silence of such intensity that I suspected a planned assault, for after the initial noise came whispers and hushed instructions I could not identify.

Moving closer to the front door, I waited for it to open. Now I heard a man's voice and a woman's gentle replies: I lifted the lamp and its yellow glow fell upon the door. The latch moved, raised from outside.

Clearly, who ever was entering believed the occupant of the house to be unaware of an assault, and was not expecting a violent reception.

The initial advantage, therefore, would be mine. I waited, tense.

Slowly, the door creaked open.

With the lamp upraised I stood motionless, contained by the thudding of my heart.

The door opened wider, pushed from outside.

Incredibly, a small child made shape on the hall floor before me. A boy, of about two years old, was staring up at me with the uncertainty of a child confronting a stranger. Raising the lamp higher in disbelief, I saw him more clearly.

He was a child in miniature, no more thantwo feet tall, and dressed in Afghan robes. The white gown he wore reached to his slippered feet; his poshteen was purple, proof of royalty, and was inlaid with silver about his shoulders: around his waist was a golden girdle.

Childlike, with a finger in his mouth, he stared up, and I stared down, for he was like a wraith appearing out of the night amid the fumes of whisky.

'It is your son, Sahib,' said a voice from beyond the door, and another stepped into the lamplight, and it was Karendeesh.

I knew him instantly, clothed as he was in the regalia of teh Afghan travelling Court, and there was about him a majesty. Like a man stepped out of an ancient dynasty he bowed, saying:

'The Dost commands, Karendeesh obeys. The King sends no mesage except to say that in Afghan law a man is responsible for his own children . . .'

I had no words for him; I was still straing down at my son.

Karendeesh added, 'Further, says my King, a child of flaxen hair and a European smile has no place in the nobility of Afghanistan. Do you understand?'

I did not reply, but put down the lamp and, kneeling, opened my arms to the child: it was as if Jonathan, my first-born, had left his tomb and was standing there in greeting.

'He is Durrani's boy?' I asked, huskily.

Karendeesh nodded, saying, 'Greet this man, child, he is

your father,' and the boy approached, first touching his forehead and breast, then bowed to me: I took him into my arms.

'His name?' I asked.

'Suresh is his name, born of Durrani. But what is a son without a mother to tend and obey him, asked the King, so he sends her also, for she is banished from our Court . . .' and another moved into the glow of the lamp.

'*Durrani!*'

She whispered, kissing my face and hands, 'This is how we planned it when we saw you through the window.'

laughing in tears, I held them both, and Karendeesh said: 'I bring her to you out of love. For her place is here, though you are not her husband; in teh next world, perhaps, her place will be with me.'

'Yours is a good love, Karendeesh,' I said.

In the morning, when Suresh awaoke between us, we dressed him in the little sailor's suit and jacket which Durrani had brought with her. Then we took him with us, hand-in-hand, up to the Big Wheatfield, to see the swallows fly away . . . as I had promised to my sone, Jonathan.

Further Reading

Signal Catastrophe Patrick MacRory: Hodder and Stoughton

Journal of the Afghanistan Disasrers, 1841–2 Lady Sale: John Murray

The First Afghan War, 1838–1842 J.A. Norris: Cambridge University Press

The First Afghan War Sir Henry Durand: Longmans and Green Co., 1879

The Sepoy and the Cossack Pierce G. Fredericks: W.H. Allen

The Indian Mutiny John Harris (Ed: Ludovic Kennedy): Granada Publishing Co.

The Afghan Wars, 1838 to 1879 T.A. Heathcote: Osprey Publishing Co. Ltd.

British Attitudes Towards India: 1784–1858 George D. Bearce: Oxford University Press

Mother India Catherine Mayo: Jonathan Cape